SIERRA MCCALLISTER

Beneath The Bond

A bond fated by stars. A truth hidden in silence.

Thread
& Thorn
BOOKS

First published by Thread & Thorn Books 2025

Copyright © 2025 by Sierra McCallister

This novel is entirely a work of fiction. The names, characters, and incidents portrayed in it are the work of the author's imagination. Any resemblance to actual persons, living or dead, events, or localities is entirely coincidental.

Sierra McCallister asserts the moral right to be identified as the author of this work.

Sierra McCallister has no responsibility for the persistence or accuracy of URLs for external or third-party Internet Websites referred to in this publication and does not guarantee that any content on such Websites is, or will remain, accurate or appropriate.

Designations used by companies to distinguish their products are often claimed as trademarks. All brand names and product names used in this book and on its cover are trade names, service marks, trademarks, and registered trademarks of their respective owners. The publishers and the book are not associated with any product or vendor mentioned in this book. None of the companies referenced within the book have endorsed the book.

First edition

ISBN: 979-8-218-76617-7

This book was professionally typeset on Reedsy.
Find out more at reedsy.com

For those who believe in magic,
in love that defies the stars,
and in the bonds that hold us fast.

Contents

Preface

I began writing *Beneath the Bond* with only two characters in mind—Aislen and Kael—and a stubborn belief that their story deserved to be told slowly, like embers catching into flame. I wanted a world that felt alive beneath the surface, where magic hums in the roots of the land, and where bonds are forged in loyalty long before they are claimed in love.

This book is more than a fantasy romance. It's a reminder that the quiet moments matter—the ones between battles and storms—when characters choose to stay, to fight, or to believe in one another even when the path ahead is unclear.

Every corner of Velastra, every breath of its forests and courts, is built on years of daydreams, stolen writing hours, and the endless encouragement of the people who love me best. To my family, thank you for letting me vanish into this world and for welcoming me back when the words ran out.

It is my hope that somewhere within these pages, you find a spark that stays with you long after you turn the last page.

— *Sierra McCallister*

Acknowledgments

To my husband, De—

Thank you for being my constant. For grounding me when I get lost in my own head, and for always being ready to help, no matter how small or strange the request. I love you more than words can say—and they can say a lot.

To Malia and Trisha—

You were the first to believe in this story when it was just scattered thoughts and half-formed dreams. Your encouragement, excitement, and unwavering support carried me through the hard days and made the good ones even brighter. I wouldn't have finished this book without you.

To the readers—

Whether you found this book by fate, curiosity, or a friend's gentle shove—thank you. Thank you for stepping into this world with me, for feeling with these characters, and for letting this story wrap around your heart the way it did mine.

I hope something here lingers with you, the way good stories always do.

Prologue

Wynmere - 10 Years Ago
(Border Village in Velastra)

The scent of sun-warmed pine needles clung to Aislen's dress as she ran, laughter bubbling up from somewhere deep in her chest. Loose curls bounced against her shoulders, catching leaves and golden flecks of dust that danced in the late afternoon light.

Kael chased close behind, his footsteps light, almost fae-like, because they *were*, even then.

"You're going to trip," he warned, out of breath but grinning.

"I'm not!" she shouted back.

But of course, she tripped.

She tumbled face-first into the mossy clearing where they always met when chores were done and grown-ups weren't looking. Twigs snapped beneath her palms, and the scent of damp earth and crushed mint filled her nose.

Kael caught up and flopped down beside her, eyes sparkling like storm clouds in moonlight. His light blue tunic was smudged with dirt and green stains, his dark hair tousled by wind and running.

Aislen could hear him still laughing beside her. She turned her head away hoping he wouldn't notice the blush creeping up her face.

For a moment, they lay in silence, staring up through the trees. Above them, the canopy filtered gold light, like something magical hung in the air.

Maybe it did. In this hidden village, with its whispered rules and fading border wards, magic always felt close, just barely out of reach.

Even the trees and gardens here felt magical.

Sunbeams painted shifting patterns across Kael's cheekbones. Somewhere above, a hawk cried, distant and fierce.

Kael turned toward her on his elbow, that mischievous tilt already forming in his smile.

"I dare you to kiss me."

Aislen blinked. "What?"

He shrugged. "Thess said kisses are gross. I want to know if she's right. I bet you'll chicken out."

His eyes shimmered with challenge.

She didn't know this yet, but the challenge in his eyes would grow to be one of her favorite things.

Heat rose to her cheeks like fireweed in bloom. "No, I won't," She said confidently. Kael knew she could never turn down a challenge.

She sat up straighter, narrowed her eyes, and leaned in, just enough to brush her lips to his. A flash. Warm, soft. It barely counted.

The world held its breath. Somewhere in the trees, a cricket stopped mid-chirp.

But when she pulled away, her heart thudded too loud in her chest. His fae ears flicked, and she just knew he could hear the beat of her heart. He had to.

She willed it to calm down, but it wouldn't.

Kael looked stunned. Not grossed out. Not laughing. Just… still.

Then he grinned. "Told you it was gross."

"Totally," she lied.

Because something had shifted.

Not between them, but something deep inside her.

Quiet, stubborn, and sure.

She'd known even then at the young age of eight, somewhere quiet and stubborn in her chest, that one day Kael would grow up and find his *mate*. And it couldn't be her. Humans didn't have mates. That's what the stories said.

She'd only be his best friend. Nothing more. Nothing *magical*.

So she laughed, punched his arm, and ran back toward the village like her lungs weren't burning and her heart wasn't already broken in a way she didn't yet have words for. Behind her, Kael shouted something, probably teasing, but the wind caught it and pulled it away.

She didn't know why, but as her feet pounded the mossy path and the wind kissed her cheeks, she felt like she was flying.

One

"Before"

꧁ꙮ꧂

Wynmere - Present Day

~ Aislen ~

The morning sun spilled soft gold across Aislen's cluttered room, catching the silver strands in her hair like tiny stars come alive. She stared at the small, half-finished gift on her desk. It was a delicate necklace woven from moonstone and wildflowers. Moonstone for Kael's lunar magic, and wildflowers because he used to always pluck them and put them behind her ear when they were kids. They became her favorite.

Kael's nineteenth birthday was only days away.

Nineteen. It was the age when fae found their mates.

The thought should have stirred something inside her. But it didn't. Or at least, she wouldn't let it. Humans did not get to have mates; that was simply the way of things.

Because for years, Aislen had buried those feelings deep. She had locked them away like a dangerous secret. Admitting them meant risking everything: their friendship, her carefully crafted life, and the fragile peace she clung to.

But now, the fear was different.

If Kael found his mate this year, would he drift away? Would she lose her closest friend and confidant? She had other friends, but there was only one him.

She pressed a hand to the crescent-shaped birthmark just above her collarbone, her heart aching with a longing she refused to name.

Outside, the cobbled lane below echoed with the clatter of a milk cart and the murmur of a neighbor's spell-marked broom sweeping itself across a porch. The morning in Wynmere was already alive.

The scent of baking bread wafted in from the shop below. The familiar chatter of market day rose faintly, tangled with the faint, ever-present thrum of ward-magic pulsing in the village stones.

Aislen bit her lip, forcing her gaze toward the window where the village of Wynmere was already waking up. The magic from the village hummed softly. Wynmere was one of the last border villages where humans and fae coexisted peacefully. There were other places though, where humans like her were seen as less than chattel. Fortunately, they resided in a place where that was not tolerated.

But others were not as lucky.

Her mind began to race as her thoughts strayed back to Kael.

She had close friends, Thess and Sion were amazing. But what she had with Kael... it was different. Special. Kael was hers, and hers alone. Aislen was not ready to give that up. Give him up.

And though she would never say it out loud, she wasn't sure how to let him go. Or if she even could.

* * *

The necklace wasn't the only thing she had been overthinking.

Half her wardrobe was now scattered across the bed. There were tunics, shawls, and even a pale skirt she hadn't worn in months. Nothing looked right. Nothing *felt* right.

It was just a birthday. Just Kael. And yet… her stomach twisted like she was walking into something that was far more fragile than just a celebration.

She finally settled on a soft linen dress in pale sage.

It was simple, comfortable, and familiar. Everything she needed to calm her nerves.

Aislen slipped it over her head, fingers lingering near the hem before turning to the mirror.

She thought of the necklace again, made of moonstone and wildflowers, and the way her heart had pounded while weaving it.

She hoped he'd like it.

A soft knock at the door pulled her from her thoughts.

"Almost ready?" her dad's voice called.

Aislen smiled faintly. "Almost."

She stepped into her boots, tied a loose braid into her hair, and slipped the wrapped gift into her satchel. Then she opened the door to find Tomas, her dad, in the hallway. His arms were crossed but his eyes danced with amusement.

"Did you change your outfit three times?" he asked, arching a brow.

"Five," she muttered, not quite meeting her dad's eyes.

He laughed. "Well, you look beautiful. Some lucky guy will fall off his chair when he sees you."

Aislen rolled her eyes. "That lucky guy has seen me in mud-covered trousers and tangled hair. I think I've ruined those chances already."

"Hardly," Tomas said, as he brushed a loose curl from her face. "You have always been someone worth noticing, my daughter."

She leaned up and kissed her dad on the cheek.

"Be safe," he said. "And if anyone gives you any trouble—"

"I'll throw a nice hot cider in their face."

"That's my girl," her dad said as he gave her a hug goodbye.

Pulling her cloak around her shoulders, she stepped outside.

The cobbled path was warm, still holding the day's heat. Fireflies blinked lazily in the hedges, like tiny stars drifting close to the earth. Someone was singing from an open window above, and the air carried the scent of roasted apples and smoke from the village hearths.

Wynmere glowed with a silent sort of magic at night.

She walked slowly, letting her thoughts catch up to her feet. Every step closer to the tavern made her heart beat faster. She wasn't sure what she was expecting from tonight.

She just didn't want anything to change.

But deep down, she already knew it would.

Two

"Flicker"

~ Aislen ~

The tavern was alive with quiet laughter and the low hum of familiar voices. Flickering lanterns hung from wooden beams, casting warm pools of light over the gathered faces. Everyone was there. Friends, family, neighbors, what felt like the entire small, close-knit village that had watched Kael and Aislen grow up together. The scent of roasting meat mingled with the tang of spilled cider, and somewhere nearby, the faint tune of a lute thrummed softly under the chatter.

Aislen stepped through the door, the gift now clutched tightly in her hands. She removed it from her satchel before she stepped inside. She wanted to be ready.

She had wrapped it in linen and twine, tucked a small sprig of silverleaf into the knot. Simple. Meaningful.

Her stomach twisted further into uneasy knots.

For something so small, so simple, she had never felt more nervous.

She had spent just about every single day with Kael for almost their entire lives, so why was this day so different?

She knew why, but she wasn't ready for that truth. Not even inside her own head.

8

Kael was across the room near the hearth, leaning back in a chair with that easy, crooked smile he wore without effort. His storm-gray eyes caught hers, and for a second, everything went quiet. Her heart stuttered.

Stop it, she willed herself.

She broke eye contact first and made her way toward the food table, pretending to fuss with a plate as if the noise and motion could drown out the storm inside her.

"Late, as usual," came a voice behind her.

Aislen turned to find Thess Lethwyn, her other close friend, leaning against the post with a cup of cider in hand and one brow raised in mock judgment. Her sharp eyes softened only slightly in concern. Thess was a human, like her. Not that it mattered here.

"I'm not late," Aislen said. "I'm... fashionably cautious."

Thess snorted. "More like emotionally avoidant."

"I don't know what you're talking about." Aislen said, though the tightening at her temples told a different story.

Thess sipped her drink. "You've had a pinched look on your face for a week. And if I had to guess, you've been up all night making that necklace."

Aislen sighed and glanced toward Kael again. "It's just a birthday."

"Sure." Thess tilted her head. "Except it's *his* nineteenth birthday. And we all know what that means."

"Don't," Aislen warned softly.

"I'm not saying anything." She smirked. "Except that if I were secretly in love with someone, I probably wouldn't spend the night hand-weaving him a moonstone necklace unless I wanted to confuse *everyone* involved."

"I'm not—" but the words caught in her throat.

"It's just a gift, Thess. That's it."

"It's beautiful," Thess said, gentler now. "But be careful. If the bond hasn't hit him yet, it will soon. You can only bury feelings like that for so long before they dig their way back up. I just don't want to see you get hurt."

Aislen didn't answer. She spotted Sion, another one of their friends, waving them over from the other side of the tavern. He was sitting with Kael at a small table by the window. The moment dissolved as they crossed the room.

Kael rose to meet her halfway, eyes scanning her face.

"You came," he said, like there had ever been a question.

"Of course I did." Her voice was quiet, and for once, she didn't quite meet his gaze.

"I saved you a seat," he added, motioning toward a spot beside his. "Only had to fight off two cousins and a drunk bard to do it. I wouldn't even let little Matias take your seat, instead he ran off playing swords with the other children."

Aislen smiled, small and tight. "I'd say how heroic of you, but here you are, stealing chairs from children."

"Defending chairs," he corrected. "Big difference."

She raised a brow. "You sure that bard didn't win?"

"Please," Kael scoffed. "He barely made it past the second verse before I challenged him to a cider chugging contest and he bowed out gracefully."

Aislen let out a small laugh. "That sounds about right."

Then, on impulse, maybe nerves, maybe something deeper, she tilted her head. "Alright then. Since you're apparently in the mood for challenges..."

Kael leaned in, smile tugging at the corner of his mouth. "I'm listening."

"I dare you to make it through this entire night," she said, voice light but laced with meaning, "without trying to charm your way out of anything."

He feigned offense. "Charm? I am naturally likable."

"Mmhmm."

He held out a hand. "Challenge accepted."

She took it, briefly, and the contact sparked more than just warmth in her palm. She pulled away quickly. Too quickly.

"You okay?" he asked, watching her closely.

She nodded too quickly. "Just tired."

A lie. She wasn't tired, she was terrified. Of what the night might bring. Of what it might not.

Despite her fears, she sat beside him, fingers curling around the edges of the gift in her lap. The room buzzed with conversation. Plates clinked, someone started a song in the corner, and time ticked forward. It was slow and heavy as it dragged her toward midnight.

Toward a bond that wasn't supposed to exist. It was unfair.

* * *

~ **Kael** ~

Kael had never liked being the center of attention.

Even as a kid, he'd preferred the edges of the room. The shadows at the edge of the clearing, the space just behind Aislen's shoulder, that's where he felt the most comfortable. But tonight, the tavern was filled with every villager who had ever taught him, scolded him, sparred with him, or slipped him a sweet roll when no one was looking.

There were streamers. And flowers. And a crooked hand-painted banner that read:

"Happy 19th, Kael! The Moon's Not the Only Thing Getting Older!"

He should've been laughing.

Instead, he felt like he couldn't breathe.

Not even the giggles of his little brother, Matias, could ease the anxiety building in him.

Kael felt her before he saw her.

Not just noticed, but *felt*. Like the air shifted, warmer, tighter in his chest. Like the low hum of magic inside him, usually steady and quiet, suddenly pulsed in time with her footsteps.

He looked up.

There she was.

Aislen moved through the crowd as if she didn't know the whole room tilted slightly toward her. Linen dress, silver light catching in her hair, clutching a small wrapped bundle like it might explode. Or like *she* might if she let go.

She didn't come right to him. Of course not. Aislen never made things that simple. Instead, she disappeared near the cider table, probably pretending to need something she didn't want, probably pretending not to look for him in return.

Kael swallowed hard, heart kicking against his ribs.

She'd come. Of course she had. And yet part of him hadn't let himself believe it until now.

Nineteen.

He was supposed to feel different tonight. Supposed to awaken to something new—some instinct, some magical pull toward the one meant for him.

And he had.

But it wasn't new.

It was her.

It had *always* been her.

And that was the problem.

Because humans didn't have mates.

He knew the stories. The rules. The way the bond felt when it started flickering to life in your soul. A bloom of magic. A soft ache when she looked away. The rush of wanting to protect, to run, to *stay*. He'd read it all, heard it in bard's songs, even seen it once or twice in court pairings.

And now, every time Aislen smiled at someone else, or pulled her hand away too fast, or looked like she might leave…

It hurt. A little too much.

Like something in him was unraveling, thread by thread.

This isn't supposed to happen, he'd told himself, again and again.

So maybe it wasn't the beginning of the bond taking hold. Maybe he was just *broken*, clinging to a childhood crush that had never really gone away.

Or maybe the magic was wrong. Maybe his bloodline was cursed.

He wasn't about to tell her that. Not when she already looked nervous just being near him. He hated that she felt that way, he never used to make her nervous.

She was walking toward him now, slow and cautious like he was something fragile.

Kael stood, forcing his voice steady. "You came."

She nodded, looking anywhere but at him. "Of course I did."

He fought the pull to reach for her. Fought the urge to ask if she felt it too, this *buzz* beneath his skin whenever she was near.

Instead, he offered a lopsided grin. "I saved you a seat. Only had to fight off two cousins and a drunk bard. I wouldn't even let little Matias take your seat, instead he ran off playing swords with the other children."

A ghost of a smile tugged at her lips. "I'd say how heroic of you, but here you are, stealing chairs from children."

And stars, he could live off that smile for days.

"Defending chairs," he corrected smoothly. "Big difference."

She raised a brow at him. "You sure that bard didn't win?"

He gave a low laugh.

"Please," Kael scoffed. "He barely made it past the second verse before I challenged him to a cider chugging contest and he bowed out gracefully."

Aislen let out a small laugh. "That sounds about right."

Then her expression shifted. It was slight, but just enough to spark a flicker of mischief in her eyes. "Alright then. Since you're apparently in the mood for challenges..."

Kael leaned in, pulse quickening. "I'm listening."

"I dare you to make it through this entire night," she said, voice light but laced with meaning, "without trying to charm your way out of anything."

He feigned offense as his grin widened playfully. "Charm? I am naturally likable."

"Mmhmm."

He held out a hand. "Challenge accepted."

Her hand touched his, just briefly. But it was enough to make him miss her warmth as she pulled away quickly. Too quickly.

He looked at her.

"Are you okay?" he asked, keeping his tone light.

"I'm just tired," she answered.

A lie.

But he didn't press.

Because if she didn't feel it...

If this was just in *his* blood, and not hers—
Saying anything could ruin everything.
And losing her completely?
That would destroy him.

* * *

Kael had been mid-conversation with one of his cousins, something about training at the border, but the words barely registered. The tavern had grown warmer, louder. Lanterns flickered against wood-paneled walls, casting shifting shadows across the room. Somewhere, someone was laughing too loud. Someone else dropped a plate.

He wasn't listening. Not really.

Because every time his gaze drifted across the room, it found her.

Aislen.

She was still beside Thess.

Still not looking at him.

Still trying to pretend this night was just another celebration.

She shifted in her seat and tucked a loose strand of hair behind her ear. It was an old habit, one that always meant she was nervous. He knew every version of her body language, every little tic and tell. He wanted to go to her. Ask her what she was feeling. Ask her if it was *just him*.

But he stayed rooted.

Because if he said the wrong thing, if he *was wrong,* he'd ruin everything.

"Kael?" Sion's voice cut through the fog. "You good?"

Kael blinked. He hadn't even realized his friend had joined him again. "Yeah. Just… thinking."

Sion looked at him for a beat too long, like he didn't believe a word of it. But he didn't press.

Kael forced a smile, excused himself, and turned toward the hearth. He needed air, but instead, he found heat. The fire crackled too loud in his ears. His lunar magic, usually cool and balanced, began to twist.

Not yet. It's not midnight yet.

He squeezed his eyes shut and breathed deep, willing the feeling away. It didn't work.

The warmth bloomed inside him, not the fire's, but something *internal.* Like a thread tugging loose inside his chest. Like his soul was being rewoven, stitch by stitch, around a name he already knew by heart.

He opened his eyes and saw her laugh.

Just a laugh. Just a moment.

And then her scent.

To Kael, her scent had always been something familiar. It was warm linen, wild herbs from the apothecary, and a whisper of pine smoke from the village hearths. *Safe. Steady.*

But tonight, something shifted.

The moment the bond began to flare to life in his chest, her scent changed. Or maybe… it had always been there, and now he was finally *attuned* to it.

She smelled like moonlit violets and summer rain on forest soil. It was like starlight caught in blooming earth. Soft, cool, and impossibly alive. There was something *ancient* in it too, something that tugged at the fae magic in his bones and whispered:

Home. Mine.

And gods help him, it made his head spin.

Every time she passed near him, the scent coiled in his lungs and settled low in his chest like heat and ache and longing all at once.

He had at least a few hours. Or so he thought.

But just before the eleventh bell rang from the village tower, the rest of it *hit* him. Not just the small feeling, not her scent, but everything all at once.

Like a wave crashing through his chest—

No, deeper. Lower. *Rooted.*

Kael staggered back half a step and gripped the edge of the hearth behind him, eyes wide. The room spun.

A warmth bloomed inside him like silver flame licking through his ribs, coiling in his lungs. Magic surged, raw and ancient and *terrifyingly right.*

15

And tethered to it. To *her*.

His mate.

Aislen.

It wasn't a whisper anymore, it was a roar.

His body reacted instinctively. His eyes snapping to her like gravity itself had shifted. She was mid-laugh with Thess, but her expression faltered, just for a heartbeat. Like maybe—*maybe*—she had felt something too.

But she didn't look toward him.

Not once.

He nearly called her name. Nearly crossed the tavern in four long strides to ask her if she *felt it too*. If she knew.

But she couldn't.

Because she was human.

Because the bond shouldn't *be possible*.

Which meant there were only three explanations:

1. Something was broken in him.
2. This was all in his head.
3. She wasn't entirely human.

And he wasn't ready to find out which.

* * *

Kael turned his face toward the fire and focused on breathing. The magic didn't fade, but it dulled, like it understood his panic and settled, waiting.

The worst part wasn't the bond.

It was the hope.

The aching, beautiful hope that he wasn't just imagining everything he'd ever wanted.

And it scared him more than anything.

He didn't want to lose her.

He couldn't risk it.

So when she finally looked over at him again, shoulders drawn tight, gift still in her lap, Kael forced a grin.

Just the easy kind. The *old* kind. The one that said, *We're fine. I'm fine. You're fine. Nothing's changed.*

Even though everything had.

Three

"Buried"

~ Aislen ~

The tavern had thinned to a low hum. A few villagers lingered in the corners, clinking mugs and humming along to a bard's sleepy tune, but the magic of the party had softened now. It settled into something much quieter.

Warm amber light pooled around the worn wooden tables, and the faint scent of spiced cider mingled with smoke from the dying hearth.

Aislen hadn't moved from the bench in over twenty minutes. Her thighs had gone numb. Her fingers curled tight around the frayed linen wrapping in her lap.

She should just give it to him already. It was his birthday. That was the whole point.

But every time she looked over at Kael, she hesitated.

What if he didn't like it?

He was talking with Sion and Thess now, laughing at something Thess had said, and yet, he kept glancing her way. Just little flickers. Almost like he didn't want to get caught.

He's being careful.

The thought stung more than it should. Careful was for glass, for fire,

18

for people you couldn't afford to get too close to.

She drew a slow breath, steeled herself, and stood.

Kael turned just as she reached him, that smile already sliding into place. It was warm, practiced, too polite.

"You didn't open your present," she said, holding it out before she could talk herself out of it. Her voice was too soft. Too small. "I made it for you."

Thess and Sion shared a look before excusing themselves to get another mug of cider.

She saw him glance at their retreating friends before focusing back on her. His smile faltered, just a little. He didn't reach for the gift right away.

"Aislen—"

"Don't make a thing out of it," she cut in, lifting her chin a little too high. "It's just something small. For your birthday. That's all." Her heart pounded so loudly she was sure his fae ears could hear it.

"Don't act like I have never given you a gift before." She looked at him with her eyebrows raised.

Kael looked at her for a long moment before finally taking the bundle from her hands. His fingers brushed hers, just barely, and her breath caught.

It wasn't the first time they'd touched. It wasn't even the hundredth. But tonight, her skin felt different. Too awake. Like there was static humming just under the surface.

She hated it. She loved it.

He peeled back the linen carefully, like he didn't want to break the moment, or maybe like he was afraid of what was inside.

When the necklace fell into his hands, Kael stilled.

Pale moonstone glimmered in the firelight, the dried wildflowers threaded between each stone catching the light like flecks of gold dust.

"You made this?" he asked quietly.

"I had help with the binding spells," she admitted, brushing imaginary dust off her skirt. "But the design was mine."

He looked up, and there was something in his eyes, something raw and unreadable.

"It's beautiful," he said, almost like it hurt to say it. "You remembered the wildflowers."

Aislen's throat tightened. "They always reminded me of you."

Kael stared at the necklace a moment longer, then slipped it over his head. The stones settled against his collarbone.

"They suit you," she said, trying to joke, but it came out a whisper.

He smiled. "Thank you. Really."

The words sounded true. But they also sounded... final.

Aislen glanced down at her hands. "You've been weird tonight."

Kael blinked. "Weird?"

She met his eyes. "Different. Quiet. Careful. Like you're trying really hard not to upset me."

He didn't answer right away. His jaw tensed.

"I didn't want to make things uncomfortable," he said finally.

"Why would it be uncomfortable?"

He looked away. "Because tonight matters. And we both know it."

Her heart lurched. "You think I don't know that?"

"I think you don't want to."

That hit harder than it should have.

"I know what happens when fae turn nineteen," she said, voice sharper than intended. "I know what tonight means. I'm not an idiot, Kael."

"I didn't say you were—"

"You're not going to find her," she blurted. "Not tonight."

Kael's eyes widened, but he didn't argue.

She swallowed, suddenly wishing she could claw the words back. "Sorry. That came out wrong. I just meant... you're not *guaranteed* to. For some it may take weeks, even years—"

"I know."

They stood in silence, the necklace between them like a secret.

What if he did find her tonight?

The thought struck like a stone to the gut. It hit suddenly, making her breathless. What would she do? Smile? Pretend to be happy? Force a laugh and offer a blessing she didn't mean?

Would she lie and say it didn't matter?

Would he see through it?

Would he let her?

Aislen looked at Kael then, really looked, and the ache in her chest bloomed sharp and quiet. No, she wasn't ready. Not to lose him. Not to stand by while someone else became his future. Not to fade into the background of her own life like she had never hoped for more.

"Thess says I bury things," she muttered. "That I lock feelings down so deep, I forget they're even there."

Kael huffed a quiet breath. "She's not wrong."

Aislen gave a shaky laugh. "I guess not."

Another beat passed. A longer one.

"I've been thinking," she said. "If you do find her soon, your mate I mean... and things change..."

Kael's posture stiffened. "Nothing has to change."

"You don't know that."

He didn't even hesitate. "I do."

"You and I, this—" he waved vaguely between them. "We don't *break* just because some ancient magic says so. You're my person Aislen, my best friend."

Silence.

Too much silence.

Kael didn't move. Didn't blink.

And then he smiled. Just a little. Not his real one.

Kael looked down at the necklace in his hands and touched it carefully. "It means a lot. That you made this."

She nodded. *So much for him not charming his way through tonight*, she thought.

Before she could say something else to embarrass herself, she added "Happy birthday, Kael."

He didn't respond right away. Just looked at her like he was memorizing something he'd never get back.

"Thanks for staying late," he said. "I know crowds aren't really your thing. I would have bailed too if it wasn't all for me."

"You're my thing," she said, and immediately regretted it. Her face burned. "I mean—ugh, stars, not like that. I just meant, you know, *my best friend thing*. My designated moral anchor. My emotional support fae."

She forced a laugh that didn't quite reach her eyes. "Someone has to keep you humble before your ego starts glowing."

Kael raised an eyebrow, but didn't call her on it. He just looked at her like he saw right through the joke and straight to the part she was trying to bury.

"I know what you meant," he said.

And gods, if his voice wasn't full of longing, she didn't know what it was. But whatever it was… it wasn't enough. It never would be.

She never would be.

Not for someone who was fated for someone else.

* * *

The night air was cool and sharp as Aislen and Thess stepped out of the tavern. The village streets were quiet now, the party's laughter and music fading behind them like a half-remembered dream.

The stars stretched across the sky, pale and distant, their light barely reaching the sleepy village.

Thess pulled her cloak tighter around her shoulders, eyes scanning the empty road ahead. "You really put yourself through the wringer tonight."

Aislen sighed, fingers absently tracing the knot on her cloak. "It's not just a party, Thess, this is… everything. What if he really does find her soon? What if this—" she gestured vaguely around her, "—all means nothing? What if I lose my best friend?"

Thess shot her a look that was half exasperation, half sympathy. "First, ouch. You would still have me. Second, that isn't going to happen. And third, you act like you're auditioning for the village tragedy queen."

"Maybe I am," Aislen admitted, voice barely above a whisper. "I'm sorry

Thess, you know I love you. I just…"

Thess stopped and turned, fixing her with a sharp glance. "Listen, burying feelings doesn't mean they vanish. They're like weeds, Aislen. The longer you ignore them, the more tangled they get. Sooner or later, you've got to pull them out before they choke everything else."

Aislen bit her lip, thinking of the years she'd spent locking away the ache of something unspoken. "And if I pull too hard? What if it all comes undone?"

"Then you're human," Thess said softly, her usual sarcasm replaced by something steadier. "Messy, scared, but real. You don't have to be perfect, or the hero of some fae legend. Just yourself. That's enough."

They started walking again, boots crunching softly over gravel, the silence settling like a blanket between them.

Aislen glanced at Thess, grateful for the fierce honesty. "Thanks, Thess. For being my person. Between you, Kael and Sion, you're all I have. I'm terrified of losing that."

Thess grinned, shoulders relaxing. "I'm more than a person, you know. I'm the most amazing person you'll ever meet. But I'll take it."

Thess bumped shoulders with Aislen, her voice softer than usual. "It may not feel like it, but it's going to be okay."

And for the first time that night, Aislen felt a flicker of something she hadn't allowed herself.

Hope.

Four

"Strain"

~~~~

~ **Kael** ~

The tavern's warmth lingered like a fading song, the last echoes of laughter and clinking mugs dissolving into the night. Kael sat by the window, the moonstone necklace heavy in his hands, its cool weight a quiet reminder of everything he couldn't yet say.

Outside, the village was settling into sleep. Lanterns flickered along the cobblestone streets, casting long shadows beneath the skeletal branches of ancient trees. And there she was, Aislen, walking away with Thess by her side, cloaked in the silver-gray night, her silhouette framed by the pale light.

He watched her every step, memorizing the way her shoulders drew tight, the careful tilt of her head as she whispered something Thess's way. The distance between them seemed to hum, a current of something unspoken stretching taut and fragile.

Kael traced a finger over the moonstone, feeling a pulse beneath the smooth surface, a heartbeat that mirrored his own. His chest tightened with a strange mix of hope and fear. The gift was more than a necklace. It was a promise, a question, a tether between them that neither dared to fully grasp yet.

But the bond, the one that had been stirring deep in his blood, was growing restless. It wanted to claim her. He could feel it in the hollow spaces of his ribs, in the jitter of magic beneath his skin. Tonight was only the beginning. The real test was still to come.

A shadow fell across the window, and Kael turned to see Sion stepping inside, hands shoved deep in his coat pockets, eyes scanning the room with his usual casual alertness.

"Still here?" Sion asked, nodding toward the moonstone in Kael's hand.

Kael forced a smile, trying to seem less tangled inside than he felt. "Yeah. Just... still thinking."

Aislen was his best friend, his most important person, but Sion was a close second. They met about four years ago during junior warrior training after Sion's family moved to the village from the Aurion Court. Thess had been part of the group even longer, ever since she marched up to Aislen at age eight and never left her side.

They spent just about every day together. The four of them were rarely seen apart.

Sion moved closer, lowering his voice. "You know you don't have to keep it all bottled up, right? Especially not tonight."

Kael looked out at the night again, reluctant. "It's not that simple."

Sion's gaze softened. "It never is. But you've got people, Kael. We're not going anywhere."

Kael laughed, low and bitter. "Doesn't make it easier."

Sion shrugged. "Nope. But it does make you less crazy."

The tavern door creaked open, and a petite figure stepped inside. It was Elara, Kael's mother. Her silver-streaked hair caught the lantern light, and her gentle smile held a wisdom that only years of watching Kael grow could give.

"Elara," Sion greeted quietly.

She gave him a soft nod before turning to her son. "It's late. I'm heading home." Her eyes flicked to the necklace in his hands. "That one looks important."

"It is," Kael admitted, slipping it into his cloak pocket. "More than I expected."

Elara's expression tightened just a bit. "I see. You'll figure it out. You always do."

Kael nodded, feeling the weight of her quiet confidence.

Elara gave him a small, motherly peck on his cheek and headed out into the night, her footsteps fading down the road.

Sion clapped a hand on Kael's shoulder. "Come on, man. Let's get you home before you start conjuring more worries."

Kael rose, shoulders heavy but resolute. One last glance out the window where Aislen had disappeared.

"Tomorrow's coming," he said quietly.

"Yeah," Sion agreed with a grin. "And with it, whatever the hell fate decides to throw at us."

Together, they stepped out into the cool night air, the village silent but alive with possibility.

* * *

Kael thought going home would help him clear his mind, but nothing could ease the roaring in his head.

He needed to move. To bleed it out.

So he went where he always did when his thoughts were too loud: the warrior's ring.

The sparring field lay quiet, bathed in silver moonlight, the torches casting long shadows across packed dirt and stone. He wasn't alone.

"Couldn't sleep either, Duskthorn?" Tavien's gravel-thick voice cut through the air like a blade. The older warrior stood at the edge of the ring, arms folded, eyes sharp even beneath his greying temples. Tavien was the head of the warriors in their village. He knew everything, everyone. Despite his age, he never missed a beat.

Kael offered only a nod, already peeling off his tunic and stepping onto the field.

Lira, lounging on a bench with her booted feet propped on a training dummy, let out a low whistle. "Stars, Kael, you're glowing. That must've been some party."

Lira was like an older sister to him. She was an entire decade older, but because she was fae, she barely looked a day older than him. When Sion was unavailable, she was his sparring partner.

"Not tonight, Lira."

"Ooooh, testy." She hopped to her feet, spinning a training staff in one hand. "Let me guess. Our dear Aislen left with tall, smirky, and annoying?"

He didn't answer. Didn't have to.

"Thought so," she muttered.

Kael threw himself into his drills. He did round after round of strikes, pivots, and defensive blocks. Each of his movements became faster, sharper, and more desperate than the last. Tavien watched silently, arms still crossed. Lira circled, stretching, warming up.

"You fight like something's chasing you," Tavien finally said.

Kael didn't stop. "Nothing is."

"Mm. That's the problem."

A beat.

"You're chasing something."

Kael slammed the blunt end of his staff into the target dummy with a grunt, cracking the wood slightly.

Lira whistled low. "Well, that dummy definitely asked about your feelings. Rude thing."

Kael spun to face her. "Can we not do this tonight?"

She only grinned, flipping her braid over her shoulder. "What? Pretend you're not moon-eyed over the girl you've loved since you were knee-high? Come on, I need entertainment."

"She's not mine. She never can be," Kael muttered.

"Woah, okay, Kael, what's with the downward spiral? What, did she finally fall for someone else?" Lira asked, her eyebrows raised.

Kael just went back to ignoring her. He wanted to feel, not talk.

Tavien stepped closer now, voice quieter but heavy with weight. "So that's why you're trying to break your own bones? You're here punishing yourself? For what?"

Kael's jaw clenched.

He continued hitting the dummy for a few minutes before he could even get a word out.

"I can't tell her," he snapped. "It'll ruin everything. I'm 19 now. She'll think I'm just some selfish male trying to trap her into something she didn't choose."

A pause. Lira's expression sobered.

"You really think she wouldn't choose you?" she asked softly.

Kael looked down at his shaking hands. "She's everything," he said. "But if I push this... if I lose her, even as a friend, I don't think I'll survive it."

Tavien exhaled through his nose. "Then you'd better figure out what kind of warrior you want to be, boy. One who runs from the truth... or one who faces it, no matter the pain."

Kael nodded, slow and grim. "Let's go," he said, lifting his staff.

Lira smirked, already stepping forward. "Don't cry when I knock you on your ass."

Kael adjusted his stance as Lira rolled her shoulders, staff spinning lazily in her hands. They knew each other's moves by the back of their hands now.

"Ready to get humbled?" she asked, flashing a grin that had spelled trouble since he was a kid.

Kael met her eyes, jaw tight. "Don't go easy."

"Oh, darling, I never do."

Tavien gave a low grunt of approval and stepped back into the shadows to watch. The ring fell quiet but for the crunch of boots on packed dirt and the low whistle of wind through the trees.

Then Lira struck first.

She was fast, always had been, but Kael met her staff with his own, the crack of wood-on-wood echoing across the field. He parried her next blow, spun, and swept low for her legs.

28

She leapt, twisting midair, and landed with a flourish. "Still slow," she teased.

"You talk too much," Kael growled, lunging again.

They fell into a brutal rhythm of attack, dodge, and counter. Kael's muscles burned, sweat beading on his brow. But Lira didn't let up, and neither did he.

Until she appeared.

Not really. Just a flicker. A breath.

Aislen at eight years old, cheeks flushed from running through the woods, curls tangled with pine needles as she dared him with that look in her eyes.

"I dare you to kiss me," he had asked.

He hadn't understood then, not the way he does now. But even as a boy, her closeness had made his chest feel too full, his skin too tight. That kiss, barely more than a brush, had etched itself into him like a brand.

Soft. Uncomplicated. But unforgettable.

And now, years later, it came back like a punch to the ribs. A memory blooming where focus should've been. One flicker too long.

Aislen's smile as she handed him the necklace. Her scent, that impossible mix of moonlit violets and rain-drenched soil, it crashed over him like a storm, stealing his focus.

And in that second, Lira swept his legs from beneath him and drove the blunt tip of her staff to his chest.

He hit the ground hard, the wind knocked out of him.

Lira stood over him, breathing heavily, brow furrowed now instead of smug.

"There it is," she said, voice softer. "You weren't fighting me, Kael. You were fighting your damn feelings."

Kael turned his face to the side, jaw clenched against the sting behind his eyes.

"I can't get her out of my head," he admitted, voice low. "It's like she's... everywhere."

Lira dropped to a crouch beside him, resting her staff across her knees. She just looked at him for a moment, deciding on what to say.

"She's your mate, isn't she?"

He nodded once.

"But how?" A pause. "I didn't think that was possible. Does she know?"

"No," he rasped. "And I won't tell her. Not yet. Maybe not ever. There must be something wrong with me, maybe my bloodline. I don't know. But I can't let this hurt her."

Lira leaned back, exhaling. "You're a stubborn ass."

"Thanks."

She nudged his side with her boot. "But I get it. Still—" she stood, offering him a hand "—you keep bottling this up, it's going to tear you apart. You think getting your ribs cracked in the sparring ring hurts? Wait 'til you break your own heart."

Kael stared up at her for a long beat, then took her hand. She hauled him to his feet with ease.

For a moment, they just stood there. Neither of them spoke. The wind moved quietly through the trees, the moon high and bright above them. The only sound was their breath, his still shaky, while hers was steady.

Kael didn't know what to say. Didn't know if anything would make it hurt less.

Lira didn't push. She didn't tease, didn't joke. Just stood beside him.

"You're stronger than you think," she said, voice quieter now. "And she's not blind, Kael. I may not understand how this happened but if she hasn't felt it yet... she will."

He brushed the dirt off his pants, glancing toward the torch-lit path that led back toward the village. Toward her.

"Yeah," he said, not quite believing it. "We'll see."

Five

"Distance"

~ **Aislen** ~

The morning sun filtered through the kitchen window, casting gold lines across the wooden floorboards. Aislen stood at the counter, slicing bread for breakfast even though she wasn't hungry. The scent of fresh herbs from the hanging bundles above her head should have calmed her, as it usually did, but today, everything felt... itchy.

Off.

She set the knife down a little too hard.

Her mom glanced up from the hearth, stirring a pot of simmering stew. "You're up early."

"Couldn't sleep."

"You've been saying that a lot this week."

Aislen shrugged. "Just a lot on my mind."

It wasn't a lie. Not exactly. It just wasn't the whole truth.

She grabbed a basket from the wall hook and headed out toward the garden without waiting for another comment. The morning air was cool on her skin, the dew still clinging to the grass. She sank her hands into the soil of the herb beds, pulling weeds, checking roots, repotting sprigs of lemon balm that didn't actually need moving.

She'd already rearranged the garden twice this week. Her dad teased that the thyme would start filing complaints.

She didn't care.

If her hands were busy, maybe her heart would quiet down. If she kept moving, maybe her thoughts wouldn't keep circling back to him.

Kael had been quiet since his birthday. Not cold, just… distant. Slippery. Like trying to hold water in her hands. He hadn't stopped by. He hadn't responded to the note she slipped into his pack days before the party. And he hadn't come to the garden even once.

He used to love watching her garden, he would even lend a hand every once in awhile.

So maybe he was done. Maybe she was overthinking. Maybe it was nothing.

Or maybe it was something more and that terrified her.

The thyme plant snapped in her fingers.

"Sorry," she muttered to it, brushing the soil back around its roots like an apology could fix it.

From behind her, the screen door creaked open.

"You planning to dig a hole to the next realm?" her dad called.

"I'm fine."

"You keep saying that."

"I keep meaning it," she said, but her voice lacked the weight to make it true.

Frustrated, she stood up.

She needed a change of scenery, she needed to escape.

With that thought, she dropped her gardening materials and made her way towards the village.

Towards him.

The market was unusually quiet for a late summer afternoon. Aislen walked slowly down the village path, trailing one hand along the sun-warmed stone wall beside the apothecary. She'd told herself this was just a walk. Just something to do.

But her feet already knew where they were going.

The bakery's bells jingled faintly in the distance. A pair of children darted past her with sticky fingers and berry-stained grins. She gave them a faint smile, but didn't stop. Her path curved instinctively toward a familiar stone house at the edge of the woods.

Kael's house.

The front gate creaked softly as she pushed it open. The garden here was tidier than hers, Elara's touch, no doubt. The rosemary bushes were trimmed back, the walkway swept clean. The door was half-open to let the breeze through.

She hesitated.

Then lifted a hand and knocked.

A moment later, Elara appeared in the doorway, wiping flour from her hands with a linen cloth. Her shiny brown hair was braided back, her expression was calm but the quiet surprise in her eyes gave her away.

"Aislen," she said, warmth threading her voice. "What a lovely surprise."

"I... I was just walking through the village," Aislen said, already hating the way her excuse sounded. "I thought I might say hello."

Elara nodded gently, stepping aside. "He's not home."

That stopped Aislen short. "Oh. I... I didn't say I was here for—"

"You don't have to," Elara said kindly. "He's out training. Has been every day since the celebration."

Aislen tried not to frown. "Training where?"

"Warrior's ring. Or out near the west ridge." Elara's eyes softened, something like knowing flickering in them. "Sometimes, when a male doesn't know what to say, he hits things until he figures it out."

That earned a small, reluctant smile.

"I'm sorry I missed him," Aislen said quietly.

"You didn't," Elara replied, folding her cloth. "He's just not ready to be found yet."

Aislen nodded, murmured a thank you, and turned back toward the village path.

She didn't go home.

Instead, her feet carried her the long way. She went down past the bakery, past the market stalls, and then up the narrow trail behind the smithy. It opened to a ridge overlooking the training fields.

She scanned the packed-dirt ring, the sparring dummies, the scattered weapons.

Empty.

Not a single soul.

Her heart sank.

He wasn't there either.

She stood there for a long moment, the wind catching at her braid, the sun warm against her skin, and still, the weight in her chest didn't lift.

He was avoiding her.

And for the first time since they were kids, she didn't know why.

With a sigh, Aislen made her way back home.

* * *

Aislen sat cross-legged on her bedroom floor, an open book resting on her lap, one she'd read a dozen times before. The spine was cracked, the pages soft at the edges, corners bent from late nights and rereads. But today, the words wouldn't settle. They blurred together, too quiet, too far away.

She closed it with a sigh and leaned back against the bed frame, staring at the ceiling.

Outside, the late afternoon light filtered through the window in golden strips, catching the edges of the pressed flowers lining her sill. They were beginning to fade. Maybe she should replace them. Maybe she should clean her desk. Maybe she should—

Her gaze drifted to the little drawer beneath her window seat. The one with the sketches she hadn't touched in what felt like months.

She pulled it open.

Inside were folded pages, smudged charcoal, soft outlines of trees and wildflowers and faces she hadn't meant to capture but had drawn anyway.

One sketch slid loose. It was of Kael, half-finished, his jawline shadowed and his eyes left blank. Unfinished.

She stared at it for a long time, then gently set it aside.

Her fingers itched to draw something else, anything else, but nothing came. No image, no motion. Just that heaviness again.

That silence.

She glanced at the unfinished sketch of Kael one more time.

Then, slowly, carefully, she slid it back into the drawer and closed it.

Out of sight. But not out of mind.

The house creaked softly as it settled. Somewhere downstairs, her dad was humming under his breath, a low tune that used to lull her to sleep as a girl. It should've been comforting. And in some ways, it was. But tonight, the quiet didn't feel peaceful. It felt hollow.

She pushed to her feet and crossed to the window. The sky outside was dimming now, streaked with lavender and rose. Lanterns were being lit along the roads. The garden shimmered in the low light.

Aislen pressed her forehead to the glass.

Maybe tomorrow things would feel normal again. Maybe Kael would show up at her gate like he used to. Maybe they'd laugh about how strange everything had felt and it would all make sense somehow.

But deep down, she knew he wouldn't.

Something had shifted between them. And no matter how much she tried to distract herself, that truth lingered.

She turned away from the window, blew out her candle, and crawled beneath the covers, pulling them up over her head like she used to when the world felt too big.

Sleep didn't come easily.

But eventually, it did.

And the last thing she dreamed before the dark took her was the feeling of Kael's embrace and the sound of her own voice saying his name like a question.

Six

~ Aislen ~

The garden had always been her escape.

Aislen crouched near the lavender patch, fingers buried in the warm soil. The sun dipped lower behind the trees, casting long amber shadows across the rows of wild herbs and stubborn roots. She should've felt calm here. This space was hers, untouched by expectations or court politics or... him.

But her chest still felt tight.

It had been almost ten days.

Ten days since his birthday.

Kael was avoiding her, and if he wasn't, then he was damn good at never being where she was.

She stabbed the spade into the dirt a little harder than necessary.

"Those weeds offend you personally, or are you just taking out your feelings on innocent plant life?"

She looked up to see her dad leaning against the fence, arms folded, expression mild.

Aislen brushed her hands off on her apron. "I'm just gardening."

He lifted a brow. "Right. The kind of gardening that requires glaring at a thyme bush like it insulted your honor."

36

She didn't answer. Instead, she sat back on her heels and sighed. "I guess I'm just... off today."

He came closer, crouched beside her with a familiar creak of old knees. "This wouldn't have anything to do with Kael, would it?"

Aislen's shoulders stiffened. "Why would it?"

"I didn't say it did." He picked a weed and twirled it between his fingers. "But you haven't mentioned him once since the party, which is... unusual."

She stared at her dirt-streaked hands. "He's been weird."

Her dad gave her a sidelong look. "Weird how?"

"Just... distant. Like he's avoiding me." Her voice dipped, quieter now. "Or like he's waiting for something."

He didn't speak right away. Just watched her carefully.

Aislen dug her fingers back into the soil, restless. "And then he went all silent again when I gave him the necklace. It was like... like he was sad. Or resigned. And now it's like he's trying not to be around me too much. And I don't—" She stopped herself, jaw tight. "I don't understand what changed."

"You two have always had a rhythm," her dad said gently. "When it shifts, it's bound to feel off."

She nodded slowly, but her mouth twisted. "But it's more than that. Something's different. And I don't know why it bothers me this much."

There it was, the edge of a truth she couldn't quite touch.

"I mean," she added quickly, "we've always been close. But lately..." she shook her head. "Maybe it's just that I miss my friend."

He didn't challenge her. Didn't tease. Just hummed thoughtfully, still twirling the weed stem in his fingers.

"Sometimes," he said slowly, "the things we don't say out loud are the ones shouting the most inside us."

She glanced at him, startled.

He smiled faintly. "Doesn't mean you have to know what they're saying. Just means they're there."

Aislen dropped her gaze. "Well, if they're saying anything, it's in a language I don't speak."

"Maybe," he said, standing with a groan, "you just haven't learned to listen

37

yet."

He left her there, quiet again, surrounded by the soft scent of earth and lavender. Her thoughts tangled like vines—tight, coiled, reaching.

She didn't know what she felt.

But maybe... she was starting to wonder.

* * *

The air was heavy with the scent of summer pine and the lingering promise of rain as Aislen ran. Her feet pounding the dirt path just beyond the edge of the garden. She hadn't meant to. One minute she was watching her dad disappear into the house, the next, she was sprinting down the trail like something was chasing her.

Maybe something was.

Her thoughts, mostly. All tangled up in Kael and that look on his face when she gave him the necklace. It had been a gift. That's all. Something simple. Something real.

So why had it felt like goodbye?

The trees blurred around her, tall sentinels that offered no answers. The wind tugged at her braid, her heartbeat thudding louder than her boots against the worn trail. She didn't even know where she was going, only that her skin itched like it didn't fit right, like she needed to *move* or she'd come apart at the seams.

It wasn't helping. She was still frustrated. Still confused.

Still—

Her steps slowed. The woods opened around her in a sudden hush of memory. A moss-covered clearing stretched ahead, lit by slanted moonlight and the shimmer of fireflies.

Her breath caught.

Of course. This place.

The stream still trickled over smooth stones at the edge of the grove. The branches of the twisted willow tree still arched overhead like the arms of something ancient and kind. She hadn't been here in years. Not since—

"Aislen? What are you doing here?"

Her heart stuttered.

Kael.

He stepped out from behind the willow, his hair tousled, his shirt loose at the collar like he'd dressed in a rush. His storm-gray eyes met hers, and this time, she didn't look away.

"I didn't mean to be," she said truthfully. "I just... ran."

Kael gave a small, almost disbelieving laugh. "Me too."

The silence between them was not quite comfortable, not quite unbearable. It just felt almost thick and full of something neither of them had words for.

They stood on either side of the stream now, the same one they'd crossed barefoot when they were kids. The memory tugged at her. Their muddy feet, shy glances, and that soft, startled kiss that had felt like the whole forest leaned in to watch.

Aislen swallowed. "We haven't been back here in years."

Kael nodded slowly, eyes not leaving hers. "I think about it more than I should."

She felt it then, that hum beneath her skin again. That... *pull*. Like invisible threads stitched between them were tightening by the second. She shifted her weight, arms crossed, trying to pretend the ache in her chest wasn't getting worse the longer he looked at her like that.

"Why now?" she asked, voice barely above a whisper. "Why are you here tonight?"

He hesitated, jaw clenching. "I didn't know where I was going. I just... needed to breathe. And somehow, I ended up here." A pause. "Guess I was hoping I wouldn't be the only one."

The air between them crackled, like something waiting to ignite.

Kael stepped forward, crossing the stream in two long strides, water splashing dark against his boots.

And just like that, they were inches apart.

The air between them tightened, as though the whole grove had drawn in a single breath.

Aislen's own lungs stilled. She swore the streams murmur slowed, the fireflies hovering midair like fleck of gold frozen in glass.

"Kael—" she started, but the words tangled in her throat. Breaking like a wave.

His gazed locked to hers, unblinking. A muscle jumped in his jaw. One hand twitched at his side, as if he had to force it to remain there instead of reaching for her.

"I missed you," he said. Simple. Honest. Like it cost him something.

She stared up at him, searching his face for an explanation she could understand. "You've been... different lately. Distant. Then *not*. I don't know what you're doing."

"I don't either," he admitted. "I'm trying to do the right thing. But I don't know what that is anymore."

"Then why does it feel like you're waiting for something to end?"

He flinched, barely, but enough for her to notice.

"I'm not trying to leave," he said, voice rough. "I'm trying not to ruin what I already have."

"Why would you ruin it?"

Kael glanced toward the water, then back to her.

The world tilted. The moonstone on his chest caught the light, and Aislen felt her heart squeeze around it.

"Kael," she breathed. "What's wrong? Why do I feel like you're lying to me?"

"I'm sorry," he whispered. "I can't. Not tonight."

They stood there in the hush of the grove, the willow branches swaying like they were listening. Aislen could feel her pulse in her fingertips, in her throat, in the charged air between them. Her hand twitched at her side, like it wanted to reach for something, or someone, but didn't know how.

Her heart beat louder than the wind, louder than the stream.

And then, before she could think to stop it, her hand lifted and touched his chest, right over the necklace. Right over his heart.

The pulse there matched hers.

And then he leaned forward, so slowly it felt like a dream, and rested his forehead against hers.

The world stilled.

Her breath hitched. She didn't close her eyes, she couldn't. Because his were open too, searching her face like it held all the answers he'd been afraid to ask for.

The heat between them wasn't just from closeness, it was something else. A pressure. A pull.

Familiar, but not.

Comforting, but dangerous.

"I've missed you," he said quietly.

The words cracked something in her chest.

"I've been right here," she whispered.

Kael's eyes closed for just a moment, like the pain of that truth cut deep.

"I know," he said.

The silence stretched again. This time, heavier.

And then Kael stepped back, just a few inches, but it was enough to make the space between them feel colder.

"I should go," he said, voice tight. "I didn't mean to... I don't want to make this harder."

Aislen blinked. "Harder for who?"

Kael didn't answer.

He just looked at her like he wanted to say something else, *so many* something elses, but none of them made it past his lips.

He turned.

Started to walk away.

And before she could stop herself—

"Kael."

He paused, just at the edge of the trees.

She didn't know what she meant to say. Didn't know what she *could* say. So instead, she just said the only thing that felt honest.

"Please don't leave me. Please. I don't understand any of this."

Kael looked over his shoulder, his face in shadow.

"I know, I'm sorry…" he said. "But one day, you will understand."

Then he disappeared into the night, and Aislen was left standing in the place where their past still lingered, and where something new had just begun to grow.

Something she couldn't name yet.

But it was there.

It was *there.*

* * *

The silence swallowed everything.

The air he'd left behind felt colder. She wrapped her arms around herself, but it didn't help. Something inside of her fractured quietly.

Aislen stood frozen, the weight of unshed words pressing against her ribs like iron. The willow swayed gently behind her, the stream still whispering, but she barely noticed.

Her breath hitched once. Then again.

And then—

She broke.

A scream tore from her throat, raw and guttural and full of everything she couldn't say.

She dropped to her knees in the middle of the clearing, fists pounding the dirt. "Why won't he just tell me? Why does everything feel like it's breaking when *nothing's even changed yet?*"

Another sob ripped out of her.

"I don't understand! I don't *know* what this is, I don't even *know* what I feel!"

The ground pulsed beneath her. Just once.

She didn't notice at first.

Until the air shifted.

"He left me," she rasped, defeated.

The breeze vanished. Fireflies winked out as if snuffed by unseen hands.

She felt something crack. It wasn't just in her chest, but somewhere deeper. Beneath it.

And then the earth *shuddered* under her palms.

The roots of the willow tree curled slightly, as if recoiling, or awakening. The stream surged, splashing hard against the stones, though no wind touched it. Nearby, several wildflowers bloomed violently, twisting open too fast, petals trembling, stems stretching toward her like they recognized something ancient in her bones.

Then a sudden pressure built in her chest. It was hot and wild.

Aislen gasped, stumbling to her feet, clutching at her heart like it might leap free from her chest.

Somewhere in the distance, the moonstone necklace she'd gifted Kael, resting against his skin, flared in sudden response, as if echoing her own magic.

The magic she shouldn't have.

And above, the moon itself flickered.

Only for a second.

Its soft light dimmed, *like a breath had passed across its surface,* before returning just as quickly, the shadows thrown by the trees stretching longer and thinner, drawn toward her like a pull she couldn't see.

Aislen stared upward, frozen. Her lips parted.

That wasn't normal.

None of it was.

Her hands were still trembling, but not from fear. From... power. From something uncoiling beneath her skin like it had been waiting, patient and buried, until emotion broke the lock.

"No," she whispered. "No, this... this isn't—"

But the clearing had already gone still again.

The flowers settled. The water calmed. The trees stilled, as though nothing had happened at all.

Only the whisper in her mind remained. It was soft, unfamiliar, and laced with stardust.

Wake up.

Aislen backed away slowly, chest heaving, a chill racing down her spine despite the summer heat. Her thoughts were shards now, scattered and sharp.

Because she wasn't supposed to be anything but human.

And yet...

Something deep inside her had just *answered back*.

$$* * *$$

~ Unknown ~

The chamber was cloaked in shadows, lit only by the pale glow of a single crystalline orb hovering above the ancient throne. He sat motionless, his hands folded like a spider's claws across his lap. Outside, the night sky stretched wide and cold, the stars blinking with cold indifference.

A sudden tremor pulsed through the magic veins of the realm. It was a surge of power, sharp and unmistakable. His eyes, ageless and piercing, snapped open. The daughter he had long watched from afar was awakening.

The power that stirred within her was rare. Dangerous. Unpredictable.

A slow smile crept across his lips. It was not one of joy, but of calculation.

So, the bloodline stirs at last.

Whispers in the Court had spoken of this day, of the prophecy woven in moonlight and earth. Some feared her power would bring ruin; others claimed it could reshape the balance of their world.

He was neither afraid nor eager to act. Not yet.

For now, he would watch. He would wait.

The threads of fate were tightening, and soon, the game would begin.

But the truth, what the Court did not see, was hidden deep beneath the veils of shadow and light.

The King's gaze softened for a fraction of a heartbeat.

She is my last hope.

And with that thought, the orb dimmed, the chamber slipping back into darkness.

Seven

"Inevitable"

~ **Maera** ~

The scent of starblossoms still haunted her dreams.

Even now, after nearly two decades, a child grown, and a heart broken beyond mending, Maera couldn't close her eyes without seeing it. The way the Celestara Court shimmered like glass spun from moonlight. The way his eyes softened only for her. The way she had once believed in forever.

She stirred the tea absently, though she wouldn't drink it. The mug sat forgotten in her lap, steam curling into the lamplit air of the cottage. Outside, the night stretched wide and velvet-dark, and something, something ancient, rippled just beneath the surface of her skin.

A pulse. A call.

She hadn't felt it in years.

Her fingers tightened around the ceramic.

It had begun again.

She stood, abandoning the tea, and walked to the window. Beyond the treetops, the moon glowed full and watchful. A wind moved through the trees. It was not sharp, but carried something strange. Familiar.

And it pulled her backward, through time, to the night her whole world had changed.

46

It had rained the day the prophecy was spoken.

The clouds over the Celestara Court never stayed long, not in that realm of shimmered skies and celestial winds. But that night, the storm had clung to the horizon, staining it bruise-purple and thunder-deep.

Maera had known something was wrong the moment she woke. The kind of knowing that sat deep in her gut, heavy and cold.

She'd slipped from his chambers before dawn, bare feet quiet on starlit marble. Her dress clung to her skin, damp from sweat and dreams, and her mind still hummed with his voice, gentle, playful, low against her throat.

"You can't keep sneaking away," he'd whispered the night before, arms wrapped around her waist, his crown discarded on the floor beside them.

"I'm not sneaking," she'd murmured, smiling. "I'm preserving your dignity."

He had laughed then, really laughed. That deep, rare sound she'd come to crave more than air.

But something had shifted in him lately. He'd grown quiet, distracted. As if he knew time was slipping through his fingers.

And he'd been right.

By midday, the seers had summoned her.

They never summoned anyone. Not unless it was dire.

Maera had entered the chamber with her chin high, heart in her throat. The air inside was heavy with incense and magic. The three star-sighted crones sat around the oracle pool, their eyes clouded silver with power.

"You bear more than a child," one had rasped, her voice thick as storm clouds. "You carry a keystone."

"I..." Maera had blinked, breath faltering. "I don't understand."

"The child will burn with two forgotten gifts," the second crooned. "One will reside in her earthsong magic and the other will be her starlight magic. The magic the child holds has not walked this realm together in a thousand years."

The third leaned forward, and her voice was barely more than breath. "She will be hunted by those who fear her. Claimed by those who would use her. Loved... but torn."

Maera had stumbled back, her fingers trembling. "No. That's not... she's not even a child. She isn't even an infant yet... there must be a mistake."

"She is a reckoning," the first hissed. "And her birth will mark the breaking of the four Courts."

The storm had broken overhead then, thunder shaking the temple walls. The seers' voices followed her into the rain.

"She will be born under moonlight, marked by wildflowers and ruin."

"She will be both salvation and shadow."

"She is the edge of balance and what falls will not rise again."

Maera ran.

She ran through the night, soaked and gasping, her heart tearing apart with every step.

He found her on the bridge, just before she crossed the threshold between realms.

"Maera," he said quiet and devastated.

She turned, rain streaming down her face. "Don't."

"You're leaving me." His voice cracked. "You weren't even going to say goodbye?"

"I *can't stay*." Her voice was sharp with grief. "They'll destroy her. They'll twist her into something she's not. You know they will."

"I can protect you—"

"You can't." Her hands fisted at her sides. "You *won't*. Not when the council forces your hand. Not when they say she's a threat."

He said nothing.

And that silence was all the answer she needed.

"I loved you," she said, voice breaking.

He stepped forward, desperation in his eyes. "You *still* do."

"Don't," she begged. "Please. If you ever truly loved me, let me go. Let me protect her *my* way."

He reached into his coat then pulling something out.

A single moonstone, carved with an ancient sigil, hung from a silver chain.

"This is hers," he said. "When she's ready... it will find her."

"Until then, wear it. Never forget your home," he begged her. His plea that followed was barely a whisper in the wind.

Maera stared at it, at him, at the life she was leaving behind.

And then she took it.

Not for him.

For *her*.

She didn't look back as she crossed the barrier into the mortal realm.

Maera blinked, the memory fading with the steam on the glass. The night outside whispered with wind and moonlight.

She could feel it again. The flicker. The hum.

Aislen's magic.

It was beginning.

Stars save them.

She pressed her palm to the window, eyes burning.

"Please," she whispered. "Don't let her be like him."

* * *

~ **Kael** ~

The bond was eating him alive.

Kael leaned against the stone wall of the barracks, fists clenched so tight his knuckles had gone white. His jaw ached from how often he kept it locked, his throat raw from holding back the things he couldn't say. Each breath was shallow, like the air around him couldn't quite reach his lungs.

Eighteen days.

Eighteen days since her scent, moonlit violets and the storm-soaked forest floor, clung to his skin long after she was gone.

And eighteen days since he began tearing himself apart, trying to stay away.

He couldn't train anymore. Couldn't eat. Could barely sleep. Everything inside him was wired to find her, to be near her, to protect her from a threat that didn't exist. At least not yet.

But the threat was him. He was the danger now.

Because if he saw her again, he didn't know if he'd be strong enough to hold the truth in.

He pressed a palm to his chest, right over the necklace she'd given him. It was warm. Always warm. Like it remembered her hands. Like it carried a piece of her magic even if she didn't know she had any.

The pull was constant now. A low, steady thrum beneath his skin. It wasn't just emotional, it was physical too. It was in his blood, in the marrow of his bones. Like threads of starlight stitched under his skin were tugging toward one name, one presence, one soul.

Aislen.

He had tried everything. Sparring, late-night walks, soaking himself under freezing waterfalls in the glen. But nothing drowned it out. Nothing dulled the ache of missing her.

Because it wasn't just longing.

It was *need*.

And it hurt.

Kael doubled over, his forehead pressing to the cool stone. His shoulders shook with a breath he couldn't hold in. The pain wasn't sharp, but it was deep. Hollowing. Like something inside him was caving in, collapsing under the weight of how badly he wanted to be near her.

Not for himself.

But because something inside him kept whispering that she *needed* him too.

And that whisper was getting louder the closer it came to her own birthday.

He had watched her from a distance once, just once. Saw her walking through the village with a basket in her arms, smiling at the baker's daughter, nodding politely to an elder. She looked... fine.

But he wasn't. And he couldn't tell if that meant anything at all.

Maybe it was better this way. Maybe it was good that she didn't feel the bond.

Because if she *had,* and she still didn't want him, he wasn't sure he'd survive it.

He'd rather lose her gently than risk breaking her with the truth.

Still, the bond didn't care about what made sense. It didn't care about what Kael *wanted.*

It just *was.*

And it was burning through him like wildfire.

He ran a hand through his dark hair, tugging hard at the roots until his scalp stung.

She was out there. Somewhere.

And every second he spent denying the bond felt like another tear in his soul.

A deep, aching growl vibrated low in his throat, instinct more than sound. His magic sparked beneath his skin, a wild shimmer just barely restrained. The Lunaris Court mark on his shoulder pulsed faintly with light, glowing beneath his tunic. As if even his blood had stopped listening to his mind and started listening to *her.*

He could feel her.

Far off.

But not far enough.

Not anymore.

Kael clenched his jaw and pushed off the wall. He couldn't do it. Not one more night.

If he stayed away any longer, he would lose himself.

And worse—he might lose *her.*

He didn't know where his legs were carrying him until he was already in the trees. Already pushing past the forest's edge, toward the places only they knew. Toward the pulse pulling at his ribs like a thread caught on the wind.

He didn't have a plan.

Didn't know what he would say.

He just knew one thing.

He couldn't stay away any longer.

Eight

"Truth"

~ Aislen ~

The summer breeze was soft against her skin, scented with jasmine and the faintest trace of cinnamon pastries. Laughter rang out from somewhere near the fountain as sunlight dappled across the cobblestones of the town square, the rhythm of daily life thrumming with easy familiarity. Aislen stood at the edge of it all, a half-circle of people around her, her smile carefully fixed in place like a mask she wasn't sure how to remove.

The only reason she was there was for her younger cousin. They were in the town square picking up ingredients for her aunt's dinner tonight. Ilyra hadn't wanted to go alone, so her mom volunteered Aislen to go with her. It's not that she didn't want to be there, she just felt distant. Tired.

She felt guilty. She wasn't really listening to Ilyra's story about the apothecary's mishap with love spells. Her laugh was delayed, hollow around the edges. Not that Ilyra's story wasn't funny, but they just weren't as close as they used to be.

Her eyes drifted without purpose over the colorful banners strung between buildings, over the merchant selling starlit sugarberries, over the pulse of the town that seemed entirely unaware of the quiet storm curling inside her chest.

It had been nearly three weeks since she'd seen Kael.

Three weeks since the stream.

Since he'd looked at her like he couldn't breathe without her... and then walked away without a word.

She replayed it endlessly. His closeness, the brush of his forehead against hers, the way his fingers had trembled just before he pulled back. She'd been sure, in that moment, that something had passed between them. Something more than friendship, more than the aching bond of shared childhoods. And yet, he'd left. Left her staring at the water, heart open, vulnerable and alone.

She hadn't seen him since. Not at training, not at the edge of the woods where he sometimes waited to walk her home, not even in passing. Nothing.

He was avoiding her.

The realization had taken root like a thorn in her chest. No matter how many times she tried to ignore it, it pierced deeper. Maybe he regretted their closeness. Maybe he was trying to spare her from something. Or maybe, just maybe, he didn't feel what she felt. Not really.

"Aislen?"

She blinked. Ilyra was watching her with a teasing smile. "That's the third time I've said your name. If I didn't know better, I'd think you were daydreaming about that cute healer's apprentice across the way."

Aislen gave a weak chuckle. "No, I'm sorry. My mind's just... elsewhere."

Ilyra rolled her eyes fondly and turned to tease someone else. Aislen let her gaze fall to her hands, twisting the edge of her sleeve between her fingers.

She had felt strange since that night. Subtle, small things like flowers blooming in her footsteps, vines curling toward her even when she didn't reach for them. It felt like something inside her was stretching, awakening. But she didn't understand it, didn't *want* to understand it, not without Kael.

A sudden ripple moved through the air.

It wasn't sound, not exactly. More like a *shift*, a disturbance in the energy around her, as if the world had just exhaled. Her head snapped up.

And there he was, as if she summoned him by thinking his name.

Kael.

Pushing through the crowd with the urgency of a storm breaking across a still sky. His cloak was slung over one shoulder, half-fastened and flapping behind him. His hair was damp with sweat, sticking to his forehead, and his breathing was ragged like he'd run the whole way from the palace.

People moved aside without quite knowing why.

Aislen's heart stuttered.

He saw her.

And in that instant, the rest of the world dropped away. The noise. The heat. The crowd. All of it blurred at the edges as silver eyes locked onto hers with a desperation that stole the breath from her lungs.

"Aislen," he said, voice hoarse, broken.

She froze. "Kael?"

Without a word, he pushed forward, closing the distance between them. His hand reached for her wrist gently, grounding, but too warm. Her skin buzzed where he touched her, something deep inside her pulling taut like a string on the verge of snapping.

"Come with me," he said, barely above a whisper. "Please. Just—come."

She hesitated, glancing at Ilyra and the others, all now watching with curious eyes and raised brows. "Kael, what are you—?"

He didn't answer. Just tugged her gently but firmly through the crowd, down a side path lined with trailing ivy and crumbling stone walls, away from the gazes, the noise, the questions.

When they were out of sight, he finally stopped. He let go of her wrist and turned to face her, chest still heaving, eyes bright with something that looked too much like panic. He looked exhausted. Pale. Like he hadn't slept in days.

"What is going on?" she asked, heart already racing.

"I can't wait anymore."

The words landed between them like thunder.

He ran a hand through his hair, pacing a short step before turning back to her. "I've tried to hold back. Gods, I've tried. I thought I could do the right thing, for both of us, but it's *hurting* me, Aislen. Every day, pretending like I don't feel it. Like it's not there."

"Kael," she whispered, voice cracking. "Feel *what?*"

He stepped closer, hands clenched at his sides, silver eyes ablaze.

"You're my mate."

The world went silent.

Something in her chest lurched, yearned.

Then the fear hit, full and fast.

Aislen stared at him, the words not computing. Her mind blanked. Her knees weakened.

"...what?"

"You're my mate," he said again, softer this time. "I've known. For a while now. I felt it deep in my soul. It's like my magic recognizes you. I don't know how it happened, I just know it did. Every part of me is drawn to you. I can't fight it anymore."

She took a shaky step back, breath catching painfully in her throat.

"No. No, Kael, don't say that."

"It's the truth."

"It *can't* be."

He frowned. "Why not?"

"Because I'm *human!*" she snapped, voice rising. "I'm not fae, I don't have a bond. That's not how this works. That's *not possible.*"

"I don't care what's supposed to be possible. Maybe you aren't fully human. I don't know," Kael said, voice fierce and trembling. "I just know what I feel. I know what I've *always* felt. And you—gods, Aislen, you *feel* it too. I *know* you do."

She shook her head, tears brimming.

"I don't... this isn't.... you can't just say that. You don't get to come here and tell me something that could rip me apart and then expect me to just what, *accept it?* After all this time? After ignoring me for days? After making me feel like I was *nothing* to you?"

"I was trying to *protect* you!"

"From *what?* From the truth? Or from *yourself?*" Her voice cracked open. "You *left* me. You didn't say a word. You made me believe I'd imagined it all."

"I was scared." His voice was rough now, the mask slipping. "I was scared of what it would mean for you. For us. You're right, you're supposed to be human, and the bond should've never been possible. But it *is*. And I love you. I've loved you for so long, I don't even know who I am without you."

Her tears fell freely now, burning hot trails down her cheeks.

"Then why didn't you tell me sooner?" she whispered. "Why wait until I was already falling apart?"

Kael stepped forward, hands trembling as he reached for her. "Please. Let me explain. Let me fix it—"

She stepped back.

"No. You broke something, Kael. And I don't know if it can be fixed."

Behind her, the ivy along the stone wall shivered and curled back like it had felt her heart break too.

And before he could say another word, before he could reach her again and make it harder to breathe, Aislen turned and ran.

* * *

~ **Kael** ~

The door slammed harder than he meant it to.

Inside the dim tavern, the scent of spiced mead and old oak drifted through the air, mingling with the low thrum of conversation and the scrape of mugs on wood. Kael didn't bother with pleasantries. He stalked toward the far corner booth that was dark, secluded, and blessedly empty.

Sion was already there, lounging like he had all the time in the world, a pint half-empty in one hand and a crooked smirk tugging at his mouth.

"You look like you punched a wall," he said casually. "Or wanted to."

Kael didn't answer. He dropped into the seat across from him, dragging a hand down his face.

"Something stronger," he growled at the passing barmaid.

Sion arched a brow, but didn't ask. Yet.

When the drink came, Kael downed half of it in one go, letting the burn center him. Ground him. *Distract* him from the way Aislen's face had twisted when he said the words. The way her eyes had shattered.

"You told her, didn't you?" Sion asked after a long pause.

Kael took a deep breath, "How did you know?"

Sion shook his head, "I always knew. I may not have known she was going to be your mate, but anyone near you both could guess you would end up together. From your reaction though, I'm assuming it went badly?"

Kael didn't look at him. "Yeah."

"Did she run?"

Kael slammed the rest of the drink.

"She didn't just run," he muttered. "She looked at me like I betrayed her. Like I *hurt* her. And maybe I did. Maybe I—*shit,* I don't even know anymore."

Sion leaned back with a sigh. "Start from the beginning."

Kael did. Every detail. Her standing in the square, the way her laughter didn't reach her eyes. The way he couldn't breathe until he touched her, like some part of him was *starving* and only she could fill the ache. The truth tumbling out, too fast, too desperate. Her denial. Her tears.

"How can she not feel it?" Kael asked, voice low and sharp with pain. "I know she's human, or I think she is. It doesn't make sense but I know I *feel* the bond. It's real. It's always been there hiding under the surface. How can she not know?"

Sion swirled the amber liquid in his glass, watching it with a thoughtful expression. "Maybe she does. Maybe she just doesn't know how to name it yet."

"She thinks I'm lying to her. Or worse, that I'm *delusional.* Like I'm using the bond to excuse everything I never said."

"And are you?"

Kael's jaw clenched. "No. I just... gods, I *waited* for her. I gave her space. I buried it so deep I thought I'd choke on it. And it still blew up in my face."

"You were never going to be able to hide it forever."

"I didn't want to lose her."

"And now you might have anyway." Sion's voice wasn't cruel, just honest. That somehow made it worse.

Kael buried his face in his hands. The ache in his chest wasn't just longing. It was *loss*. A grief still blooming.

"I don't know what to do," he murmured. "I've trained my whole life to protect the people I care about. And now the one person I can't live without thinks I've shattered her."

"She used to laugh when I stole apples from her basket and blamed one of the stray dogs." Kael wanted to, but he couldn't even summon the barest of laughs at the memory.

Sion was quiet for a long moment, then set his drink down gently.

"You've been her shield since you were old enough to lift one. Maybe now... you need to be her anchor."

Kael looked up, frowning. "What's that supposed to mean?"

"It means stop trying to *control* how she feels. Stop protecting her from the truth. Let her be angry. Let her fall apart. And be there when she needs someone to help her stand again."

Kael let the words settle.

He didn't want to wait. Didn't want to sit with this pain. But deep down, he knew Sion was right.

"I'm losing her," he whispered.

Sion leaned forward, voice steady. "Not if she's your mate, you're not. Not forever. Bonds like that don't unravel. They strain. They bend. But they don't break."

Kael stared into the dregs of his drink.

"I hope you're right."

"I'm always right," Sion smirked.

"Her birthday is next week... do you think she'll feel the bond then too? Or does it only work that way for us fae? I feel like I'm losing my fucking mind. I never should have stayed away."

Sion just gave a small smile and finished off the rest of his drink.

Nine

"Unraveling"

~❦~

~ Aislen ~

Darkness wrapped around her like a second skin.

Not cold. Not suffocating. Just… still.

Aislen stood barefoot on a floor made of light. There were silver strands of starlight woven into patterns that pulsed beneath her feet like a heartbeat. Above her, constellations shimmered across a sky that felt both endless and close enough to touch. She reached for one without thinking. Her fingers brushed the air, and the stars rippled like reflections in water.

She wasn't afraid. Not yet.

The silence was not empty. It *watched.*

Then he stepped from the shadows.

Tall. Cloaked in twilight. His features were veiled, almost indistinct. It was like moonlight caught in smoke, except his presence filled the space like gravity. A faint glow edged the lines of his form, soft and ethereal. Power radiated from him. It was not in menace, but in memory. Like she *should* know him.

But she didn't.

He didn't speak at first. Just looked at her with eyes like violet galaxies. Galaxies that were deep, ancient, and aching.

"Who are you?" she asked, but her voice sounded far away, like it echoed through a dream.

The figure tilted his head, considering her. "You don't recognize me yet."

His voice wrapped around her like velvet and thunder. Familiar. Impossible.

"I've waited a long time, little star."

Aislen took a step back. Her heart beat faster. "What do you mean?"

"When the time comes," he said, "you will seek me out. And when you do... I'll be waiting."

"I don't—"

He lifted a hand, not quite touching her cheek, and the silver light flared around them.

"Your magic is waking. The bond cannot hold it back anymore."

Before she could ask anything more, the stars shattered.

And she woke up screaming.

* * *

Reality hit like a wave.

Aislen sat bolt upright, drenched in sweat, breath ragged.

Her room was *alive*.

Vines curled across the stone floor and up the walls, blooming violently with wildflowers that opened and closed like lungs. Starlight pooled unnaturally in the corners, *thick* and *watching*, not cast by any obvious source of light. The very air buzzed with raw, chaotic energy.

"Aislen!"

Her mom's voice sliced through the dream haze. Maera was shaking her by the shoulders, eyes wide with panic.

"Wake up. Gods, please wake up."

"I—I'm awake," Aislen gasped. Her hands were trembling, glowing faintly with green light that flickered into pale starlight at her fingertips.

Maera stepped back like she'd been burned.

Aislen blinked at her hands, then at the vines that crept up her bedposts, responding to her breath. "What... what's happening to me?"

Maera's face crumpled.

She sank to the edge of the bed, pressing a hand to her mouth as if to hold back the words. But it was too late. The moment had come. The secret was cracking open.

"I should have told you sooner," she whispered.

"Told me *what?*" Aislen's voice was high and ragged. "Why is this happening? What's wrong with me?"

"There's nothing wrong with you." Maera looked at her with a strange mixture of awe and grief. "This is who you are."

Aislen's throat tightened. "Then tell me."

Maera's next words came soft. Terrible. Final.

"You're not fully human. You never were."

Aislen stared at her mom as if she'd spoken in another language.

Not fully human?

Her heart still thundered from the dream with the man in starlight, the way he'd spoken like he knew her. And now her room looked like something out of a fae-touched legend: flowers blooming from the floor, shadows moving on their own, her hands glowing with magic she didn't understand.

"No," she said softly, shaking her head. "That's not... what do you mean I'm not human? What are you saying?"

The sudden feeling of nausea didn't escape her.

Maera didn't answer. Her mouth opened, then closed again. Her eyes were glassy with tears.

Without a word, she stood up and left the room.

The vines began to retreat slightly, like they sensed her unease growing.

Aislen curled her arms around her knees and stared at the floor, chest heaving. Her skin still buzzed, like magic was a second pulse under her own.

Moments later, Maera returned with an old book cradled in her arms like it might break.

It was thick, bound in worn leather, the deep navy cover etched with fading silver swirls. Dust clung to it in patches. Her hands shook as she set it gently on Aislen's lap.

"What is this?" Aislen asked.

Maera sat beside her again. She looked older now, like the weight of the past had caught up to her in one night.

"This hasn't been touched in nineteen years," she said quietly. "I promised myself I wouldn't open it again. That I wouldn't let the past become your future."

She brushed the dust away and opened to a page filled with images. There were photos that looked real, but shimmered faintly like illusions caught in stillness.

They weren't normal pictures. Some were taken beneath a twilight sky where no stars Aislen recognized existed. Others showed a palace made of mirrored crystal, standing tall among silver trees that pulsed with light.

Aislen's breath caught. "Where... is this?"

Maera's voice was soft, but steady. "The Court of Celestara. Of starlight."

Aislen's eyes widened. "That's not real. That's a myth. It was part of the continent once, wasn't it? But... it disappeared. It was forgotten."

Her mom's eyes met hers.

"Not forgotten. *Hidden.* On purpose. After what happened."

Aislen felt like the floor was tilting beneath her. "What are you saying? That you lived there? That I'm from—*there?*"

Maera nodded slowly. "I was born in the Aurion Court. My own mother was part fae, but my father was human. I never quite took after my mother. The human counterpart was the strongest between them, which is why I am human despite some of my heritage," she paused as she looked at her daughter. "But I traveled often between the realms. I was a healer, invited to the Celestara Court after the king's wife passed away. He was grieving. The Court had lost its queen, its heart. I was supposed to stay a season. But then... I stayed longer."

Aislen's voice dropped to a whisper. "Why?"

Maera smiled softly, eyes distant. "Because I fell in love with the king."

A long silence stretched between them.

Aislen's hands tightened on the edge of the book.

"I didn't know what it was at first," Maera continued. "He never made me feel small for being mortal. Never made me feel like a guest. And when the bond clicked into place, I knew. I was his second mate, his second chance."

"That means…" Aislen hesitated before continuing.

Her moms solemn eyes met her own.

"You were supposed to be queen," Aislen finished numbly.

Maera nodded. "The coronation was planned. The Court had begun to heal. Until the prophecy."

Aislen looked up sharply. "What prophecy?"

Maera's lips trembled.

"When silver blood meets mortal flame, a child shall rise without a name. Born beneath moon, cloaked in sun, neither wholly fae, nor wholly none. Veins of starlight, heart of earth, magic split by hidden birth. She shall awaken with tear or flame, and kingdoms lost shall speak her name."

Aislen's heartbeat stuttered. "Me."

Her mom nodded. "I was pregnant with you, it was all so new. And then the vision spread. Some wanted to protect you. Others wanted… other things."

Her voice went hoarse.

"So I left. I ran. I didn't tell him until he caught me about to go over the border. I chose protecting you over bloodshed. And I came here where no one would look. Where you could grow up with dirt on your knees and books in your hands and not a crown on your head."

Tears pricked Aislen's eyes.

"And dad?" she whispered.

Maera's expression softened. "Tomas is a good man. He found me when I was alone, scared, and sick with the pregnancy. He offered me a home, a name, and a future I wouldn't have had otherwise. He's been your dad ever since. Not by blood, but by *choice*."

Aislen closed her eyes. "You lied to me."

"I did," Maera whispered. "To protect you. And I would do it again."

* * *

The garden was the only place that didn't feel like it was lying to her.

She sat cross-legged in the soft dirt near the lavender patch, hands buried in the soil. It was damp from the morning dew, cool against her overheated skin. Around her, leaves fluttered lazily in the breeze, wildflowers tilted toward the sun, and vines curled along the stones like they were listening.

Aislen dug her fingers deeper into the earth, willing it to anchor her.

She'd come out here to *breathe*, but even that felt difficult now.

Nothing made sense.

Not the dream.

Not the vines that had overtaken her room like they belonged to her.

Not the male in silver who claimed he was waiting.

And definitely not her mom's voice saying *"You're not fully human."*

She yanked a weed from the soil with more force than necessary, tossing it across the path.

"I don't even know who I am anymore," she muttered.

A small tangle of ivy lifted its leaves in response. Aislen flinched.

It hadn't been doing that before, *not like this.* Maybe she had been imagining the small things, or maybe she'd been ignoring them. But after last night, there was no more pretending. The magic wasn't going away. It was waking up. It was waking up because *it was hers.*

She sat back on her heels, rubbing at her arms. Her skin felt too tight for her bones, like something inside her was pressing outward, waiting to be *released.*

And worse than the magic, worse than the dream or the shadows or her even mom's secret... was the question she kept trying not to ask:

What if Kael was telling the truth?

She squeezed her eyes shut. "Gods, I was so awful to him..."

He had looked frantic. Desperate. Not like someone playing games. And now, with her magic flaring and her mom's words circling like vultures, she couldn't deny it any longer.

She wasn't really human.

Not fully.

Not like she thought.

Then what does that mean for the bond?

Her birthday was next week. Her nineteenth. The day Maera had always treated like it mattered more than just cake and candles. She used to think it was superstition. Old magic, maybe.

But now she wondered.

Does the bond... click into place then?

Has Kael truly been feeling it this whole time?

Will I?

And what if she didn't? What if she never could? Would she still lose him?

Her chest ached just thinking about it.

She picked at the hem of her sleeve, trying to hold the emotion back. She didn't know if she was more angry at her mom for hiding the truth, or at herself for not seeing it sooner. She had wanted so badly for the world to be simple. For love to be easy. For Kael to be wrong so she didn't have to choose.

But now?

Now everything felt too big to hold.

"I don't have enough answers," she whispered.

The wind stirred the petals around her. A few lavender blossoms leaned in like they were trying to listen.

Not enough answers... but the questions aren't going away.

Ten

"Anchor"

~ Tomas ~

He spotted her through the garden gate before she heard him approaching. Her knees were drawn up, hands buried in the soil like she was trying to root herself to the earth.

She looked so much like her mother in that moment it made his chest ache.

Tomas stepped softly over the threshold, letting the familiar scent of lavender and damp earth wrap around him. This garden had been her safe place since she was old enough to walk. She used to talk to the marigolds like they were friends. Now, the flowers seemed to lean toward her like they *were*.

"I had a feeling I'd find you here," he said gently.

Aislen didn't look up right away, but her shoulders shifted. They tensed before slumping as if she'd expected someone else.

"Let me guess," she murmured. "Mom sent you?"

"No." He crouched beside her, the ache in his knees sharper than usual today. "I talked with her, yes. But I came because I knew *you'd* need someone."

She didn't respond. Just kept her eyes on the dirt, her fingers trembling

66

slightly as they dug small lines in the soil.

She was hurting and there was nothing he could do to fix it.

Not this time.

He waited, giving her silence without pressure. It was something he'd learned to do over years of scraped knees, quiet tears, and school yard heartaches. Eventually, her voice came small and raw.

"You knew, didn't you?"

Tomas didn't flinch.

"Not everything," he said. "But I knew there was more to your mother's past than she let on. She carried it in her shoulders like it weighed a thousand years. And I knew you were special. Even before the flowers started following you."

He smiled faintly, watching a single vine curl toward Aislen's ankle. She scowled at it like it had betrayed her.

"I chose both of you," Tomas said quietly. "All those years ago. I didn't need to know her whole story. I just knew she needed help. And you, as soon as you came out, you were going to need a home. That was enough for me then. It still is."

Aislen finally looked at him, and he wished she hadn't, because her eyes were glassy, lost, and way too old for someone her age.

"I don't know who I am anymore," she whispered.

"You're still my girl," Tomas said. "Still the same kid who tried to save every injured bird you found. Who cried the first time someone stepped on a beetle. Magic or not, you're still you."

She closed her eyes, and for a second he thought she might cry. But instead, she asked:

"Kael told me something... and I was awful to him. I thought he was lying because I thought I was just a human... what if Kael was telling the truth?"

Tomas drew in a slow breath. So that was where her thoughts had gone.

"He said I was his mate," she continued, voice trembling. "I thought he was just... confused. But if I'm not fully human, if what mom said is true, what if he wasn't wrong? What if it *is* real?"

Tomas didn't know much about fae bonds or ancient magic, but he knew people. And he knew Kael. He didn't want his girl with anyone, but if it had to be someone, Kael was a good one.

"I've seen the way he looks at you," Tomas said. "Like he's trying not to break. Like you're the only thing in the world that steadies him."

Aislen shook her head, but it wasn't denial, it was fear. Her voice cracked.

"I'm scared of what it means. If he's right… then everything I thought I knew about myself, my family, my life, it's all a lie. And if he's wrong, and I *let* myself believe it… I don't know if I'll survive it."

Tomas reached over and took her hand in his, dirt and all.

"You don't have to decide right now," he said. "Not what you are. Not what you feel. But I want you to remember something."

He waited until she looked at him.

"You are *not* a mistake, Aislen. Not some prophecy gone wrong. You're my daughter. And I will stand beside you, magic or no, no matter what comes next."

Tears finally slid down her cheeks.

Tomas let her cry, let her fall into his arms like she did when she was little and the world felt too big.

And for a few quiet minutes, the garden held them both.

Tomas held her gently, feeling her tremble beneath his fingers. After a moment, Aislen's voice broke the quiet.

"Do you know… who my real father is?"

He swallowed hard, looking away toward the garden gate as if the answer might be waiting there. There was only so much she could know, and he knew that. But he also hated it

"Not really, no." He said softly, hating how easily the lie rolled off his tongue. "Your mother never told me. Not everything, anyway. I don't even know his name. Just that he was from somewhere far beyond here. Somewhere dangerous."

Aislen's brow furrowed, eyes searching his face.

"What about the prophecy? What did it say?"

Tomas shook his head slowly. "I've only heard bits and pieces. Enough to know it wasn't safe for your mother to stay. That you both would have been targets. That's why she left. Why she fought so hard for a normal life for you."

He squeezed her hand, wishing he had more to offer. "I'm sorry I can't tell you more."

Aislen swallowed, biting her lip. After a pause, Tomas said gently, "You need to talk to Kael. Not just because of what he said about being your mate, but because he's been part of your life for so long. If you won't talk to him... then please talk to someone else. Thess, maybe. You need a friend right now, someone who understands. Who isn't a grumpy old man."

Aislen nodded slowly, her eyes distant but thoughtful.

"You're not alone," Tomas said. "And whatever you decide to do next, I'll be here."

* * *

~ Aislen ~

The wind tugged at her cloak, but it couldn't chase away the pounding in her chest. Every breath felt like fire, and tears pricked at the corners of her eyes as she hurried along the forest path toward Thess's cottage.

Her footsteps faltered when she finally reached the weathered wooden door. Her hands shook so badly she barely managed to lift the knocker. The quiet click echoed in the still afternoon air.

When Thess opened the door, concern instantly clouded her face.

"Aislen? What's wrong? You look like you've run all the way here." Thess's voice was soft but concerned.

Aislen barely managed a nod, blinking rapidly as the tears she'd been holding back threatened to spill free. She stumbled inside, closing the door behind her and swaying slightly before sinking onto the cushions by the fire.

She swallowed hard, fingers twisting nervously in her lap. For a moment, she couldn't speak.

Thess knelt beside her, eyes wide and searching. For a human, her senses had always been sharper than most.

"Talk to me. Whatever it is, I'm here," she said gently.

Aislen's breath caught. She wanted to explain, but the words tangled and slipped away. Panic fluttered in her chest like a trapped bird.

"I... I don't even know where to begin," her voice trembled.

Thess reached out, brushing a stray strand of hair back from Aislen's tear-streaked face.

"Start anywhere. I'll listen."

Aislen drew in a shaky breath and began, the words pouring out like a river breaking a dam.

"It started with Kael's birthday." Her voice faltered but she pressed on. "He'd been avoiding me for days. I thought maybe I'd done something wrong, but I couldn't figure out what. Then, a few days later, I was by the stream where we first kissed all those years ago. I thought we were going to again... but then he left me there. Alone."

Her eyes grew distant, remembering.

"But just yesterday he showed up suddenly. He was out of breath and frantic. He told me he couldn't wait any longer. He pulled me aside and that's when he told me... that I was his mate."

She choked back a sob.

"I didn't know what to say. I told him it couldn't be true. That I was human, that it wasn't possible. I cried and told him that he'd hurt me by waiting so long to say anything."

Her hands clenched tightly.

"We fought. I said a lot of horrible things and I really, really hurt him. I cut him deep... I told him I felt like he'd shattered me, like he'd made me believe in something that wasn't real."

Tears spilled down her cheeks, and she wiped them roughly.

"And then I ran away. I just ran."

Aislen closed her eyes, struggling to hold the memories steady.

"But it didn't end there." She took another shaky breath. "That night, I had a dream. A man came to me, someone I didn't know, but he said he'd been waiting for me. That when the time was right, I'd seek him out."

Her voice dropped to a whisper.

"Then mom... she told me the truth. My room was covered in vines and shadows. She was frantic, shaking me awake."

Aislen swallowed hard, the fear still raw.

"She told me I'm not fully human. That I'm from... somewhere else. That my real father is someone I don't know. She was once going to be queen, but a prophecy forced her to leave everything behind to keep me safe."

Her voice cracked.

"I don't know who I am anymore. I don't know what's real. I don't know if I can trust Kael, or even myself."

She looked at Thess, desperation shining in her silver eyes.

"Have you ever felt your whole world fall apart? Like the ground just gave way beneath you?"

Thess pulled her into a gentle embrace, letting her cry without words.

Aislen closed her eyes as Thess's arms wrapped around her. They were a steady, warm presence amid the chaos swirling inside her. She wanted to unravel, to let all the fear and confusion spill out and drown her. But beneath the sorrow was something else, fragile and strange. It was a flicker of hope, a faint whisper that maybe she wasn't as alone as she felt.

Who am I if not the girl I thought I was? she wondered. *If magic runs through me, if I'm connected to something far bigger and darker, what does that make me? A threat? A mistake?* The questions churned, a storm of doubt and longing tangled in her chest.

Her breath hitched with every tear that fell. *Kael said I'm his mate,* she thought, *but can love grow from broken trust?* And yet, beneath the doubt, a deep ache pulsed. It was an echo of something ancient and unyielding, pulling at her soul.

Maybe the prophecy is real, she thought with trembling uncertainty. *Maybe I am part of something I don't understand. But how do I find my way back when the path is shrouded in shadow?*

The quiet crackle of the fire and Thess's heartbeat against her ear grounded her, pulling her back from the edge.

Thess's voice was soft, steady, and full of gentle conviction.

"Aislen," she said, her fingers tracing soothing circles along Aislen's back, "no one expects to have their whole world turned upside down overnight. But you are not defined by what others say you are, or by the magic inside you. Even if I don't quite understand how any of this happened, you are still the same person I've known. You're strong, kind, and brave in ways you don't always see. I love you for who you are, and I know Kael does too."

She pulled back just enough to meet Aislen's eyes, her gaze unwavering.

"This prophecy, your bond with Kael, the secrets your mom kept, they don't change the heart I see. You don't have to have all the answers right now. You only have to take it one moment at a time."

Thess smiled gently. "And you don't have to face this alone. I'm here. We're here. Whatever comes next, we'll face it together. You always have me, Aislen. I may not be fae like apparently the rest of you are, but I'll kick anyone's ass to keep you safe."

Aislen let out a half hearted chuckle as she let the words sink in, feeling the first real weight lift from her chest.

For the first time in days, maybe weeks, she allowed herself to believe that even the darkest nights eventually give way to dawn.

Eleven

"Fated"

~∞∞∞~

~ Aislen ~

Sunlight spilled across the garden path outside the window like gold-threaded lace, but it did little to calm the fluttering nerves in Aislen's chest. Her birthday. Her nineteenth. The day that had once meant nothing more than pastries, a few gifts, and her mom's off-key singing.

Now it loomed like a turning point in a story she hadn't realized she was living.

"Do I look like I'm about to spontaneously combust?" Aislen asked, standing stiffly in front of the mirror in Thess's cottage, hands clenched tightly around the folds of her dress.

Thess smirked from behind her, sitting cross-legged on the bed with a comb and a crown of dried moonblossoms balanced in her lap. "A little," she admitted, then added, "but only in a tragic, ethereal kind of way."

Aislen groaned, dropping onto the stool beside the mirror.

"I hate this."

"You hate looking beautiful in a dress?"

She swallowed as she looked at herself in the mirror. She really did look beautiful. Her dress shimmered like starlight caught on water, every movement sending ripples of pale silver and faint lavender through the air. She'd never worn anything so fine, not in all her nineteen years.

"I hate not knowing what's about to happen," Aislen muttered. "I hate waiting for something I can't control."

Thess stood and crossed the room, placing the flower crown gently in Aislen's hair and adjusting the strands of silver that had begun to show even more than usual at her temples. The rest of her hair had been coaxed into loose waves. The pale violet of her eyes seemed sharper against the delicate flush blooming across her cheeks.

Someone, Thess, most likely, had dusted a faint shimmer along her collarbone making the birthmark there gleam faintly beneath the scooped neckline. The bodice fit snugly, shaped to her frame without making her feel trapped. The skirt flowed down in layered panels that whispered across her ankles when she shifted.

"That part, I get," she said, meeting Aislen's eyes in the mirror. "But you've faced scarier things than a birthday party."

"Like finding out my entire life has been a lie?" Aislen offered dryly.

"Exactly." Thess smiled. "And you're still here. Still standing. Which means whatever happens tonight, bond or no bond, you'll survive it."

Aislen swallowed thickly. "I haven't seen Kael in days."

"I know," Thess said gently. "He stopped by twice. I told him you needed space. He didn't argue."

"He didn't try to push?"

Thess shook her head. "No. But he looked like hell both times."

Aislen turned away from the mirror, pressing her fingers into her temples. "I don't know what I want him to do. Show up? Stay away? I'm terrified, Thess. What if... what if the bond does snap into place? What if I feel everything all at once and it's too much? What if nothing happens at all, and Kael realizes I'm not enough?"

Thess moved closer and crouched down so they were eye level. "You are enough, Aislen. Whether you're half fae, half human, or something the world's never seen before. You're enough just by existing."

Aislen tried to smile, but her lips trembled.

"What if the bond doesn't want me?" she whispered.

Thess reached for her hand and gave it a firm squeeze. "Then screw the bond. You're not just something to be claimed. You're not just someone's mate. You're *you*. And that matters more than any ancient magic."

Silence stretched between them, soft and heavy.

Aislen let her gaze drift back towards the window. Somewhere beyond the trees, people were already gathering. The instruments tuning, lanterns being lit, laughter rising in the early evening breeze. A party to celebrate her.

A party to mark the moment everything might change.

"Let's go before I change my mind," Aislen said, rising to her feet.

Thess grinned. "That's the spirit."

As they stepped outside, the wind shifted. Somewhere in the distance, she felt it—something stirring in the threads of her magic, like a current pulling beneath the surface of a still lake.

Aislen didn't know what the night would bring.

But she knew this: whatever came, she wouldn't face it alone.

* * *

The garden near the village center had been transformed.

Paper lanterns floated between trees, casting soft golden light over swaying vines and flower-strewn tables. Someone had enchanted the blossoms to open slowly as night fell, releasing waves of perfume — honeysuckle, night jasmine, moonlilies — and it was almost too much. Too beautiful. Too dreamlike.

Aislen stood near the edge of the gathering, her breath shallow, fingers curled nervously into the folds of her dress. She hadn't been able to eat. Not much. The sweets on the dessert tables blurred together. Voices drifted past her, friends from the village, familiar laughter, polite congratulations, but everything felt distant. Like she was watching from the outside.

Thess hovered close, a comforting shadow at her side. She didn't speak, didn't press for once. Just stayed close.

And Aislen was grateful.

Because something was happening.

The closer it crept to midnight, the more the feeling grew. Her skin tingled like her blood had turned to starlight. The wind carried her name in a thousand hushed whispers only she could hear. The ground hummed faintly beneath her feet. Flowers leaned toward her without reason. And the shadows? They didn't threaten but they curled like they *knew* her.

This is what it feels like when magic wakes, she thought, fingers twitching as she felt it surge beneath her skin.

And still... Kael hadn't come.

She kept searching the crowd without meaning to, hoping for a flash of dark hair, the glint of silver eyes, the tilt of a smile she knew by heart. But there was nothing. Not a sign of him. Maybe he'd decided she needed space, or maybe he feared what would, or wouldn't, happen just as much as she did.

The more she searched, the more she couldn't shake the feeling that someone was watching her in return.

She could feel something on the wind. It was like a breath held just out of reach.

Maybe he hadn't come because she *wasn't* his mate after all.

Her chest ached, sharp and hollow, as the bells from the old chapel tower began to chime.

Twelve.

Twelve strikes. Midnight.

The exact moment the bond should, by every fae law, awaken, if it was ever meant to at all.

The final bell echoed and faded.

She exhaled slowly, blinking tears from her eyes. *I guess... nothing's changed.*

But then—

She felt it.

A pull.

Not a physical sensation, more like gravity itself had shifted. Her spine straightened. Her breath caught.

Her head turned of its own accord, her gaze pulled through the swirl of partygoers. Lanterns blurred. Laughter dulled. She didn't register movement or sound, only *him*.

A pair of stormy gray eyes, rimmed in silver, watching her from the far edge of the garden.

Kael.

She had no idea how or when he arrived, but none of that mattered any longer.

The moment their eyes locked, the world *broke open*.

The bond snapped into place with the force of a tidal wave crashing into her soul.

Everything inside her *recognized* him, his heartbeat, his breath, his scent. Her limbs moved before thought could catch up.

"Mate," she whispered, her voice not her own, but something ancient, something aching and certain.

And then she ran.

The crowd blurred as she moved, skirts flying behind her. She reached him in seconds, launched herself into his arms, and he caught her like he'd been waiting for this very moment his entire life.

She buried her face in the hollow of his neck, inhaling *him* through the bond. He smelled of warm honey, fresh earth, and something wild. It was like the scent of home. Gods, the way it *fit*. Like a missing piece of herself had fallen into place and finally made her whole.

Kael held her so tightly it stole her breath, but she didn't care.

"I've been waiting for this day," he murmured, voice raw and reverent. "For so long."

Then his mouth found hers.

And the world shattered.

Magic burst from them in a flood. It was light and shadow, starlight and silver flame. It curled around their bodies in glowing tendrils, weaving, twisting, claiming and binding as one. The garden fell silent. All eyes turned. No one spoke.

Aislen's body hummed like a struck chord as Kael kissed her. It was slow, deep, and desperate. She felt the bond in every breath. Every heartbeat. Every inch of skin where they touched.

They didn't need words. Not now.

When they finally pulled apart, both breathless and shaking, the magic still danced around them. Threads of it crackled in the air between them like lightning caught mid-strike.

Kael looked at her, eyes wide, lips parted slightly in awe.

"I knew it," he whispered, reaching up to brush a strand of moonlit silver from her face. "I *felt* it in you. Your magic... it's alive. And powerful."

She blinked, dazed. "You can feel it?"

He nodded, gently taking her hand. "I can feel *you*. It's different now. Like it's not just mine anymore."

They stood there, held together by fate and magic and every quiet moment that had led them to this.

For the first time in her life, Aislen didn't feel torn between who she was and who she was meant to be.

In Kael's arms, with the stars watching overhead and her soul fully awakened, she was exactly where she belonged.

For a while, there was nothing but the sound of her breath against Kael's, the beat of their hearts in perfect time.

But slowly, too slowly, awareness began to creep back in.

The laughter and music had fallen away. The hum of voices was replaced with a stunned hush. And when Aislen finally turned her head, still wrapped in Kael's arms, she realized why.

They were *staring*.

Everyone.

Villagers and fae alike. Friends. Elders. Strangers. Wide-eyed children clutching their parents' sleeves. Even the lanterns seemed to hover in the air with held breath.

Then someone gasped.

"*Gods*, she's fae."

A murmur rippled through the crowd like wind through tall grass.

More voices chimed in... "Did you see that magic? It was like her magic *merged* with his!"

A few people clapped. Someone whooped.

Then all at once, the moment shattered into noise and color again. Voices rose in surprise, delight, even awe.

"Congratulations!"

"I didn't even know she was fae!"

"That was *stunning!*"

"Did you *see* the light around them?"

"She didn't have magic before, did she?"

Aislen's cheeks burned as a small cluster of people rushed forward, friends from the village who'd come with nothing but lighthearted gifts and sweets now crowding her with wide eyes and half-whispered praise.

"Ilyra's going to lose her mind when she hears her cousin has *magic*," someone said.

Another woman leaned in. "When you kissed, it was like the stars themselves answered. That was... powerful."

Aislen looked helplessly at Kael, who stood beside her like a silent shield. His hand found hers again, grounding her.

"Too much?" he asked quietly.

She nodded once, throat too tight to speak.

Thess arrived next, pushing through the crowd with her eyebrows raised nearly to her hairline. "I leave you alone for *one* moment at this damn party and you go full High Fae in front of the whole village," she said with mock outrage.

Aislen huffed out a breath that was half-laugh, half-sob. "I didn't mean to..."

Thess pulled her into a quick hug. "You didn't have to mean to. It was *real*, and it was beautiful. Everyone felt it."

Kael stepped slightly in front of Aislen as another person tried to press too close. His voice was calm but firm. "She needs air."

That was all it took. People began to back up a step, giving her a little space.

Aislen turned back toward Thess, her voice barely a whisper. "They're all looking at me like I'm something else now. Like I'm not me anymore."

"You're still you," Thess said gently. "You're just... more. Just like we talked about."

Another wave of congratulations and curious glances swept over them, and Aislen clutched Kael's hand tighter. Her magic buzzed under her skin, alive and tangled with his. She could feel his calm trying to wrap around her anxiety through the bond, a gentle pulse of reassurance.

Kael leaned in close, brushing his lips against the side of her head. "We can leave whenever you're ready. One word and we're gone."

But for a brief second, Aislen stood still and let it all wash over her. The murmurs, the awe, the truth of it.

They saw her now.

All of her.

Not just the girl in the garden.

Not just the human child of a secret past.

She was fae. She was powerful. She was *claimed.*

And the moment the bond clicked into place... she had never felt more like *herself.*

She turned toward Kael, eyes soft but steady.

"Not yet," she said. "Let them see."

He nodded. "I'll stay by your side." His eyes glanced around before coming back to hers. "But as soon as we leave, I need to know everything. How you found out... just everything. I feel as if I have missed so much these last few weeks."

His eyes cast downwards.

"I missed you Aislen. Not just because of the bond. I missed you."

Her eyes began to water as she gently lifted his head to look into his eyes.

"I promise to tell you everything. But first, this," She said as she leaned in for another kiss.

There were still so many questions, but this. This right here made more than sense. It felt right. It felt like home.

* * *

As the magic settled into a quiet shimmer around her, Aislen's gaze flicked across the gathering. Lanterns were glowing, villagers were still staring, and voices rose in waves of stunned awe. And then she saw her.

Maera.

Her mom.

Standing just beyond the edge of the lanternlight, half-hidden behind a tall hedge of moonlilies, her mom's eyes were locked on her. The did not hold surprise, or even celebration, but something deeper. Older.

Fear.

Not fear of Aislen, but fear *for* her.

Their eyes met for only a second, but it sent a jolt through Aislen's chest. There was a storm behind Maera's gaze. Not doubt. Not shame. Just the weight of everything she hadn't said.

Then the moment passed, and her mom looked away.

Twelve

"Unveiled"

~ **Maera** ~

Maera clapped with the rest of the crowd, her smile soft and bright, but her heart was racing.

She stood beneath a paper lantern strung between the trees, its golden glow brushing her face like sunlight through fog. Around her, laughter bubbled and voices rose in delighted disbelief. Magic still shimmered faintly in the air, coiled like silver smoke. Her daughter stood wrapped in Kael's arms, glowing with magic and something deeper, older, it was something Maera hadn't seen since the night she ran from the Starlight Court.

The bond had awakened.

It was beautiful. It was terrifying.

She swallowed past the lump rising in her throat and forced herself to keep smiling. People were watching. This was a celebration. A fae coming into her magic, a true mate bond revealed under starlight, it was the stuff of songs.

But all she could hear was the last half of the prophecy.

"One breath may break the bind thread, one choice may leave the courts in dread.

The veils shall thin, the truth laid bare, all shall change if she does dare. She holds the ruin, she holds the rise. A crown in shadows. Fire in skies. Should love prevail, the land shall heal. Should hate consume, the void shall steal. So guard her path or shape her fall, the Veilborn comes to challenge all."

The guilt ate at her knowing she kept the ending of the prophecy from her daughter. She just wanted to protect her.

She had been so sure she could outrun it. That raising Aislen in the quiet edges of the human realm, burying the truth, hiding her magic, would keep her safe. But the prophecy hadn't faded. It had simply waited.

Maera's gaze drifted to the silver in Aislen's hair, now glowing like moonlit silk. Her daughter looked radiant, transformed, but Maera knew better than anyone that power this pure never came without consequence.

The moment the crowd thinned, Maera turned away and slipped between the trees.

* * *

The gathering room inside Elara's home was warm, but Maera felt chilled to the bone. A soft fire crackled in the hearth, casting long shadows across the carved wooden walls. Tomas was already there, leaning against the mantle with furrowed brows. Kael's father, Fenric, stood stiffly beside the window, arms crossed. And Elara, sharp-eyed and graceful, set down a tray of tea with hands that trembled slightly.

"You saw it," Elara said, breaking the silence. Her voice held no judgment, just gravity.

Maera nodded slowly, sinking into the nearest chair.

"She's awakened," Fenric said flatly. "And it wasn't quiet."

Tomas shot him a look. "She's just a girl."

"She's not *just* anything," Elara murmured. "She's special. And you both know it."

Maera's throat felt tight. "I thought we had more time."

"You should've told us," Fenric said. "The rest of it. Years ago."

Maera met his eyes. "I did what I had to do to protect her. You know what that prophecy said. If word of her bloodline spreads, the courts will come looking. They'll try to use her, or worse, destroy her."

"She's bonded now," Elara said softly. "To my son. We expected this, but given their situation this changes things."

Maera's chest clenched. "It *doesn't* change the danger."

Tomas's usual composure was thinned but not broken. He looked at each of them in turn, then focused on Maera.

"She deserves the truth," he said simply.

Maera nodded, barely able to speak around the ache in her ribs. "I'll tell her. All of it. Soon," she hesitated. "I owe her that much."

Tomas moved toward her, placing a steadying hand on her shoulder.

"She's strong, Maera. She's not alone in this."

"But she *is* marked," Maera whispered. "And once the other courts sense that kind of magic... they'll know. They'll remember the prophecy. And they'll come."

Elara's eyes narrowed. "Then we prepare. We shield her. We make sure she's not a pawn to anyone."

Fenric's voice was steel. "Or worse, the match that ignites a long awaited war."

The room fell into a heavy silence.

Maera's gaze drifted toward the window, where the party lights still glowed in the distance. Aislen stood among the crowd, radiant and unaware of the storm gathering at her back.

"She's in love," Maera said softly. "Truly. I saw it in her eyes. I *want* this for her."

Tears pricked her eyes, but she didn't let them fall.

"But the courts don't care about love. They care about power. And Aislen... she might be the key to all of it."

"Maera, if they learn not just who she is, but who helped conceal her, they'll come for us all," Elara said, somberly.

* * *

~ Aislen ~

Aislen sat beside Kael on the long velvet-cushioned bench in Elara's sitting room, her knees barely an inch from his. A tea service sat untouched on the table between them, its steam long gone cold. She could feel the heat of Kael's leg close to hers, steady and solid, but her own fingers were woven so tightly together in her lap, they were starting to ache.

Across from them sat four of the most important people in their lives, her mom and dad to their left, Elara and Fenric to their right. The room was warm from the hearth, but the air was thick with something heavier than heat. Expectation. Fear. Uncertainty.

"I believe you both know what comes next," Elara said softly, her hands folded with a kind of ceremonial grace in her lap.

Aislen looked toward her, brows furrowed. "Next?"

Kael nodded beside her, his voice low and quiet. "The mating ritual."

Aislen's heart did a strange little twist. "Right," she said slowly, her voice dry. "I've heard of them. Like a wedding... right?"

"In many ways," Elara replied. "It's not just symbolic, it's sacred. An ancient fae tradition, bound by magic and witnessed by your chosen circle. It's meant to affirm the bond and protect it."

"It's also not optional," Fenric added, his voice like stone cracking. "For true bonds, the ritual must be completed, or the magic becomes unstable. Too long without formal recognition and both bonded souls begin to unravel."

Aislen blinked. "Unravel?"

"It starts small," Fenric said. "Dreams. Restlessness. Mood swings. Then it worsens to pain when separated, sickness, disorientation. The bond doesn't tolerate limbo," he cleared his throat. "If we wait too long, it could even end in death of the bonded."

A quiet chill passed through her. She turned her head slightly, catching Kael's profile. His jaw was tight, his throat moving as he swallowed hard.

"I've already felt it," he said without looking away. "The restlessness. The way my chest tightens when I'm not near you."

Her heart squeezed. "I thought that was just me."

Kael gave a small, sad smile. "It's both of us."

A silence settled between them. Then Fenric cleared his throat again as he continued.

"Usually the ritual is small," he said. "Friends. Family. A feast, some words, a symbolic joining. Afterward, you're expected to live together. To start your life."

Aislen sat back slightly, as if that sentence had knocked the wind from her.

"I'd be moving out?" she said, looking at her mom in alarm. "Just like that?"

Maera's smile was gentle, but her eyes were tight around the edges. "It's tradition. Once a bond is confirmed and honored, you start your life together. You will build a home, deepen the connection. You grow into it."

Aislen felt the walls tilt around her. Kael's hand brushed hers again, and she clung to it this time, grateful for something to anchor her.

Elara leaned forward slightly. "It's a joyful occasion, Aislen. The bond is rare. It's worth celebrating. But there are… other things you should know."

Maera went very still.

Aislen noticed it immediately. How her mom's hands, resting delicately on her knees, had curled into her skirts. How she didn't meet anyone's eyes.

"Elara," she said, a note of warning in her voice. "Not yet—"

"They need to know," Elara said gently. "She deserves to understand."

"Understand what?" Aislen asked, her voice trembling.

Maera's shoulders lifted with a breath. Her lips parted. But no words came out at first.

So Elara continued.

"All mating rituals, especially those involving fae with strong magical signatures, are recorded. It's part of the royal registry. It's law."

"Law?" Aislen repeated. "You mean like… written down?"

Fenric answered with a firm nod. "Documented, stamped, and sealed. Copies sent to each of the Courts for record-keeping. But the primary report is always sent to the Sun Court. It's where the royal family resides."

Kael straightened slightly. "Why does the royal family care who bonds with who?"

"Because every bond holds power," Elara said. "And some of them... carry consequences."

Maera exhaled slowly, then lifted her head. "They'll know," she whispered.

Aislen turned toward her. "What?"

Her mom finally met her eyes, and the look there made her breath catch.

"They'll know who you are," Maera said quietly. "Or at least... they'll suspect."

The words fell like stones into a still pond.

Kael sat up straighter. "Wait. You mean—"

"When your bond is registered, your magic is cataloged. Traced," Maera explained. "Every magical pulse leaves a signature. Hers is rare. Unique. Once it's on paper, once it reaches the castle... someone might recognize it. Someone from the Aurion Court."

"Recognize it as what?" Aislen asked, her voice rising.

"As bloodline magic," Maera said. "Old. Powerful. Forbidden. You already possess both starlight magic and earthsong magic this makes you a trifecta of danger. Dangerous or not, that's how they will see you."

"Earthsong magic, as you probably have realized is nature-aligned. It's why you have always had an affinity for gardening. Not only can you create nature, you can speak it's very own language. It isn't as common as it used to be. I wasn't sure at first if you had inherited your fathers starlight magic. It's a deep and powerful magic. It may appear as shadow at times, but it's actually the opposite, your magic offers the absence of light, often triggered by fear."

Maera looked down nervously.

Her hands began to shake.

She sighed, "Most do not inherit the bloodline magic, not anymore."

"I don't understand. Aislen said there was a prophecy, but she is just now coming into her powers. I can't see it being that dangerous," Kael challenged.

Maera looked at him. His voice sounded confident, but the way he possessively held her daughters hand made her think he was more scared than he let on.

"It's because—" Maera started.

Fenric cut in, "They will only see it as a challenge to their throne. That kind of bloodline magic only appears in royal fae lines. 300 years ago, the fae lands were all divided. Each court had a high lord or a high lady. They each ruled their own lands, they did not fall under one ruler. Even though they ruled separately, the high lords and high ladies held each other in high regards. They were considered Kings and Queens in their own right. They were equals."

His eyes closed and he cleared his throat before he continued, "A powerful royal bloodline from the Aurion Court began a campaign throughout each of the courts. The campaign was to "unite" all courts under one High Crown. It was allegedly to protect against rising human threats and magical chaos, but they were power hungry. All of the courts were in agreement except for one. The Celestara Court. They argued that it was not to bring together the courts, but to divide them further. Because the Celestara Court disagreed, The Sun Crown from the Aurion Court claimed they were dangerous, traitorous and corrupted by bloodthirst and bloodcraft. This led to the entirety of the court being banished, sealed, and erased from recorded fae history."

Aislen let out a small gasp as she covered her mouth.

"They lied?" She glanced to her mom who finally met her eyes

Maera gave her a brief nod before taking back over, "Yes, they lied. They didn't want the Celestara Court to dismantle them from their throne. They held fear in their hearts. The fear grew and grew as it was passed down from one king to the next. It'll only became worse when they heard of a prophecy. Of a girl who could tear down their whole world."

"They have been patiently waiting for her ever since. Waiting for you Aislen."

A beat of silence.

"I thought you left the Court," Aislen said, eyes wide. "To hide me. You said we were safe."

"I left to protect you," Maera whispered. "And I succeeded for nineteen years. But if you go through with the ritual, if you let them see what's inside you, they'll know you're not just *any* bonded fae."

Kael leaned forward. "What will they do?"

Maera shook her head. "I don't know. It depends on who sees it. On what they want."

Tomas reached for her hand. "We'll protect her. We always have."

But Maera's eyes were still locked on Aislen's.

"They will send someone," she said. "Maybe not tomorrow. But once that bond is entered into the registry, the ripple will reach them. And when it does... your life will never be the same."

Aislen felt her world tilt. She pressed a hand to her chest, breathing shallow.

"And if we *don't* do the ritual?" she whispered.

"You'll suffer," Fenric said bluntly. "You'll fracture. Or worse, your bond could fail altogether and you would die."

Aislen turned toward Kael. His eyes were burning silver, watching her as if she might vanish.

"I don't want to lose you," he said quietly. "And I won't push you into something that puts you in danger." Kael hesitated before continuing, "but doing this I can keep you safe. If we don't, we could risk losing everything altogether."

Aislen closed her eyes.

She could feel it, the pull of the bond humming like a song beneath her skin. The promise of love. Of purpose. Of finally knowing who she was meant to be.

But there, in the shadow of it, stood the truth: stepping forward meant stepping into the fire.

Her voice was barely audible as she asked:

"What happens if they find out?"

Her mother didn't answer right away.

And that, more than anything, terrified her.

* * *

That night, when Aislen closed her eyes. She dreamt of him.

And this time she knew who he was.

The moonlight in the dream was different this time. It was cooler, deeper. It didn't just shine; it shimmered, refracting through the air like light through a prism. Aislen stood barefoot on a stretch of midnight-colored stone, surrounded by towering spires carved from crystal and stardust. The wind whispered in a language she didn't understand but somehow still *felt*. Every breath she took hummed with magic.

And he was there again.

The male from her dream.

He stood at the edge of a wide platform, cloaked in robes that moved like water, the silver embroidery across his chest glowing with every shift of his body. The wind didn't touch him, but the stars seemed to bow to him. It was like he was made of the same ancient light they were.

But this time, Aislen *knew*.

"You're him," she said softly, her voice echoing across the endless sky. "You're my birth father."

The man turned slowly, and when his gaze met hers, something clicked into place in her chest, painful and beautiful all at once. His eyes were her eyes, only deeper. Older. Timeless.

"I am," he said, his voice smooth and resonant, like a low chord plucked on a harp made of stars. "You've finally figured it out."

Her throat tightened. "Why didn't you tell me before?"

"I couldn't," he replied. "Not until the magic further awoke in you. Not until the bond anchored your soul. Until then, you wouldn't have been able to hear me, not truly."

Aislen took a cautious step closer. "What do you want from me?"

He studied her for a long moment, expression unreadable. Then, gently, "To keep you alive."

Her breath caught. "What—?"

"You felt it," he said. "The moment it happened. When your bond with the Lunaris Court male snapped into place. When your magic surged and bloomed in front of them all. That light didn't go unnoticed."

A dark pulse rippled behind his words, and suddenly the sky in her dream flickered, just once, like a shadow had passed in front of the stars.

"Someone felt it," he continued. "Someone who has been watching. Waiting. The ones who were responsible for tearing your mother from the Court... they know. And now they know *you* live."

Aislen's knees nearly buckled. "What do they want from me?"

"Power. Control. Erasure." His jaw tightened, a rare flash of emotion breaking through. "They will not let you rise."

She shook her head, her voice barely above a whisper. "But I didn't *choose* this. I didn't ask for any of it."

"No," he said softly. "But it chose you."

A thousand questions burned on her tongue, but only one made it out. "What do I do?"

He stepped forward, slowly, until they stood just a few feet apart. The air around him shimmered like heat, but colder, sharper, like starlight formed from ice.

"You come to me," he said. "You come home."

"The Celestara Court," she breathed.

He nodded. "You are half of it, Aislen. Born of Earth and Space. And if you want the truth, if you want answers, protection, *freedom,* you must come to the place that knows who you truly are."

"But I don't even know the way," she said. "And my mom, she left for a reason. She'll never let me go."

"She can't stop what's already begun." His voice turned grave. "The Aurion Court will come. Their letters. Their messengers. Their chains wrapped in silk. When they do, you must be gone."

Her pulse thundered in her ears. "And you'll be there?"

His hand reached out, not quite touching her, but close enough that she felt the cold warmth of it on her skin.

"I've been waiting your whole life."

The stars flared behind him, bright, blinding.

And then she woke up.

* * *

Aislen jolted awake with a gasp, lungs straining like she'd broken the surface of deep water. Her sheets were tangled around her legs, sweat cooling on her skin despite the chill threading through the air. The dream clung to her like smoke. She could still hear his voice, the starlight, the warning.

They know.

Without thinking, she scrambled from the bed and tore down the hallway in Kael's home barefoot, heart hammering as if it were trying to claw its way out of her chest.

"Mom!" she shouted, her voice cracking with panic. "Mom, where are you?!"

Doors opened behind her, footsteps following, Kael's voice rising in confusion, but she didn't stop.

Elara emerged from her bedroom down the hall just as Aislen nearly collided with her. "Your mom isn't—" she stopped abruptly as she saw the panic etched in her face.

"What is it?" Elara asked sharply, catching her shoulders. "What happened?"

"I saw him again," Aislen panted. "I saw my father in my dream. I *recognized* him this time. And he—he said they know. The ones who drove her away, the ones who wanted to erase me, they *know* I'm alive. I felt it, Elara. We're not safe. None of us."

Elara's face drained of color. She didn't ask Aislen if she was sure. She didn't ask for details. She just went *still*.

"Get Maera and Tomas. NOW." She yelled as Fenric ran out the door.

Kael appeared in the doorway, tunic half-tugged over his head, confusion turning to alarm as he took in the scene.

"What's going on?" he asked, voice low and tense.

Aislen was in too much of a panic to respond. She bent forward with her hands on her knees trying to keep the nauseous feeling at bay.

What felt like hours later, she heard her moms voice as she entered the home.

She came rushing in, breathing heavily, with Tomas right on her heal. They were both disheveled and still in their night clothing.

"Fenric filled me in," she hesitated before looking at each of them in turn, her lips parted like she might deny it, like she might try to soften the blow.

But then she said quietly, "I knew this would happen."

The hallway went silent.

Maera stepped back, rubbing a hand over her face. "The wards around the Celestara Court didn't just keep the other Court's out, but they *shielded* those within. As long as she was hidden, even half a realm away, that protection remained. But the bond... the magic... It's all awakened now. And when that happens, when a fae born of royal blood comes into their power, the ripple carries."

"So they felt it?" Elara asked. "Someone in the Aurion Court?"

Maera nodded. "Or someone watching for the signs. Either way, the dream confirms what I feared. We have no time left."

Kael stepped closer to Aislen, touching her back gently. "What do we do?"

Maera's eyes were sharp when they lifted. "We leave. Tonight."

"Leave?" Fenric echoed. "Where?"

"The only place she'll be truly safe now," Maera said. "The Celestara Court."

Everyone stilled.

"You're the only one we know of who has traveled there in nearly 300 years," Elara said carefully. "And even then, I heard the path was—"

"Dangerous," Maera finished. "I know. It winds through the Hollow Mountains just after you pass through the Veiled Vanor. The journey could take weeks." She glanced at Tomas, "but I remember the way. I might be the only one who does."

She turned to Aislen, her voice softer but iron underneath. "We'll need to pack what we can carry. Nothing more. Food, water, cloaks, weapons if we have them. We need to be gone before sunrise."

Aislen's hands trembled, her breath ragged. "Why before sunrise?"

Maera didn't blink. "Because that's when the Aurion Court wakes."

Elara let out a breath, her expression tight. "You really think they'll move that fast?"

"If they already know she's alive, then yes. The letters will come first. The questions. The summons disguised as courtesies. But soon after... worse."

Aislen looked between the faces of the people who had shaped her life, her mom, Elara, Kael, Fenric, and saw it there: the truth. The quiet, grim acceptance. The danger was real. And it was already here. She wasn't ready for this.

"We'll help however we can," Elara said firmly. "Whatever you need."

"Agreed," Fenric added, crossing his arms. "You won't be traveling alone."

Kael met Aislen's eyes and took her hand, gripping it tight. "Wherever you go, I go."

And just like that, everything shifted again.

Not just a dream, not just a prophecy.

A flight.

A journey into the heart of the danger they'd tried to outrun for nineteen years.

And there would be no turning back.

Thirteen

"Warning"

~OͼOͼOͽ~

~ Sion ~

The stars were still out when Sion finally slipped away from the village green. Lanterns flickered low, casting soft gold across the trampled grass and abandoned mugs. The celebration had thinned to silence, but the magic still hung in the air like fog. It was electric, unsettled.

He walked alone, hands deep in his pockets, boots scuffing the dirt path toward home. Aislen's bond had awakened tonight. Everyone had felt it. Seen it. And while joy had filled the space around her, something else had coiled in Sion's gut.

A chill.

He shook it off as he reached his door, pushing inside to the warmth and quiet hum of his family's cottage.

"Sion!" two voices whispered in unison.

He turned, startled, just as twin blurs flung themselves at his legs.

"Vessa. Runa," he groaned, laughing despite himself. "You're supposed to be in bed."

Vessa crossed her arms and looked up with exaggerated seriousness. "We tried. But the lights outside were too pretty. Runa thought they were stars falling."

Runa, wild-haired and barefoot, nodded solemnly. "They looked like stars."

Sion dropped to one knee, ruffling both of their hair in turn. "They were magic. But the kind that's not always safe."

Vessa tilted her head. "Is it because Aislen glowed?"

His hand paused in Runa's hair. "Yeah," he said softly. "It's exactly because of that."

The girls leaned into him, and for a long moment, Sion let them stay with his arms wrapped around their tiny shoulders, anchoring himself in their warmth.

Eventually, he whispered, "Back to bed now, both of you."

They groaned, but obeyed, padding down the hall with sleepy protests and tangled braids.

Sion watched until their door clicked shut.

Then, with a weary breath, he headed to his own room.

If sleep would ever come, he thought.

Sion lay staring at the ceiling, the worn beams above his bed faintly outlined in moonlight. The village was quiet now, truly quiet, but his skin wouldn't stop crawling.

Magic itched beneath the surface, restless and sharp, like invisible threads pulling in every direction. He rolled onto his side. Then his back. Then his side again. The feeling wouldn't leave. It was like being covered in tiny bugs, wriggling just beneath his skin, and no matter how he adjusted, it followed him.

He pressed a hand over his chest, willing his pulse to slow. *It's nothing*, he told himself. *Just the aftermath. The bond. All that magic stirring the air.*

But the words felt empty.

Eventually, exhaustion dragged him down into sleep, but not peace.

His dreams were jagged, splintered things.

Smoke curling through endless trees.

A silver moon split in half.

A river of ink instead of water, flowing backward.

Hands reaching from the ground. A face with no eyes. The sound of bells that never stopped ringing.

He wandered through the chaos barefoot and unseen, every step heavier than the last. The air was wrong. It was too thick, too quiet. Even his magic recoiled, retreating to the edges of his limbs as if it didn't want to be here either.

Then, in the final flicker of the dream, the forest opened.

The trees stilled. Even the wind vanished.

Aislen hovered in the center of a clearing, suspended in midair.

She glowed, not with warmth, but with terrifying brilliance. Her hair whipped around her like a halo of light, her arms limp at her sides. Power pulsed from her body in waves, cracking the earth below. She didn't speak. Didn't move.

But her eyes were open.

And they were filled with sorrow.

Sion jolted awake with a gasp, chest heaving, sweat dampening the collar of his shirt. The room was still, moonlight pooling across the floorboards, but the pressure hadn't left.

The crawling was gone, but something colder remained.

He swung his legs over the side of the bed, grounding his feet to the wood.

That hadn't been a dream.

Not really.

It was a warning.

He didn't know what his magic was trying to tell him, only that it hadn't lied to him before.

Sion's magic had given him feelings before, just small pulses that pushed him in certain directions. But he had never had a full-blown dream before, this was the strongest his magic has been regarding the future.

He didn't know what was coming, but he knew one thing with bone-deep certainty: *if he stayed still, if he waited too long... he would regret it.*

He got up and left.

* * *

~ Thess ~

A knock at the door startled Thess awake.

She blinked, groggy, heart already pounding as she reached for the dagger under her pillow out of instinct. More knocking, three firm raps. Not quite urgent, but steady. Familiar.

She threw the covers off and padded barefoot across the room, pulling open the door with a whisper of air.

Sion stood there, breath misting in the cool of night, eyes wide and unsettled in a way she had never seen before.

He didn't speak right away.

But he didn't have to.

Thess took one look at him, at the way he gripped the strap of his travel bag like it was anchoring him, at the silent fear vibrating in his bones and said, "What happened?"

"There's something wrong," he said, voice low but taut. "I don't know what exactly, but I felt it. Something's coming. And I think Aislen and the others might already be caught in it."

Thess stared at him for a beat, absorbing the weight of his words. He wasn't the type to panic. Or to act on shadows.

And he'd never lie about them.

Never lie to her.

"Okay," she said simply. "Give me two minutes."

Sion blinked. "You believe me?"

Her hand paused briefly on the doorknob, knuckles pale. But when she turned, her face was set.

She began gathering her cloak and boots. "Of course I do. You look like you've seen a ghost and swallowed it whole. If your gut says move, we move."

He exhaled, shoulders easing just slightly. "Thanks, Trouble."

She glanced back with a crooked smile. "Don't thank me yet. I'm gonna complain the whole way there."

"Wouldn't be you if you didn't."

She stepped out the door, slinging her satchel over one shoulder. "Alright, let's go save our friends."

And just like that, they disappeared into the dark, side by side. They were two sparks on the wind, moving before the storm could catch them.

Fourteen

"Departure"

~ **Aislen** ~

The house was a flurry of quiet movement. It was too tense for panic yet too fast for calm. Shadows stretched long across the floors as candlelight flickered against hurried hands and grim expressions.

Kael was already in his traveling gear, packing rations into worn canvas satchels while Tomas checked a folded map near the hearth. Maera moved quickly but efficiently through the hallway, gathering potions, healing salves, and a wrapped bundle of cloaks.

Aislen stood in the center of it all, clutching a small pouch of herbs and staring around at her life one last time. The pressed flowers on the windowsill. The worn books stacked by Kael's bed. What her life could have been, here. In Kael's home.

Her world, reduced to what could be carried.

Outside, the stars had begun to dim, that thin gray veil of pre-dawn creeping in along the treetops.

"We need to be gone within the next half hour," Maera said, stepping into the room and gently pressing a cloak into Aislen's hands. "Once the light hits the eastern ridge, any temporary cover we have is gone."

Aislen nodded and threw it over her shoulders, fingers trembling slightly at the silver stitching lining the hem. "This was yours," she whispered.

Maera smiled faintly. "It'll keep you warm through the passes."

Just as Aislen turned to grab her boots, a knock came, three sharp raps at the back door.

Everyone froze.

Elara's hand drifted toward the blade at her hip. Kael moved to Aislen's side in a breath. Tomas stepped cautiously toward the back hall, his steps silent as snowfall.

But then came a muffled voice.

"It's just us! Don't stab anyone, please."

Aislen blinked. "Thess?"

Tomas opened the door cautiously, and there they were: Sion, breathless and wide-eyed, and Thess wrapped in a travel cloak, her braid falling over one shoulder.

"What are you doing here?" Kael asked, stepping toward them with brows drawn tight.

Sion scratched the back of his neck. "Okay, this is going to sound weird, but… I had a dream."

Aislen and Kael exchanged a glance.

"A dream?" Maera asked warily.

"Yeah. I don't know how to explain it," Sion said. "It wasn't like a normal dream, it felt more like a vision. Or a warning. I think I was at the stream you always talk about. The one in the forest. Except it was night and everything felt… heavy. Dangerous. I felt like something was coming, and I had to get to Kael. So I checked on Thess first, since she was closest—"

"I didn't want him going alone," Thess interrupted, her expression serious. "He was shaken. I couldn't ignore it."

"And now we're here," Sion finished, motioning to the satchels and weapons. "Which… clearly wasn't just paranoia."

Aislen stepped forward slowly. "You *felt* something?"

"Yeah," Sion said, then shrugged helplessly. "Not like I understood it. Just… that something bad was going to happen. And if I didn't move, I'd regret it."

Maera eyed them both. "Dream-warnings don't happen by accident. Not around her."

Sion glanced at Aislen. "Are you leaving?"

"Yes," Aislen said quietly. "Before sunrise."

She turned to her mom, "We can trust them."

"Trust us with what?" Thess said.

Maera nodded in agreement, "I trust them if you do, we're going to the Celestara Court."

Thess's eyes widened. "The *Celestara Court*?"

Kael nodded. "It's the only place she'll be safe right now. There isn't much time to explain, we just have to go there. Soon."

For a long beat, the only sound was the wind pushing softly against the shutters.

Then Thess stepped forward. "Then we're coming with you."

"What?" Aislen asked.

Thess's chin lifted. "You're my best friend. And if someone's trying to hurt you, they'll have to go through me."

Sion nodded, though less confidently. "I'm not the best warrior in the village, but I sure as hell can fight. Or... distract. Or make jokes when things get bad."

Maera hesitated, then gave a sharp nod. "If you're serious, get ready. Quickly."

As Thess and Sion darted inside, Kael moved beside Aislen again, brushing a loose strand of hair from her cheek.

"Looks like our circle just grew."

She gave a breathless laugh, but it trembled. "I don't know what's waiting for us."

Kael touched her jaw gently. "Whatever it is, we'll face it together."

And somewhere in the distance, a golden ray of light began to kiss the horizon.

* * *

The room was still and quiet as the group gathered once more. This time they were in a circle, beneath the low beams of Elara's sitting room. The air thrummed softly with magic, the faint scent of jasmine and earth lingering like a promise.

Aislen and Kael stood side by side, hands trembling but clasped firmly together. The weight of all eyes felt like a thousand breaths pressing down on them, yet their gazes remained locked.

Maera stepped forward, voice steady but gentle.

"This ritual is more than a formality. It seals your bond, not just before those who love you, but before the magic that ties your souls. It will steady the unrest growing inside you both."

Tomas nodded, his eyes warm but serious.

"The bond is a living thread. If left unclaimed, it frays and tears. This ceremony binds it whole again."

Elara approached with two delicate silver bowls, their surfaces catching the candlelight like liquid starlight.

"Drink this," she said softly. "Water from the Veiled Vanor spring, blessed for strength and clarity."

Kael lifted his bowl first, the cold water a sharp, clear contrast to the warm room.

Aislen followed, the water soothing the fire of nerves in her chest.

Elara began an ancient chant, the sound weaving through the silence like a gentle breeze through leaves.

The water in the bowls shimmered and lifted, forming a glowing arc of light between the two of them.

Maera took Aislen's hands in hers, squeezing gently.

"Remember, no matter what darkness may come, this bond will protect you both. It is stronger than fear."

Kael's voice was low, raw with emotion.

"I vow to stand by you. To face whatever shadows fall, together."

Aislen's breath hitched, but she met his eyes with fierce resolve.

"And I vow the same. No matter the cost."

A thread of silver light braided itself between their hands, pulsing like a heartbeat. The warmth spread through their bodies, gentle but unyielding.

The room seemed to hold its breath until the light slowly dimmed, leaving the steady pulse of the bond beneath their skin.

"Wait, what's that?" Maera stepped closer to Kael.

A faint glow pulsed along the side of his collarbone, it was an identical mark to the one on Aislen's

"They're both glowing," Maera whispered, her breath catching. "It's the same."

Elara tilted her head. "Do you think...?"

Maera hesitated, eyes tracing the marks. "I think it could be," She murmured. Then to Kael and Aislen: "There is a chance your powers might merge once your bond reaches its full strength. Not only are your bodies bound, but so are your souls."

Aislen turned to Kael with wonder and unease. *Who are they? And what are they about to become?*

Kael caught her gaze and offered a small, lopsided smile, the kind that said he already knew what she was thinking.

The ritual had done more than seal the bond.

It had given them a piece of each other.

A piece that allowed them to feel each other's emotions, and always, always find their way back, no matter the distance, no matter the darkness.

The group began to shift, scattering to finish packing and give them space. But Aislen stayed still, her hand still wrapped in Kael's. Something... was different.

The magic buzzed faintly beneath her skin, like a second heartbeat thrumming in time with her own. She looked up at him, and from the startled flicker in his eyes, he felt it too.

A strange warmth moved between them. It was not physical, not quite emotional either. Just... presence. A knowing. She could feel the weight of his thoughts, the edges of his fear, the low hum of longing buried deep beneath his calm exterior.

"Is this..." she whispered, barely audible.

Kael nodded slowly. "The bond. Strengthened."

He reached for her cheek, but stopped short, like he wasn't sure if touching her again would ease the intensity or make it worse. She didn't move either. It was too much and not enough all at once.

Then Maera cleared her throat behind them.

They jumped.

Tomas and Elara had apparently not moved far either. Elara was trying to look vaguely interested in her satchel, and Tomas pretending to check the same rope for the fifth time.

"It'll settle soon," Maera said gently, though her lips twitched in amusement. "But just know, it only gets stronger after... well." She gestured vaguely, then crossed her arms. "After you've sealed it fully."

Aislen went crimson.

Kael looked like he might spontaneously combust.

Tomas looked everywhere but at them. "Right. So. Horses. I believe Fenric is already out at the stables, I'll check on them."

"Good try," Elara muttered to him as they both walked away.

Kael exhaled a laugh under his breath, dragging a hand down his face. "Fae rituals and parental commentary. A winning combination."

"I want to crawl into the earth," Aislen mumbled, mortified.

"Please don't. I'd have to dig you out."

Despite herself, she snorted, and the tension softened between them once again.

* * *

They were about to head outside to follow the others when Thess stepped forward, grabbing Aislen's elbow. Her voice was soft but steady.

"We may not know or understand everything, but we're here."

Sion's expression was grave as he added, "Neither of you are alone in this."

Kael nodded at them both in appreciation as they walked out the door in silence. Aislen paused to give them both a quick hug. She knew she was surrounded by the best people possible.

They all turned as they heard the chanting.

Fenric moved to the doorway, beginning the warding ritual. His hands traced ancient runes in the air, silver light spilling from his fingertips like liquid moonlight.

Elara's voice rose in a melodic chant, weaving through the night air, powerful and commanding.

Their magic coiled around the threshold, a glowing web of protection expanding outward, shimmering and twisting like smoke caught in the breeze.

Aislen felt the magic tingle across her skin, a warm electric pulse.

"This ward will hide your trail, your scent, your magic," Elara explained quietly. "It will confuse those who hunt you. This is the only way I know how to keep you safe from here."

Fenric's voice was steady, a low promise.

"It won't last forever, but it buys us time. We now have precious hours, maybe even days. Thank you, my love."

Maera's eyes scanned their faces, each etched with quiet determination and fear.

"We don't know what waits ahead. But together... we might have a chance. Your devotion is more than enough."

Elara's face fell as she nodded in understanding.

Kael stepped close, voice barely a whisper.

"I agree. Just like everything else we have ever faced, we face this side by side."

Aislen squeezed his hand, the bond humming like a living thing beneath their skin.

A pale dawn mist clung to the grass as final preparations buzzed quietly through the village square. Tomas tightened the straps on a satchel with the same careful tension that lined his brow. The weight of what lay ahead pressed on every shoulder.

Kael stood near the stables, his cloak draped over one arm, gaze flicking between Aislen and his mother. Elara crouched down beside a small boy bundled in thick wool, his cheeks flushed and his silver-streaked hair curling softly at the edges.

"Are you sure you don't want to come?" Kael asked, voice low but strained.

Elara shook her head with a gentle smile, tucking a wisp of hair behind her ear. "I've had enough of battles for one lifetime," she said. "And someone needs to keep this one out of trouble."

The boy grinned up at Kael, eyes gleaming with mischief and complete trust. He looked so much like Kael had at that age it tugged something sharp inside Aislen.

"I can fight too," the boy declared, puffing out his chest.

Kael knelt and ruffled his hair. "Next time, little shadow. You'll have to keep Mama safe for me, alright?"

The boy, Matias, nodded solemnly and threw his arms around Kael's neck. For a moment, she saw Kael let himself hold on too tightly.

When he stood, Elara was waiting. She stepped close to Aislen, resting a warm hand on her arm. Her eyes, so much like Kael's, searched Aislen's face with something that wasn't quite sorrow... or hope... but some quiet ache that seemed to live between the two.

She leaned in and whispered something, just a few words, low enough that even the wind didn't catch it.

Aislen stiffened, her eyes widening a fraction. When she looked at Elara, it was with something fragile and unsure flickering beneath the surface.

Then Elara turned, pressing a kiss to her younger son's head and guiding him toward the cottage with one last glance over her shoulder.

Kael approached Aislen as they prepared to leave, his brow furrowed at the conflicted look on her face.

"What did she say to you?" he asked quietly.

Aislen blinked, then looked away toward the path that wound into the trees.

"I... I can't tell you," she said softly. "Not yet."

Kael stared at her for a beat, trying to read the meaning behind her words. "Why not?"

She looked away.

"She asked me not to," Aislen said as she glanced back at him, her voice almost a whisper.

The silence stretched between them, heavier than before.

Then Kael simply nodded, jaw tight.

With one last breath, they stepped into the shadowed night, bound by ancient promises and uncertain futures.

* * *

~ **Kael** ~

The moment was heavier than anything he'd imagined, a weight that pressed down on his chest and squeezed until it hurt. His mind spun with the enormity of what was happening, the prophecy, the ritual, the looming danger, and yet here, now, all he could see was her. Aislen.

His fingers twitched, his breath caught in his throat. How was he supposed to protect her when the world was closing in? When every shadow felt like a threat? When the one person he couldn't bear to lose was the very person who might be the center of all this chaos?

Then her hand landed on his shoulder. Warm. Steady. Like a lifeline thrown in a storm.

His heart jolted. The panic inside him softened, quieted by that simple touch. She was here. Right now. And maybe that was enough.

He met her gaze, voice low and raw. "I love you."

The words tumbled out before he could stop them. "I know we haven't said it out loud, maybe even to ourselves, but I have loved you since long before I understood what love even was. Before I knew there were words for it. I was terrified of the day I found my mate because it meant I could never leave. I've left before. I've lost before. And the thought of leaving you, losing you, it would've broken me."

He swallowed hard, emotions catching in his throat. "But I didn't have to choose between my duty and my heart, because I have you. It was always you. Even when I didn't know it was you. I will choose you every day, no matter what."

His voice cracked on the last words, but he kept his gaze steady, searching hers for a sign.

Aislen blinked, her breath trembling. She reached up, fingers tracing the line of his jaw softly, grounding herself as much as him.

"I—I don't know what to say," she whispered. "I've been scared too. Scared that this bond is more curse than blessing, that all of this—" she gestured around, the weight of their situation pressing in "—will tear us apart. That loving you means risking everything."

"I just… what if I'm not enough for this? What if I ruin it because I am still learning who I am?" Aislen's voice cracked. "I never thought I'd have a mate. Everything is just so new, but despite it all, I always wanted to be yours one day."

Her eyes glistened in the firelight, shining with unshed tears and fierce determination.

"But hearing you say that… It's like a light in the dark. Like maybe, just maybe, we're not alone in this. That even if the world wants to pull us apart, we'll hold together."

She squeezed his shoulder gently. "I don't have your strength yet, but I want to learn. To be your partner. Your mate."

Kael's breath hitched as relief and hope bloomed inside him. "You already are. And we'll face whatever comes. Together."

Their foreheads met, a silent vow passing between them stronger than any words could say.

Kael leaned in, his breath mingling with hers, cool and sharp like mountain air, laced with the faintest hint of mint from the tea they'd barely touched. His pulse raced as the space between them shrank, the world tilting and sharpening. Every sound, every scent, every flutter of a heartbeat amplified in vivid clarity.

Their lips met. It was soft, tentative at first, a question whispered in warmth and light. The kiss deepened, slow and searching, the heat of her mouth igniting something fierce and tender inside him. His hands found her waist, pulling her closer as the outside world melted away. The flicker of candlelight caught in her hair, turning it into a halo of moonlit silver and shadow.

Time stretched and folded around them. The quiet rustle of fabric, the subtle scent of lavender, the faint taste of honey lingering on her lips. Every sense was alive, every nerve ending singing with the electric charge of their connection.

Their bodies were moving against each other, trying to erase every inch of space. Affection turned into something more desperate, primal, their bond thrumming between them like a living thing. Kael's grip tightened at her waist, pulling her flush against him until he knew she could feel the solid, aching length of his desire through the thin barrier of fabric. His breath hitched against her lips, the sound raw, almost pained, and his finger flexed as he fought the urge to explore more.

Her hands slid up his chest, feeling the rapid drum of his heart beneath her palms. He was holding himself back, even if barely, and the restraint only made the air between them burn hotter. He was one breath away from forgetting every promise he'd made to himself, from crossing the fragile line between wanting her and taking her.

Just as the moment threatened to spill beyond the confines of whispered promises and touches, a soft clearing of throats behind them shattered the fragile spell.

They both pulled back, breathless and wide-eyed, as the footsteps of the others approached.

"I'd say get a room, but we're kind of surrounded by trees." Thess smirked.

Kael's cheeks flushed, the weight of reality settling heavily on his shoulders. "Soon. You will be mine in more than one way," he murmured in her ear, his voice thick with longing.

Aislen blushed as she smiled, her fingers still curled lightly in his. "Later, I plan to make you the same," she promised.

With everyone's eyes on them they straightened, smoothed their clothes and started following the others' trails through the trees.

* * *

They walked for hours, boots kicking up dust from the winding forest path. The trees offered little shelter from the morning sun, which climbed steadily overhead, pressing heat into their shoulders and backs like a weight meant to be carried.

Aislen's braid clung damply to the back of her neck, and sweat slicked her collarbone. She didn't complain, at least not out loud, but her limbs ached with every step, and the pack over her shoulders had long since started to dig.

By the time Tomas called for a stop, the sun was nearly at its peak.

They all scattered beneath the trees, grateful for the fractured shade. Thess dropped beside a moss-covered stump and immediately pulled off her boots. Sion followed, stretching out on his back like he planned to nap before even touching his food.

Aislen moved farther off, settling under a twisted pine whose branches arched like open arms. She unwrapped a bit of bread and fruit from her pack, tearing into the bread absently. Her thoughts wandered, not to the path ahead, but to the soft words Elara had whispered hours ago, the words she still hadn't been able to shake.

Across the clearing, Kael leaned against a tree, arms crossed. His cloak was slung over one shoulder, and sweat gleamed along the edge of his jaw.

They had barely talked as they were walking. Everyone was quiet, trying to conserve their energy for the unknown.

Their eyes met across the space between them, just for a heartbeat. Just long enough for something tight to wind up in her chest.

Then he pushed off the tree and walked toward her.

Aislen tried not to track his steps, but she felt every one. The weight of him. The heat.

"Mind if I sit?" he asked, already kneeling beside her before she could answer.

"Was that really a question?" she asked, raising a brow.

A small grin tugged at the corner of his mouth, but it didn't reach his eyes. "Figured it was polite to ask."

They ate in silence for a moment. Close. Closer than they had to be.

Then Kael reached over and plucked a crumb from the corner of her lip with his thumb.

Aislen gasped.

His touch was light, barely there, but her skin ignited beneath it. Her breath caught. So did his.

For a heartbeat, neither of them moved. Kael's thumb lingered just a second too long. His pupils dilated.

Then a shimmer of silver flickered across his fingertips. Moonlight, faint and ghosting like breath on glass.

He jerked his hand back and stared at it. The glow faded as quickly as it came, but the silence that followed was heavier than anything the forest could offer.

"...that new?" she asked, voice rough.

Kael's jaw clenched. "No."

"Why haven't I seen it before?"

"Because I usually have better control."

Aislen looked down at her half-eaten fruit, pulse hammering in her throat. "You don't have to—"

"I do," he said, voice suddenly hoarse. "Because if I don't..."

He didn't finish. Didn't have to. The unspoken burned between them like summer sun through glass.

A rustle in the distance broke the spell. Tomas calling for the group to move on.

Kael stood first, holding out a hand. She took it without thinking.

Their palms met, hot skin on hot skin, and for one brief, unbearable moment, his magic brushed against hers. Not full force. Just a whisper. A silver hum curling beneath her skin where their hands touched, like a promise waiting to be broken.

Then it was gone.

They didn't speak as they rejoined the others.

But Aislen could still feel the warmth of his touch long after the sun had begun to fade.

Fifteen

"Undercurrent"

~ Kael ~

Ever since they stopped to eat, Kael hadn't left her side. Not for more than a few breaths at a time.

Every chance he got, every shared glance, every brush of skin, he let himself take one more moment. One more tether to her. One more excuse to linger.

And yet, it was never enough.

The bond had only strengthened since her birthday, humming like a second heartbeat in his chest, *pulling* him toward her with a force he didn't know how to resist. Not really. Not anymore.

He should have been better than this. Stronger. More in control.

But when her fingers accidentally grazed his as she passed him the waterskin, he didn't flinch. He didn't pull away. He let it happen. *Wanted* it to happen. Because the whisper of her skin against his own was the only thing that silenced the screaming in his head.

And now she walked just ahead of him, sunlight catching in the loose strands of her hair, her shoulders tense from the weight of the morning. She glanced back once to make sure he was still there, and gods help him, he almost reached for her again.

They stepped out of the trees into the soft rushing sound of water, quick and clear.

The forest broke open to reveal a narrow river threading through smooth rock and shimmering roots. It wasn't wide, but the water ran fast, silver in the midday light. A few flat stones jutted along the edge where the forest thinned.

Kael's instincts screamed. The river wasn't the danger. *The open space was.*

"We need water," Tomas said, gesturing to the stream. "But keep your eyes sharp."

Kael didn't answer. His focus had already narrowed. Aislen crouched beside the bank, cupping water to her lips. Stray droplets clung to her skin, to her throat, catching in the hollow at the base of her neck.

He swallowed hard.

Don't look. Don't think. Don't touch.

But then she turned to him, brushing her damp hands over her arms as she removed the dirt that built up from travel. "It's clear," she said. "Cold, but clean."

Kael moved before he could stop himself, kneeling beside her. "Let me help you," he murmured, dipping his handkerchief into the water and gently pressing it to the back of her neck.

Aislen startled slightly but didn't move away.

Her breath caught.

He felt her body go still under his touch, felt the way the bond *reached* for her even through the thin cloth. Her skin was warm beneath the cool water, and when he dragged the cloth down between her shoulder blades, she shivered, but not from the cold.

He wanted to press his mouth to that spot. To sink his fingers into her hair and pull her close. To tell her he couldn't take it anymore.

Instead, he stood. Too fast. Too sharp.

She looked up at him, lips parted, confusion and something deeper flickering in her eyes.

Kael turned away before he did something he'd regret. Something he'd *love.*

Sion came up beside them, glancing down at the water. "We need to cross."

Kael scanned the small river. There were stones in places, but most of the narrowest points were deceptively deep. The current was fast enough to sweep someone off balance if they stepped wrong. Worse, the terrain offered no real cover on the far bank. They'd be exposed for a good twenty paces.

"No bridge?" Kael asked.

Fenric shook his head from further down the river. "Not for a mile upstream. Too far to detour. We'd lose daylight."

Kael's eyes flicked to Aislen again. She was already pacing the bank, eyes narrowed, searching for the best crossing point.

He should be thinking about safety, about shadows and cover and enemy scouts. But all he could think about was the curve of her spine as she bent to test the edge with her boot.

And the fact that if she slipped, he'd dive in after her without hesitation.

He couldn't keep doing this.

He couldn't keep pretending he didn't want to whisk her away, press her against the nearest tree, and make the bond undeniable.

But not like this. Not with everyone so close.

And gods, was it *killing him.*

* * *

~ **Thess** ~

Thess stepped over a gnarled root, squinting against the sun as it flashed across the surface of the river. The water looked calm enough from a distance, but up close, the current tugged at the banks with a hungry sort of rhythm. It whispered promises of soaked boots and bruised pride.

"Lovely," she muttered. "Wet socks and certain death."

She picked her way along the edge, eyes scanning for anything that resembled a solid path. A cluster of stones near a bend looked promising, so she stepped out onto the first one, testing her balance.

"Let's see what happens..."

The second stone wobbled slightly under her boot. The third felt steadier — until her foot *slipped*. Her arms flailed, and for a breathless moment she teetered, staring down at the rush of cold water waiting to drag her under.

She caught herself at the last second, one knee hitting the stone with a sharp *crack*.

"Ow. Okay. *Not* this way," she called over her shoulder. "Unless you're into surprise baptisms and broken ankles."

Sion snorted from the far bank. Kael didn't react, he was too busy not blinking at Aislen like she was about to vanish.

Thess stood, brushing grit from her palms. "Seriously. Someone else please try dying first, I'm taking a break."

Before anyone could answer, a low, guttural growl rolled through the trees.

Her body went still. Every muscle tightened.

She turned slowly, heart suddenly beating somewhere near her throat.

Behind them, in the shadows just beyond the treeline, something was moving. Branches cracked. Leaves shivered. And then she saw it, eyes gleaming low to the ground. Too many legs. Too many teeth.

"Um... guys?" Thess called, backing toward the water. "Tell me you see that."

Kael had already drawn his blade, putting himself between Aislen and the trees.

Another growl. Closer. This time, it wasn't just one.

"We have to cross," Tomas barked, voice firm. "*Now.*"

"But the current—" Aislen started.

"*Now,*" Kael snapped. "Go!"

There wasn't time to argue. Whatever it was, it was fast and closing in.

Thess didn't hesitate. She splashed into the water, teeth gritting against the cold as it surged around her thighs. "Let's find out how much I hate this."

Behind her, shouts rose. Metal rang out. The sound of claws tearing through bark.

And as the water hit her waist, Thess knew one thing for sure:

This was going to suck.

* * *

~ Aislen ~

The moment the growl echoed through the trees, her blood turned to ice.

She didn't have to see it to know that something fast, something wrong, was coming for them. The kind of sound that stirs ancient instincts and screams *run*.

Kael was already moving, sword drawn, stepping in front of her like a shield. The forest behind them cracked open with snarls and clawed feet, and she didn't wait to see what came next.

"Go!" Kael barked.

Aislen plunged into the river.

The cold stole her breath instantly. Water surged around her thighs, then her hips, dragging at her like it wanted her to stay. The rocks were slick, uneven beneath her boots. Ahead, Thess was almost across, swearing colorfully as she fought the current.

"Keep moving!" Tomas shouted, gripping Maera's elbow as she struggled forward beside Thess. Sion waded beside them, steady as a wall, bracing against the current as he helped Maera forward.

Aislen turned to help Kael, but her foot slipped.

The river caught her like a lover with cruel intentions. It took her breath away.

She fell sideways, her arms flailing. Breath gone in a rush icy panic. Cold water closed over her head. The current yanked her away from the others, tumbling her downstream with terrifying speed.

She didn't scream, she couldn't.

The breath was ripped from her lungs, and panic surged as she flailed for purchase. Stones tore at her palms. The world narrowed to rushing water and spinning light.

Then there were hands.

Strong, familiar hands. Kael's arms wrapped around her from behind, pulling her tight against his chest as the current fought to drag them both under.

"I've got you," he gasped against her ear, breath ragged.

His grip was iron. His warmth bled into her frozen skin. But the river wasn't letting go.

Suddenly, she felt it. His magic.

A pulse of energy like moonlight beneath her ribs. The current around them shimmered faintly, and the water seemed to split around their bodies. Not enough to stop the flow, but enough to ease it. To guide them.

Her magic pulsed in response to his.

Kael's voice was low and fierce, murmuring words she didn't understand as his magic poured into the stream. Silver tendrils coiled around them like ribbons, pushing them toward the far bank.

Her ears rang. Her limbs buzzed with cold. She couldn't stop shaking, but Kael was there.

They hit the shallows hard, coughing and soaked, but alive.

Kael didn't let go until she was on her knees in the grass, breath coming in gasps. She turned to look at him, and something inside her twisted at the way he looked at her. He looked at her like he'd almost lost her. Like he still might.

Before she could speak, a roar split the air behind them.

She twisted around in time to see Fenric, still on the opposite bank, sword glowing as he fought the creature back. The monster was massive. It was low to the ground, all sinew and shadow and too many teeth. Fenric ducked a swipe, slashed across its side, and turned—

Then dove into the water.

Aislen's breath caught.

He hit hard, and the current seized him instantly. But he was strong, fast. His strokes cut through the water with brutal precision.

Within moments, he reached them, dragging himself into the mud with a grunt, blade still in hand.

"Everyone across?" he panted.

Tomas nodded from farther up the shore. "We're here."

"Good," Fenric growled, pushing up to his feet. "Next time, let's avoid streams with death beasts, yeah?"

Aislen would have laughed, should have, but her limbs were shaking too hard. And Kael was still holding her hand. Still watching her with a gaze so intense, it felt like it might burn her alive.

"Thank you," she whispered.

He didn't answer, just brushed a strand of wet hair from her face, his fingertips lingering long enough to make her breath hitch.

And that one, simple touch felt more dangerous than the river ever had.

* * *

~ **Maera** ~

Her legs still trembled.

The rush of the stream had soaked through her cloak, and her hands wouldn't stop shaking. Not from the cold, but from the memory of that growl. Of those eyes in the trees.

Maera stood just beyond the others, trying to still her breath as she watched Kael check Aislen over again, his magic still humming faintly around his fingers. Thess and Sion were wringing water from their sleeves with dry sarcasm. Fenric stood watch a few paces off, ever silent.

And Tomas, gods bless him, was suddenly there, wrapping his arms around her from behind.

She leaned into his chest, eyes fluttering closed as he held her. Solid.

Steady. Warm.

"We're okay," he murmured against her hair. "We're okay, Maer. We'll be okay."

She wanted to believe him.

But her voice cracked as she asked, "How did it find us?"

Tomas didn't answer right away. His hands stilled on her arms, tightening just slightly.

"We were supposed to be warded," she whispered. "No beasts. No scouts. Nothing should've been able to track us, not out here."

"I know," he said, voice low. Thoughtful. Troubled. "I don't know how it found us."

Maera swallowed hard and turned her head just enough to look at him. "But something did."

His jaw tensed. "Yes."

The shadows between the trees deepened as the sun slid lower, and a chill crept over her skin that had nothing to do with water.

She wrapped her arms around Tomas's waist, holding him close.

Maera briefly glanced at Fenric. Something felt off.

She just didn't know what.

Just that something had found them.

And it wouldn't be the last.

Sixteen

"Watched"

~ Aislen ~

The fire crackled low, casting warm golden light over the quiet clearing. Trees arched protectively overhead, their branches heavy with the hush of night. They were just a few miles from the Veiled Vanor, but it already felt like the forest was watching.

Aislen pulled her cloak tighter around her shoulders, the chill of damp clothes clinging stubbornly to her skin. Her hair was still damp from the river, braid still falling apart as tendrils curled free along her cheeks.

They'd made camp on the outer edge of a wide glade, the brush thick enough to feel hidden, almost safe.

Tomas stirred the pot over the fire, the hissing of the pot mixed with the scent of herbs and root vegetables curling upward in steam. Fenric sat sharpening his blade a few feet away, silent as ever, while Thess handed out hunks of bread with exaggerated flair.

"Chef Thess," she announced, tossing Sion a piece. "Made with zero talent and less patience."

"Delicious," Sion deadpanned, biting in. "Tastes like anxiety and unwashed socks."

A soft laugh rippled through the group. It was strained, but real.

Aislen took her bowl without speaking, sitting beside Kael as he stared into the flames. His body was still coiled tight with tension. He hadn't strayed more than an arm's length from her.

Not that she minded.

As the meal wound down, Tomas glanced toward the shadows beyond the trees. "We'll need someone for first watch."

"I'll take it," Kael said immediately.

Aislen looked up from her half-eaten stew. "I'll come too."

Thess raised an eyebrow. Sion smirked.

"I mean, it's not like I wasn't going to anyway," Aislen said, shrugging like her heart wasn't racing. "Two pairs of eyes, right?"

"Of course," Thess said, not bothering to hide her grin. "Totally about that."

Kael ignored them, standing and gathering his weapons. "Let's move."

They waited until the others had settled all bundled in cloaks, whispering quietly before sleep took them. Maera's soft voice murmured to Tomas as they lay down, and Fenric took a spot near the fire, blade resting across his lap even in sleep.

Then it was just Aislen and Kael.

They stepped beyond the glow of the firelight and into the dark hush of the woods.

The night air was cool, tinged with the sharp scent of pine and earth. The moon hung low through breaks in the canopy, spilling fractured silver across the forest floor.

Kael walked beside her, silent. Focused.

But every time their hands brushed, accidentally or not, Aislen felt it. The tug. The electric tension that lived in the narrow space between them.

She cleared her throat. "Do you think we're close enough now? To the Veiled Vanor?"

Kael nodded. "Close enough to be nervous."

Aislen swallowed. "What do you remember of it?"

"I was young," he said. "My mother took me there once..." He trailed off, gaze fixed on the trees ahead. "It was beautiful. And dangerous. Like it knew more than it should."

They walked in silence for a few steps. The hush between them wasn't empty, it was thick with unsaid things. Heavy with the weight of their bond, the ritual, the river.

Finally, Kael exhaled and spoke without looking at her. "I thought I lost you today."

Her steps faltered.

"I felt the bond strain when you went under," he said. "It was like... like something inside me started tearing. I've never felt anything like that. Not even when—" He shook his head. "I don't think I could survive losing you."

Aislen turned to face him, heart hammering.

"You didn't lose me."

"No," he agreed, stepping closer. "But I almost did. And I keep thinking... if I don't say it now, if I don't—"

She reached up, pressing her fingers to his lips.

"Kael," she whispered. "I know."

His eyes searched hers in the dim light, something wild and desperate flickering beneath the surface. "Then don't stop me."

"I wasn't planning to."

His breath hitched.

And then, slowly and deliberately, Kael reached out and took her hand, guiding it to rest over his heart.

"Feel that?" he murmured.

She nodded. "Like thunder."

"That's what you do to me."

Aislen's throat tightened. Her voice was barely a breath. "Kael—"

His hands cupped her face, thumbs grazing her cheeks as he leaned in slow, aching, reverent.

She rose onto her toes and met him halfway.

The kiss started soft. Familiar. But it deepened quickly, sharpened by everything they hadn't said. Her hands curled in his shirt as his fingers tightened at her waist. Their bodies pressed together, every line and curve fitting like something inevitable.

Kael groaned into her mouth, and she felt it vibrate all the way down her spine.

He pushed her gently back against a tree, breath ragged, lips ghosting along her jaw.

"I want you," he whispered. "But not here. Not like this. You deserve more than a stolen moment in the woods."

"I don't care where," she said, clutching his cloak. "I just care that it's you."

A sound escaped him, somewhere between pain and hunger. His forehead dropped to hers, his magic crackling faintly beneath her fingertips.

"When it happens," he said, voice low and rough, "it won't be rushed. Not like this. It'll be *everything*."

Their mouths met again, slower this time. Lingering. A promise instead of a demand.

Reluctantly, they finally pulled apart.

They stood like that, tangled in shadow and moonlight, as the forest exhaled around them and something in the dark kept watching.

* * *

~ Kael ~

Something shifted.

It wasn't the breeze, though the wind had stilled. And it wasn't the trees, though their branches no longer rustled with night creatures.

It was something else. A silence that didn't belong.

The silence was deafening, as if the night itself were listening, watching.

Kael's breath slowed, sharp with instinct. He stepped back from Aislen, reluctantly releasing her hand. His eyes scanned the trees, but it wasn't his sight he trusted now, it was the pulse beneath his skin, the subtle thread of magic that had always whispered warnings before his senses could catch up.

And right now, it was screaming.

"Aislen," he murmured, his voice quiet but taut. "Get behind me."

She didn't argue. She stepped close to his back, her presence steady, grounding, but it did nothing to soothe the twisting in his gut.

He closed his eyes and let the magic flow outward.

Moonlight tingled down his arms, spreading through his fingertips in pale threads. The forest around them lit faintly in his mind, lines and shapes and movement. Every flicker of a moth's wing, every curl of mist rising from the soil.

But nothing was there.

Nothing.

And that was the problem.

The woods were too still. Too quiet. Like something had stepped into the clearing and smothered the natural rhythm of the night.

He pushed his magic farther, straining past the outer edges of the camp's wards, through the trees and across the river they'd crossed earlier.

Still nothing.

No creatures. No movement. No scent of magic besides their own.

But the wrongness didn't go away.

Aislen touched his elbow lightly. "What is it?"

Kael opened his eyes, jaw tense. "Something's watching us."

Her hand tightened. "Can you sense where?"

"No." His voice was a low growl of frustration. "That's the problem. It's like they're there and not there at the same time. Too close to be nothing, too far to strike."

He took a slow step back toward camp, guiding her with him.

"We should wake the others," she whispered.

"Not yet," he said. "Let's move closer. If it's watching, it might back off once it sees we're alert."

Or it might not.

He didn't say the second part out loud.

They moved in silence, the leaves beneath their boots barely stirring. Kael kept his senses wide, every muscle pulled tight like a drawn bow.

Still... nothing.

Yet the weight of unseen eyes never lifted.

By the time the firelight flickered back into view through the trees, Kael's heart was hammering.

He cast one last sweep of his magic outward, but the wrongness had already vanished.

No trace. No whisper. Just the cool hush of forest and flame.

Like whatever had been watching them had retreated the moment they stepped back into the light.

Kael let out a slow breath, jaw clenched. His fingers brushed the hilt of his blade. "It's gone," he murmured. "But it was *there*. I know it."

Aislen nodded slowly. "I think I felt it too. It was eerie. I don't know how to describe it, but something changed."

They stood there, just outside the circle of campfire warmth, surrounded by trees that no longer felt like shelter.

And though the danger hadn't struck, not tonight, Kael couldn't shake the feeling that this was just the beginning.

Something had found them.

And next time… it wouldn't just watch.

* * *

~ **Unknown POV** ~

In the heart of a far-off chamber bathed in flickering gold and crimson light, she stood still as stone.

A basin carved from obsidian sat before her. It was filled with liquid that shimmered red as rubies, blood, ancient and potent, swirling with magic that pulsed to the rhythm of a stolen heartbeat.

She leaned over it slowly, hands splayed at the edges, her long fingers crusted with dried scarlet. Her eyes were distant, fixed on the vision scrying within: the flicker of firelight, the movement of shadows, and the pair of silhouettes lingering just beyond a small camp's edge.

The girl.

The boy.

The bond.

Virel's lips curved into something sharp and cruel.

"So… you're running," she murmured, voice like sun-scorched silk. "And toward *them,* no less."

Her golden eyes glowed brighter as she leaned in, blood magic coiling behind her gaze like smoke. Across the distance, through illusion and projection, she had watched them walk the border of their camp. Had *felt* the boy's magic ripple across her tether. He'd sensed her, not clearly, not enough to see, but enough to stir unease.

He was stronger than she expected.

But *not* beyond her reach.

Behind her, a soft whimper broke the silence.

She didn't turn.

The body hanging from the rafters trembled slightly, what remained of the messenger who had failed to stop them at the stream. Their legs were bound in iron, feet dragging just inches from the blood-slicked marble below. Magic crackled along the chains, feeding the basin, feeding *her.*

"Almost useful," she said aloud, as if the dying thing could still hear. "But even failures have their purpose."

She raised one hand, and the blood in the basin surged. The image within fractured briefly, then cleared again, settling on the girl's face. It was so strikingly familiar, so *infuriatingly* radiant.

Her blood. Unclaimed by the court that birthed her.

But her power was awakening now. She could taste it.

"You don't even know what you are yet," she whispered. "But you will."

She dipped a finger into the basin and drew a sigil in the air, the scent of iron thick in her nose. The magic sparked gold and red, vanishing with a soft hiss.

Then she turned, at last, to face the bound figure.

They moaned faintly, twitching at her gaze.

She stepped closer, her robes trailing through the blood on the floor, and cupped the dying creature's face.

"I've seen enough," she said softly. "Sleep now. Your work is done."

She kissed their forehead like a mother blessing a child, and then burned the life from their veins with a single word.

The body went still.

She turned away, eyes once more fixed on the basin.

"Find her," she murmured to the blood. "Follow the bond. Burn everything in your path."

Then she smiled.

"All the stars in the world can't save her now."

Seventeen

"Marked"

~ Aislen ~

Something warm bloomed.in her chest. It was gold and violet, curling like mist through her ribs. She reached for it, half-asleep, half-aware, and found herself standing barefoot in a field of silver grass.

The stars above shimmered like they were falling. They were drifting slowly, softly, until they melted into the roots of the trees that rose up around her. Vines pulsed with light, not green, but hues she didn't have names for. It looked like starlight tangled in earthsong.

She turned slowly, unsure of where she was or how she had arrived.

The forest was silent.

But then... a voice. Low. Gentle. Distant.

"You are not lost, Aislen. You are only returning."

Her breath hitched.

"Daughter of the lost Court. Blood of the broken sky."

The trees leaned closer, as if bowing toward her. One of them cracked open, not splintering, but unfolding like petals. And at its center, light. A heartbeat.

She stepped forward, drawn as if by invisible strings. Her fingertips trembled. She could feel the pulse of magic in the soles of her feet, humming through the earth and into her bones.

"Seek me when you're ready," the voice said. "I have waited long enough."

She reached for the glowing bark.

The moment her fingers brushed it, the dream fractured like glass.

A gasp tore from her lips as she sat upright, drenched in sweat and tangled in her bedroll. Her chest was tight, her heartbeat too loud in her ears. The cold air of the forest hit her skin like ice water.

She blinked hard, disoriented.

Her wrists stung faintly. She yanked back her sleeves and froze.

Silver vine-like marks shimmered along the insides of her forearms, fine and delicate, glowing like soft moonlight etched into skin.

She stared, wide-eyed, breath caught.

The marks pulsed once.

Then slowly faded, vanishing into her skin like they'd never been there at all.

The fire was low, casting faint flickers across sleeping forms. Fenric was still sitting upright nearby, unmoving except for the rise and fall of his chest. The others were tucked close together, curled in cloaks and blankets. Maera, her mom, was on watch.

Kael stirred beside her. A faint crease formed between his brows even in sleep.

She didn't dare move.

Something had changed.

The air felt charged. Like the dream had followed her into the waking world and refused to let go.

Aislen pressed her hand against her chest, fingers curling into the fabric of her cloak. The ache hadn't gone away, it had sharpened. A tether pulled at her from deep in the woods ahead, soft but insistent, like a half-heard melody calling her name.

The Veiled Vanor wasn't just close.

It was calling her.

The pull in her chest wouldn't quiet.

Aislen rose silently, brushing loose strands of damp hair from her face.

Kael shifted but didn't wake. The fire had dulled to embers now, a soft orange glow tracing the edges of the trees.

She stepped away from the bedrolls, heart thrumming.

A lone figure stood at the edge of camp, silhouetted by the moonlight, her mom. Still awake, still watching.

Aislen crossed the clearing slowly, boots crunching softly over needles and moss. Her mom didn't turn, but she spoke as Aislen neared.

"Couldn't sleep either?"

Aislen shook her head. "Dream again."

Maera's mouth pressed into a thin line. "Was it him?"

"I think so," Aislen whispered. "He called me daughter of the lost Court. He said… he's waiting for me."

Maera closed her eyes for a breath, pain flickering through her expression.

"I saw these marks," Aislen added, pulling back her sleeve. "They faded, but they were real. Silver vines. They *glowed.* I could feel them. The forest was… listening. I don't know how to explain it."

Maera turned at last, her face weary and illuminated by starlight. "You don't have to explain it. I believe you." Maera hesitated before continuing, "the forest has a tendency to mark the ones they choose."

"Then tell me what it means."

A beat of silence.

"I can't," Maera said softly. "I don't know how your magic works. I've seen earthsong. I've seen what it can do in others. But what's growing in you, it's something else. Something more." Her voice broke slightly. "No one here has seen starlight magic. No one knows how it intertwines with earthsong, not until *you.*"

Aislen swallowed hard. "Then who *can* help me?"

Maera hesitated, then answered with a voice thick with old grief. "The male who gave it to you."

"My father," Aislen whispered.

Maera nodded.

They stood there, wrapped in quiet for a long moment.

Finally, Aislen spoke again. "Are you okay with this?"

"With what?" Maera asked.

"Going back," Aislen said. "To the Court you left. The Court you *ran* from. You left to keep me safe... and now you're returning for the same reason."

Maera's eyes glistened, but her shoulders stayed straight. "I swore I would never set foot in that Court again."

Aislen's heart sank.

"But I'd walk through fire if it meant keeping you alive," Maera finished. "And maybe... maybe going back means facing what I couldn't before. For your sake."

Aislen stepped closer. "Do you hate him? My father?"

Maera didn't answer right away. Her gaze turned toward the treetops, where stars blinked through shifting clouds.

"I loved him," she said at last. "And I hated him. And I mourned him. But I never stopped fearing what being his daughter might mean for you."

Aislen's throat tightened. "And now?"

Maera looked at her with something fierce and soft in equal measure. "Now I'm just hoping I was wrong."

Aislen hesitated, then asked, "And dad? I mean, the one who raised me. What does he think about you returning? About... *him?*"

Maera gave a soft, almost sad laugh. "He knows."

"About everything?"

"Mostly," she said. "I told him the truth years ago. About the Court, your father, who I was. Who I could have become."

Aislen blinked. "You were almost made queen."

Maera nodded slowly. "They called it the Starbinding. He wanted to name me heir beside him, crown me with light and gold. I would've ruled at his side. And then the prophecy came along and I was scared. I was scared he would agree with them. I didn't know what it might do. What it might do to *us.* So I left. I thought I was walking away from a life... not building a temporary one only to return."

Aislen lowered her gaze. "And dad accepted all that?"

Maera's lips curved softly. "Tomas loved me before I ever said a word.

He raised you like his own from the moment I placed you in his arms. He's never once asked me to pretend that I was someone else."

Aislen met her mother's eyes. "But you're going back to the Court... with him."

"I asked him if he could bear it," Maera whispered. "Returning with me. Facing the past I fled. Walking beside the shadow of someone I once loved."

"And?"

"He said, 'I've already done the hardest thing. I watched you hurt and held you through it. I can face anything else, as long as you're still beside me.'"

Aislen's throat burned.

"He doesn't see me as divided," Maera added. "He sees me whole. Even when I don't."

The silence between them thickened. It was aching, yet comfortable.

Then Maera reached out, brushing Aislen's hair back from her damp cheek. "Don't be afraid of loving more than one truth. Of being made of more than one thing. That's not a weakness, Aislen. It's your strength."

Aislen closed the space between them and let herself fall into her mom's arms, if only for a moment.

And in the distance, the stars above the Veiled Vanor pulsed faintly brighter, like they'd been listening all along.

* * *

~ **Kael** ~

The morning mist clung to the earth like it didn't want to let them go.

Kael stood near the edge of camp, adjusting the straps on his satchel, but his eyes never left Aislen. She was walking slowly beside Maera, heads bent together in quiet conversation. Whatever they'd spoken about, Aislen's expression had shifted. She was calmer, but somehow distant, like she was carrying something too big for words.

He recognized that look. He'd worn it for years.

They broke camp with little fanfare, the air thick with unspoken tension. The trees loomed closer the deeper they walked. The once-golden light of morning struggling to pierce the dense canopy overhead, and the further they went, the more Kael noticed how *wrong* the forest felt.

It wasn't threatening, not exactly.

It was watching.

His magic stirred restlessly beneath his skin, moonlight gathering at his fingertips like mist around steel. He stretched it outward, quietly, letting it drift like a pulse through the trees.

Shapes shimmered where there shouldn't be shapes. Paths shifted, subtly, underfoot. Roots curled slightly inward when they passed. The bird song that usually greeted sunrise had fallen silent, and even the insects had gone still. Not even a leaf stirred on the breeze.

The Veiled Vanor wasn't just a place. It was a presence.

A memory, dreaming with its eyes open.

And it was awake.

Kael shifted closer to Aislen. "Do you feel that?"

She glanced up at him, brows drawn as she nodded. "It feels almost like it's pulsing. Like a heartbeat. I thought it was just me."

"It's not." His jaw tightened. "The pulsing in the air, along with the trees being eerily still, doesn't make sense. Like they're sentient and listening."

Thess let out a low whistle behind them. "Either I'm going mad, or that log just moved."

"You're not mad," Kael said grimly. "Stay close to the path. If there even is one."

They pressed forward in a tight line. Tomas and Fenric were leading, Sion and Thess in the middle, Maera and Aislen just ahead of him. He kept to the rear, watching the shadows, the subtle sway of branches that *shouldn't* be moving.

His magic pulsed again. It was an echo, almost like a warning. A ripple through the forest, too faint to explain, but loud enough to set every nerve on edge.

Tomas walked ahead, blade in hand but lowered. "We're close now," he said quietly. "From what I've read, the outer veil of the forest is alive. It changes with need, with mood. With memory."

Kael's voice was low. "And right now, it must remember something it doesn't trust."

He looked at Aislen again. Her steps had slowed. Her hands were curled tight at her sides. Her eyes weren't on the forest at all, they were somewhere deeper. Farther. Drawn forward by something only she could feel.

He reached out, letting his fingers graze hers. She didn't pull away.

"We'll be okay," he said, though he wasn't sure if it was for her or for himself.

She gave a faint nod. But her hand trembled in his.

And ahead, the forest narrowed into a corridor of trees so thick the light could barely reach the ground. The canopy sealed shut overhead, blotting out the sky.

Kael felt it then. Certainty.

The Veiled Vanor wasn't just watching.

It was *deciding.*

* * *

~ Sion ~

Sion didn't like trees.

He'd never admit it out loud, of course he had a reputation to uphold, but he firmly believed forests should stay where they belonged: in fairy tales and background scenery. Not *sentient.*

Not *breathing.*

And definitely not *judging* him.

The Veiled Vanor judged.

Every step they took felt heavier than the last, like the forest itself was measuring their worth. Roots twitched beneath his boots. Branches closed in, narrowing the path until it was barely wide enough for single file. The light had gone green and strange, filtering through the leaves in a way that made everything feel submerged. Almost like they were walking underwater.

He didn't like it. Not one gods-damned bit.

Thess was just ahead, muttering under her breath as she ducked under a low-hanging bough. Sion kept pace behind her, blade in hand, eyes flicking to every flicker of movement.

"I swear," Thess hissed, "if one more vine brushes my ankle, I'm setting the whole forest on fire."

Sion opened his mouth to respond with something appropriately sarcastic, then he froze.

A vine had curled over the edge of the narrow path ahead. It was small, green, and seemingly harmless, but something about it sent every instinct into overdrive.

Thess stepped toward it.

"Don't—"

Too late.

Her boot caught the vine.

And the forest *reacted.*

The ground shuddered. Trees groaned. Vines snapped to life like whips, curling around limbs and legs. One lashed across Sion's side before he could blink. It was sharp as a blade and hot with magic. He hit the ground hard, vision flaring white as pain bit deep into his ribs.

"Sion!" Aislen's voice, sharp with panic.

He barely registered Kael yelling something. He saw Fenric move like a shadow into a defensive stance, blade flashing.

But all of it blurred into background noise as the forest surged again. Bark split. Roots snapped. Vines reached.

And then, everything stopped.

Not gradually.

Like a held breath.

The vines froze mid-lash. The wind halted mid-gust. Even the trees seemed to *lean back.*

A soft glow bloomed in the air, warm and wild. Earthy and celestial all at once.

Sion blinked.

Aislen stood in the center of it, hands raised not in fear, but in command.

Her eyes shimmered with starlight. The air around her pulsed with silver and green, like vines and constellations had begun to *weave together* around her. Her magic poured from her like breath, raw, unrefined, but unmistakable.

The forest *listened.*

The vines recoiled, uncoiling from limbs and weapons. The air released its grip. The corridor ahead slowly widened, the trees pulling back like curtains.

Silence returned.

Only now, it was reverent.

Sion coughed and sat up slowly, wincing. "Remind me never to piss her off," he muttered.

Thess helped him to his feet, wide-eyed but grinning. "Starting to feel like we've been following the wrong Chosen One."

Kael rushed to Aislen's side, hands skimming her arms, checking for injuries. She barely seemed to hear him, gaze still fixed on the space where the vines had writhed seconds before.

Sion watched her warily.

This wasn't just magic.

He could feel it. It was something more, something older.

His side burned. Not a deep cut, but sharp enough to sting with every breath.

Sion had been injured plenty of times in his life, but this wasn't a normal wound. The vine had bitten like it *knew* where to strike. Not to kill, but to warn. To punish. His cloak was torn, sticky with blood, but the bleeding had slowed.

What lingered wasn't just pain.

It was awe.

He'd seen powerful magic before, Kael's lunar magic being one of the strongest. But what Aislen had just done wasn't refined or trained, it was *instinctual*. Like the forest knew her. Like it bowed to her.

She hadn't shouted. She hadn't begged.

She had simply *been*.

And the forest had bowed to her.

Sion stood slower than usual, testing his ribs with a grimace. Thess gave him a once-over but said nothing, her focus flicking warily between Aislen and the still-shifting trees.

He looked at her sideways. "You okay?"

"I think so," she whispered. "But I was wrong. She's not our Aislen anymore, not entirely."

"No," Sion agreed. "She feels different."

The others gathered around cautiously, no one wanting to break the strange hush that lingered in the air. Even the birds were silent again, like the forest was still watching through a different kind of lens now.

Kael hovered close to Aislen, hands brushing hers. She didn't seem hurt, but her breathing was shallow, her eyes glazed like she was listening to something only she could hear.

"Are you alright?" Kael asked softly.

Aislen blinked. The light in her eyes dimmed slowly. "I... I think so. I'm not sure how I did that. It didn't feel like casting. It felt like *responding*. Like something opened and poured out."

Maera stepped forward, her voice quiet. "The Vanor let you pass."

Tomas glanced between the trees. "Or tested you and decided you were worthy."

Fenric said nothing. But for the first time in their journey, he looked at Aislen not like a charge to protect... but like a force he couldn't afford to underestimate.

Sion looked around the group and saw the shift settle in.

No one said it outright.

But they all knew.

This had changed things.

Aislen wasn't just a girl walking toward a prophecy anymore.

She *was* the prophecy.

And the Veiled Vanor had just marked her as its own.

Eighteen

"Interrupted"

~ Aislen ~

The trees parted as if exhaling.

They'd been walking for hours. Twisting through shadowed paths, slipping between groves that seemed to breathe and shift around them. The forest hadn't attacked again, but it hadn't relaxed, either. Every step deeper into the Veiled Vanor was a test of nerve, patience, and trust.

And then… the cabin appeared.

It stood at the center of a quiet glade, its silhouette stark against the dappled green. Moss grew thick along the roof. One shutter hung crooked on its hinge. The wood was weathered and darkened by age, worn as if no hands had touched it in decades.

But it didn't feel abandoned, not really. It just felt lonely.

The air pulsed faintly, like the moment between a held breath and a whispered word. Kael's hand drifted toward his blade. Tomas stepped forward first, eyes narrowed, cautiously moving towards the threshold.

"It wants us to go inside," Aislen murmured.

Thess frowned. "Or it wants us *trapped*."

Sion snorted. "Same difference at this point."

But the path behind them had already closed. Vines grew silently over the trail, sealing off the forest as if to say *this way is done.*

They had no choice.

When they crossed the threshold, the magic hit like warmth.

"Something is wrong with how right this feels." Maera muttered.

Inside, the cabin defied logic. What should have been a cramped, musty room opened into an elegant, multi-room sanctuary. Wood-paneled walls glowed with gentle firelight. The hearth crackled with real flame, casting shadows over lush woven rugs. Shelves were lined with jars of herbs, books, and crystals that shimmered faintly in the light.

The kitchen was fully stocked. It held bowls of fresh fruit, loaves of bread still warm, honey and cheese and meat arranged like a banquet waiting for guests.

A faint, floral scent hung in the air. Not overwhelming, but soft. Familiar.

Kael's brow furrowed. "This doesn't make sense."

Tomas drew his blade. "It's a glamour."

"Or a test," Maera added softly, her gaze scanning the ceiling beams. "The forest doesn't give anything for free."

Aislen stepped cautiously into the center of the room. "Or a trap."

Sion gave the rug under his feet a suspicious tap. "If I fall into a pit, someone tell my mother I died complaining."

Thess nudged him. "She already assumes that."

They explored room by room. Each one was fully furnished with a bed waiting for every traveler. Clean linens. Fire-warmed floors. Soft light without any visible source. Even the water in the washbasins was warm.

Aislen lingered at the threshold of a smaller room tucked at the end of the hall. The air inside felt heavier, older, like it remembered things. A book lay open on the bed. The words glimmered faintly, written in a script she didn't recognize, but somehow *understood.*

She turned away.

When Fenric reached for the door again, it didn't budge.

Not locked with a key, but *sealed.* Magically.

His jaw tensed. "It's warded. Hard."

Tomas tried next. Nothing.

Kael laid his hand against the wood. "It's not letting us leave."

Silence stretched.

"It's a cage," Thess said quietly.

"It could be a sanctuary," Aislen whispered. "Or both."

Sion sat heavily at the end of the long dining table. "Well, if it *is* trying to fatten us up, it picked the wrong group of traumatized idiots."

Aislen moved toward the hearth, arms wrapped around herself. The flames danced higher as she neared, as though greeting her. The warmth seeped into her skin, into the ache in her chest that hadn't eased since the forest began to move.

Kael came to her side. "You okay?"

She nodded, but her voice was barely audible. "It feels like it was waiting."

Kael's eyes flicked to the room behind them, to the walls too wide for the cabin's exterior, to the hush that wrapped the space like a secret.

"So what now?" Thess asked.

"We eat," Tomas said at last. "We rest. We don't waste the gift, whatever it is. Not until we understand it."

The group exchanged wary glances, the firelight flickering in their eyes.

The door remained shut.

The food remained warm.

The beds remained waiting.

And with nowhere left to run, they did the only thing they could.

They stayed.

* * *

~ **Kael** ~

Their room was warm when they stepped inside.

A soft golden glow lit the carved walls, flickering gently from a lantern that didn't burn oil but light itself. The bed was impossibly wide, draped in deep green blankets that shimmered faintly like leaves under starlight. The air smelled faintly of pine, smoke, and something floral that Kael had come to associate with her: moonlit violets and summer rain on forest soil.

Aislen paused in the doorway, eyes scanning the space. "This is... definitely a choice."

He tried to summon a reply, but his throat was dry.

The cabin gave them one room.

Thank the gods.

"Should we—" she began, but didn't finish.

Kael stepped past her slowly, his hand brushing hers, and the touch sent lightning through him. They hadn't been alone since the forest. Not like this. Not after what happened between them that night on watch, or what she did with the vines. Not with her magic humming so loudly it made his own rise to meet it, breathless and unbidden.

Silence fell between them, thick and charged. Her eyes, gods, her eyes, were searching his like they could read every battle inside him.

Then she whispered, "I don't want you to sleep on the floor, so I hope that's not what you're thinking..."

He didn't move.

He couldn't, not until she did.

And she did.

Her hands were steady despite the hesitation in her eyes, she reached up and unfastened the clasp of her cloak. It slid from her shoulders and pooled onto the floor, leaving her in a simple tunic and trousers, but he swore it was the most powerful magic he'd ever seen.

His voice was hoarse. "Aislen..."

She crossed the remaining space between them and laid her hand against his chest, right over where his heart thundered. "I know you feel this," she whispered. "I can feel it through our bond."

He couldn't deny it, not that he would.

But if he didn't kiss her now, he'd burn alive from the inside out.

He covered her hand with his and leaned in, slowly and reverently, as if breaking this distance might undo him completely.

Their lips met in a breathless hush.

Her lips were soft, familiar, but different now. This wasn't a stolen kiss in the dark or a moment they'd regret come daylight. This was fire breaking past the dam.

Kael kissed her like he was dying and she was air.

She responded just as desperately.

Her fingers curled in his shirt, pulling him down as she rose to meet him. Their mouths moved with purpose now, hungry, claiming, *real.* He groaned when she bit gently at his lower lip, and he responded by pressing her back against the wall, his hands sliding to her hips to anchor her there.

"You don't know," he whispered, breathless between kisses. "You don't know what you do to me."

"I think I'm starting to," she murmured, tilting her head to kiss the edge of his jaw, the line of his throat. "I think I like it."

His hands trembled as they slid up her sides, beneath the thin fabric of her tunic. She was warm and soft. She was my mate. Mine.

The tunic came off slowly. She lifted it over her head, revealing skin kissed gold by the sun and dappled in firelight. His breath caught in his throat.

"You're... you're beautiful."

She rolled her eyes faintly, cheeks flushed. "You always say that like it surprises you."

"Because it *does,* every time," he said, brushing his thumbs over the curve of her ribs. "You're all I see."

He kissed down her neck, each inch a vow, and felt her shiver under his mouth.

When her fingers slipped beneath his shirt and lifted it over his head, the cool air hit his skin like a dare, and he loved the feeling of a good dare. She dragged her hands down his chest slowly, memorizing him, and he swore softly when her palms smoothed over the muscles of his stomach.

Her mouth followed, kissing along his collarbone, her teeth grazing lightly at his skin.

Kael's restraint was splintering.

"I should hold back, I should slow this down, but I can't," he took a deep breath. "I need you more than I need air, Aislen."

He backed her toward the bed, guiding her down until she lay beneath him, her hair fanned across the plush bedding like some vision pulled from the gods' dreams. He braced himself above her, drinking in the sight of her bare skin, the way her chest rose and fell, the raw vulnerability in her expression.

"We can stop," he whispered. "Say the word and I'll stop."

"I don't want to stop," she breathed. "Gods, I never want to stop."

He groaned and dipped his head to kiss her again. It was deeper this time, anchoring his hands beside her head as her thighs parted beneath him. Their bodies aligned with too much ease. Her skin was velvet against his, burning hot and impossibly soft.

His hands explored every curve, waist, hip, the dip of her spine, as her nails raked lightly down his back. She let out a low, breathless sound as he kissed lower, tasting her skin like he could memorize every inch.

She was gasping now, her body arching into his touch.

Every moan was a reward. Every shift of her hips was a plea.

Kael's mouth found the swell of her breast, and he sucked gently, groaning when she tangled her fingers in his hair and pulled. His tongue traced circles. Her back arched. Her name was a prayer on his lips.

He was gone. Entirely undone. Everything else in the world had fallen away.

Just Aislen.

Only Aislen.

They were both shirtless, their legs tangled together, breath hot and ragged in the heavy hush of the room. His hands slid down her thighs and back up again, thumbs stroking the sensitive space below her hips. She was trembling beneath him, he could feel her need.

He reached for the ties of her trousers, hands already moving to strip away the last barrier between them when—

Knock. Knock. Knock.

They both froze.

Kael's head dropped to her shoulder with a long, pained groan. "No."

She buried her face against his neck. "Tell me that was thunder."

The knock came again.

Louder this time.

Knock. Knock. Knock.

Aislen swore under her breath. "Who in the seven hells—"

Kael pulled back reluctantly, brushing her hair from her face with a shaking hand. "If we don't answer it, they'll go away."

But the knock came a third time, persistent and pointed.

He let out a soft curse, rolling off her and dragging a blanket over her chest. "If it's Sion, I swear I'm throwing him into a tree."

Aislen quickly pulled her shirt back on, cheeks flushed, her eyes still glazed with heat.

Kael yanked on his shirt and stumbled to the door, every part of him still hard and aching. He flung it open, frustration boiling beneath the surface, until he saw who was standing there.

Maera.

Her expression was unreadable. In her hand was a folded piece of parchment glowing faintly gold around the edges.

"This appeared on the table," she said calmly. "It's from the Aurion Court."

Kael stared at the letter. Then back at her. Then over his shoulder at Aislen.

Every part of him that had been on fire now went still.

The Aurion Court.

And everything they'd just shared... it was going to have to wait.

Nineteen

"The Cost"

~~~~~

~ **Aislen** ~

The letter felt heavier than it should.

Though the parchment was fine, smooth and delicate, sealed in shimmering gold wax that still pulsed faintly with heat, something darker clung to it. As if the paper remembered where it had come from. As if the queen's presence still lingered in the ink.

Kael stood beside her, shirt hastily pulled on, jaw tense and unreadable. He hadn't said a word since Maera had handed over the envelope and retreated down the hallway with that look in her eyes, that quiet blend of dread and fury only a mother could master.

Aislen's hands trembled as she broke the seal.

Inside, the handwriting slanted with elegance that felt too perfect, too sharp:

To the child of stolen blood and borrowed name,
You step into the Veiled Vanor like it might not recognize you.
But I have watched you, little starlight. I have felt the pulse of your magic singing
through the roots and shadows. You do not yet know what you are, but I do.

148

And I am waiting.
Every flicker of power you release sings my name. You do not need to find me,
child.
I will find you.
Burn brightly, if you dare.
— Sun Queen Virel Solanar
Queen of the Aurion Court and Ruler of the Fae Realm

Aislen let the parchment fall to the floor as her hands angrily curled into fists.

The cabin, so warm moments ago, suddenly felt too close. The magical hum of the hearth turned oppressive. The very air pressed against her skin like a warning.

"She knew," Aislen whispered. "She felt me. Here in the Vanor."

Kael's eyes were already scanning the room, magic brushing against the walls like a net cast in panic. "We have to assume she can track you any time you use your power now."

"She said every flicker sings her name," Aislen echoed, breath shallow. Which meant...

"I can't use it," she said numbly. "Not here. Not again. Not unless I want her walking straight through that door."

Aislen sat frozen, her thoughts racing as Kael gently lifted the fallen letter. He didn't say anything at first, just reread the curling script, eyes narrowing, mouth set in a hard line.

"We should tell the others," he finally said.

Aislen hesitated, but nodded. "They need to know."

They stepped into the hallway, the tension between them still humming, but now overshadowed by the gravity of what Queen Virel's words meant. The warmth they'd shared just minutes ago had been swept away like ash on the wind.

The main room was dim, the lanterns lowered. A few voices still murmured beyond the far arch, Maera and Tomas, perhaps. Sion sat by the hearth sharpening a knife, and Thess had her feet propped up on the edge of the table, a book open in her lap.

When they entered, everyone looked up at once.

Kael didn't waste time. He dropped the letter on the table.

Tomas read it aloud. His jaw clenched. "She knows."

"She *feels* her," Maera added, voice quiet and bitter. "That means every time Aislen's magic flares, it could be giving Queen Virel a path straight to us. Or worse, one of her monsters."

Fenric crossed his arms, unreadable as always. "Then the girl can't use her magic. Not unless we're ready to fight."

"She *saved* us with that magic," Thess snapped, sitting up straighter. "She kept the forest from killing Sion."

"And as true as that may be, it is also how the Sun Queen found us," Kael said flatly. "I felt something watching us even before the river. That could've been her reaching through."

A heavy silence settled.

Aislen swallowed hard. "So what do we do?"

"We get out of this gods-cursed house first," Sion muttered. He stood and crossed to the front door, gripping the handle.

Still sealed.

He tried harder, then Tomas joined him.

Nothing.

Fenric walked over and placed a hand to the wood and muttered a low spell. The door shuddered, but held.

"We're not getting out tonight," he said grimly.

"We rest," Maera said, though it sounded like a reluctant order. "We need clear heads tomorrow. If the forest is giving us a reprieve, we take it. Whether we like it or not."

Thess closed her book. "What a charming vacation this has turned out to be."

Aislen tried to laugh, but she couldn't.

The group slowly began to disperse, each person retreating to their rooms with quiet murmurs and sidelong glances.

Kael waited by the door to theirs, his expression unreadable.

They stepped inside together.

The bed was still unmade, still tangled with the heat and promise of what had almost happened. Aislen stood frozen near the foot of it, unable to look at him, unwilling to pretend they could pick up where they left off.

She heard him move behind her, the soft sound of his boots being toed off, the creak of him lowering onto the bed.

"Aislen," he said gently.

She turned to face him, voice soft and raw. "Will you just... hold me?"

No hesitation.

He pulled back the covers and opened his arms.

She crawled into the bed beside him, curling close as his arms wrapped around her. His warmth settled around her like a shield, like something sacred. She rested her cheek against his bare shoulder and closed her eyes.

The fire flickered low.

His voice broke the silence after a long while. "I meant every word. Earlier."

She smiled faintly, eyes still closed. "So did I."

They didn't speak again.

And though nothing had happened the way it was meant to, though the bond between them had been interrupted again, this, *this,* was enough for tonight.

***

~ **Maera** ~

She was in the glade again.

Not the Vanor, no. This place was older. Sacred.

The stars above moved slowly in impossible patterns, their silver light dripping like molten silk across the forest floor. Trees arched high around her, their bark the color of moonlight, their leaves humming with soft

151

music only dreams could hear. The air was heavy with the scent of jasmine, blooming even though no vines grew near.

She hadn't seen this place in fifteen years.

And she knew, with bone-deep certainty, she hadn't come here on her own.

Maera turned slowly.

And there he was.

Alarion.

The Starlight King stood in the clearing like a memory given flesh. His silver-blond hair fell in waves over his shoulders, untouched by time. He wore a tunic of dark midnight blue threaded with constellations, a cloak draped behind him like a living piece of night. But it was his eyes, those violet eyes, that caught her. Still bright, still deep, still looking at her like she held the cosmos in her hands.

"You're late," she whispered, voice catching on the wind.

"I'm early," he replied, stepping toward her. "You just didn't know I'd be waiting."

Her breath hitched. "It's been over fifteen years."

"I know. You stopped dreaming of me."

His voice held no accusation, only sorrow. "Or perhaps you stopped letting yourself."

She crossed her arms to hide the tremble in them. "I had to let you go. For her. She was getting too big too fast."

"I know," he said again. "And you were right to do it."

Silence settled between them, soft but brimming.

He moved closer, slow and deliberate, until they stood a breath apart. "You look the same," he murmured.

She gave a sad smile. "That's a dream's mercy."

"No," Alarion said. "That's *you*. You were always the strongest thing in any room."

Maera's heart twisted. "You could have stopped me. That day I left."

"I couldn't," he said quietly. "Because I loved you. And I knew what the prophecy meant. If I'd begged you to stay, you would have… and it would

152

have broken you."

She looked down. "It still did. I am returning. It's ironic really."

His hand lifted, fingertips brushing her cheek. The touch felt warm and wrong and perfect all at once.

"You're returning home," it felt like he stared through her.

"It's not my home anymore, Alarion."

He chose to ignore her words.

"I never chose another," he said, voice low. "I never even tried."

"You're a king," she said bitterly. "You *should* have."

"No one could be you."

She shook her head. "I married. His name is Tomas, he's kind. He took care of both of us."

"I know." He didn't flinch. Didn't draw away. "He's a good man. I've seen the way he guards you. And Aislen."

"She calls him 'dad.'"

"As she should," Alarion said gently. "He earned it."

Her chest ached with the weight of two lives. One of them lived, one abandoned.

"I loved you," she whispered.

"And I never stopped," he replied.

Silence again.

"But this isn't why you came," Maera said at last, steadying herself.

"No." His expression grew grave. "There's something on your path, something that hides even from me. It moves between your lot and my Court. It doesn't wear a name I know, but I feel it. Watching."

"Virel?"

"She's watching too, yes. But this... this is older. Deeper. The forest stirs around it, but doesn't reveal it."

Her mouth went dry. "Then we go around."

"You can't," he said. "It's not a creature. I do not know for sure, but I think it's a truth. And if I am right, a truth can't be avoided. Only faced."

He stepped back, the light around him growing softer.

"She's waking," he murmured. "The girl. She shines like dawn, Maera."

"She's not ready," Maera said.

"No," Alarion agreed. "But soon, she will be. And when she comes, when she finds her way to us, I will be waiting."

He met her eyes once more, all the centuries of his immortal life flickering behind them. "I do not ask you to come back to me, Maera." He sighed, "Pain was the last thing I ever wanted to give you."

She blinked quickly. "Then why now?"

"I came to remind you of who you are," he said, voice like wind and stars. "Because soon, she will need that female again. Not the mother. Not the wife. But the force that walked away from a king for the sake of a child. The female who would have made the most beautiful, benevolent queen to my people."

"I was terrified."

Maera tried to reach for him.

But he was already dissolving into light.

And then she woke with her unshed tears finally falling down her face.

* * *

~ **Tomas** ~

The first thing he noticed was that she was moving.

Not the restless shifting of someone trying to find comfort, but the full-body tremble of a mind caught somewhere far away. Beside him, Maera twisted in the sheets, her brow drawn tight, lips parting to whisper broken fragments into the dark.

Tomas blinked the sleep from his eyes.

"Maera?" he murmured, reaching out to brush her arm.

She didn't stir. Didn't even flinch at his voice.

Instead, she muttered something low, first too soft to catch then again, louder:

"…Alarion…"

The name hit him like a blade.

Tomas froze.

It wasn't the first time he'd heard the name spoken. He knew who Alarion was, *what* he was. King of the Celestara Court. The man Maera had loved before she ran. Before Aislen. Before *him*.

But it had been years, at least a decade, since the name had passed her lips.

Dreaming of him.

Calling for him.

Tomas sat up slowly, watching her chest rise and fall in uneven rhythm. Her fingers clenched the blanket. Her mouth moved again, but the words were slurred and lost to the shadows.

His heart ached.

He didn't doubt her love. Not truly. Not after all these years spent side by side, building something real out of ash and silence. She had chosen him, again and again.

But love didn't erase what came before.

And now, as they traveled toward a place Maera had fled, toward a king who had once been her everything, Tomas felt something he hadn't in a long time.

Fear.

Not of Alarion himself. No. He was a king, yes, but Tomas knew how to stand his ground, magic or not.

He feared the memory. The weight of what still lived in her heart. The way her soul might stir at the feel of starlight after so long in shadow.

And what it might mean for them.

Maera shifted again, this time turning toward him, her hand reaching blindly in the space between sleep and waking.

He caught it gently and brought it to his chest, holding it there like a vow.

"You came back once," he whispered to her sleeping form. "Just… come back again."

He didn't sleep for the rest of the night.

Outside, the Vanor pulsed. Watching. Waiting.

Twenty

"Reflections"

ᘿᘾᘿ

~ Aislen ~

The morning light was dim, filtered through heavy mist and branches that wove tighter than they had the day before. The air held a hush like the forest had stopped breathing.

Aislen hadn't slept well. Not truly.

She'd drifted in and out of strange, shapeless dreams, flashes of starlight and cold marble and something ancient watching her from just beyond her vision. When she awoke, Kael was still holding her, one hand resting protectively over her ribs like his body had molded to hers in the night.

But the comfort didn't last long.

They gathered in the main room, drawn together by a pressure none of them could name. The hearth burned low, casting flickers of gold across tense faces. No one ate. No one spoke.

Then Maera stepped forward.

"I had a dream," she said quietly, folding her hands in front of her. "He came to me."

No one asked who. They all knew.

"The king of the Celestara Court."

Aislen sat up straighter. She noticed it immediately, that deliberate

156

phrasing. Not *Alarion*. Not his true name. Maera didn't look at her when she said it. Didn't look at Tomas, either.

Her mom rarely lied outright, but she was excellent at telling only part of the truth.

"What did he say?" Tomas asked, voice calm, but not soft.

Maera hesitated just a breath too long. "He warned us. There's something in the path ahead, something he couldn't see clearly, but dangerous. Old. Hidden. He couldn't fully name it, only sense an idea of what it is."

Fenric's arms were crossed, his expression unreadable. "So we just walk into a threat that even a fae king fears?"

"We've done worse," Thess muttered, rubbing her temple.

"He said to keep our eyes open," Maera continued, ignoring the snide comments. "The path ahead won't let us turn away. Only forward."

Aislen didn't miss the way her mom's voice dipped at that last line, like it carried weight beyond the words. Like it was meant for her ears, not the others.

Her fingers clenched at her sides.

Kael leaned in, murmuring near her ear. "She's holding something back."

"I know," Aislen whispered.

Before anyone could speak again, a sound split the silence.

Click.

The front door, sealed tight since the night before, creaked open with an almost theatrical slowness. Hinges groaned. Cool air flooded inside.

Everyone stilled.

Sion moved first, blade already in hand. He stepped to the doorway and pushed it open wider, peering out.

"The path is new," he said.

They followed one by one, the tension thick enough to cut.

Outside, the forest had changed. Again.

Where twisted branches had formed a cage the day before, now a trail stretched ahead, narrow, winding, and glowing faintly beneath the moss-covered ground. Not with light, exactly, but with memory. Like it had always been there, waiting.

Aislen followed the others outside. She stepped onto the grass and turned to look back, but the cabin was gone.

No door. No porch. No stone chimney. Only mist and trees and silence.

As if the whole thing had been a dream stitched into the forest's edge, real only as long as they'd needed it.

She reached back, half-expecting her fingers to find a hidden wall. There was nothing.

Gone.

Erased.

The others exchanged quiet, uneasy glances. But no one spoke.

Aislen felt it, deep in her bones, the magic here was old.

Whatever was ahead, they couldn't go back now.

The Vanor had chosen their path.

* * *

The trail wound deeper into the Vanor, each step pressing into moss-covered roots and earth that pulsed faintly beneath their boots. The trees leaned closer, branches laced so tightly overhead they barely glimpsed the sky.

It was too quiet.

No birdsong. No wind.

Even the air felt like it was holding its breath.

"We should stop for a drink," Tomas said, pausing near a pond tucked behind a tangle of brush. The surface shimmered dark and glassy, untouched by wind or ripple.

The others nodded in agreement. One by one, they knelt to scoop water into waterskins or palms. Aislen dipped her fingers into the surface, expecting coolness, but the moment her skin touched it, the world changed.

The pond rippled once.

Then everything shattered.

Aislen blinked and suddenly, the forest was gone.

She stood in the center of a garden.

Her mom's garden, the one from her childhood home. Flowers bloomed wildly, sun spilling over stone paths, laughter echoing from the cottage.

She heard her own voice, soft and young.

"Kael, wait!"

A boy darted past, dark-haired and grinning, followed by a younger version of herself. Her breath caught. They were so small. So unaware of what was coming.

Aislen turned, confused.

What was this?

Why was she here?

The illusion twisted again.

Now she stood before the Council of the Lunaris Court, robed and radiant. Magic shimmered at her fingertips, but her arms shook. They waited, Kael, her mom, her friends, all their eyes filled with hope and expectation.

"You're the Starlight Heir," someone said. "Step forward."

She took one step—

And the world cracked.

Fire. Screams. Her mom sobbing in chains. Kael, bloodied, reaching for her as figures cloaked in sunfire magic dragged him away.

"You could have stopped this," a voice hissed.

It was hers.

She turned as she faced herself. Older. Wilder. Power blazing like a second sun in her veins. The version of her who had *accepted* it all. Who had stopped running.

And she hated her.

"Why won't you let me live?" the other Aislen snarled. "Why do you keep hiding from what we are?"

"I didn't ask for this!" Aislen shouted back. "I never wanted any of it!"

The other smiled, sad and sharp. "But you *are* it."

And the garden was gone.

The Court vanished.

Everything fell away into darkness.

She was falling.

Falling.

Then—

A voice, soft and real.

"Aislen."

Kael.

His voice was distant, but steady. Anchoring.

"Aislen, come back."

She fought the illusion, heart pounding. The darkness clung to her, whispering her doubts, her fears, her refusal to become the girl the prophecy named.

You're not ready.

You'll lose everyone.

You're not enough.

But Kael's voice cut through it again, firm and aching.

"You are not alone."

She opened her eyes.

Real ones.

The forest snapped back into place, harsh and vivid.

She was on the ground, trembling, her face damp with sweat. Kael knelt beside her, arms around her shoulders, his magic pulsing faintly where their skin touched.

She gasped. "How long—?"

"Too long," he said, holding her tight. "You were the last one. We couldn't reach you."

Around them, the others were shaken but recovering. Tomas sat beside Maera, rubbing his temples. Sion leaned against a tree, breathing heavily. Thess stood watch with a blade drawn, eyes darting at every shadow.

Aislen pushed herself up. Her body ached like she'd run for miles.

"What happened?" She asked warily.

"It was an illusion, meant to disorient us. I believe it came from the pond." Fenric said from near the pond. He was staring down at it, almost inspecting it. "It took our memories, twisted them into our fears."

"It was an illusion..." she said hoarsely. "But it felt so *real*."

"It wanted to trap us," Maera said, voice grim. "It tried to bury us in our own truths, or variations of it."

"What did you see?" Aislen asked her quietly.

Maera hesitated. "A past I thought I buried."

Thess looked pale. "Mine wasn't sunshine and tea," she muttered. "But hey, at least nobody died. Yet."

"Can you not joke for once? Seriously?" Sion stomped away angrily.

The others cast weary glances at each other.

They didn't need to say more.

The Veiled Vanor had given them their first test.

Not with blades or monsters.

But with themselves.

And it had almost worked.

Aislen looked up at Kael, who hadn't moved from her side. "I saw... I saw what I could be. And I hated her."

He frowned. "Why?"

"Because she didn't hesitate," Aislen whispered. "Because she was everything I'm afraid of becoming. Powerful. Unstoppable."

Kael cupped her face gently. "You are going to become exactly who you are meant to be."

She closed her eyes, breathing him in.

She wasn't ready to believe that yet.

But for the first time... she wanted to try.

The forest was still watching.

But now Aislen was watching back.

* * *

~ Kael ~

Kael hadn't let go of her.

He couldn't.

Even after she woke gasping from the illusion, her body trembling like a leaf in a storm. Even after she whispered his name and assured him she was back, he hadn't loosened his grip.

His arms wrapped around her like armor, like prayer.

They'd stopped for a moment of rest beneath a wide-boughed tree, the entire group rattled and quiet. The only sounds were the rustle of leaves above and the faint lap of water from the pond, deceptively peaceful now. Kael sat with his back to the bark, Aislen curled into his side, her head tucked beneath his chin.

His magic flickered faintly at the edges of his skin, still agitated. Still searching.

They needed a breather before moving forward, but even now, Kael didn't let himself relax.

Not when the memory of what he'd seen still burned behind his eyes.

The illusion had been perfect.

Too perfect.

Aislen, safe and smiling in a garden that never withered. Their lives already entwined. There was no more waiting, no danger, no prophecy. Just her lips on his, her laughter in his ear, the warmth of a world without fear.

He'd believed it for one long, aching moment.

He *wanted* to believe it still.

And that was the trap.

The forest hadn't conjured horrors for him like it had for some of the others. No chains, no flames, no bleeding regrets.

It had offered a dream.

The thing he wanted most.

A life with her. One without danger.

Real. Whole. *Easy.*

He exhaled through his nose, trying not to tighten his hold on her too much. She was safe. She was here. But he still hadn't shaken the feeling that part of him was back in that false reality, standing at the edge of an illusion and wanting to stay.

He turned slightly, brushing his fingers through her hair. "Are you okay?" he murmured.

Aislen nodded without speaking. Her fingers curled against his chest, steadying herself with the rhythm of his heartbeat.

He didn't push. Not now.

Across the clearing, the others sat in varying degrees of silence. Tomas and Maera shared a quiet conversation. Thess had her knees hugged to her chest, staring at the pond like it might shift again. Sion stood a few paces away, turning a blade slowly in his palm, brow furrowed in deep thought. His own father was passing among the trees.

No one else asked what each person saw.

And none of them volunteered.

But the silence said enough.

It had been different for all of them, tailored illusions spun from the rawest parts of their hearts.

Kael's jaw tensed.

This was just the beginning.

Whatever force had created those visions, whatever magic lived in this cursed forest, it was intelligent. Strategic. It didn't want to kill them.

Not yet.

It wanted to *weaken* them.

Chip away at their resolve before they even reached the true danger.

Kael pressed a kiss to Aislen's hair, closing his eyes briefly.

He wouldn't let that happen.

He didn't care what waited ahead, sunlight or shadow, ancient king or vengeful queen.

He would walk through fire before he let anything take her from him.

They just had to survive long enough to face it.

Twenty-One

"Confessions"

~ Kael ~

They walked in uneasy silence, the weight of the illusions still pressing like fog against their backs. The path had widened, the roots beneath their boots strangely soft, almost like they were being guided again, coaxed forward by something unseen.

Too easy.

Kael hated it.

Beside him, Aislen walked with her jaw tight and eyes alert. Her fingers brushed his occasionally, each touch a small reassurance they were still themselves, still *real*.

The trees began to thin.

A clearing opened ahead, round and quiet, with a ring of moss-covered stones at its center. The light here was strange. It was not sunlight or even starlight. Just a soft golden shimmer that hung in the air like dust that never settled.

For a heartbeat, it felt... calm.

Peaceful, even.

Too peaceful.

Kael's instincts screamed.

"Something's wrong," he said, his voice cutting the hush.

But it was too late.

The earth trembled beneath their feet, soft at first then it grew. The moss curled back from the stone ring as something massive stirred just beneath the surface.

Then, with a terrible grinding sound, a figure *rose.*

It was neither man nor beast.

At first glance, it resembled a statue. It had stone-like skin, hunched and broad-shouldered, its eyes glowing faint gold beneath a heavy brow. Moss clung to its joints. Runes were carved deep across its chest and arms, glowing faintly like embers trapped beneath granite.

It stood taller than a house.

And it *smelled* of old magic and something long dead.

Sion stepped forward, blade drawn. "What in the gods—"

The creature's voice echoed through the clearing. It was low, grinding, and almost mournful.

"One question for each of you."

They froze.

The creature's eyes swept slowly across them.

"Answer honestly... you pass.

Lie... and you die."

The last word thudded like a death bell.

"Gods," Thess whispered.

Kael pushed Aislen slightly behind him.

The creature raised one hand. A pulse of golden light snapped through the clearing and they could no longer move.

Their feet stayed rooted.

Mouths silenced. Eyes fixed.

Only the voice remained.

It turned to Sion first.

"What do you fear most?"

Sion's jaw clenched. For a moment, Kael thought he'd lie.

But then he spoke and his voice came out harsh, raw.

"…Being forgotten by the ones I love."

The golden light flickered. And the grip released—for *him.*

Sion staggered back, breathing hard, free to move.

Next, it turned to Thess.

"Who do you love?"

She flinched. "No one."

She glanced at Sion a moment too long and the light *hissed.*

Kael's heart stuttered.

But then the runes pulsed faintly… and the creature moved on.

She had told the truth. Or at least part of a truth.

Tomas was next.

"What do you regret?"

"…Not telling her sooner." His eyes flicked to Maera.

The glow passed. Safe.

Maera.

"If he asked, would you go back to him?"

The silence was unbearable.

She didn't look at anyone as she answered.

"…Yes."

No one spoke.

The creature turned to Fenric.

"What would you sacrifice to win?"

"…Everything."

The runes flared. Acceptance.

Then—

Kael.

"Do you believe you deserve her?"

His blood ran cold.

The answer rose up, unbidden, bitter.

"…No."

Aislen choked behind him, but the light passed.

Then came her.

The creature's golden eyes bore into her like sunlight through fog.

"Who are you?"

Aislen didn't answer right away.

The light pulsed around her as it waited.

Kael turned toward her, heart pounding.

She took a breath.

Then another.

"...I don't know yet," she said. "But I'm ready to find out."

The runes pulsed once.

Then the creature *bowed.*

"You may pass."

With that, it stepped aside, melting slowly into the stone ring as if it had never been.

The silence left in its wake was deafening.

They didn't speak as they crossed the clearing.

No one dared.

They had passed the test.

But Kael knew some of their questions would haunt them far longer than the path ahead.

* * *

~ **Maera** ~

The path narrowed again, winding through gnarled trees whose branches hung low like listening ears. Moss brushed her ankles as she walked, but Maera barely noticed. Her thoughts were louder than the forest.

She stayed near the back of the group, steps slower than usual, letting the others drift ahead.

Tomas didn't speak.

He hadn't since the creature's voice echoed her truth through that cursed clearing. Since she'd said *yes.* Not to anyone in particular, not to any present face, but to the past that still lived in her chest like a second heartbeat.

If he asked, would you go back to him?

The words still rang in her ears.

And she hated how easily she'd answered.

She hated herself for how *true* it had been.

The others moved ahead, giving them space. Whether out of mercy or discomfort, she didn't know.

Tomas walked beside her, his silence a weight more suffocating than shouting. She felt it in every step, every breath between them.

Her fingers curled into fists.

"I didn't mean to hurt you," she said suddenly.

He didn't stop walking.

Maera bit her lip. "I didn't even know that answer was inside me until it was already out."

Still nothing.

The wind whispered through the trees, brushing her hair into her face like a veil. She pushed it away, heart hammering.

"I love *you*, Tomas," she said, more forcefully now. "I chose this life. I chose you. I would never leave what we built."

He slowed just slightly.

"But... he was my past," she added softly. "And he never stopped being a part of me."

Finally, Tomas looked at her.

And she braced for whatever came next.

Tomas stopped walking.

The weight of it hit her harder than any shouted words could have.

He turned slowly to face her, his expression unreadable in the half-light beneath the trees. She held her breath, waiting for anger, for sorrow, for something that would splinter everything they'd built.

But it didn't come.

He just looked at her.

"I know you love me," he said softly.

Maera blinked, startled by the calm in his voice. The steadiness of it.

"I've never doubted that," he added.

Her throat tightened. "Then why won't you say something? Anything."

"I am." He tilted his head slightly. "You think I didn't know? That when I married you, I didn't see the shadow of him in the corners of your eyes?"

Her heart thudded.

"I've always known," Tomas said, quieter now. "I just hoped... maybe one day, it wouldn't hurt."

Her lips parted, but no words came.

"I don't regret you," he said firmly. "I never have. You saved me from a life I didn't know I was missing. And you gave me *her*. Aislen. My reason. My everything."

The way he said their daughter's name unraveled something inside her.

But then his voice dipped, almost imperceptibly.

"So yes... hearing you say you'd go back, it stung."

Maera winced. "It wasn't a promise."

"I know." His eyes didn't waver. "It was the truth. And I'd rather hear that than silence."

The silence that followed was louder than any illusion.

"I just need to know," Tomas said, barely above a whisper now, "that I still matter. That I'm not just the quiet choice after the storm."

Maera stepped forward before she could stop herself.

"You do," she said, voice shaking. "You've always mattered. You *always will.*"

He searched her face for a heartbeat more, then lifted a calloused hand to her cheek.

And with that one touch, she knew:

They would be okay.

Not unscarred.

But *okay.*

* * *

169

That night, when he came to her in a dream, she ignored his calls. She ignored the way her body recognized the place she once called home.

She let it all go.

She didn't want to lose the life she built, the life she loved with every fiber of her being.

The stars above the dream palace faded. And in their place, the scent of moss and firelight, the life she chose, wrapped around her like a promise.

Twenty-Two

"Unbound"

~ **Aislen** ~

The Veiled Vanor finally fell away behind them.

There was no grand moment. There was no shift in light, no magic flaring at the borders. One moment the forest stood tall and endless around them, the next, it thinned into scattered trees and tangled underbrush that gave way to open terrain.

They had made it through.

Aislen hadn't realized she'd been holding her breath until she stepped into the sunlight and the weight on her chest finally loosened.

The others emerged behind her, silent, cautious. Even the breeze felt hesitant, like the world itself wasn't sure what came next.

They'd been walking for a week.

Seven days of watching the trees, feeling eyes that weren't there. Of dreaming dreams that didn't always belong to them. Of magic that bent too close to the bone.

But now the forest was behind them and ahead the land stretched wide and open, leading toward jagged silhouettes that cut the horizon like teeth.

The Hollow Mountains.

Dark. Vast. Waiting.

They wouldn't reach them until morning. For now, the group stopped just beyond the forest's edge. A patch of tall grass and flat stone made for a good resting place. No illusions. No traps. Just sky.

Kael dropped his pack and ran a hand through his hair, eyes scanning the mountain line. "We'll make camp here," he said quietly.

No one argued.

Aislen sat slowly, grateful for the stillness. Her body ached. Her mind even more.

She glanced back at the forest once. Its edge loomed like the mouth of a story they'd somehow escaped.

Despite the warmth on her skin, something told her it wasn't done with them.

It was an unfamiliar sensation after so long in the shade of the Vanor. For the first time in days, there were no illusions nipping at the edges of her vision. Just the wind. The scent of dry grass. The low hum of insects beginning to stir as evening crept closer.

She dug into her pack, fingers brushing over the moonstone necklace she gave Kael. She tucked away days ago to keep it safe during their trek. It felt heavier now, like it had absorbed some of the forest's magic... or maybe just its memories.

Across the makeshift camp, Thess and Sion were unpacking rations, quietly bickering over who forgot to grab more dried fruit. Tomas was crouched by a flat patch of earth, digging a shallow fire pit with a curved blade. Fenric had climbed a nearby outcrop to get a better view of the trail ahead, his silhouette sharp against the setting sun.

Kael was only a few paces away, inspecting their remaining supplies. His brow was furrowed, but the tension that had strung him tight for days seemed to be slowly easing. She watched the way the light caught in his hair, the way he turned instinctively toward her every few moments, just to check she was still there.

It made her chest ache in a way she didn't have words for.

Maera approached quietly and handed her a blanket. "Rest while you can," her mom said. "You'll need it before the climb."

Aislen nodded. "Do you think it'll be worse than the Vanor?"

Maera didn't answer right away. "Not worse," she said. "Just different. The mountains have their own kind of danger. More stone than shadow. More silence than illusion."

"But still dangerous."

"Always."

Aislen pulled the blanket over her lap and looked to the jagged line of peaks ahead. They rose like ancient sentinels, guarding secrets only fools, or desperate souls, tried to uncover.

"I don't know if I'm ready," she whispered.

"You don't have to be ready," Maera said, brushing a hand through her hair. "You just have to keep going."

Maera placed a soft kiss on her forehead before walking away.

* * *

Night settled softly over the clearing.

One by one, the others drifted into sleep, their breathing steady in the hush between fire crackles and wind. Even Thess had gone quiet, curled under her cloak with a hand on her dagger. Only the mountains stood fully awake now. Watching, waiting.

But Aislen couldn't sleep.

She lay on her blanket with her eyes wide open, staring at the stars through gaps in the clouds. Every time she closed her eyes, the weight of the past week rushed in—the illusions, the monster's question, her own voice saying *I don't know who I am yet.*

And worst of all… the truth of it still clung to her like damp air.

A rustle beside her broke the silence.

Kael sat up, glancing down. "I know you're not asleep. I can feel your frustration."

She shook her head, "I just can't sleep. So much has happened I just—"

"Me neither." He looked around, then offered his hand. "Come walk with me?"

She didn't hesitate.

The forest was gone now, but a copse of trees still ringed part of the field. They slipped away from the camp quietly, their boots muffled by grass and moss, the moon casting long silver shadows across the open ground.

No illusions here.

Just them.

Kael didn't speak until they were far enough that the glow of the fire had vanished behind them.

"You've been quiet since whatever happened back there," he said softly.

Aislen shrugged. "Trying to figure out who I am."

He reached for her hand, fingers brushing hers with a gentleness that belied the storm in his eyes. "You don't have to figure it out all at once."

"Feels like I do."

Kael stopped walking and turned to face her, his hand catching her waist to steady them both.

"You were brave in there," he said. "And honest. That's more than most can say."

Her breath caught at the warmth in his voice, at how close he stood, his thumb grazing the curve of her hip like it was instinct.

She didn't move.

Didn't want to.

The air between them shifted, heavy with want and unspoken things.

"Kael," she breathed.

He leaned in slowly, testing the space between them, but she met him halfway.

Their kiss was soft at first. Patient. But her fingers found their way into his hair and he made a sound low in his throat, and the hunger spilled loose.

He backed her gently into the shadows beneath the trees, hands skimming beneath her cloak as her body arched toward his.

Kael's mouth was fire against hers, all slow hunger and barely reined-in restraint. His hands traced her sides like he was memorizing her, mapping each inch of her body with reverence and possession tangled together.

Aislen gasped as he pushed her gently against the trunk of a wide tree, its bark cool against her back. His cloak shielded them from the warm breeze, but it was his body, his heat, that wrapped around her like armor.

His lips moved to her jaw, then her neck, where he lingered just long enough to make her knees threaten to buckle. "Gods," she whispered, fingers gripping his shirt. "Kael—"

He growled softly. "Say it again."

"Kael."

The sound of her voice on his name undid him.

His hand slid down, skimming over her thighs, lifting the edge of her tunic with slow, maddening care. He kissed her again, harder this time, and then pulled back, breathing hard.

"I want you," he said, forehead pressed to hers. "You know I do."

"I know."

"And I will have you," he murmured. "All of you."

Aislen whimpered, dizzy from the ache in his voice, from the way her body pulsed in anticipation.

"But not here," he added. "Not rushed. Not half hidden behind a tree while the others sleep yards away."

Disappointment flickered through her, but before she could argue, he dropped to his knees.

Her breath caught.

He looked up at her, eyes lit like moonfire. "But I can give you a taste. If you'll let me."

She nodded, unable to speak.

Kael slowly slid her trousers down to her ankles. He couldn't help but stare at the apex between her legs as he pulled her legs apart with sure, tender hands, lifting one over his shoulder. The first brush of his mouth against her was like lightning, stealing the breath from her lungs. She bit her knuckle to keep from crying out.

He didn't rush. Every stroke of his tongue was deliberate, devoted, like worship, like promise. Her hands tangled in his hair, her head falling back against the tree as heat coiled deep inside her, building, burning.

And when release crashed over her, he held her through it, never letting go.

When he finally rose, lips slick, eyes dark with hunger, he kissed her slow and deep, letting her taste herself on his tongue.

"You'll come apart for me like that every time," he whispered. "And next time... I won't stop there."

Both of their marks were glowing in the night.

Aislen trembled in his arms.

She couldn't stop trembling. Even as Kael pulled her cloak gently back into place and rose to his feet, the air around them felt electric, like the Veiled Vanor had left sparks in her skin, and only he could draw them out.

Aislen leaned into him without thinking, her forehead resting against his chest. His heartbeat was rapid, strong. Familiar. She could still feel the ghost of his mouth on her, every nerve attuned to the space where they touched and the promise of more just beneath the surface.

Kael wrapped his arms around her, cradling her like she was something precious, not fragile, but sacred.

"That was..." she began, but words failed her.

His voice was low and rough against her hair. "Just the beginning."

Heat rushed to her cheeks, and she buried her face in his chest to hide it. "So that's what you meant by a taste..."

He laughed quietly, breath warm against her temple. "Didn't want to leave you wondering."

Her fingers curled into the fabric of his tunic. "Kael?"

"Yeah?"

"Have you ever..? If you have, I might rip their head off. But I have to know. Have you done that before?" It came out of her mouth quickly, too quickly.

He chuckled.

"No Aislen. I mean, I have had offers, but I always turned them down. You were my first kiss and after that day, I knew I wanted you to be my first anything." Kael pulled her in close as he kissed her forehead.

"It will always be you. You're mine."

"I love you Kael. I will never let you go, especially not after that. If I was wondering what being with you was like before, that's all I'm going to think about now." A blush crept up her face at the truth of how she felt.

His breath caught. He pulled back just enough to look at her, brushing her hair behind her ear with reverent fingers. "You don't have to wonder," he said softly. "I'm yours, Aislen. Every reckless, devoted, inconvenient part of me."

She swallowed hard, eyes shining. "You say that like it's a bad thing."

Kael grinned, eyes gleaming. "Oh, it absolutely is."

She laughed then, really laughed, and it broke something in her that had been wound too tight for too long. It wasn't just lust coursing through her now. It was safety. Warmth. Longing that had finally found somewhere to land.

Kael kissed her again. It was slow, sure, and full of everything he planned to show her.

When they finally started back toward camp, their hands were still linked.

And even in the cool mountain air, Aislen's body still burned for him.

* * *

~ **Fenric** ~

From his perch near the edge of the camp, Fenric watched them return.

Kael's hand held Aislen's as they walked side by side, heads bowed close together in the dark. A quiet intimacy lingered between them. It was unspoken, but unmistakable. Anyone with eyes could see it.

Fenric's jaw tensed.

They thought they were alone in the trees. They weren't.

He hadn't meant to stay awake. But sleep never came easy anymore, not with the mountains so close, not with the weight of what lay ahead pressing harder with each mile.

And not with the female glowing like that.

She didn't even know it. But her power crackled in the air around her now, as natural as breath. Not just earth and starlight, but something older. Something wild.

Kael didn't see it.

Or maybe he did, and loved her in spite of it.

Fenric rubbed a hand along his jaw, eyes narrowing slightly.

He didn't hate her. There was no hatred in him for Aislen. She was kind, bright, brave when it mattered. His son loved her, she was his mate.

But she would change everything.

Kael wouldn't be the same the longer this bond continues on. None of them would.

Fenric exhaled through his nose and looked back toward the mountains.

He'd spoken the truth to that creature in the Vanor. He *would* do anything to win. He had been waiting for the moment he feared would come.

But what he hadn't said... was that he didn't know what he would do when it arrived.

Not yet.

Not fully.

His son was in love.

And the world would pay the price if that love burned too brightly.

Twenty-Three

"Faultline"

~~~

~ Aislen ~

The mountain loomed above them, its base spread wide like the jaws of something ancient and sleeping. Craggy slopes stretched upward, steep and uneven, marked by jagged cliffs and narrow ledges carved by wind and time. The air here felt different, thinner, crisper, and clean in a way that made her lungs ache from the unfamiliar clarity.

They stood at the edge of the ascent, packs tightened, cloaks drawn against the sudden chill. For the first time in days, the trees weren't closing in. The sky stretched vast above them, brushed with streaks of soft lavender and silver from the rising sun.

"This feels... weirdly good," Thess muttered, rolling her shoulders as she adjusted her gear. "Like I can finally breathe again."

"You say that now," Sion said with a dry smile, "wait until your legs start screaming."

Thess elbowed him, but even that had less bite than usual. The tension of the Vanor had lifted, replaced by a quiet determination.

Kael stepped up beside Aislen, his hand brushing hers briefly before falling to his side again. "You ready?" he asked.

She nodded. "I think so."

179

Behind them, Tomas checked the ropes while Maera scanned the rocky slope ahead. Fenric stood at the rear, silent and steady, as if already bracing for the next trial.

They began the climb slowly. The terrain was uneven, boulders jutted from the slope like bones, and loose gravel made every step a test of balance. But the sky was wide open, and the sun, though pale, was warm on their backs.

Their breathing was loud at first, unsteady from days of poor sleep and tighter lungs, but no illusions waited here. No magic tugged at the edges of their minds.

Aislen placed one hand against the cool surface of the stone and felt it humming faintly. It was not like in the forest, not as dangerous. Just old. Steady. Like the heartbeat of the mountains themselves.

"We'll find a ridge to stop at by nightfall," Maera called up the line. "Keep steady footing."

"Easier said than done," Thess grumbled, skidding briefly on a patch of gravel.

"Need help?" Sion asked, grinning.

"I'll let you know when I'm about to fall to my death."

Their banter carried up the slope, light enough to feel like relief.

Kael climbed beside Aislen, occasionally offering a hand or pointing out a better foothold. They didn't speak much, but every shared glance, every breathless smile, felt like a promise: *We made it this far. We'll keep going.*

Aislen paused at a ledge halfway up, catching her breath. Below them, the valley stretched in patchwork green and gold. Ahead, the path twisted upward toward the waiting shadows of stone and sky.

The ledge wasn't quite big enough for camp, which means they had to continue until they reached the ridge far in the distance.

The climb wasn't easy, but at least they had sunlight.

There were no illusions here. No enchanted trees whispering threats. Just the bite of stone under their boots, the occasional gust of mountain wind tugging at cloaks, and the burn in her calves that reminded Aislen she was still alive.

180

The Hollow Mountains stretched ahead, a jagged promise etched into the sky, but she no longer felt like she was walking toward her own unraveling. She felt hopeful.

"Do you think we'll find a magically friendly goat at the top who offers to carry our supplies?" Thess asked dryly as she adjusted the pack on her back.

"If we do," Tomas replied from a few paces ahead, "I'm naming it Lunch."

Aislen rolled her eyes. "Morbid, dad."

"Practical," he corrected with a grin over his shoulder.

Kael chuckled beside her, and Aislen felt a soft flutter in her chest at the sound. The tension in his shoulders had loosened some since they left the forest. Even with the climb, the open sky and crisp air seemed to do something good to him. To all of them.

"Pretty sure I'd take a mildly sarcastic goat companion over most of the things we've met lately," Sion added, wiping sweat from his brow. "At least the goat wouldn't ask riddles or try to kill us with our own secrets."

"Unless it's an illusion goat," Aislen said with mock seriousness. "Then we're doomed."

Kael raised a brow. "Illusion goat?"

"You never know in this realm," Thess muttered.

The path narrowed again and curved upward. Wind whipped around them, tousling hair and tugging at cloaks. Aislen paused to catch her breath, stealing a glance behind her.

The view was breathtaking with layers of forest fading into mist, the path they'd taken now barely visible. They had come so far.

"I missed this," she said quietly.

Kael glanced at her. "The altitude?"

"The air," she said. "The sky. Being able to see everything again. It feels like… we're finally moving forward."

They shared a small smile.

"Don't get too sentimental," Thess said, brushing past them. "You'll make me cry, and I only packed one handkerchief."

Tomas gave her a pat on the shoulder as he passed. "I'll trade you half a sock for it. Freshly worn."

Thess gagged. "Never mind. Keep your feelings and your foot fabrics to yourself."

Aislen laughed, and the sound surprised even her. It felt good having laughter without fear biting at the edges.

Maybe the mountains would test them, too. But for now, the sky was open, the path was clear, and the laughter was real.

The wind tugged at her cloak as they climbed, sharp and brisk at this altitude, but clean, so much cleaner than the stifling magic of the Vanor. The sky was impossibly blue above them, and sunlight spilled across the jagged ridge like a promise. They were only a few hours into the climb, and while the path was steep, the mood had shifted.

Or so she thought.

It happened so slowly.

Thess was cracking jokes behind her, snarking at Sion for over-packing again, and Tomas had launched into a very serious debate with Maera about which trail food was truly the worst.

Aislen smiled, her fingers brushing the cool edge of the stone beside her as she climbed.

Then her dad slipped.

It happened in the blink of an eye. One moment, Tomas was reaching for a foothold, the next, his boot skidded against loose gravel and he pitched sideways, the drop yawning open below him.

"Dad—!"

Aislen's scream tore from her throat before her mind could catch up. Her hands shot out instinctively, not toward him, but to the mountain.

The stone answered.

There was no incantation. No conscious call.

The ridge beneath Tomas shifted with a low groan, a slab of rock jutting out from the cliffside like a hand. Dust exploded outward as the slab caught him.

Tomas's chest was heaving from panic.

He was moments from having disappeared into the void.

Everyone froze.

No one moved.

Even the wind seemed to hold its breath.

Aislen couldn't breathe either. Her heart thundered as the echo of magic pulsed through her veins. It felt warm, wild and alive. Her hands trembled where they hovered above the stone, her fingers glowing faintly gold.

She hadn't meant to.

She'd just... reacted.

Kael was the first to move. He scrambled to the ledge, reaching down to grab Tomas's arm and haul him carefully back up onto the path. Once her dad was safely beside them, Aislen dropped to her knees.

"You're okay dad," she gasped. "Are you okay?"

Tomas stared at her, his eyes wide. It was not with fear, but awe.

"You... you caught me."

Aislen blinked back the rush of tears and nodded. "I didn't think. I just... did it."

"You did good, love," he whispered, voice rough with emotion. He reached out, brushing her hair from her face with a hand that trembled. He pulled her into a tight embrace.

Behind them, the others had gone silent.

Even Thess looked shaken.

Aislen could feel the magic still humming in her bones. Her earthsong, deep and ancient. She hadn't drawn from it... it had risen to meet her. To protect what she loved.

Kael knelt beside her and touched her back gently.

"You saved him," he said, reverent. "You didn't even hesitate."

Aislen raised her eyebrows as she met his gaze, "You sound surprised." Her voice softened. "It felt like the mountain moved before I could."

He smiled. "Maybe it did."

But across the ridge, Fenric stood still as stone, watching. His expression unreadable.

And Aislen, for all the warmth thrumming in her chest, couldn't shake the feeling that her magic had just drawn a line in the sand, one that could no longer be ignored.

* * *

~ **Kael** ~

They made camp higher up the ridge, the sun just beginning to tip westward behind a jagged peak. The air was thinner here, but somehow crisper, cleaner. Birds circled in lazy spirals far above. Below them, the Veiled Vanor stretched like a distant shadow.

Kael sat near the edge of the ridge, polishing the edge of his dagger with a cloth, but he wasn't paying attention to the blade. His mind was still replaying the moment Aislen moved the mountain.

She hadn't even thought about it.

It was instinct.

Raw, untrained earthsong magic, reaching through stone and shadow to save the man she called dad.

She had only just come into her magic, yet she was already so strong. So natural.

Pride burned in his chest.

So did worry.

"Walk with me."

Kael looked up. Fenric stood a few feet away, arms crossed. His voice was even, unreadable. He didn't wait for an answer before turning and starting down the very narrow stretch of trail that curved along the ridge.

Kael sighed, sheathed the dagger, and followed.

They moved just barely out of earshot, the wind tugging at their cloaks. Finally, Fenric slowed, gaze fixed on the distant horizon.

"She's powerful," Fenric said, almost too casually.

Kael nodded. "She is."

"You love her."

It wasn't a question.

"Yes," Kael said simply. "She's my mate. I thought we already established this, father?"

Kael looked at him with disbelief. Unsure as to where this was leading.

Fenric let the word hang in the air before turning to face him. "Then you need to be careful."

Kael frowned. "What does that mean?"

"I'm not saying don't love her." Fenric's jaw worked. "I'm saying love like this, bonded love, it burns hot. Fast. Bright. And sometimes it blinds you to what's coming."

Kael stiffened. "You think I can't protect her?"

"I think," Fenric said carefully, "that the magic waking in her is older than either of us understands. And if it goes unchecked, if something goes wrong, loving her may not be enough."

Kael's fists clenched. "She's not dangerous."

"Did I say she was?"

"You're dancing around it."

Fenric's expression didn't change. "I'm trying to prepare you."

"For what?"

"For the possibility," Fenric said, voice lower now, "that your love for her might put you in the path of something far bigger than a bond."

The words hit Kael like a slap.

For a moment, neither of them spoke.

Then Kael took a step back. "I don't need your warnings."

"You need perspective."

"I have it. I know what I'm risking."

"I'm not sure you do."

Kael shook his head. "Then I guess we disagree."

Without waiting for more, he turned and started back toward camp.

Fenric didn't follow.

But Kael could still feel his father's gaze pressing into his back. It was heavy with the weight of unspoken truths.

And doubts Kael wasn't sure he wanted to name.

His father's words burned in his chest, but all he could think about was her. He had to get back to her.

* * *

~ Aislen ~

Aislen had just finished smoothing the base of the fire pit with her palms when she felt Kael's presence storming toward her like a wave of heat.

His expression was unreadable. His lips tight, eyes blazing, and there was something barely restrained coiled beneath his skin.

"Kael?" she started, rising to her feet.

He didn't say a word, but his magic pressed against her like heat from a fire, crackling along her skin.

The closer he got, the hotter it burned.

He grabbed her hand, his grip firm but not harsh, and pulled her away from the others.

"Kael—wait—what's going on? Why are you—?"

She barely got the words out before he stopped, spun, and kissed her.

It wasn't soft. It wasn't careful.

It was fierce, breathless, like he'd been drowning in his thoughts and she was the only air that could fill his lungs.

Aislen froze for a heartbeat, startled by the sudden heat of him, but then she melted into it, arms wrapping around his neck, her body arching to meet his. His hands cupped her face like she was something breakable, precious, and yet the kiss was anything but gentle.

Every brush of his lips sent another spark of heat racing down her spine, leaving her dizzy and aching for more.

When he finally finished kissing her, his chest was heaving, and she could feel the tremble in his fingers where they still touched her cheeks.

For a second, he hovered there. He was close enough that his lips still brushed hers when he spoke, his voice shaking in restraint.

"I needed you," he said, voice low, hoarse. "Gods, I needed you."

186

Aislen swallowed hard, dizzy from the fire still crackling between them. "Kael... what happened?"

He hesitated, dragging a hand through his hair as he stepped back half a pace, like he needed room to breathe, or to not say something he'd regret.

"My father," he said tightly. "He pulled me aside and told me to be careful with you. That I'm too close, too consumed."

Her breath caught.

"He doesn't understand. Doesn't see you the way I do." Kael's jaw clenched. "He thinks this bond—*you*—will destroy me."

Aislen's eyes stung, but she held her ground. "And what did you say?"

He looked at her then, really looked at her.

"I told him it would. That you *have* changed me. But not into something weak." His voice cracked, raw with emotion. "You make me want to be more. For you. For us. And if that terrifies him, then maybe it should."

She stepped closer, touching his face again, this time with aching tenderness. "Then let him be afraid. But don't carry it."

Kael leaned into her touch, his anger softening beneath the weight of her presence.

"I won't," he whispered. "Not when I have you."

Twenty-Four

"Tension"

The Hollow Mountains rose like jagged sentinels, their slate-gray peaks slicing into the sky with cold indifference. Wind howled between narrow ravines, echoing through stone like whispered warnings. The path carved into their side was uneven and narrow, little more than a trail of flattened rock skirting cliffs that dropped into mist-choked gulches below. Snow still clung to the shaded crevices despite the warm season, crystalline and untouched, while patches of stubborn moss gripped the stone like nature's quiet defiance.

Every step echoed, their boots against stone, gravel skittering into the void. Above, the sky was a pale, washed-out blue, veiled in thin cloud layers that shifted like smoke. The air was thin and sharp, scented with frost and minerals, and every breath tasted like stone and cold iron.

Far below, where the foothills still held green, the trees looked like dark smudges against the land, both distant and irrelevant. Up here, in the silence of the heights, there was only rock and wind and the quiet hum of ancient magic buried deep in the bones of the mountains. The kind of magic that watched and waited, unconcerned with the hearts of those who walked its paths.

The climb grew steeper as the sun edged higher, casting long slashes of light across the sheer stone. Loose shale shifted beneath their boots, and sharp outcrops jutted from the path like the ribs of some ancient beast. The higher they climbed, the less forgiving the mountain became. The narrow switchbacks tested their balance, and silence fell over the group, not from fear, but effort.

The path wove between towering stone spires, some curved and leaning as though frozen mid-collapse. Others stood tall and jagged, spearing the sky like broken spears. Insects were scarce. Even birds kept their distance. Only the wind remained, relentless and whispering, curling through crevices and keening across the cliffs.

Their boots left only fleeting prints on the frost-dusted stone, quickly swept away by gusts that whistled low and mournful through the cracks. The cliffs were gray and glinting in the light, some areas dotted with crystal deposits that sparkled faintly like stars embedded in rock.

Now and then, the trail would widen enough for two to walk side by side. In those moments, conversation flickered to life again with short, quiet exchanges about footing, supplies, or the distant shape of the next ridge. But mostly, they walked in near-silence, the mountain demanding their focus with every step.

By midday, thin clouds had begun to drift in, brushing across the peaks like a veil. Shadows shifted with the wind, sometimes making the path appear to vanish altogether. More than once, they paused to recenter, checking the trail markings, drinking from flasks, breathing deep to keep lightheadedness at bay.

At one point, a narrow stone bridge stretched over a ravine, its edges worn smooth by time and erosion. It creaked under their weight. Not from instability, but from age, like the mountain itself groaning in protest.

They crossed it one by one, slow and measured. No one spoke as they passed over the yawning drop. Far below, mist churned like something alive.

On the other side, the incline steepened again. The air thinned further, and sweat beaded beneath cloaks despite the cold. Muscles burned. Joints ached. Every heartbeat echoed in ears dulled by altitude.

And still, the mountain rose.

It offered no welcome, no comfort, only the constant question: *How far will you climb?*

* * *

~ **Kael** ~

Kael kept his gaze on the trail ahead, boots crunching against loose stone, but his mind was far from the path. The burn in his thighs, the ache in his shoulders, the thinning air, none of it touched the storm churning beneath his ribs.

He couldn't get the taste of her out of his head. He never wanted to stop tasting her, not for a heartbeat.

If he could do it again right now, he would… sooner, harder, longer…

There was no doubt when it came to Aislen.

He wanted to grab her and lose himself in her until neither of them remembered where one ended and one began.

But every time he looked at her, she was talking to one of the others. She was prying smiles and laughter from each of their faces, trying to make the best out of an unsavory situation.

As if his thoughts summoned her, she looked back.

Over her shoulder, her eyes caught his and gods, she smirked, one brow arched in a silent dare.

Kael held her gaze without flinching. Daring her right back.

Holy hells, he loved her. Fiercely. Stupidly. Entirely.

Anything he threw at her, she met with fire. Matched him. Matched *everything*. He'd always dreamed of finding an equal. He never imagined she'd be this perfect.

How could his father ever doubt her?

But still his father's voice echoed with every step.

"The magic waking in her is older than either of us understands."

"Loving her may not be enough."

"Your love for her might put you in the path of something far bigger than a bond."

It had sounded like a warning, but not the kind born from fear of Kael being hurt. No, it was something else. Strategic. Veiled. As if his father wasn't telling him everything.

Kael adjusted the straps of his pack and pushed forward, the wind tugging at the edges of his cloak. The air thinned with every hundred feet they climbed, but he didn't slow. He needed the burn. Needed something to focus on other than the creeping suspicion taking root in his gut.

He trusted his father. He *wanted* to trust his father.

But he had never spoken like that before. Not even when Kael first began showing signs of moon-bound magic. Not when war had knocked on their borders. Not even when Kael nearly lost his arm during sparring as a boy.

And now, after everything, after watching Aislen wield magic that could move mountains… *now* he warns him to be careful?

Why now?

Kael's eyes flicked up to where Aislen walked several paces ahead, her braid trailing behind her, catching bits of sun. She was laughing at something Sion said, her shoulders loose for the first time in days. She looked alive. She looked free.

He would follow her into fire. Into war. Into the dark without a torch.

But his father… what did he know that he wasn't saying?

Kael clenched his jaw.

Maybe his father wasn't worried about *Aislen*.

Maybe he was worried about who might be looking for her.

Maybe, Kael thought, he needs to be even more careful. Not everyone can be trusted, not anymore.

* * *

~ Sion ~

The wind had a bite to it up here. It was thin and sharp, like the mountain itself was warning them to turn back. It threaded through the folds of his cloak and bit into the skin beneath his collar, but Sion barely noticed. His legs ached from the climb, his boots were damp from a trickle of snowmelt that had somehow found its way into his left heel, and every breath scraped down his throat like cold smoke.

Still, he walked with steady steps, just a hair behind Aislen and Thess as they led the group along a narrow bend in the trail. The ridge dropped away sharply to the left, nothing but mist and sky below, while jagged spires of stone rose like broken teeth to their right. The path curved like a scar carved into the mountain's side, winding forward toward another stretch of shadows.

Aislen was talking again. She was making light of the climb, of the cold, of the very real possibility that something worse still waited ahead.

"I'm just saying," she declared between breaths, "if we die on this mountain, I want it on record that I was the funniest one here."

Thess scoffed, rolling her eyes with all the dramatic flair she could muster. "Sweetheart, if we die on this mountain, I'm haunting you first just to correct that lie."

"You'd haunt me?" Aislen gasped, pressing a gloved hand to her chest. "I'm touched."

"I'd haunt you with passive-aggressive commentary. You'd never sleep again. I'd float above your bed just to judge your life choices."

Sion arched a brow, lips twitching. "I'm sorry, are we ranking ghost strategies now?"

"Only if I'm winning," Thess replied without missing a beat, tucking a windswept strand of hair behind her ear.

Aislen grinned sideways. "You'd be the kind of ghost who rearranges furniture and groans when people use the wrong tea mug."

"Exactly. Standards are eternal."

The laughter between them was soft, quick, but it echoed across the stone like a balm. Sion didn't laugh often. He didn't need to. It was enough to

192

listen. To walk behind them and let their voices fill the silence. The wind could scream and the mountain could loom, but when they talked like this, it drowned out everything else.

It felt like home.

Not the kind built with hearths or stone walls. Not the kind with roots or permanence.

But *this,* the quiet rhythm of footsteps, the sarcasm slicing through the cold, the way Aislen's face lit up even when her legs were shaking with exhaustion... this was the kind of home he'd never known he needed.

And gods help anything that tried to take it from him.

He adjusted the strap on his pack, eyes scanning the horizon. The trail ahead narrowed again into a crooked pass where the cliffs seemed to lean toward one another, casting long shadows over the path. Up above, clouds hung low and heavy, their undersides tinged gray-blue with ice.

Aislen's laughter faded into a breathless hum as they rounded the bend, her eyes flicking toward a pair of hawks circling high above the peaks.

She was trying to keep the mood light. He could see it in the way she smiled too quickly. In the way her hand occasionally brushed against the stone wall beside her, as if grounding herself without realizing it.

Thess was a sharper thing, all edges and retorts, but Sion could tell she was watching too. She always did, pretending not to care while her eyes missed nothing.

The farther they climbed, the more Sion felt it creeping in again. That heaviness in the air, like a storm building beneath the surface of the sky. No thunder. No threat. Just that quiet tension before something snapped.

He didn't know what lay ahead.

Didn't know how long this path would stretch before it broke beneath them or turned into something worse.

But he did know one thing:

If anything came for his friends, if even a whisper of danger touched their shadows, he'd tear it apart with his bare hands.

Because for the first time in a long while, he didn't just feel useful.

He felt *anchored.*

And he'd fight the gods themselves if it meant keeping that.

Just as he was thinking that, a gust of wind curled down from the upper ridge, sharp enough to sting the skin beneath his collar. The path narrowed again ahead, crumbling slightly at the edges where frost had splintered the stone. Aislen moved cautiously but not slowly. She was determined, focused. Tired, maybe, but not hesitating.

Until her boot clipped a jagged edge.

She pitched forward with a startled gasp, arms swinging out for balance. Sion didn't think.

His hand shot out, catching her by the elbow and steadying her with one sharp tug. His other arm braced around her back instinctively, keeping her upright as her momentum faltered against him.

"I'm fine," she said quickly, breath hitching. "I'm okay."

Her cheeks were flushed, and not just from the cold. Embarrassment, maybe. Or the sudden brush with danger.

Sion didn't let go right away. He waited until he felt her weight shift back into her own feet, solid again on the uneven path. Only then did he release her, stepping back with a silent nod.

She gave him a sheepish smile and murmured, "Thanks."

He gave the faintest shrug. "One of us has to be coordinated."

From behind, he could feel Kael's eyes watching them.

Sion turned around. Kael's eyes found Aislen first, checking her over with a glance that flickered like lightning. Then his gaze lifted, met Sion's across the narrow trail.

And for a heartbeat, something unspoken passed between them.

Kael didn't say a word. He didn't have to.

The look in his eyes was all Sion needed: quiet, intense, filled with gratitude.

Thank you.

Sion nodded once in return. Just a flick of his chin.

I've got her.

Then the moment passed. Kael turned forward again, Aislen steadied her pack, and the climb resumed like nothing had happened.

But the mountain had shifted.

And so had something between them.

* * *

Sion fell back into step behind the girls, his eyes scanning the rocky trail ahead, watching each careful placement of Aislen's and Thess's boots as they moved. He didn't need to hover, just be close enough. Just in case.

But a few steps later, his foot caught on a patch of loose gravel. He caught himself, barely more than a shift in balance, but it jarred something loose in his mind.

He would keep them safe. He *had* to.

That part was never in question. He'd made that promise to himself before they left the village, before Aislen stepped further into something ancient, and Kael's heart gave itself away in its entirety, and their world changed shape beneath them. He could carry the weight. He *wanted* to.

But some weights didn't stay neatly packed.

His thoughts drifted, uninvited, to back home. Back to the tiny house just off the west field where the shutters stuck and the firewood pile always leaned crooked. He imagined the smell of his mother's cooking, heavy with herbs and always a little burnt at the edges. His father's laugh: loud, rough, always followed by a cough when he drank too fast. The clang of steel from the training yard behind the house.

And his sisters.

Twin whirlwinds with tangled dark curls and the kind of shrieks that could rival banshees. Only three, but somehow they ruled the entire house with sticky fingers and wide, gap-toothed smiles.

He could still feel the sting of ink on his chest, heap market dye that took two days to fade. They'd snuck into his room during an afternoon nap and drawn "armor" across his arms and stomach, complete with squiggly "runes" and what looked suspiciously like a cat riding a sword.

"You're magic now," one of them had whispered with great solemnity, holding up the inkwell like a sacred artifact. "You can't die."

He'd let them finish. Sat perfectly still while they painted him like a warrior-prince from one of the storybooks. And when they were done, he'd picked them both up, one on each shoulder, and ran laps around the yard until their laughter turned breathless and bright and filled the whole sky.

Aislen's soft laugh brought him back.

He blinked and refocused, catching her up ahead as she brushed her fingers along the stone wall beside her. Thess leaned close to whisper something, probably something sarcastic, and Aislen snorted in reply, muffling it behind her hand.

Sion smiled, but it didn't quite reach his eyes.

He trusted his parents. Gods, he *respected* them. They were two of the fiercest warriors the outer rings had ever seen. If anyone could keep those girls safe, it was them.

But still.

Still.

The world felt heavier now. And darker. The things they were running from weren't just old stories anymore. They had teeth. And reach.

He exhaled slowly, adjusting the weight of his pack.

Let them be safe, he thought again. Not a prayer. Not quite. Just a desperate hope tied up in a promise he'd have to keep from hundreds of miles away.

He looked back to Aislen and Thess, still laughing, still walking like they weren't on the edge of the world.

He couldn't protect everyone. He knew that.

But *he would die trying* if it meant they never had to feel the kind of fear that lived in the pit of his stomach now.

And gods help anything, magic, monster, or man, that came between him and the people he loved.

Twenty-Five

"Unleashed"

~ Aislen ~

The wind stilled.

It had been howling just minutes ago, tearing at cloaks and hair as they crested the last ridge, but now it was quiet. Too quiet. The kind of quiet that wrapped around your spine and whispered that something was watching.

Aislen stood near the edge of the narrow path, staring into the yawning mouth of the cave. It rose before them like a wound in the mountain's face. It was tall, jagged, and pulsing with cold air. Not just with wind, but the kind of cold that felt purposeful. A warning sent shivering down the spine.

She swallowed hard, her hand drifting toward the stone wall beside her. The mountain had welcomed her before, steady and strong beneath her magic, ancient but not cruel. But this... this felt different.

This part didn't want them.

Kael stepped beside her, silent and still, his gaze locked on the darkness ahead. His shoulders were taut, his jaw clenched, but his hand brushed against hers for just a moment. Just long enough to say *I'm here.*

Tomas and Maera stood a few paces back, their expressions unreadable but wary. Thess muttered something under her breath that sounded like a prayer and a curse all rolled into one. Sion had gone quiet too, his eyes narrowed as he studied the edges of the cavern, like he expected it to reach out and grab one of them. Fenric was in the far back, muttering to himself quietly out of reach.

Aislen took a breath.

The air that drifted from the cave was damp and thick. It scented of minerals, old moss, and something fainter underneath. Like rot. Or death. Like the breath of a place that had been sealed off from the world for centuries. Maybe longer.

"There's no other way," she said, the words barely above a whisper.

No one disagreed.

The cliff behind them was too steep to climb. The trail had ended here, carved with unnatural precision into a dead end that left no doubt: someone, or *something*, wanted them to enter.

Aislen squared her shoulders and stepped forward until her boots kissed the shadowed edge.

She couldn't see far into the cave. Just a few feet of stone, slick and uneven. It swallowed the light like a living thing. Her heart pounded, full of panic and unease.

She glanced back once at the others.

At Thess's furrowed brow.

At Sion's quiet readiness.

At her mom's stillness.

At Kael.

Then she turned toward the dark.

And stepped inside.

The cave swallowed sound.

Aislen hadn't realized how loud the world was until it vanished behind her. The wind, the rustle of cloaks, the crunch of boots on gravel, it was all gone. In its place was a stillness so deep it pressed against her ears like pressure beneath water.

Their footsteps echoed faintly at first, but even those seemed to fade the deeper they walked.

"Sion? Light it up will you?" Thess said shakily from somewhere behind her.

Sion raised one hand.

A low breath left his lungs as he whispered the summoning phrase under his breath, one he'd used a hundred times before to summon his flame.

Nothing.

He tried again. This time louder. The others paused, looking in his direction.

A tiny spark flickered to life in his palm before it blinked out as if snuffed out by unseen wind.

"That's... not right," he muttered, frowning.

"It's like the air here doesn't want it," he said, voice tight. "Somethings fighting me."

"You've never had trouble before," Thess said, her voice hushed but steady.

"Not unless I was drunk or half-dead," he answered dryly, but there was no humor in it.

Kael conjured his own light, orbs laced with moon instead of flame. They held steady, flickering faintly but intact.

Sion cursed under his breath. "Something in here's suppressing fire magic."

"Or just yours," Fenric muttered, almost too low to catch.

Aislen ignored the jab at her friend, but the unease in her chest sharpened.

The cave wasn't just old, it was warded. Alive.

The tunnel walls were rough-hewn, not naturally formed. Carved. Intentional. Dark stone gleamed in places with veins of silver or crystal, but the shimmer died almost instantly under the weight of shadow. Whatever light filtered in from the outside vanished after only a few yards, and even the glow of their conjured orbs flickered like candle flames in a storm.

Kael walked beside her, his hand occasionally brushing hers, grounding her. Behind them came the others. They were silent now, their breath shallow and weapons already drawn.

The air changed.

Not colder, just heavier. Like it was filled with things it shouldn't be, even though nothing looked off.

But the *smell.*

What she first thought was rot, wasn't, not exactly. It was older than that. Dust and stone and the faint, bitter tang of something decayed *centuries* ago. It clung to her tongue and left a coppery aftertaste in her throat.

They passed an archway where strange markings lined the walls. Not runes, at least not any she recognized. The grooves looked burned into the stone rather than carved, blackened and half-melted at the edges. Something magical. Something wrong.

Kael touched her shoulder gently, pointing to the ground. Old footprints, long faded, led ahead.

There were bones. Just a few. They were small, maybe from an animal. Hopefully.

As they inched forward, no one spoke.

And then—

A whisper.

It came from *everywhere* at once.

Not loud. Not sharp. Just a slither of sound across the stone.

"You should not have come."

Aislen stopped so suddenly Kael nearly collided into her. Her breath caught. The air pressed in, colder than before, not in temperature but in absence. Like the space had been hollowed out just to let the voice echo inside her bones.

The others froze too.

Even Thess, who always had something to say, went completely still.

"So many years… so many dead… and still you bring more."

It wasn't yelling. It didn't need to.

Each word slithered through the stone like smoke through a keyhole. It almost sounded female. Young. Ancient. The cadence shifted with each syllable, refusing to settle into one shape. One voice.

"Your light does not belong here, daughter of stars."

Aislen's blood turned to ice. She didn't know how she knew, but the voice was speaking to her.

"A child of prophecy. A thread unraveled too soon."

Kael moved in front of her now, hand gripping the hilt of his blade, his body tense and ready. Sion shifted beside them, shielding Thess instinctively.

Aislen's heart hammered so fast she thought it was going to explode.

The air had grown icy. Not just windy, but cold.

Maera stepped closer to Tomas, her eyes glowing faintly as she whispered something under her breath. A prayer, maybe. It seemed fitting.

"You walk with power you do not understand..."

"A child filled with starlight, stumbling toward a gate that will devour you."

The voice now dry, cracked, but almost amused, echoed again. This time from directly behind them. Aislen spun, but there was nothing there.

Kael stepped closer, his breath steady but low. "We're not here to trespass," he said, voice firm. "We're here because we have to be."

Darkness closed in.

"Then perish as they did. Lost, forgotten... alone."

Silence.

And then all they could hear was screaming.

Not human. Not animal.

The unmistakable sound of metal-on-stone and hollow-boned fury as something charged from the shadows. It was fast, loud, and there were *too many*.

The smell of death.

There was nothing else it could be.

The undead.

Figures rushed toward them from the darkness. They were bone-white, half-armored corpses with shattered blades and empty sockets glowing with faint green fire. They must have been long-dead warriors, risen from whatever slumber they were entombed in.

Kael shouted something, a command or maybe a warning, and the sound broke the trance.

Steel rang.

Aislen raised her hands and let her magic fly.

The cave became pure chaos.

Aislen barely had time to think.

The first of the undead lunged from the darkness, shrieking as its rusted sword arced toward her. She ducked low, instincts flaring, and slashed upward with her blade. She had never been more thankful for the sparring lessons Kael made her endure.

Steel met bone with a sickening crack. The thing staggered, but didn't fall.

She threw out her other hand, palm open.

Magic surged.

Her earthsong answered her panic. It was not soft and steady this time, but sharp, like the mountains themselves had flinched. Stone cracked beneath the warrior's feet, and a jagged spike erupted from the ground, impaling the creature mid-step. Its body crumpled with a rattling shriek.

She turned to find another already rushing her.

Kael appeared in a blur of motion, his twin blades catching the undead mid-swing. His expression was unreadable. It held pure focus, pure fury. Moonlight shimmered faintly around him, his magic bleeding through in brief, glowing veins across his arms and neck.

"Aislen!" Thess shouted. "Left!"

She pivoted just in time to meet a skeletal warrior dragging a jagged spear. It swung wide. Aislen jumped back, stumbled, brought her blade up in a desperate parry.

The impact sent a shock through her arms.

"Watch your footing!" Tomas barked from across the cavern, slicing down another attacker with a roar.

He moved like a man half his age, wild-eyed but sure-handed. Nearby, Maera hurled handfuls of potion glass into the shadows, some igniting on contact, others bursting into acid-green smoke.

It wasn't the time to be impressed, but Aislen was glad her mom remembered some things from her time with her father.

Thess was on the move. She was spinning, ducking, striking with a small blade in one hand.

Sion stood like a wall between her and the shadows, his axe a blur of steel. Every swing sent bones scattering. He wasn't as fast, but he was relentless. Unshakable.

They were holding their ground. Barely.

But there were *so many.*

Aislen turned, heart thundering, and raised her hands again. The stone beneath the undead's feet rippled, just slightly, but enough to send one crashing to its knees. She lunged and drove her blade straight into its exposed spine.

Her breath was ragged. Her arms ached. But she kept going.

Magic sparked from her fingertips like gold-threaded lightning. It might have been wild and untamed but it was *hers.*

Another undead screamed, and Aislen whirled around just in time to see Maera stumble, her leg catching on rubble. One of the corpses raised its rusted sword over her.

"No!"

Aislen reached out with both hands, her entire chest alight with panic and power.

The ground answered.

A wall of stone rose between Maera and the blade just in time, the undead crashing into it with a sickening crunch. Aislen's knees buckled from the force of the draw, but she didn't fall.

She wouldn't fall.

Not while they were still breathing.

Aislen's pulse thundered in her ears.

The cave was chaos, screams, steel, shattering bones, but her focus narrowed to one thing: Thess.

Across the cavern, her friend had slipped. Blood dripped from her temple, and one of the undead had already closed the distance, sword arcing toward her exposed side.

There was no time.

Aislen's feet were already moving, but she wouldn't reach her in time.

"NO!"

The word tore from her throat and something answered.

A blast of light erupted from her chest. Not the golden shimmer of her earthsong. This was colder. Brighter. *Older.* It burst outward like a shockwave, throwing every undead in a twenty-foot radius to the ground in a violent ring of raw magic.

The cavern went still, just for a breath.

Then the stars appeared.

Tiny specks of silver light flickered to life in the air around her. Dozens at first. Then hundreds. They hung there, suspended like a constellation stitched into shadow. They shimmered along her arms, her collarbone, and even her fingertips. It was her starlight magic passed down from her father finally singing with power.

Kael froze mid-strike, his head snapping toward her.

Sion lowered his blade in awe.

Even the undead who were still standing hesitated, as if sensing something they weren't meant to touch.

The cave itself seemed to pulse in response. The walls were humming faintly as the stone beneath their feet glowed with soft, silver light.

Aislen stood at the center of it all, her breath ragged, her heart a wildfire.

She was afraid. Still trembling. But in the fear, something steadied. Something claimed her back.

She didn't think. She just did.

She raised one hand, and the starlight followed. It laced through her fingers and coiled outward, spinning like threads of silver wind. She threw it forward and it hit the nearest undead with no sound at all.

Just light.

The body crumbled. It was silent, instant, and just *gone.*

The magic wasn't like her earthsong. It didn't move with weight or crack with power. It was unmade. Not with violence. But with light.

The undead weren't meant to exist. And her magic sensed that.

They screamed.

More surged forward, but the air around Aislen shimmered like a shield. She threw both hands out and the light shot from her palms, spearing through three more corpses and burning them to ash.

Kael was at her side now, panting, staring at her like he'd never seen her before.

"Aislen..." he breathed. "Are you—?"

"I don't know," she whispered. "I think so. Whatever this is, it's mine."

Behind them, the last of the undead reeled back and the moment cracked again.

The light grew brighter.

The cave shuddered.

And Aislen lifted her hand one last time.

The final wave of starlight poured forward like a tide and wiped the rest of the undead from existence.

When it was over, there was no sound but the ragged breathing of the living.

No bones.

No weapons.

Just silver motes, still drifting slowly through the dark like snow made of stars.

* * *

~ **Maera** ~

The air shimmered with light that should not exist.

Maera stood still, her hand braced against the cold cave wall, breathing through the sharp, aching swell of magic that hadn't touched this world in generations. The fight was over. The undead gone, *unmade,* not simply defeated. And at the center of it all stood her daughter.

Aislen.

Bathed in starlight.

It clung to her skin like a second layer, flickering gently along her arms, her hair, her lashes. Like the very threads of the cosmos had been sewn

205

into her. The others were still catching their breath. Tomas gripped her shoulder as Thess wiped blood from her own brow. And then there was Kael looking at her daughter like she was the only thing in the world.

But Maera...

Maera watched in silence.

Her heart thundered with pride. And terror.

She's more like him than I ever thought.

That thought slipped unbidden through her mind, and it left a bitter taste on her tongue.

She had always known Aislen would be powerful. She'd seen it in the way her daughter moved through the world, with gentle hands and a stubborn heart, as if kindness itself was a form of rebellion. But this... this was beyond even Maera's fears.

Starlight magic wasn't meant for mortals.

It was prophecy and blood and court-forged legacy.

And it was Alarion.

She looks just like him.

The memory of him came unbidden: violet-eyed, ageless, smiling at her like she held all the gravity in his world. He had once been gentle. Warm. He'd once pressed his forehead to hers and whispered that their love would change everything.

But the more power he gained, the more she saw another side of him.

He began to *change.*

Not suddenly. Slowly. Quietly. Like moonlight slipping into shadow. Every choice became strategy. Every word a weapon. He still loved her and she believed that. But he began to love power too much.

She hoped when she became his queen that she could bring love and peace back to a court, a people, where it felt diminished.

Until everything changed and she couldn't even try.

And now... Aislen bore the mark of him in every glimmer of her magic.

Please don't lose yourself to it, my girl.

Please don't let it twist you into something beautiful and terrifying and alone.

Maera blinked, and the cave came back into focus.

Aislen was still standing where the final burst of magic had left her. Her hands were trembling now, the light beginning to fade. The glow in her veins was dimming. Her shoulders sagged under the weight of what she'd done, or what had been done *through* her.

And she looked *so young.*

Still just a girl, unknowingly trying to carry a crown the stars had placed on her head before she even knew what it meant to wear one.

Maera stepped forward.

She moved slowly, boots crunching over scattered rock and ash, until she reached her daughter. Aislen didn't speak. Didn't move.

She was still staring at her own hands like they weren't hers anymore.

Maera didn't say anything at first.

She simply reached out, wrapped her arms around her, and held her close.

Aislen inhaled sharply, and then let out a shaky breath that sounded like it had been stuck in her chest for hours. Her body folded into Maera's with the familiarity of home.

Maera pressed her lips to her daughter's temple and closed her eyes.

"You were extraordinary," she whispered. "And I've never been more proud."

Aislen didn't answer, but her fingers clutched Maera's cloak just a little tighter.

And for the first time in a long time, Maera let herself cry.

Not because she was afraid of what Aislen was becoming.

But because she was finally beginning to see who her daughter truly *was.*

And it terrified her just as much as it made her proud.

Twenty-Six

"Calculations"

❧❧❧

~ **Aislen** ~

She stood in the village again, though it was quiet now and drained of sound and color. The trees were grayer than green, the sky a muted silver. Smoke curled from chimneys without scent. The people were gone. Or maybe had never been there at all.

Aislen turned slowly, her feet crunching softly on the frost-laced path that led away from the garden.

This wasn't real.

But it felt *close.*

She reached the edge of the clearing, just outside Elara's home. The door creaked open, slow and deliberate. Inside, candlelight flickered. It was too bright for the pale world beyond it.

Aislen stepped over the threshold.

Elara was there, standing with her back to her, her long hair in a braid draped over one shoulder, her hands busy tying something closed. Bandages maybe? A satchel?

She turned at the sound of Aislen's steps, her eyes crinkling at the corners. Not smiling exactly, but her face softened.

Just like she had been that morning. The day they left.

"Come here child," Elara had said then, and now again, her voice echoing, layered.

The memory was folding into the dream now, and Aislen let it happen.

She stepped closer, and Elara reached for her. It was not to pull her into a hug, but to touch her face gently. Her thumb brushed over Aislen's cheek, and for a moment, all the tension of the journey, the magic, the fear, slipped away.

"Before you go," Elara said softly, leaning in.

"There's something you should remember."

Aislen blinked, and the dream shifted slightly. Shadows curled at the edges of the room. The fire dimmed.

Elara leaned closer, and her lips brushed just beside Aislen's ear, just like they had before.

"Be kind to Fenric. But never give him your full trust."

The words landed like a stone in her chest.

Even in the dream, Aislen stiffened.

"He was once a good man," Elara whispered, "but he's made too many quiet choices."

A pause. A weight.

"Kael believes him to still be good. Let him hold onto that hope until he no longer can. Be careful, but love fierce Aislen."

Elara pulled back. Her eyes were still kind, but now shadowed.

And Aislen remembered. She remembered how Elara had held her gaze a little too long that day. How her hand had lingered on Aislen's arm. How Kael had noticed too, but hadn't pried.

Too many quiet choices.

The words echoed, and the dream began to fade.

The fire went out.

The house dissolved.

And Aislen woke up.

The darkness was different now.

Not the kind that pressed in from all sides like it had during the battle, but softer. Still.

Aislen opened her eyes slowly, blinking against the faint silver glow that lingered in the air, the last breath of starlight flickering out like the final embers of a dying fire.

They were still in the cave.

Sometime after the undead had fallen and her magic had faded, they'd made camp in a wide alcove along the tunnel wall. Just enough space for a few bedrolls, a small, carefully shielded fire, and their bodies, still trembling from the fight.

The group had eaten what little they could stomach, exchanged barely a dozen words, and collapsed into restless sleep.

Aislen hadn't meant to dream.

And now, awake again, she wasn't sure if she *had* or if Elara's voice had truly found her in the dark.

Too many quiet choices.

She stared up at the cavern ceiling, heart still racing under the stillness. The cave was silent except for the soft crackle of fire and the slow breathing of those around her. Kael's arm was draped protectively around her waist, his body curved warm against her back.

But something felt off.

She didn't move, not right away.

Just listened.

And then she felt it, *that hum on the back of her neck.*

The sensation of being watched.

Her eyes shifted, just barely, toward the far wall of the cave.

And froze.

Fenric was awake.

He sat with his back against the stone, arms resting on his knees, face unreadable in the low firelight. He wasn't sleeping. He wasn't even pretending to rest.

He was watching *her.*

Their eyes met across the cave, and for a breath, neither of them looked away.

His expression wasn't cold. It wasn't cruel. But it wasn't soft, either.

Just still.

Observing.

Calculating.

The fire cracked softly between them.

Aislen's heart thudded once, slow and heavy.

Then, without a word, she turned her head away and tucked herself back into Kael's chest. His arms tightened around her in his sleep, instinctive even now.

She closed her eyes.

And pretended she hadn't seen anything at all.

* * *

~ **Fenric** ~

She saw him.

He knew it the moment their eyes met across the cave.

Aislen hadn't flinched, at least not visibly, but the way her breath caught, the subtle tension in her shoulders before she curled back into Kael's chest... it was enough.

She was beginning to wonder.

Good.

She *should* wonder.

Fear would make her cautious. Predictable.

Fenric sat perfectly still against the wall, his hands resting on his knees, his sword laid carefully across his lap. Not in threat, but in ritual. A warrior's quiet prayer. A habit he couldn't shake.

The cave was dim, but his vision had long since adjusted. Every breath, every shifting shadow, every heartbeat was a note in a song he'd been hearing his entire life.

He let his eyes linger on Aislen just a moment longer.

Starlight.

He'd known it the instant her magic erupted. Not just earthsong, not the quiet hum of nature-bound power. No, what she wielded had been celestial. Damn near ancient, if not worse. The kind of magic only the oldest courts whispered about. The kind his father used to tell stories of by the fire, before the war came and burned all those fairy tales to ash.

And now it was *real.*

Alive.

Sleeping in the skin of a female who didn't yet know what she carried.

A female his son loved.

A female he claimed as his mate.

Fenric's gaze drifted to Kael, still wrapped around her like she was the center of his world.

He didn't doubt Kael's love. That part was real. Raw. Unshakable.

But love couldn't keep a family safe. Not from famine. Not from politics. Not from war.

Fenric had spent decades as a blade for hire, a soldier, a protector of people who never remembered his name. He had watched kings fall and common men rise. He had seen what power could do and what it could *buy.*

The Celestara Court.

That was the key.

A Court forgotten by most, hidden for generations. Aislen was their lost heir, whether she knew it or not. And if she stepped through their gates, *doors would open.*

Not just for her.

For Kael.

For their entire family.

For Fenric.

If he played this right, if he found a way to contact the Sun Queen first, to bring her proof of Aislen's existence, he could offer something no one else could. He already destroyed the ward his mate placed upon them. That was the first thing he did.

An heir wrapped in prophecy. A girl born of both earth and stars. A chance to control the old blood before it woke up all the way.

And in return?

A place of power.

Wealth beyond the struggling village life they'd scraped through for years.

A guaranteed seat at the side of the most feared ruler in the realm.

Maybe even a place in the Sun Queen's personal guard.

He would be seen. Respected. Untouchable.

And Kael would never have to bleed in a battlefield again.

Fenric's jaw tightened.

He *did* love his son.

But love wasn't enough. Not when power was on the table. Not when futures could be bought with secrets.

He just had to be careful.

He couldn't move too soon. Aislen was watching now. Elara had seen it too, that much was clear. That old warrior female had always been sharp beneath her calm. She'd never said anything outright, but her silence had teeth.

But she would forgive him.

He was her mate, she would always come back to him. Always.

Still, Fenric could wait. Watch. Position himself.

And when the time came?

He would do what needed to be done.

For the family.

Even if it meant betraying the girl his son would die for.

Twenty-Seven

"Darkness"

~ **Aislen** ~

Morning didn't come in the cave. Not the way it did outside.

There was no sun breaking through the trees, no birdsong or shifting breeze. Just the low flicker of their small fire, nearly out now, and the hollow drip of moisture from the ceiling. Slow, rhythmic, and distant.

Aislen opened her eyes to stone and shadow.

Her body ached in places she hadn't known could hurt. Her limbs felt heavy, like they'd been carved from the same rock they slept on. Magic still hummed faintly beneath her skin, but it had dimmed. Quieted, as if it were waiting.

Kael was still curled against her back, steady and warm. She didn't move. Not yet.

The rest of the cave was eerily still.

Sion sat near the fire again, sharpening a blade, though the sound was muffled by cloth. Thess was lying down but not asleep, one arm over her eyes and the other draped across her stomach, as if willing herself not to speak. Maera sat apart from them, legs crossed, head bowed in meditation, or maybe even exhaustion. Tomas was still resting quietly at her feet.

214

And Fenric…

He wasn't where he'd been last night.

Aislen scanned the edges of the cave and spotted him standing near the tunnel entrance, watching the stone ahead like it might shift beneath his gaze. The firelight didn't quite reach him, and he looked like part of the cave itself. Rigid, silent, waiting.

Her stomach twisted.

She still wasn't sure if the dream had been memory or something else. But Elara's voice clung to her like cobwebs.

Never give him your full trust.

Kael stirred behind her. She felt his hand slide across her waist, his breath warm near her shoulder.

"You're awake," he murmured, low and rough with sleep.

"Barely."

She turned just enough to look at him, their foreheads nearly touching. He brushed a strand of hair from her face and gave her a faint smile, but it didn't quite reach his eyes.

"You okay?" she asked.

Kael hesitated.

Then nodded. "We're alive."

Aislen didn't point out that *alive* wasn't the same as *okay.*

Not today.

Sion glanced up at them, his eyes flicking between them before returning to his blade. He hadn't spoken since last night. Not even a quip. And that silence… it weighed more than his axe.

From his spot near Maera's feet, Tomas sat up slowly, wincing as he rotated his shoulder. "How's everyone feeling?" he asked, voice gravelly.

"Like we were dragged across the edge of a cliff and then set on fire," Thess muttered, still not looking up.

"That good, huh?"

"Would've been better if the undead had sent snacks."

A faint, humorless chuckle passed through the group. Even that felt wrong.

The cave held its breath around them.

Aislen sat up fully now, brushing dust from her clothes, and tried to shake the cold from her bones. Her magic was still there, resting, but she felt *different*. Not broken. Not whole. Something else. Like a cup filled too high, and one wrong movement might make it spill again.

They had to keep moving.

This place, it had let them live, but it hadn't welcomed them.

She could feel that now. Whatever power still lived in the bones of this mountain, it was watching.

And it wanted them gone.

They moved with the slow, mechanical rhythm of people who hadn't yet processed what they'd survived.

Bedrolls were rolled and tied with half frozen fingers. Loose stones were cleared from the edge of the camp. The fire was smothered beneath layers of ash and earth. No one spoke more than necessary.

Even the clinking of buckles and armor felt too loud.

Aislen knelt to gather her pack, her fingers trembling slightly as she tightened the leather straps. Her chest still hummed with the echo of power. No longer active, but present. The magic was like a second heartbeat now, pulsing just beneath the surface of her skin.

Maera stood nearby, eyes scanning the group as they moved. She didn't speak, but Aislen could feel her watching. Not judging. Not afraid. Just... alert. Like she was trying to memorize every expression, every hesitation.

"We need to move before the hour changes," Fenric said flatly from the mouth of the tunnel. "Magic like that doesn't go unnoticed. Not in these mountains."

Aislen's head snapped up.

It wasn't what he said that bothered her, it was *how* he said it. Not in fear. Not even in anger. Just a statement of fact, as if he'd expected this all along.

"I didn't mean to draw anything," she muttered.

"You didn't have to," Fenric replied, his gaze sharp. "The earth remembers. It will pass it along to others of the earthsong magic. Anything watching will do the same."

Kael, who had been silently strapping on his chest plate, looked up. His expression flickered full of anger, protectiveness.

Sion stepped between them as he adjusted the length of rope tied to his belt. "Can we argue about consequences after we're not sitting in a haunted cave?"

Thess scoffed. "You say that like the next cave won't also be haunted."

Tomas stood and adjusted his pack. "Let's just try to reach open air before we start getting philosophical again."

They all fell into motion gathering, shouldering, and double-checking supplies. But Kael didn't move.

Not until he walked over and gently brushed Aislen's hand with his fingertips.

She looked up at him.

"Walk with me," he said softly.

Before she could ask why, he was already turning away and walking down the narrow curve of the tunnel they'd entered from, where the shadows swallowed the path beyond.

Aislen hesitated for only a moment, then followed.

The others didn't stop them. No one had the energy to ask questions.

Kael moved just far enough down the tunnel that the embers of the dying firelight behind them disappeared. The sound of packing faded behind the curve of stone, replaced by the quiet drip of water and the faint, echoing hush of ancient earth.

When he stopped, he turned to face her.

His eyes were storm-dark.

"You can't do that again," he said quietly.

Aislen blinked. "What?"

"Not without warning. Not without knowing what it costs."

"It saved our lives, Kael."

"I know." His voice cracked, just slightly. "But it *lit up the continent.* Do you understand that? That wasn't just magic, Aislen. That was a beacon. If anyone felt it, if *she* felt it—"

He didn't say the Sun Queen's name.

217

He didn't have to.

Aislen swallowed, her back straightening.

"I didn't ask for this. I didn't *want* it."

"I know." He stepped closer, his hand reaching for hers.

They stood in silence for a beat.

Then she whispered, "I'm scared."

Aislen didn't look away from him.

She couldn't.

Kael's hand was still wrapped around hers, rough fingers curled so gently against her knuckles it felt like a promise. His jaw clenched once, hard, before he spoke again. It was lower this time, as if the truth might break something between them.

"I'm scared too," he said. "More than I've ever been."

His honesty. The raw way he looked at her.

It stole her breath.

"I know how to fight, Aislen. I've trained my whole life. I'd face monsters. Entire Courts. Even fate herself if it meant protecting you."

He stepped closer.

"But I don't want to die for you."

Her heart stuttered.

"I want to live with you. Together."

The cave seemed to pull back around them, less stone and more silence. More *space.*

"I want to take you somewhere quiet," he whispered. "Somewhere green and sunlit. A place where we don't have to watch our backs or guard every word. Somewhere I can fall asleep with you beside me and not wonder if someone is tracking our magic or waiting for us to slip."

"I want us to have a family of our own. I want to watch the love in your eyes as you look at them."

Her breath hitched.

"That's all I ever wanted. To *begin* with you. Not like this. Not in fear. Not while running."

Aislen's chest ached at the rawness in his voice. She reached up slowly, her fingers grazing the edge of his jaw, the curve of his neck. "Kael..."

"I'll fight to the death if I have to," he said, voice thick. "But gods, Aislen, I don't want to."

Neither of them moved for a heartbeat. Their breathing had shifted. Ut was now too fast, too shallow, caught in the space between emotion and instinct. Kael's gaze dropped to her lips. Then back to her eyes.

And in that one look, she realized they were alone. Or alone enough.

Her hand slid to his chest, curling in the fabric of his shirt just as his arms wrapped around her waist and pulled her against him. Their mouths met in a rush, not frantic, but *hungry*. Desperate in the way that said they'd waited too long. Held back too much.

Aislen's whole body hummed with satisfaction.

The magic in their bond stirred. It was just under her skin. It flared, not dangerous, just alive. Responsive. Like it had been waiting for this too. The kiss deepened, heat rising between them faster than either of them could contain. His hands skimmed up her back, pulling her closer, and her fingers found their way into his hair, tugging just enough to make him groan softly against her lips.

When they finally broke apart, breathless and dazed, he pressed his forehead to hers and whispered, "I love you."

She didn't need to answer.

He already knew.

Kael's mouth returned to hers with a growl low in his throat, and Aislen's knees nearly buckled.

His hands were everywhere. They were spanning her waist, trailing up her back, pulling her in like he needed her closer than closeness allowed. She rose onto her toes, pressing herself against him, not caring about stone walls or watchful shadows. Not here. Not with him.

His lips dragged from her mouth down the curve of her jaw, breath hot against her throat. She gasped, fingers curling into his shirt, tugging him down to meet her again.

"Aislen," he murmured against her skin like a prayer. "You feel perfect."

She whimpered at the sound of her name on his lips. Raw, reverent, undone.

Magic flared between them, warm and shimmering, dancing across her skin where he touched her. His thumb brushed just beneath the hem of her shirt, and her stomach fluttered at the contact. Gods, every nerve in her body was awake singing for him, for this, for the life they weren't allowed to have yet but *desperately wanted.*

Kael leaned his forehead against hers again, breathing hard. "Tell me to stop."

She didn't.

He kissed her again deeper, slower this time, but no less intense. One hand tangled in her hair, the other cradled her hip, like he was trying to memorize the way she fit against him.

She gasped softly as his mouth brushed along the shell of her ear and his hand began its descent into the band of her trousers.

And then—

"Hey! Did a monster get you two or are you just making out with the rocks down there?"

Thess's voice echoed like a slap down the tunnel, laced with sarcasm and concern in equal measure.

They froze.

Aislen let her forehead drop against Kael's chest, groaning. "Of *course* it's her."

Kael huffed a quiet laugh, arms still around her. "She has excellent timing."

"Worst timing," she muttered, not moving.

Another shout: *"I'm not coming down there to rescue you from sexy cave monsters. Just saying."*

Kael leaned down and pressed a final kiss to her forehead. "We'll finish this later."

Aislen looked up at him with a flushed smile, still breathless. "Promise?"

"On my life," he whispered.

Reluctantly, they stepped apart, though his fingers lingered at her waist until the very last second.

They walked back toward the others together, hearts still pounding, lips

220

tingling, and magic singing softly between them.

Twenty-Eight

"The Edge"

~ Aislen ~

They had walked for hours.

Ten, maybe more. Time had lost its shape in the cold belly of the mountain, stretched thin between uneven steps and the constant echo of boots against stone. No one spoke much anymore. There wasn't energy for words, only the quiet crunch of gravel and the occasional rustle of fabric or scuff of a boot dragging just a bit too slowly.

The air grew colder the deeper they went, damp and heavy like the weight of forgotten centuries pressing against their lungs. Shadows clung stubbornly to the walls, even where their torches flickered. Each footstep sounded too loud. Too alone.

They stopped only a handful of times. It was only to sip water, shift gear, and to stretch out aching calves. Never long. Never enough.

And then—

A glow.

It started faint, barely more than a whisper of silver on the jagged tunnel floor.

"Wait," Sion murmured from ahead, raising a hand to still the group.

Everyone halted, breath held.

There, far in the distance. Not torchlight. Not magic.

Daylight.

Real, warm, natural light spilling in faint streams through the narrowing mouth of the tunnel ahead.

Aislen felt her chest tighten with cautious relief. Her legs ached, her shoulders burned beneath the weight of her pack, but her pace quickened.

The others followed, quiet but eager, their steps quickening with a kind of silent desperation. The exit was still a ways off, but they could see it now. It was real.

A sliver of freedom.

Kael fell into step beside her, and their eyes met just briefly, wordless understanding passing between them like a spark. They'd made it through. Somehow. Again.

Behind them, Tomas shifted his pack and let out a slow exhale. "I was starting to think this place didn't have an end."

"It still might be a trap," Fenric muttered from the rear.

Thess let out a dry snort. "If it is, I vote we at least enjoy the fresh air before the next nightmare shows up."

Aislen smiled faintly but said nothing. Her hand brushed the cave wall as they walked, as if to say goodbye to the strange magic that lingered in the stone. The walls were narrowing now, sloping inward just before they widened one final time into a jagged mouth of shattered rock and sunlit fog.

They were almost out.

But something still pressed at the edges of her magic. It was faint, distant, like a whisper under the surface of her skin.

The Hollow Mountains weren't finished with them yet.

She could feel it.

* * *

~ Thess ~

The light was blinding after hours inside the cave.

Thess blinked against it, one hand rising to shield her eyes as her boots crunched onto sunlit stone. But whatever warmth she'd expected from the sunrise drained from her the moment she looked ahead.

There it was.

A bridge.

If you could even call it that.

Wooden slats, half-rotted and warped, stretched across an impossible drop. The ropes holding them together looked brittle with age, strands frayed like hair, snapping gently in the wind. Whole sections of the planks were just… missing. Not broken, but gone like someone had plucked them free with greedy fingers.

And below?

A chasm.

Vast. Silent. Unforgiving.

The ravine yawned beneath them, so deep the shadows at the bottom felt like the edge of another world. Mist crawled along the jagged rocks far below, a slow-moving blanket that did nothing to soften the threat of the fall.

"Absolutely not," Thess said, her voice dry and brittle as she lowered her hand. "Nope. I'm declaring mutiny. We live in this cave now."

Aislen stepped beside her, equally frozen. Her silence said enough.

Kael emerged next, his face hardening as he took in the sight. He moved closer to the start of the bridge, testing the ropes with a slow pull, and the entire structure groaned in response.

Sion went to help Kael inspect the bridge. After inspecting, he looked right at Thess.

"Funniest person first," he said, "That's you, right?" He added with a smirk.

She blinked. "Excuse me? You're volunteering me for the Trial of Utter Doom?"

"You know Sion? I think you're right. Thess is pretty funny," Kael replied, a smirk of his own now.

"Oh, I see. So now I'm the sacrificial goat," she muttered, but her feet were already moving.

Aislen reached out and gripped her arm. "You don't have to, they were just joking."

"Yeah, I do." Thess gave her a crooked smile that didn't quite reach her eyes. "We're not turning back. And someone's gotta see if the ancient rope nightmare is walkable."

She took a deep breath and stepped up to the edge. Her heart thudded hard. It was fast, loud and everywhere. The first wooden plank dipped beneath her boot.

It creaked.

She froze.

"Okay," she whispered to herself. "Just don't look down. Don't look—"

She looked down.

Cold sweat beaded along her spine as her gaze dropped into that endless space. The mist below writhed like it was alive. Like it was waiting.

Thess squeezed her eyes shut. One step. Then another.

Her boots landed on old wood that bowed under her weight and whispered against the ropes. The bridge swayed, slow at first, then stronger with the next gust of wind. She grabbed the side ropes so hard her fingers ached.

Her breath hitched.

Each step was a small act of rebellion against fear.

A dance between balance and gravity.

Halfway across, a board cracked beneath her heel.

She yelped and lunged forward, catching the side ropes in both hands as splinters flew and the board dropped into the abyss below with a sickening snap.

She stayed frozen there, heart pounding in her throat.

Behind her, someone shouted her name, but she couldn't answer. Couldn't even breathe.

You're not falling. You're not falling.

But you *could have.*

Her mind wouldn't stop whirling.

Her eyes burned.

She forced herself upright, legs shaking now, and took another step. Then another.

And another.

Each time she crossed a missing slat, she had to jump, the ropes groaning and jerking under the motion. Every time, she swore it would be the one that tore loose. That she'd plunge into the dark and disappear before anyone could reach her.

But then—

Solid ground.

She stumbled onto the ledge and fell to her knees, chest heaving.

It took her a few seconds to realize she was laughing. That half-hysterical kind of laugh that came when you'd stared death in the face and didn't die.

"Totally fine!" she called back to the others, voice still trembling. "Totally did not pee myself!"

Aislen let out a nervous laugh. Even Kael smiled faintly.

But Thess just knelt there, fists pressed to the earth, soaking in the miracle of standing.

As each of them crossed in turn, Kael first, followed by Aislen, then the others, she remained still. Watching. Breathing. Hiding how close she'd come to freezing.

It wasn't the height that got to her.

It was the silence below it.

Like the ravine had no end. No mercy. Just *waiting.*

And yet… she'd done it.

For them. For this mismatched, stubborn, beautifully doomed little group.

Because they were hers now.

And she'd cross a thousand damn bridges if it meant they made it to the other side.

Although, she really didn't want to.

But at least she passed the Trial of Utter Doom.

* * *

Finally the bridge was behind them and the path picked up again. It was narrow, winding, and carved into the side of a cliff like the mountain had grown tired of offering comfort.

Thess trailed at the back now.

Usually, she kept ahead. Made herself loud. Visible. Hard to ignore.

But something about that bridge… about standing at the edge of death with nothing but fraying rope and blind faith beneath her feet, it had pulled something loose in her. Unraveled a thread she'd been pretending wasn't there.

The path before them was steep and unforgiving, but her eyes stayed on the people ahead. Aislen, brushing back windblown hair and checking on Kael with a soft smile. Kael, tense but alert, always one hand near his weapon, the other touching Aislen. Tomas walking a bit stiffly after the cave, Maera quiet and watchful as ever. Even Fenric… well. He existed. Sion was the only one who seemed to notice her absence. He glanced back at her with raised eyebrows and eyes full of concern.

She shook her head at him. He nodded as he turned around and continued moving.

This mismatched band of runaways, misfits, and warriors… they were the closest thing to family she'd ever felt seen by.

Thess stuffed her hands into the pockets of her coat and kept walking, boots scraping against the stone trail. Her legs still trembled a little from the bridge, but she'd never admit that out loud.

The youngest of eight kids didn't get to be soft.

Not in her house.

Growing up, if you wanted to be heard, you had to be *louder.* If you wanted love, you had to earn it through jokes, through antics, through

227

being the comic relief when everything else felt heavy. The loud one. The strange one. The one they all laughed at but didn't look too closely at.

It worked. Sort of.

Until it didn't.

Her family had love, sure. But not the kind that made space for all the feelings. Not the kind that noticed when she needed it most.

So, she learned to speak in sarcasm.

To hide pain behind eye rolls and raised eyebrows.

To make people laugh before they asked too many questions.

But these people?

They didn't look away when she got quiet.

They noticed when her hands shook. When her smile faltered.

Kael always checked in with a nod. Aislen shared warmth like she'd never run out. Sion? He treated her like her chaos wasn't a nuisance but a rhythm he trusted. Even Aislen's parents joked with her like they meant it. Like she belonged.

And maybe… maybe she did.

The wind picked up again, pulling at her hair and stinging her eyes. She blinked hard.

No crying.

She didn't cry.

Only losers cried on mountain trails after not dying.

"Gods, I'm getting sentimental," she muttered, kicking a loose pebble down the slope. "Must be the altitude. Or I'm dying. That's also a possibility."

Ahead, Aislen turned just slightly, as if sensing her voice even through the wind. She didn't say anything, just gave her a small, knowing look. The kind that said: *You're not alone.*

And for once, Thess didn't crack a joke.

She just smiled. Soft, real, and quiet.

And kept walking.

She'd nearly died today.

But she'd also survived.

And not just the fall.

The loneliness too.

* * *

By the time the sky began to bruise with sunset, the trail finally evened out. The air, still thin, had grown colder with elevation, and every step made Thess's muscles burn like they were being carved out and replaced with fire.

But they'd made it.

The narrow path spilled out onto a rocky plateau that curved along the side of the mountain like a waiting palm. It was sheltered on three sides by jagged walls and outcroppings, and just barely flat enough to be considered safe for camp.

Thess dropped her pack with a dramatic groan and flopped backward onto a patch of moss-dappled stone.

"If I die here, tell people I went out looking awesome," she muttered to the clouds.

Kael walked by and arched a brow. "You're not dying."

"I might be. My legs have officially detached from my body and are filing complaints."

Sion chuckled nearby, tossing down his gear. Aislen smiled faintly and lowered herself onto a stone beside her dad. The group was tired, beyond tired actually, but something about this spot felt like relief. Temporary, yes. But real.

They had crossed the top of the Hollow Mountains.

And they were still breathing.

Thess turned her head to look at the drop-off on the edge of the plateau. The view took her breath away. The endless skies melting into a distant valley, forests sprawling far below like spilled ink... the world looked small from here.

But her chest felt big.

Bigger than it had in years.

"I can't believe we're almost on the other side," she said quietly, not really meaning to speak aloud. "Feels like we've been climbing forever."

"You've done well," Maera said from where she was unrolling a blanket. "We all have."

Thess looked over, startled by the gentleness in her voice. For a woman who carried secrets like armor, Maera's praise felt like rare sunlight.

"Thanks," Thess said, a bit awkwardly. She didn't know what to do with real compliments. Usually she deflected them. Threw a quip like a shield.

But maybe she didn't have to tonight.

The others settled in slowly, lighting a small, controlled fire that gave off more glow than heat. They shared water and dried food. Quiet talk replaced the usual banter.

Even Thess didn't feel like filling the silence.

She wrapped herself in her cloak and leaned back against a boulder, eyes trained on the stars beginning to peek out between clouds.

For the first time in forever, she didn't feel like she had to perform. No jokes. No noise.

She just… existed.

And they let her.

She watched Aislen laugh softly at something Sion whispered. Watched Tomas lean into Maera's side as they sipped warm broth. Watched Kael stare silently out over the ledge, his posture sharp but his presence steady.

These people. This ragtag, stubborn group.

She'd die for them.

And maybe, just maybe, they'd fight for her, too.

The thought made something ache in her chest in the best way.

Home wasn't a place. Not for someone like her.

But maybe it could be *this*.

Thess became lost in her thoughts as the fire grew dim.

She closed her eyes to the wind and let it wash over her face, stealing the sting of old memories and leaving something new in its place.

By the time she opened her eyes, the fire had long since burned low. Most of the group was asleep, curled up in their cloaks beneath the overhang, breaths slow and even against the hush of the wind.

But Thess couldn't sleep.

She lay with her arms behind her head, staring up at the stars and listening to the shift of gravel as someone approached.

Sion.

He didn't say anything at first. Just stood there at the edge of her bedroll, arms crossed, gaze sharp in the moonlight. Thess arched a brow.

"Can't sleep either?" she whispered.

He crouched down, close enough that she could see the flecks of gold in his eyes. "It's been a while," he murmured, voice low. "Since we... last blew off steam."

Thess smirked. "You mean since I got bored?"

Sion's lips twitched. "Exactly that. Any chance you're bored again?"

She didn't answer right away. Just held his gaze, watching how he waited for her to answer.

That was what she liked about him. Always had. Sion never expected more than what she was willing to give.

And right now?

Right now, the tension from battle and fear and near-death clung to her skin like sweat. Her muscles were tight. Her heart still hadn't fully slowed since the cave.

Maybe she *was* bored.

Or maybe she just needed to *feel* something good for once.

"Maybe I could use a little entertainment up here," Thess said as she looked up at him through her lashes.

He leaned closer. "Let me make sure."

Her pulse thudded in her ears. She sat up, tossed off the blanket, and stood, brushing gravel from her leggings. "Ten minutes."

Sion rose with her, a small grin tugging at his lips. "I'll make you forget the last ten hours."

She followed him up a narrow incline, just beyond sight of the others, the stars overhead like sharp white blades in the navy sky. The cold bit at her cheeks, but the heat rolling off Sion's body made her forget it entirely.

He turned the second they were alone, grabbing her waist and pinning her against the stone wall behind them. His mouth found hers, urgent and hungry, his hands already tugging at the layers of her cloak.

She responded with teeth and tongue and a low sound of need that made him groan against her mouth.

"You always this worked up after a fight?" she murmured against his lips, tugging his shirt free of his trousers.

"You always this mouthy when you're about to come undone?" he shot back, nipping at her jaw.

"Try me."

He spun her around, her palms bracing against the cool stone wall. One hand slid up her thigh, dragging her trousers down just enough, the other covering her mouth forcefully.

"Unless you want to wake them up?" he asked, voice hoarse and trembling with restraint.

She shook her head quickly, biting her lip.

"But if I bite your hand, don't finish early on me," she whispered, voice full of heat.

Gods—she needed this.

The first thrust knocked the breath from her lungs. Her knees buckled slightly, but his grip was there as his hips moved against her with a rhythm honed from pure need.

It wasn't soft.

It wasn't careful.

But he knew just what she needed.

Thess gasped against his hand, her body arching back to meet every movement, every stroke that sent sparks up her spine. The stone was cold beneath her palms, but everything else was heat. Her core was burning, her breath ragged, and her thighs trembling.

Sion kissed the nape of her neck, bit gently at her shoulder, and pressed deeper.

232

She moaned against his palm, and he growled low in her ear, "You're trouble, you know that? Now be a good girl and don't wake the others or we won't be able to finish this."

Her body clenched at his voice in her ear. The low and throaty way he spoke to her.

The pressure built inside her, pulsing and rising with each thrust. She barely held back a cry as her release crashed over her, muscles tensing and pleasure rolling in waves so fierce her legs nearly gave out.

Sion wasn't far behind.

He cursed softly, gripping her hips tighter, his body trembling against hers as he spilled inside her with a final, breathless thrust.

For a long moment, they didn't move. They just stood there, hearts pounding in time, breaths ragged against the mountain air.

Then, slowly, he let his hand fall from her mouth, brushing a kiss across her cheek before pulling her back against him.

Thess closed her eyes for a second, letting herself feel less alone.

The kind of touch that didn't ask her to be anything more than what she already was.

"I thought this was just because you were bored," he murmured against her hair.

She chuckled, breathless. "Maybe I was. Maybe I'm just glad it was you and not some hairy monster in the cave."

His arms tightened for half a beat. "If you're ever bored again, you know where to find me."

"Oh, I will," she said with a smirk, adjusting her cloak.

They walked quietly back toward camp. No strings, no regrets.

But even as she lay back down and pulled her blanket over her again, Thess didn't sleep right away.

It didn't mean anything.

They were just two warriors looking for ways to release the tension.

But the ache in her chest said otherwise.

Twenty-Nine

"Inheritance"

~ Kael ~

They awoke the next morning feeling hopeful. They made it through the first half of the mountain, how hard could the second half be?

He shouldn't have even questioned it.

The path down the far side of the mountain was steeper than the climb had been, the rocks sharper, the ledges narrower. Gravel shifted beneath Kael's boots with every step, a quiet warning that the mountain would not suffer carelessness. The air was colder now, thinner, and charged with something he couldn't name.

He kept Aislen just ahead of him, close enough to reach if she slipped. Her braid swayed with each step, and he caught glimpses of the curve of her cheek as she turned to glance back at Thess and Sion, who bickered quietly behind them.

At first, it was subtle.

The wind shifted. A strange hush fell across the ridge, as if the mountain itself was listening.

Kael paused mid-step.

The clouds that had drifted lazily overhead just hours ago were now churning. Thick, dark, unnaturally fast. They gathered over the valley

234

below like a beast curling in on itself, swallowing the sun one greedy mouthful at a time.

He glanced up. "Something's wrong."

Aislen turned toward him. "What do you mean?"

"The sky." His voice was low. "It wasn't like this before. Not this fast."

Sion reached his side and squinted upward. "Storm's coming. But that's not just weather."

"It's magic," Maera said from a few feet up the path. Her hand hovered near the dagger at her belt, fingers twitching.

Kael's gut twisted. The energy in the air was unmistakable. It was like standing beneath a lightning storm that hadn't struck yet. And still, they had no shelter. Just jagged cliffs, narrow switchbacks, and a trail that looked increasingly unforgiving.

Behind him, Fenric spoke for the first time in hours. "We need to move. Fast."

Kael bristled at his tone, but said nothing. Not yet.

Aislen's brow furrowed as she stepped toward him. "Do you think it's another trap?"

"I don't know." His hand found hers, briefly. "But we're exposed out here. We keep moving until we find cover."

Lightning split the clouds above, but no thunder followed.

The sound was swallowed whole.

The first drops came like warning shots. They felt like sharp, cold slashes against their skin.

The wind howled, bending even the brittle alpine shrubs flat to the ground. It ripped at their cloaks, whipped loose hair into eyes, and turned the narrow path into a gauntlet. The storm chased them like a predator, fast and too deliberate to be natural.

"Down this way!" Maera called over the roar, pointing toward a jagged break in the stone off the main trail.

Kael followed her lead, guiding Aislen behind him, their boots sliding on wet gravel. Sion had Thess by the arm, practically dragging her across a patch of slick, crumbling earth. Both fathers were at the rear, scanning the storm's edge like they expected something, or someone, to step out of it.

They rounded a bend—and there it was.

Half-buried in stone and shadow, the remnants of a once-great structure jutted from the mountainside like the bones of a long-dead god. Ancient stone archways, shattered columns, moss-cloaked staircases leading nowhere. The carved edges were worn with age, some blackened as if touched by fire long ago.

The air carried the scent of moss and scorched stone, like rain on old ash, with a trace of something unexpected. It was sweet and ancient, like starlilies blooming in a forgotten tomb.

"What the hell is this place?" Aislen whispered as they ducked under what remained of a roof held up by two splintered support beams.

Kael didn't answer. He couldn't. The magic that clung to these stones was faint, but old, older than anything he had ever felt. It hummed underfoot, low and broken, like the memory of something sacred.

Sion was already scanning the area for weaknesses. "There's enough cover here to wait out the worst of it."

"If it holds," Tomas muttered, glancing upward at the cracked ceiling above them. "This place is ancient."

A burst of wind drove rain in sideways, forcing them deeper into the shadowed remains. The walls were crumbling, but still standing. The stone was carved in places. It held barely legible patterns and figures etched into the damp surface, obscured by grime and time.

Kael brushed his fingers over one of the walls, trailing across the faint lines of a mural. He froze.

"Aislen."

She turned, still catching her breath. He stepped aside so she could see.

Even diminished over time, the image was unmistakable.

A fae with pale, radiant eyes. She had starlight pouring from her hands, cloaked in vines and crowned in moonlight. She stood before all of the courts. Between them, a ravine split the land.

A war was brewing in the mural's strokes. But the center, the figure of the female, was what drew the eye.

Aislen's breath hitched.

"It's me," she whispered. "Or... it's someone like me."

Kael's voice was quiet. "This is the Celestara Court's history."

"What's left of it," Fenric said, suddenly beside them. "Burned. Buried. Forgotten for a reason. We must be getting close if we are finding their old ruins."

Kael shot him a look. "Or hidden."

"The Celestara Court was vast, we are still no closer than we were yesterday, Fenric. The mountain itself used to be a trading post between the Courts. Before they were all divided. This must have been all that was left," Maera said quietly as she bowed her head in a silent prayer.

Another crack of lightning split the sky behind them. The storm screamed outside the broken archways.

Inside the ruins, the silence was heavier.

Rain tapped against the fractured stone overhead, a steady rhythm as Kael crouched beside the small fire. The flames danced in low, flickering light, casting shifting shadows against the hollowed ruin walls. Aislen had excused herself a moment ago, whispering something about feminine duties. Kael watched her move deeper into the ruins, following her scent. The others were still quiet. They were eating, checking gear, murmuring in pairs, but soon Kael's eyes tracked one figure specifically.

His father.

Fenric sat a little apart, back braced against a moss-draped pillar, sharpening a blade that didn't need sharpening. His movements were slow. Measured. Calculated. Like always.

Kael stood, brushing his hands on his cloak, and crossed the distance in a few strides.

"We need to talk," he said quietly.

Fenric didn't look up. "We're talking."

"Not like this." Kael folded his arms. "What happened in the Vanor, what you said about Aislen... it's bothering me. Why did you say that? I thought you loved Aislen. She is just as much as part of our family as I am, and that was before I knew she was my mate."

Fenric paused in his sharpening. "You want me to lie? Tell you there's nothing to worry about? Things have changed, son."

"No. I want you to tell me the truth." Kael's voice was low, tight. "Not riddles. Not warnings without answers. What is it you're not saying? What has changed, father?"

A beat of silence stretched between them.

Kael knelt across from him, closer now. "You've always been a hard man, but you were never cryptic. Not like this."

Fenric met his eyes, and there was something unreadable in the lines around his mouth. Ignoring his questions, he finally gave his son a response, "Because this is bigger than you, Kael."

Kael's jaw tensed. "Then make me understand."

"You think I don't want what's best for you? For our family?" Fenric's voice was still quiet, but laced with something more intense now. "But sometimes what's best comes with hard choices. You can't save everyone, Kael."

"You're talking in circles."

"I'm talking like a male who's seen too many mistakes made for love," Fenric replied, gaze sharpening. "And I'm watching my son walk the same path."

Kael leaned in slightly, tone dark. "Then tell me, what mistakes are we walking toward? What do you know about the Celestara Court that you're not saying?" Kael paused, "Was my mother a mistake? Your mate? I have witnessed you stand by her side time and time again."

Fenric's mouth tightened. Only answering one of his son's questions, he said, "I know it was forgotten on purpose. And maybe it should've stayed that way."

"That's not an answer."

"It's the only one I'll give."

Kael's heart pounded harder. He could feel his magic stirring beneath his skin.

"You're hiding something. Something big. I can feel it every time you look at her." He took a breath. "Are you planning something? I need to know because if you are, you need to know that my choice will be her. It will always be her."

That did it.

For the first time, Fenric's eyes flared. "Be very careful with your words, son."

"Why? Because it's the truth?"

Fenric stood slowly, towering even in the flickering firelight. His voice dropped to a low, warning rumble. "There are truths you aren't ready for. Not yet. And if you love her the way you say you do, if she's truly your mate, you'll trust me when I say some doors don't need to be opened."

Kael stood too, fists clenched at his sides.

"I'm not a child anymore. And this isn't just about me. You're not just my father now. You're a male with secrets in a world that's burning and she's the one who keeps me from going up in flames."

Fenric didn't blink. "Then hold tight to her. But don't be so naive as to think the fire won't come for you anyway."

They stood there for a long moment, rain still pattering softly on stone, the fire snapping low between them.

Kael finally turned away, his jaw set.

He didn't have answers. Not yet.

But his father was lying, maybe not with his words, but with everything else.

* * *

~ **Aislen** ~

The others were settling in. They were laying out cloaks, checking gear, and lighting a careful fire where the wind couldn't reach. But Aislen excused herself and drifted toward the far side of the ruins, drawn by something deeper than curiosity.

The storm still raged beyond the fractured walls, a silver fury blurred by rain and shadow. But in here, beneath the broken ribs of some ancient structure, the silence felt sacred. Not peaceful—no, it hummed with expectation. Like the stones were holding their breath, waiting for her.

She stepped over a fallen arch, careful not to disturb the fragile remains. Vines curled around shattered columns. Ferns and moss had crept into the cracks. But further down the narrow corridor, the air felt warmer, still charged. Less touched by time.

And then she saw it.

Half-concealed beneath soot and vines, a mural stretched along the curved inner wall of a broken rotunda. What remained was fragmented with chunks missing and whole faces erased, but it pulsed with something familiar.

She stepped closer, brushing a hand over the moss to reveal faint strokes of white and silver pigment. A line of stars traced a female's brow. A pattern of light spilled from her hands into the earth. A shape behind her held a crescent throne, carved in stone and shadow.

Aislen stared.

It wasn't her. Not exactly. But it could have been. The shape of the figure. The arch of her brow. The curve of her cheek. And the way the figure stood... not commanding, but present. Whole.

"Gods," she whispered.

Because this was once connected to the Celestara Court. Or what was left of it.

And she was, by bloodline, the daughter of its king.

A princess.

The thought made her stomach twist.

She sank slowly onto a chunk of broken stone, gaze still fixed on the mural. Water dripped steadily nearby from a crack in the ceiling, echoing like a ticking clock in the hollow space.

She hadn't said it aloud. Not to Kael. Not even to her mom. But the truth settled heavier with every passing day.

She was a princess to a Court no one remembered. A Court no one wanted to remember.

A Court swallowed by time and war and silence. A Court where the king had once loved her mom and lost her. A Court that is hopefully still be watching. Waiting.

Would they recognize her?

Would they care?

She didn't feel like royalty. She felt like a female who bled and broke and laughed too loud. She felt like someone made of soil and starlight, but unsure where either ended and she began.

And what terrified her most, what made her chest ache in a way she couldn't name, was the fear that being a princess would mean she had to stop being Aislen.

Would she still be allowed to grow wildflowers in cracked teacups? To race Kael through the trees? To cry when the world felt too heavy and still be strong the next morning?

Would they expect her to be a weapon? A symbol? A perfect, polished reflection of power?

She wasn't that. She didn't want to be.

But maybe, just maybe, she could be something else entirely.

Something new.

Her fingers traced the edge of the painted figure's hand, where vines curled into stars. Earth and sky, bound as one.

A strange sense of calm bloomed in her chest.

"I'm not her," Aislen murmured. "But maybe I'm not just me anymore either."

The storm growled above them, distant thunder rolling through the stone.

She took a steadying breath and stood.

Whatever waited at the Celestara Court, whoever she was supposed to become, she'd meet it head-on. As herself. Not some perfect heir. Not some weapon of prophecy.

Just Aislen.

And she hoped that would be enough.

As Aislen walked back, she could hear the rain finally letting up. Not a lot, but enough to finally make out the voices on the other side of the ruins.

She could hear Kael's voice, not his words, just the deep timbre of his voice. That alone brought her comfort she didn't know she needed.

After hearing his voice, she'd meant to head straight to Kael, to tell him what she'd seen. The beautifully tragic fragments of stars and thrones and something that looked hauntingly like a crown carved into stone, but the images still swirled too loud in her chest. She wasn't ready to say them aloud yet.

Instead, her eyes sought out her mom.

Maera stood just beyond the flickering firelight, her cloak drawn tight against the cold, speaking softly to Tomas and checking the packs for damage. Her movements were practiced, steady. Almost regal.

Aislen saw a glimpse of the leader her mom could have been. If it wasn't for her and this damn prophecy.

"Mom," Aislen said, her voice softer than she intended.

Maera turned immediately, eyes searching hers.

"Can we... walk? Just us?"

Maera didn't hesitate. She gave Tomas a small nod and followed Aislen without a word, slipping between the shattered arches and crumbling walls like someone returning to a long-lost place.

They didn't speak as Aislen led her deeper, through vines and rain-slick moss, to where the remnants of the mural waited. The broken pieces of forgotten grandeur. A history the wind had nearly erased.

Maera stepped closer to one of the walls, her fingertips brushing a jagged edge of painted stone. Stars shimmered faintly beneath her touch. They were long ago faded, but still somehow present. Still waiting.

Aislen watched her mom take it all in, the tension in her shoulders drawing taut. Maera didn't speak either. Not at first. She just stared at the mural as if it might move, as if the past might unspool itself all over again.

Finally, Aislen broke the silence.

"Is this what you were trying to keep from me?"

Maera didn't answer, but her eyes closed briefly.

Aislen pressed on. "Was this the life you walked away from?"

Maera turned to face her, and in her gaze was something Aislen hadn't seen before. Not fear. Not guilt. But grief.

Aislen's breath caught. She hadn't expected that.

"Am I supposed to stay here?" she asked, her voice cracking now. "Is that what all this has been leading to?"

Maera frowned, eyes narrowing slightly. "Stay?"

"In the Celestara Court," Aislen whispered. "As a... princess?"

The word tasted foreign on her tongue. It sounded ridiculous. Absurd. But also terrifying.

Aislen stepped back from the wall, heart pounding. "Because I can't. I won't. I don't want this. I thought I could try, but I didn't ask for it. I'm not meant to sit on a throne or wear something heavy and jeweled and pretend to rule over anyone."

Her hands trembled as she wiped them against her cloak. "I don't want to be anyone's symbol. I don't want to be the hope of a dying Court. I want to be Aislen. I want a life that is mine mom."

Maera crossed the distance between them and cupped her daughter's face in both hands, thumbs brushing the dampness beneath her eyes.

"You don't have to be anything you're not," she said gently. "I didn't run from the Court to trap you into returning to it."

"Then why does it feel like the mountain is pushing me there anyway?" Aislen whispered.

Maera's voice was soft, but firm. "Because you are powerful, and good, and you care so deeply. That alone makes you dangerous to people who only know how to hoard power."

Aislen closed her eyes, her mom's touch grounding her as the wind shifted around them.

"I don't know what's coming," Maera admitted. "But I do know this: you are not your father. You are not his Court. You are not anyone's heir unless you choose to be."

Aislen opened her eyes slowly.

"You are mine," Maera whispered, her forehead resting against her daughter's now. "You are starlight, yes, but also earth and wildflowers and courage. If this place asks something of you, you get to decide what answer you give."

Aislen swallowed hard and leaned into her mother's embrace.

The ruins whispered around them.

And in the echo of stone and stars, Aislen wasn't sure what answer she'd give yet.

But she knew she wouldn't be forced into becoming anything she didn't recognize.

Thirty

"Taken"

⚜

~ Aislen ~

The descent was quieter than the climb, eerily so.

Where once there had been breathless laughter, soft conversation, and the occasional sarcastic quip to break the monotony, now there was only the steady crunch of boots on gravel and the low rustle of leaves above. It wasn't silence, exactly, it was a hush. The kind that pressed into your ears and settled along your spine, too heavy for mere quiet. As though the mountain itself was listening. Waiting.

They had been walking for nearly a full day since leaving the shelter of the ruins behind. Every step down the far side of the range seemed to carry them deeper into something unnatural. Once they were a little more than halfway down, they came across a forest.

The forest that met them wasn't wild in the usual way. It was… watchful. Similar to the Veiled Vanor in a way.

The canopy overhead grew thicker with each mile, trees twisting into unfamiliar shapes, their trunks wide and gnarled, bark split like old scars. Moss hung from the branches like limp fingers, and the deeper they walked, the darker it became. Even though the sun had yet to set.

The light that filtered through the trees was cold. Tinged with gray and green. It bent unnaturally, pooling in places it shouldn't, vanishing entirely in others. Every shadow seemed too deep. Every branch too still.

Kael moved near the front, eyes constantly scanning. The tension in his shoulders hadn't eased since morning, and his hand kept twitching toward the hilt of his sword with each stray gust of wind. Aislen stayed at his side, her senses on high alert. Every now and then, her fingers would brush against her own blade, or hover just slightly above it in the air, feeling something no one else could.

Sion and Thess followed close behind, unusually quiet. Even Thess's usual irreverent commentary had dulled to wary muttering. Her eyes darted constantly between the path and the surrounding trees, and she kept one hand on the dagger at her hip like it was a promise she might need to cash in at any moment.

"I don't like this," she finally whispered under her breath.

Sion grunted. "That makes two of us."

Maera and Tomas walked just behind them, eyes sharp and weapons visible. Fenric brought up the rear, more stoic than the rest, though his gaze scanned the trees like a predator hunting something it couldn't yet name.

It wasn't just the quiet. Or the unnatural light. It was the air itself.

It felt *old.*

Too old. Like it had been sealed away and forgotten for centuries, only now disturbed by the careless presence of intruders. It pressed against their skin with a clammy sort of weight, thick with damp earth, mildew, and something else... something metallic. Like rust. Or blood.

The birds had gone silent hours ago.

Even the insects were missing. No buzz, no hum. Nothing but the steady, distant dripping of water and the muted snap of their boots breaking twigs beneath the mulch. Time felt strange here. Like the sun had decided not to bother keeping track anymore.

The trail narrowed as they went on. Trees pressed closer. Vines crawled over the rocks like veins, pulsing faintly with some unseen rhythm. Even the stone beneath their feet seemed different now. It was slicker and worn smooth in places where no water had flowed in years.

Then, the symbols began to appear.

At first, they were subtle. A spiral here. A crude shape etched into a branch. But then they became more frequent and obvious. They were burned into bark, chiseled into stone, half-erased by time but still present enough to chill the blood.

They weren't a language. Not exactly.

Just teeth. Claws. Eyes. Shapes that didn't belong in any natural order.

Kael touched one gently with his fingers, his brow furrowing. "These are warnings."

"Or rituals," Maera said grimly.

Sion muttered, "Well that's comforting."

Thess elbowed him. "Shut up."

They pushed forward.

No one wanted to be the one to suggest turning back. There was nowhere else to go, and going back through the mountains meant revisiting the cave they'd barely survived. So they continued, deeper into the thickening woods, each step laced with the quiet understanding that something unseen was watching.

And *waiting*.

At one point, Tomas paused and tilted his head toward the trees. "Did anyone else hear that?"

They froze.

No footsteps. No breathing. Just silence.

Kael scanned the trees, hand tightening around his blade. "What did it sound like?"

"Breathing," Tomas replied slowly. "But not ours."

They needed to pick up their pace.

Aislen glanced at her dad and noticed a limp as he moved.

She tucked that away for later. As soon as they made it through whatever this was, she was going to ask him about it.

Now it was time to move.

Not running, not yet at least. But they were walking faster, shoulders taut, eyes scanning the trees and shadows with sharpened urgency.

By the time the sun began to set, though it was nearly impossible to tell through the suffocating canopy, they had not stopped even once to rest. It wasn't until the shadows stretched long enough to blur the path entirely that they agreed, reluctantly, to pause.

Just for a moment.

To breathe.

To listen.

And that's when Aislen felt it.

* * *

The path twisted downward like a ribbon unraveling from the sky, slick with melting frost and scattered stone. Each step was a careful negotiation between balance and momentum, and the air carried a weight that pressed against Aislen's skin. It was not just from the altitude, but something else.

It was subtle at first. A prickle at the edge of her thoughts. Like a whisper just beyond hearing.

She paused mid-step, her boot crunching against loose shale. The others kept walking, their movements steady and focused, but Aislen stood still. Her eyes drifted to the trees that clung stubbornly to the cliffside. Those ones were crooked, silver-barked, and their leaves darker than any she'd seen below the mountain. Their branches curled inward, as though listening too.

She placed a hand against one of the larger stones lining the path, and the moment her fingers met the cold surface, something stirred beneath it.

A hum.

Not sound. Not really.

It vibrated through her bones like memory. It was ancient and low and pulsing, like a heartbeat buried in the earth.

Her breath caught in her throat.

She stepped back quickly, heart racing. But the magic didn't follow, it stayed, rooted in the stone, in the earth beneath her feet.

The wind shifted, carrying with it a strange scent. It was a mixture of damp moss, scorched minerals, and something older, like the first fire ever burned. It filled her lungs and made her skin tingle with awareness.

"Do you feel that?" she asked suddenly, turning toward the others.

Kael looked up from where he was adjusting a strap on Sion's pack. "Feel what?"

"The magic." Her voice was low, urgent. "It's... it's everywhere. In the stones. In the air. Like it's waiting."

Kael straightened fully now, frowning. "I feel something. Barely. Like... pressure in the back of my mind."

"It's more than that," Aislen said, her hand now hovering near the rocks again. "It's... speaking to me. Not in words exactly, but my magic understands it. Like it knows the language."

The others had stopped, watching now.

Maera was the first to respond. "Magic this old can leave traces. Echoes."

"But it's not just echoes," Aislen insisted. "It's aware."

Sion rubbed the back of his neck, visibly unnerved. "I don't feel anything."

"Neither do I," Fenric added, casting a wary glance up the path behind them. "Whatever it is, it's clearly tuned to her."

Tomas crossed his arms, his brow furrowed. "Could it be from the mountain itself? You said the Veiled Vanor had its own kind of sentience."

"This feels different," Aislen whispered. "More direct. Like it's searching for something. Or someone."

Kael stepped toward her slowly. "And your magic... understands it?"

She nodded, unable to look away from the earth beneath her feet. "Yes. It's like I'm remembering something I never knew. Like my power recognizes it, and it's trying to answer."

For a moment, no one spoke. The silence wasn't empty as it pressed in from every side.

Kael reached out, fingers gently brushing hers. "Then whatever this is... you're not alone in it. I think I can feel the edge of it too. Not clearly, but enough to know you're not imagining it."

Their magic pulsed faintly between them where their skin met, a soft glimmer that only they could sense.

Aislen's shoulders dropped slightly, tension bleeding out at his touch. But even with his comfort, the pull of the mountain's magic remained.

It was still there. Whispering, calling, waiting.

Whatever it was, it had found her.

Soon, the mountain air shifted.

What had once been crisp and cold was now thick with something heavier. It was damp and clinging to their skin, like a warm breath held too long. Aislen felt it first in her chest, the same way she sensed an oncoming storm or a spell about to break. Her magic stirred beneath her skin, uneasy and twitching like it too could feel the change in the wind.

They had been walking for hours, muscles aching, silence blanketing the group heavier than snow. No one had spoken much since the ancient ruins. Whatever peace they'd gained there had faded quickly as the descent grew more treacherous.

Aislen glanced up from the path just as a shiver rolled down her spine. Ahead, the mountain dipped into a narrow pass choked with jagged rocks and frost-burned moss. But it wasn't the terrain that made her pause.

It was the fog.

At first, it was little more than a thin veil creeping between the trees. But within seconds, it surged forward—too fast, too thick. A swirling wall of white that looked like it swallowed stone and sound alike.

"Kael—" she started, reaching out.

He was already at her side, sword halfway drawn, his eyes narrowing at the sudden change.

"Stay close," he warned, voice low.

Then the fog consumed them.

It wasn't just fog. It felt *alive* as it twisted between their legs, curled up their backs, and whispered against their skin like silk soaked in magic. It was colder than it should've been. Colder than the wind, colder than the snow, and it carried a scent Aislen couldn't name: damp stone, old blood, and something older still. It was like forgotten spells clinging to the bone, but not quite.

They kept moving, slower now, trying not to lose sight of one another. She could hear Sion muttering behind her, his voice strained. "This isn't normal. Something's wrong."

"No shit," Thess muttered beside him.

And then—

Silence.

Not just quiet, but *absence*. No footsteps. No rustle of gear. No voice.

Aislen froze, heart pounding. "Thess?"

No answer.

"Sion?" Her voice sharpened.

"I'm here," he replied quickly from somewhere to her left.

"Kael? Mom? Someone else answer me please," Aislen was beginning to sound frantic. Her senses felt cut off, she couldn't see anything.

"I'm here sweetheart, I have your dad and Fenric with me," she could hear her mom somewhere in front of her. Her tone sounded just as worried as she was.

She felt someone touch her shoulder. Startled, she turned around only to feel the warmth of Kael's hand, "I'm here too. I've got you," he whispered.

Her relief only lasted seconds. Only one person hadn't responded.

Thess.

Aislen turned in a slow, frantic circle, mist clawing at her cloak.

"Thess!" she shouted, louder now.

Nothing.

Kael's hand gripped her elbow. "We have to stay calm—"

"She was *right here*," Aislen snapped, wrenching free and stumbling forward further into the fog. "She was just—she was—" Her voice cracked.

Aislen began to run.

"THESS ANSWER ME RIGHT NOW!" She yelled as she ran. She could hear the sound of boots chasing her. In the moment, it didn't matter who it was as long as she found the person she was looking for. "THESS!!"

Moments later, the fog began to thin. She was in a clearing somewhere.

Aislen frantically turned around in a circle looking for her friend. Within seconds, both Kael and her dad appeared, they had followed her into the fog.

As quickly as it had come, the fog began to peel back in strips, torn by the wind and fading light.

Desperately, with some sight regained, she began running back in the direction they came. Soon, she could see her mom and the others. Their backs were facing her and they were all looking down at something.

Once she got there, she pushed through their bodies to see what they were looking at, hoping to the gods there wasn't a body lying there.

Her heart shattered.

There wasn't a body there. It was even worse.

There, where Thess had stood, her pack lay on the stone.

Untouched. Unscorched. Just... left.

Aislen stared at it like it might vanish too.

"No," she whispered, rushing forward. She dropped to her knees, fingers trembling as she touched the familiar stitching on the side. Thess's work. A threadbare patch she'd sewn on herself in the shape of a crooked star.

"No, no, no."

Her breath hitched as her fingers clenched the fabric. "She was just here. I should've felt something. I should've known—"

Her voice cracked. "I didn't feel it coming. I didn't even sense the danger, I should have."

Kael crouched beside her, reaching for her shoulder.

"Aislen." His voice was steady but soft. "Don't. Don't go there. This wasn't your fault. None of us sensed it. We couldn't have stopped it."

Behind her, Sion's breath was ragged.

"She wouldn't—she wouldn't just leave it," he said, voice too tight, too raw.

Kael crouched beside them, scanning the surrounding slope, every muscle tight.

"She didn't leave," Aislen said, her voice shaking. "She wouldn't leave us. Something had to have taken her."

A heartbeat passed.

Then Sion's fist slammed into the stone, hard enough to split his knuckles. "Gods—"

Kael grabbed his shoulder, steadying him, but it was Aislen who met Sion's eyes.

"There's no blood," she said quickly, hope clawing through the fear. "No signs of a fight. Just fog and... and *silence*. That means she's alive. She has to be... right?"

Sion didn't respond at first. He stood slowly, shoulders rising and falling in sharp, jagged breaths. Then he nodded once, barely.

Aislen stood too. Her fingers were numb, but not from the cold.

From the *wrongness*.

From the ache in her bones that told her this mountain, this forest, wasn't done with them yet.

"We're going to find her," she said softly.

We have to, she thought.

* * *

~ Sion ~

Sion stood just outside the thinning fog, jaw tight, arms crossed against his chest like a dam holding back something more dangerous than the storm.

The pack lay where it had fallen. Still. Innocent. Too quiet.

He hadn't picked it up. Couldn't. Not yet.

Aislen's face was pale, voice cracking each time she spoke. Kael had already begun checking the area, marking footprints, confirming what they already knew. There were no tracks beyond theirs. Nothing to show *where* she'd gone.

Just the damn fog. Here, then gone. And Thess with it.

Sion scrubbed a hand down his face, fingers pressing hard into his eyes.

He didn't understand why his chest felt like it was caving in.

She was annoying. She was chaotic. She never shut up and pushed every one of his buttons just to get a reaction.

She was also gone.

And that fact was burrowing into him like a thorn that refused to be ignored.

"She has to be nearby," Maera said, voice even. "Magic like that doesn't just… whisk someone away."

"We don't *know* what kind of magic this is," Tomas replied. "That fog wasn't natural."

"How do you know anything about that fog? You don't, Tomas." Maera snapped. It must have been the stress of everything, because she is usually the most soft-spoken one of them all.

Tomas gave her a weary look, but didn't respond. He walked away as he continued looking for any clues.

"We should split into pairs," Fenric offered. "Fan out. Check the surrounding ridges and forest line."

"No," Kael cut in. "Too dangerous. If something took her, it could still be watching."

"I agree," Aislen said quickly. "We can't lose anyone else."

"But we *have* to move," Fenric argued. "We wait too long, and her trail will be cold."

"There *is* no trail," Tomas snapped from his place a few feet away. "She vanished, remember? We don't even know what direction she—"

"She's not *dead*," Sion growled, louder than he intended.

The group turned toward him. His fists were clenched, breath tight.

He didn't mean to be the center of attention. Gods, he hated it. But the way they were talking, as if they were planning for loss, hedging their bets, it made something crack inside him.

"You all standing around arguing isn't going to bring her back faster," he said, voice low but heated. "So either we *do* something, or we shut up until we have a plan."

A heavy silence followed.

Maera folded her arms, her voice taut. "Whatever that fog was, it didn't take me. And I was nearest her."

Fenric tilted his head slightly. "Maybe it didn't take you because of your bloodline. Your connection to the Celestara Court."

A beat of silence followed.

Aislen looked at the pack, brows drawn. "But Thess... she's the only one of us without a magical tie. No bond. No Court."

Sion's voice was low. "You're saying it went for the easiest target."

Kael's jaw tensed. "Or the most vulnerable."

The idea left a chill in its wake, more biting than the fog ever had.

Fenric moved a few paces back from the group, arms crossed, watching the trees like he was no longer fully with them. Like his mind was already somewhere further down the path.

He saw Kael glance at his father before speaking again.

"We'll search," Kael said at last. "Together. No one alone. We stick to the path as best we can, branch out in short sweeps. We mark our trail."

Sion exhaled through his nose, nodding.

Good. That was good.

Except it wasn't.

It wasn't fast enough.

* * *

They started moving.

Slow. Deliberate. Silent.

The pack was now strapped to his back, heavy with her scent, her energy—chaotic and warm and impossible to ignore.

He wasn't letting it go.

As they crept along the edge of the trees, eyes scanning for signs of a trail that didn't exist, something tugged at the back of his mind. A flicker. A flicker of her.

A memory.

She'd been sitting on a fallen log near the stream one afternoon, absently braiding wildflowers into her boot laces, humming some off-key tune she claimed was "probably from a dream."

He'd walked by, fully prepared to ignore her until she tossed a daisy at his face.

"You know you're a little scary when you brood too long," she'd said without looking up. "Makes people think you're scheming instead of sulking."

"I'm not sulking either."

"Sure you're not. That's why your eyebrows are fighting again."

He'd blinked. "Fighting?"

Thess had finally looked up at him, grin wide and wicked. "Left one's clearly winning."

And gods help him, he'd laughed. Just once. Just enough that she blinked in surprise, like she hadn't expected it to actually work.

Then she tossed another flower at him. "Don't worry. I won't tell anyone you're soft."

Now, in the still-dark woods, his lips twitched involuntarily.

He hated her for that. For worming into places she had no business reaching.

For not being here.

Aislen slowed up ahead, waving them to pause.

The fog had lifted completely, but the woods were unnaturally quiet. No birds. No rustle of leaves. Just the distant wind high in the cliffs above.

"I don't like this," she murmured, glancing to Kael.

"Me neither," he said. "But we keep moving. She's out here. Somewhere."

Sion didn't say a word.

He just tightened the straps of her pack against his shoulders and kept walking, every step a silent promise—

You better still be alive, Trouble.

~ Thess ~

Darkness pressed in on all sides.

It was thick, alive somehow, like the air itself had weight. Like it breathed without her. Damp and suffocating, it clung to her skin like wet cloth. The scent was what hit her hardest. Rot and mildew. Old blood and older death.

She wasn't in the woods anymore.

Her hands trembled as she reached out blindly, fingertips brushing something stone-cold and slimy. It was too smooth for rock, too curved. She recoiled, heart thundering in her ears.

A scraping sound echoed in the distance.

She stilled. Waited.

Nothing.

Just silence.

It was wrong. Everything was wrong.

She didn't know how she got here. One second they were walking, the fog creeping in like it had a mind of its own and then... nothing.

No light. No voices. No trail.

Just this nightmare.

She hugged her arms to her chest, crouching low against a wall she couldn't see, trying to slow her breathing. A single tear carved down her cheek as her voice cracked into the emptiness.

"Someone..."

She swallowed hard.

"Please... someone help me."

Her whisper vanished into the dark and the dark, it seemed, had already made it's choice.

Thirty-One

"Fallout"

~ Sion ~

They didn't move for a long time.

The air still shimmered faintly with the ghost of the magic that had taken her, the fog having retreated as if smug with its prize. No one spoke. No one dared to.

They had searched for hours after Thess vanished. They called her name until their voices were hoarse, combed the rocky edges of the path and peered into every crevice. Her pack was still strapped tightly to his back, a cruel reminder that she had been there only moments before.

Now, the group sat in the dim mountain light, gathered near a low outcrop of stone where they'd paused to rest. But rest didn't come easily. Not when one of their own was missing.

"We can't stay here forever," Fenric said at last, his voice gruff, hollowed out like the caves they'd come from. "She's gone. She'll find her way out eventually. We need to keep moving."

Aislen's head snapped up. "You think we should just leave her?"

"She's resourceful," Fenric said with a shrug, not meeting anyone's eyes. "Wasting daylight helps no one."

Sion stood.

Not suddenly, not with a shout, but slowly. It was like the fury was building in his bones with each second Fenric's mouth stayed open.

"You've had a lot to say lately about who we leave behind," Sion said, his voice low. "And a whole lot less to say about what the hell is wrong with you."

Fenric glanced at him. "Careful."

"No," Sion growled. "You don't get to say that. Not when one of us is missing and you're acting like it's an inconvenience. Like she was just... excess weight."

Kael tensed at Sion's side, but didn't speak. His eyes locked on his father, unreadable.

Sion stepped closer, the air between them tightening like a drawn bowstring.

"Why don't you want to find her?" he asked, voice hard. "What's really going on with you? And what happened between you and Kael? You've been treating him like he's a burden, your own son, and we've all been too polite to say anything."

Fenric's expression didn't change, but his posture did. His shoulders straighter, stance rigid. "You know nothing about my family."

"I know enough," Sion snapped, fists clenched. "I know you're hiding something. I know your son is twice the man you'll ever be. And I know Thess matters. She matters to all of us. If you can't see that—"

Fenric shoved him.

It was sudden and brutal and broke the tension like glass shattering on stone.

Sion staggered back, but recovered fast, lunging. Their fists collided with the sickening crack of rage long held in. The others shouted, scrambling to intervene, but it was too late. The fight had begun.

Kael moved first, seizing Fenric's arm and yanking him back. Aislen and Tomas rushed to pull Sion away, who was bleeding from the lip but still snarling like a feral wolf.

"Enough!" Maera's voice cut through the chaos like a blade. "We are falling apart, and that is *exactly* what whatever took Thess wants!"

Everyone froze. They were caught in surprise at yet another outburst from Maera.

The tension was high.

Sion's chest heaved, fury and grief warring behind his eyes. Fenric shook Kael off with a cold glare, lips pressed tight.

A silence fell, raw and exposed.

And Thess wasn't there to crack a joke and lighten the mood.

Not now.

* * *

~ Kael ~

The sun was beginning to dip, a haze of gold brushing the jagged rocks as twilight crept up the mountainside. It should've been beautiful.

But Kael couldn't feel anything but the echo of fists and words.

The group had settled a short distance away, murmuring low as they attempted to resume planning. No one mentioned Fenric's name. No one even looked at him. He'd retreated to the edge of the camp, like always. He was close enough to loom, far enough to isolate.

Kael's jaw still ached from gritting it.

Sion sat apart too, legs stretched out, back against a slab of stone. His knuckles were bloodied, his lip split, and one eye already starting to bruise. He was silent as he cleaned his wounds with a piece of cloth and water from his canteen. Efficient. Detached.

Kael approached without a word, dropping into a crouch beside him. Sion didn't look up.

"That was a hell of a punch," Kael said quietly.

"Which one?" Sion muttered, dabbing at his temple. "I lost track."

Kael huffed softly through his nose. "The one that got his shoulder to jolt. He doesn't do that unless he feels it."

Sion gave a dry, bitter smile. "Good. I meant it to hurt."

Silence again. Not awkward. Just... tired.

Kael let it linger a moment before asking, "You alright?"

Sion shrugged, wincing as he pulled at a cut. "Physically? I'll live. But just so you know, your dad is a complete dick."

"I feel like I don't even know who he is anymore. It's like he's a different person out here," Kael admitted.

Emotion flickered behind his eyes. Guarded, but not invisible.

Kael leaned back onto his heels. The air smelled faintly of smoke and damp stone. The kind of scent that lingered long after the fire died.

"But I didn't know he'd get under your skin that much," Kael said, voice low.

"I didn't either," Sion replied, finally glancing his way. "But it's like... something about him just grates. Like he's constantly sizing us up and finding us lacking."

Kael didn't answer right away. That wasn't entirely wrong.

"I think he's scared," Kael said after a beat. "And too proud to admit it."

"He's something, alright," Sion muttered, tossing the bloodied cloth aside. "I'm just trying to understand why he's acting like she doesn't matter."

"She does," Kael said. "To all of us."

Sion nodded, jaw tight. His voice was rougher when he asked, "You think we'll find her?"

"I don't know," Kael admitted. "But I know we'll never stop trying."

The words landed like a vow.

Sion looked away again, toward the cliffs where the fog had first rolled in, where Thess' laughter had last echoed.

"She's tough," Kael added, more gently now. "If anyone can make it back to us... it's her."

Sion's throat bobbed. He didn't speak. But his hand clenched where it rested on his knee.

The quiet between him and Sion settled into something almost steady, if still tense. Like a cracked shield holding together by sheer will.

Then soft footsteps crunched over loose rock.

Kael turned.

Aislen approached, her cloak tugged tight around her shoulders, her expression drawn but focused. The wind caught a few strands of her hair, tugging them across her face like the mountain itself didn't want to let her go.

She paused just a step away, eyes flicking from Sion's bruised face to Kael's tensed posture. Her voice was soft but firm when she spoke.

"We can't stay like this."

Sion lifted his head. "No one's planning to."

She exhaled, kneeling beside them. Her eyes shimmered with exhaustion, but beneath that was a spark Kael had come to recognize as reckless determination. It made his stomach twist.

"You have something," he said.

"I might." She glanced at Sion, then back to Kael. "It's probably stupid."

"That's our specialty," Sion muttered.

She offered him a wan smile before continuing. "I've been thinking... that fog wasn't natural. It wasn't just fog, it was targeted magic. Like it knew who to take."

Kael tensed. "You think it's sentient?"

"I think," Aislen said carefully, "that maybe someone used their own magic to create the fog. And that it took her somewhere on purpose. We can't follow it the usual way."

Sion frowned. "So what? You want to yell into the wind and hope it answers?"

She shook her head. "No. I want to use my magic."

Both Kael and Sion stiffened.

Kael's voice was tight. "Aislen—"

"I know it's dangerous," she interrupted. "I know it could lead others to us. But if I'm right about this, they have been tracking us the entire time. I think they want to see where we're going. If they wanted to hurt us, I think they would have before now. Whatever this is, my magic... it hears it. Like it's part of it somehow. I'm not sure if ancient magic could do something like this... but I think it's worth trying to figure out."

Sion looked at her with wide, wary eyes. "What do you want to do? Call to it?"

Aislen's hands trembled slightly as she clasped them together. "Not exactly. But I want to let whatever magic this is, whatever person who is dealing it, to know that I am here. That I know they're here too. Maybe I can follow the thread they left behind."

Kael moved toward her, his voice low but insistent. "Absolutely not. What do we do if they try to take you too?"

She met his gaze squarely. "Then you come find me."

Silence. Sharp. Shaking.

Kael wanted to argue. Gods, he wanted to say no again. No way in hell. But the fire in her eyes stopped him. She wasn't asking for permission. She was telling them she wouldn't sit still while Thess was out there, scared and alone.

Sion sighed, rubbing a hand down his face. "This is insane."

"Probably," Aislen agreed.

Kael finally spoke, quiet but certain. "Then we do it together."

Aislen gave a small, grateful nod.

She looked like a female willing to burn the world for her chosen family. And Kael knew, deep down, that if anyone could find a way through the impossible, through ancient magic and mountains that hungered for secrets, it would be her.

* * *

~ Aislen ~

The fire burned low, casting soft gold against the stone and tired faces that surrounded it. Aislen sat with her arms looped around her knees, her body sore, her mind far away. The flames crackled and popped, the sound almost soothing. Almost. But even in the hush of momentary stillness, everything felt sharp-edged. Off-kilter.

They were supposed to be searching for Thess.

Instead, they were here. Waiting. Resting. Planning.

Bringing her less than sane plan to life.

Tomas sat across from her, the firelight flickering over the creases in his brow as he studied a worn map stretched across a flat stone. Maera was beside him, her arms folded, mouth drawn in a thin line as they traced a path she had once traveled alone. A different time. A different world.

"If the trail hasn't shifted," Tomas murmured, "we're about a week out from the edge of the Starlight Court's outer wards. Maybe less."

Maera didn't respond at first. Her gaze was distant. But then she nodded, slowly.

"Depending on the magic. The terrain was unstable then. It could be worse now."

Their voices faded into a hum around her. Aislen stared into the fire, its amber glow licking at the shadows beyond, and for a moment, she let herself pretend it was just another quiet night at home. That Thess was beside her, cracking jokes. That Kael was sitting so close their knees touched. That her mom wasn't watching her like she was about to disappear.

But none of that was true.

She looked around the fire one last time. At Maera's guarded gaze, at Tomas's tight jaw, at Kael's steady presence. At the absence of Thess' laughter. And the silence inside her finally broke.

She drew in a breath and stood slowly, brushing ash from her palms.

"I think…" she said softly, the words strange on her tongue, "I have another idea. A way to find what took her. Or to at least find something."

All heads turned toward her. The air shifted.

Maera's voice was wary. "Aislen."

"I want to try and find him," Aislen said, meeting her mother's eyes. "My father."

The silence was instant. The fire popped sharply. Tomas stilled.

Aislen's heart thudded once, hard and steady. "You said he came to you in a dream too. He told me… I'd come find him when I was ready. Maybe that means I can dreamwalk too. Maybe I can try."

"You think now is the time?" Maera asked, her voice a low murmur, careful and tight.

"I don't know," Aislen admitted. "But I feel it. Something is changing. I think he might be the only one who knows how to help us, how to help me."

Tomas shifted, his jaw tense. "Isn't dream-travel risky? You've barely scratched the surface of your power. You don't know what waits for you in there."

"I won't be alone."

She turned to Maera fully now. "You'll come with me."

Maera blinked. "Aislen…"

"You know the Court better than anyone. You were there. I am the proof that it meant something. I don't know what yet, but I *know* it does."

A heavy breath escaped her mom's lungs. Her shoulders sagged. She didn't argue, not this time. But Aislen noticed the way her mom's body held hesitation as her fingers tightened on the hem of her cloak.

Kael said nothing, but Aislen felt his presence behind her, solid and steady. The bond between them thrummed faintly at her back like a tide waiting to rise. She could sense his unease.

She glanced over her shoulder at Kael. Their eyes met and a war seemed to fight inside him. With some hesitation, he nodded.

"That settles it. We'll do it tonight." Aislen said, her voice barely more than a whisper.

The group didn't speak. No one needed to.

Aislen turned her gaze upward. The stars above the mountain glittered sharp and endless, like the sky was watching. Waiting.

And for the first time, she let herself hope her father might be, too.

Thirty-Two

"Veil"

~ Aislen ~

Aislen looked around the fire at the faces she trusted most in the world, her hands clenched around her knees and heart pounding with the weight of what she'd just suggested.

"Does anyone even *know* how to do a ritual for dreamwalking?" she asked quietly. "Because I don't. I just— I felt like it was something we could try, but I don't know where to start."

The silence that followed was broken only by the distant chirp of insects and the crackling of the flames. Kael's jaw flexed. "I wish I did," he said. "But I've never... dreamwalking isn't something the Lunaris Court teaches anymore. Not in at least a decade, if not more. It's considered too unstable. Too dangerous."

Of course it was. Everything she needed seemed to be buried in forgotten bloodlines and half-spoken warnings.

But before disappointment could fully settle in her chest, Sion shifted where he sat beside the fire, rubbing the back of his neck. "I might... sort of... know how."

Aislen's brows lifted. "You *might*?"

"I read about it," he said, glancing at her and then away again. "Years ago.

266

It was part of the old northern records. Rites tied to the realm between sleep and memory. I never tried it because, well, I didn't think I'd ever need to."

Maera leaned forward slightly. "But you think you can do it?"

"I think I can guide the ritual, at least," Sion said. "But you'll be the ones crossing over. The dreamworld is drawn to blood and intent. Your bond to the Celestara Court, and hers"—he looked at Maera—"that will be the bridge."

Aislen exhaled slowly, trying to steady the way her heart beat against her ribs. "So we really could do this."

"You could try," Sion confirmed. "But you should know... dreamwalking isn't just memory. It's magic, and it *feeds* on emotion. If you're not careful, it'll show you what you *want* to see instead of what's real."

Kael's hand found her shoulder. "You don't have to do this, Aislen. You've done enough."

"I haven't," she whispered. "We might as well be lost in these mountains, one of our own is missing, and I'm still walking around with magic I barely understand. I need answers. And if I can reach my father, if he has any insight as to what took Thess, I might finally get them."

Maera's expression twisted, torn between fear and something softer. Hope, maybe. Or the ache of old wounds reopening.

"Then let's prepare," she said.

Sion stood, brushing dirt from his palms. "We'll need space. The circle has to be traced by hand, with ashroot dust. Blood will need to be exchanged, but only a drop, between you and your mother. And you'll need a tether. Something to anchor you here."

Kael took the necklace from around inside the pack and offered it to Aislen. "This brought me back to you once. Now it's your turn."

She took it, the smooth moonstone warm against her skin.

The group moved in a quiet rhythm after that, each task carried out with reverence and weight. Sion gathered what herbs and materials he could from their supplies, murmuring protective incantations as he mixed them into the circle. Tomas laid down extra cloaks for warmth. Maera sat beside

Aislen and braided a strip of her hair together with her daughter's, binding them with a slender thread of gold.

"This is the bond I swore I'd never break," Maera whispered. "Even when I ran."

Aislen didn't speak. Her throat was too full, her heart too loud.

When the circle was complete, they knelt across from one another within it. The earth beneath them was soft but solid, the mountains standing sentinel around them.

Sion stepped to the edge of the circle. "Are you ready?"

Aislen met her mom's gaze, and in that moment, she saw not the female who had raised her, but the female who had once led an entire Court.

"Yes," they said in unison.

And the ritual began.

The moment Aislen's eyes fluttered closed inside the circle, the world tilted sideways.

Not in the way it did when she was dizzy or tired, but as if the very *edge* of reality had been pulled away, and something else had slipped into its place.

No sound. No scent. No warmth.

Only blackness.

Here, the laws of the waking world didn't matter. Time was fluid. Distance, meaningless. Emotion shaped everything, even the truth.

She felt the tug of Maera's hand still in hers. Felt her mom's breath catch, just once, before silence swallowed it too. They were both standing on something smooth and cold beneath their bare feet, like glass or polished obsidian stretching endlessly in all directions. It reflected nothing. No stars above. No wind or sky. Just a vast void with a heartbeat of its own.

Aislen turned toward her mom, finding Maera beside her, eyes wide as she scanned the nothingness.

"You alright?" Aislen asked quietly.

Maera nodded once, lips drawn tight. "I'm with you. Wherever this is."

They walked slowly forward, fingers still linked, each step quiet and unreal. The dreamworld moved like a living thing, shifting in texture, in weight, in feeling with every emotion they carried into it.

"Do we... call him?" Aislen asked, voice uncertain.

"I don't think we have to," Maera murmured, slowing. "He already knows you're here."

Aislen barely had time to register that before the void shimmered.

Like a curtain parting across the stars, a silver seam of light split open ahead of them. And through it stepped *him*. He was tall, commanding, his form made of starlight and shadows, hair streaked in silver like constellations, eyes a mirror of her own.

Alarion.

Maera stiffened.

Aislen felt the shift immediately, the rise of old tension between them, a past too big to ignore. Maera's fingers tightened slightly in hers, a tight inhale slipped her lips.

Alarion's gaze moved to Maera first.

"You brought her," he said gently. "Even now, you still walk between duty and love."

"She is my daughter," Maera said, her voice firm. "She is not yours to command. And this is *her* choice."

His eyes softened. "Then let us speak plainly."

He stepped forward, turning to Aislen. "You're growing stronger. I felt it the moment you crossed the veil."

Aislen's throat closed. All the questions she'd prepared were gone. All she could manage was:

"I need your help."

Alarion's expression grew serious. "Tell me."

"It's my best friend, Thess, she was with us near the end of the Hollow Mountains. She was taken. I—" Her voice cracked. "I don't know how to find her."

Alarion's eyes flickered with something like pain. "I feared this. Your magic woke something. Not just in me, but in her."

Maera's breath hitched softly beside her. "You mean the Sun Queen."

"Her? The Sun Queen?" Aislen was confused. "But why?"

269

He nodded. "Virel has creatures, twisted things she calls *pets*. They don't kill, not right away. They ensnare. Lure. She knows what drives you, Aislen. Your empathy. Your loyalty. Thess was taken to pull you away. She's bait, nothing more."

"No," Aislen whispered.

"She's still alive, she would be too valuable to kill right away," he added, "but if you go to her blindly, it will be into Virel's trap."

Aislen trembled. "I don't care about her games, I just want my friend back."

"You must be smarter than that," Maera said gently, stepping closer, pain lacing her voice. "You can't throw yourself blindly into fire just because someone you love is caught in it."

"I'm not leaving Thess!" Aislen snapped.

"You won't," Alarion said calmly. "But you must go with *understanding*. Virel wants to cut you off before you remember who you truly are. Before you become what the Court needs."

Aislen shook her head, voice barely a whisper. "I never asked to be part of this."

Maera turned toward her slowly, eyes filled with sorrow and pride.

"No," she said, "but you were born to it. And now... you have to decide what to do with it."

The silence that followed was heavy.

Alarion stepped forward, his gaze soft. "The way to your friend's prison lies along the path you already walk. There's a place where the wind stills and shadows listen. Trust your instincts, Aislen. And trust those who would bleed for you."

Aislen swallowed hard. "Would you have come here to help me? If you could, I mean."

He reached out, brushing her cheek with a touch of magic and memory. "If the opportunity had not been taken from me, I would have been there as you grew up, my daughter. I will always be watching, even if from a distance."

Then the world began to fracture, the light splintering beneath their feet like glass catching fire.

Maera let go of her daughter's hand as the dream collapsed, the scent of ash and starlight burned away into nothing.

Aislen awoke first, her gasp dragged through dry lungs as if surfacing from a frozen river. For a second, she wasn't sure if she was still dreaming until Kael's hand found hers, solid and trembling.

Her mom followed seconds later, but those seconds stretched like a lifetime in the void. They sat up slowly, as if their bodies were still reorienting themselves. At some point during the ritual, they must have fallen over to their sides. The campfire was flickering around them, Sion leaned forward to steady the circle stones, and Kael was already pulling Aislen into a tight embrace.

* * *

~ Maera ~

Maera did not wake when Aislen did.

She felt it, the moment her daughter slipped from her grasp. A warmth, then a cold ache where her hand had been held. A flash of light as the dream began to crack, as though the stars themselves were splintering beneath her feet.

And yet... Maera stayed.

Or maybe she *couldn't* leave.

Because Alarion stood there, still whole in a world unraveling. His form shimmered like twilight held together by memory and magic. It was unchanged, unreadable, and *undeniably him.*

"You let go," he said softly, not accusing, just observing.

"No," she whispered. "She did."

The void shuddered. The dream was ending. But this moment... this one fragment between breaths and waking... it *held.*

Alarion took a step forward, the floor beneath him fracturing, but he did not fall.

"You stayed longer than I thought you would."

"I didn't plan to," she said, her voice barely audible. "I meant to follow her. I *tried* to."

"But your heart wanted something else."

Maera's chest ached. Not just from the weight of this place but from the sharp, sudden awareness of everything she hadn't allowed herself to feel for almost two decades.

She turned away from him slightly, her arms folding over her stomach like she could shield herself from the truth clawing its way to the surface. "Don't do this."

"I'm not doing anything," Alarion said gently. "You're here, Maera. You stayed. So ask yourself—why?"

The silence between them trembled, fuller than words.

And finally, slowly, Maera turned back to him. Her eyes shimmered. Not with starlight, but with unshed grief.

"I hated you for not trying harder to stop us."

His expression didn't change, but a crack ran through the space beside him.

"I know," he said.

"I *needed* you. Not as a king, not as some figure from prophecy, but as the male who said he loved me."

"And I did," he said, stepping closer now, the dream distorting around him. "I *do*."

Maera closed her eyes for a beat, forcing the tears to stay in. "Then why did you let me go?"

"Because you were afraid. We were both afraid. I wanted what was best for our daughter and at the time, I did not think it was me. You were right, Maera, she stood a better chance at fighting if she was away from me. And now look at her, look at what she has become because we gave her that chance."

He sighed, "I am not ashamed to admit that at the time, I might have been too proud to chase someone who was running away from me. From us. I understand it now, but then my pride won out."

She laughed softly, bitterly. "So that's what we were in the end? A contest of pride?"

"I would not change the choices we made, Alarion. They gave me our daughter and they kept her safe from a prophecy long enough for her to be able to understand it." Her voice lowered, "Now answer my question. In the end, was it just a contest of pride? Did you not want your Court to come to learn that their future queen left them? Because if you must know, the guilt of leaving them has weighed on me every day since," her voice broke. "I just couldn't leave her there, Alarion. I couldn't. She needed someone to protect her, and I did my best. Every single day. I tried to move on. I tried to be happy. I tried."

"Maera," he said. "Look at me. I have made mistakes, we both have. I wanted to leave with you and if it weren't for my duties, this damn curse, I would have. But someone had to keep our people safe in a world where we weren't allowed to exist. I know you needed me, but so did they, Maera. I knew you would keep her safe. We both had our own jobs that night."

His hand lifted, hovering between them but not quite touching. "I watched you leave. I stood at the border of the Court, waiting, hoping you'd turn around. But you didn't. And I didn't stop you. Because I thought maybe that was love too—*letting go.*"

"And it *wasn't*," Maera whispered. "It was fear and pride. From both of us."

The ground beneath her began to fracture faster. Time was slipping. The dream was collapsing.

"I raised our daughter in secret," Maera said, voice tight. "I taught her to fear her own magic. I made her *small,* because I was afraid of what would happen if the Court ever found her. If *you* ever found her."

Alarion's expression cracked. It was not with anger, but with pain.

"I wanted to hate you," she said, voice breaking now. "I wanted to hold onto that anger because it was easier than remembering what it felt like to love you."

She met his gaze fully then. "But I never stopped. I tried. I *swore* I did.

But I never could."

The dream shook violently now, light bursting through the cracks.

"And I have never stopped loving you," Alarion said, his voice low and reverent, "not even for a breath."

She took a step forward, and suddenly the years fell away. The years of silence. The loneliness. The fear. She was no longer the female who had run, she was the female who had once *loved boldly.*

And still did.

But there was no time left.

The dream shattered around them, like glass exploding beneath moonlight.

Alarion looked at her one final time. "When you reach the Court, meet me at our spot. Where the trees meet and the ladybugs fly free."

Then everything broke and Maera jolted awake with a ragged inhale.

The world was cold and too loud. The fire crackled beside her. Kael knelt beside Aislen, checking her pulse, his face full of worry.

But Maera sat up, motionless in the dirt, her hands gripping her knees, her chest rising and falling in uneven gasps.

No one saw the tears that slipped down her cheeks, quiet and unrelenting.

She had let him go once.

But now... she wasn't sure she could do it again.

But she also wasn't sure if she could pick between them.

Her first love, and the man who put her back together again.

Instinctively, she glanced at Tomas.

His eyes were already on her as he watched her from near the fire, the weariness of what just happened flowing off of him.

He looked away, unable to ask her what happened with Alarion.

And she couldn't even blame him.

She watched as he repositioned himself with a soft grunt, a hand pressed to his lower back. He had been walking stiffly since their attack with the undead.

Maera sighed.

She needed to talk to her husband.

Thirty-Three

"Hunted"

~ Aislen ~

The fire crackled low, casting long shadows across the camp as dusk melted into night. Aislen sat on the ground, her knees hugged tight to her chest, the cold creeping through her clothes as if it was trying to burrow into her bones.

No one spoke. Not yet.

Sion had already extinguished the remains of the ritual circle, covering the ashroot with dirt. Kael crouched nearby, elbows resting on his thighs, hands fisted so tightly his knuckles had gone pale. Her mom sat beside Tomas across the fire, still gripping the map they'd spread out in the dirt, though she hadn't looked at it since waking. There seemed to be more distance than usual between her mom and Tomas.

Aisle eyed them carefully before she broke the silence.

"It was her," she said softly. "The Sun Queen."

All eyes shifted to her.

"She sent something. It was some kind of creature, a pet that she's twisted to do her bidding. It took Thess. And she's using her to get to me. It's a trap." Her voice barely held. "But she's still alive."

Maera sat up straighter. "The Starlight King said the creature wouldn't

275

kill her right away. Thess is being kept... for leverage."

Kael stood abruptly, pacing like a panther too long in a cage. "So we're being hunted. We already suspected we were being followed. Now we know who, and why."

"That means something else," Sion added. "We're not even the target. Aislen is."

The quiet returned, but this time, it was charged. Frantic beneath the surface.

Aislen gritted her teeth. "She came with us. Thess followed me into this madness, knowing there'd be danger. And now she's being used like... like a pawn. Like a message."

Kael's pacing intensified. "Then we need to change everything. We can't keep walking around blind. We need to fortify, track whatever's following us, create distance. If Virel wanted to bait you, she's probably watching how we respond."

"We can't waste time setting up camp after camp," Sion argued. "She's out there now, damn it. Every moment we hesitate could be the last one we get."

"I'm not saying we don't act!" Kael snapped. "I'm saying we don't walk straight into the Queen's claws with no plan at all."

"And what exactly do you propose?" Sion stood now too, squaring off with him. "We wander in circles until she drops Thess on our doorstep?"

Kael's voice lowered into something colder. "We don't let emotion drive us off a cliff."

"Emotion is the reason any of us are here," Aislen cut in, standing. Her hands trembled, but she kept her voice firm. "Not all of us are soldiers. We're damn sure not rulers." She glanced at her mom who was pointedly avoiding her daughters eyes. "We're just people trying to protect each other the only way we know how."

She looked directly at Kael, then at Sion. "I won't be the reason we fall apart. But I'm not going to abandon her either."

Kael turned to her, the muscle in his jaw jumping. "No one is saying we leave her, gods Aislen, I just think we need to pause to do this safely. We shouldn't do anything reckless."

"If I were to remind you, the last reckless idea I had is what got us answers. Stop treating me like I'm broken porcelain," she said. "She's my best friend, Kael, my sister in every way that matters. I'd burn the sky if I thought it would bring her back."

He stepped forward, brushing a curl from her face, his touch soft but his voice ragged. "And if you get taken too? What then?"

"Then you'll come for me," she whispered. "Because that's what we do."

The moment hung between them, a tension woven of fear and something deeper.

Maera cleared her throat gently. "The Starlight King said we're already walking the path that leads to her. There's a place where the wind stills and where shadows listen. That's where we'll find the trail."

Tomas nodded, pulling the map back toward him. "It's only about a week's journey to the outer ridgeline. From there, we'll keep our eyes sharp. Look for signs of this... stillness."

"But how do we know she'll still be alive?" Kael asked.

"We don't," Maera admitted. "But I believe she will be. If Virel wanted her dead, she would have left the body."

Sion's eyes flared. "We've fought monsters before. But we've never gone up against something like this. Not a queen."

Aislen turned to him. "That's why we don't separate. We stay together. If the path splits, we camp until we agree. No one vanishes into the fog alone."

Her chest burned with fear, but she pushed through it. She had to.

Fenric, standing a few paces back with his arms crossed, finally spoke. "And what's the plan once we find it? Fight whatever's guarding her with half-trained magic and emotions running wild?"

Kael spun on him. "You've had something to say at every turn but offer nothing. If you're not going to help, why are you even here?" Barely biting back the other question he had for his father. He wanted to ask him whose side he was even on.

Fenric didn't flinch. "To keep you alive."

"You sure about that?" Sion muttered under his breath.

Kael started toward him again, but Aislen stepped between them, throwing up her hand. "Enough! All of you!"

The fire snapped behind her like it agreed.

A long silence followed.

She turned slowly. "I don't need protection. I need partners. Thess is missing. The Sun Queen is using whatever monsters at her disposal to hunt me. And my magic..." She glanced at her hands. "My magic is pulling me toward something I still don't understand. But I won't back down. Not now. I need you all with me on this, I can't do it alone."

Kael's voice was rough when he spoke again. "Then we make the plan together. No more secrets. No more fights. We do it together."

Maera pointed at the map. "We'll head east first light. I remember this trail—I admit, not as much as I'd like—but it should lead toward the pass I used when I left the Court."

Maera leaned closer, tracing the line again. "It's risky, but faster. If we're careful... we might be able to intercept her trail and stay one step ahead of the Sun Queen's spies. Maybe."

The wind whispered through the trees like an omen.

Aislen looked up at the stars overhead, her stomach twisting.

Thess, hold on. I'm coming.

They were all coming.

* * *

~ Kael ~

The flames snapped and hissed as the wind shifted, scattering tiny sparks across the packed dirt like fireflies that had lost their way.

Kael sat just outside the ring of light, his elbows resting on his knees, his fingers digging into the worn leather of his gloves. His eyes weren't on the fire. They hadn't been for hours.

They were on her.

Aislen.

Her silhouette flickered between firelight and shadow, head bent toward her mother, the pale curve of her cheek catching the glow just right. She looked so calm, so impossibly composed for someone who had just agreed to walk willingly into a trap.

But he saw the tension in her shoulders. The tremble in her fingers when she thought no one was watching. The exhaustion behind her eyes.

He knew that look.

It was the look of someone holding the world together with trembling hands and pretending they weren't bleeding underneath.

And gods, he loved her for it.

He loved her for the way she never backed down, for the fire in her voice when someone she cared about was in danger, for the way she'd walk headfirst into darkness if it meant dragging someone back out.

But he hated it, too.

Because it meant she'd never stop putting herself last. Never stop running into the storm with no shield but her heart. And he didn't know how many more storms she could survive.

He clenched his jaw, forcing himself to breathe.

She shouldn't have to be this brave. Not alone.

You were supposed to protect her.

The thought came unbidden, sharp as a blade. He'd sworn in every quiet moment they'd shared, in every look he'd given her when she wasn't watching, Kael had made a promise.

He would protect her.

Even if she had never chose him.

Even if she had never realized she was his mate.

Even if the bond, so loud now in his blood, never fully awakened in her.

He would still protect her. Even if it killed him.

But the truth he was starting to realize… was that he couldn't protect her from everything.

Not from fate. Not from the pull of prophecy. Not from the choices she'd made to chase after those she loved.

And he wouldn't try to.

Because trying to cage her strength would only break it.

He ran a hand down his face, the weight of it all pressing hard against his chest.

She was his heart, yes, but she was also her own. A storm of wild magic and stubborn hope, spun from stars and soil and the soft, aching parts of the world most people never noticed.

She wasn't something to guard. She was someone to stand beside. To believe in. To fight with, not just for.

Even when it terrified him.

Especially then.

Kael watched as Aislen touched the moonstone pendant around her neck, the one he'd given her to wear during the ritual, the one that once anchored him back to her in his darkest hour.

Now it was her turn.

He didn't know what was coming next. But he knew this: whatever hell the Sun Queen had waiting, Aislen would face it with or without him.

And he'd be damned if he let her go alone.

Kael stood slowly and crossed the firelight, his boots whispering over the ground. Aislen looked up at him, her eyes soft but tired, a flicker of question behind them.

He knelt beside her and reached for her hand. She didn't hesitate.

"You don't have to go alone," he said quietly. "Not ever."

Her fingers tightened around his.

And in the silence that followed, as the fire crackled and the shadows pressed in, something unspoken passed between them. Something older than words. Stronger than fear.

She leaned into him, and Kael could finally breathe again.

He kept breathing until they had been sitting for minutes or maybe even hours, with their foreheads together and their eyes closed.

When they finally opened their eyes and were released from their trance, the fire had burned down to its last stubborn embers.

The others were scattered around the camp, some curled beneath cloaks, others keeping a wary half-watch from where they sat in silence. Even Sion had settled into a light doze against a rock, one arm slung over his pack, his brow still furrowed like he was fighting ghosts in his sleep.

Kael hadn't slept. Couldn't.

Not after what they'd learned.

Not with the image of Thess's frightened eyes burned into the back of his mind, or the memory of Alarion's warning echoing like a curse.

He picked Aislen up and laid her down on their shared bedroll.

Grabbing their cloaks, he draped them over her body to keep her warm.

He might not have been able to rest, but she could.

And she was beautiful.

She lay on her side, curled beneath two cloaks just outside the edge of the firelight, her dark lashes fluttering against her cheeks as her breath rose and fell in steady rhythm. Kael watched her for a long time, unwilling to break the fragile stillness that had finally settled over them.

She looked peaceful in sleep. Softer, in a way he rarely got to see.

The weight she carried—the prophecy, the power, the fear—it fell from her shoulders in dreams, even if only for a little while.

And gods, he needed that. Needed her peace to remind him there was still something to hold onto in all this madness.

Silently, he lowered himself next to her with slow, careful movements. He didn't want to startle her.

But the moment he settled in behind her, her body shifted ever so slightly as her back pressed against his chest. He felt her breath hitch just once before falling back into rhythm.

She didn't wake.

She didn't need to.

Kael slid an arm beneath her head and tucked the other around her waist, his hand splaying gently against her stomach. Just holding her. Just... *being* with her.

He closed his eyes and exhaled, his forehead pressing lightly to the back of her neck.

281

She was here. She was warm. She was breathing.

And so was he.

That was all that mattered right now.

Not the prophecy. Not the Courts. Not the trap tightening around them like a noose.

Just her.

Just this.

The scent of her... wildflowers and soft earth and that faint, elusive shimmer of starlight that always clung to her skin, filled his senses and quieted the roar in his chest. Her magic was still thrumming softly beneath her skin, no longer surging, just... present. Steady. Like it knew it wasn't alone.

He tightened his hold just a little, not enough to wake her, but enough to let the bond hum between them.

And in that quiet hum, he found peace.

It didn't matter how strong the storm was, or how clever the trap.

She was his.

And he would follow her into the dark, again and again and again, just to make sure she came back out.

* * *

~ **Unknown POV** ~

From the edge of the clearing, just beyond where the firelight bled into night, the forest held its breath.

A branch shifted, too slow for wind. A shadow detached itself from the deeper black, slinking low to the earth, unseen.

It watched.

It listened.

The girl burned too bright. She was glowing even when her magic was still tethered, her power humming just beneath the surface like a storm not yet touched down.

The others surrounded her like shields. The moonborn. The wild one. The lost queen.

But none of them saw the eyes in the trees.

None of them noticed the soft scuttle of claw on bark. Or the breathless hush that followed, like the forest itself was waiting for something terrible.

The scent of blood still clung to the path behind them.

They were ready.

Thirty-Four

"Instinct"

~ Sion ~

The sky was still streaked in that sleepy shade of gray and blue when Sion stirred from the stone he'd leaned against. Morning hadn't quite broken yet, but the fire had long since burned to ash, leaving the air colder than it should've been.

The others were waking slowly, reluctantly, like their dreams had offered better company than the path ahead.

He rolled his shoulder, stiff from sleeping half-upright, and glanced toward the bedroll near the base of the trees. Aislen was curled beneath her cloaks, Kael beside her, one arm protectively draped over her waist. Sion looked away quickly.

That wasn't his to watch.

Not because he felt anything for Aislen that way, he didn't, but because he recognized that kind of devotion. He envied it. The way Kael held her like she was an anchor and compass all at once. The way Aislen, in sleep, allowed herself to rest in it.

Sion had never been anyone's compass.

He stood, dusting off his hands, and walked the perimeter of their small camp. His steps were quiet, cautious. He hadn't told the others, but he hadn't slept much. Not because of dreams, but because of what he'd heard.

Or... hadn't.

The forest had gone too quiet in the hours after the dreamwalking ritual. No bird calls. No rustling of creatures. Just stillness. Like the world had drawn in a breath and forgotten how to let it go.

They were being watched. He felt it in his bones, in that old part of him that magic had carved hollow and alert.

His magic was on edge.

He wanted to do more, but what could he even do? His healing powers, thankfully, haven't been needed much. His illusions were of no use right now, unless he wanted to have everyone imagine they were actually relaxing in a bed of water somewhere.

It's not like he could shadow walk like Kael, or god knows what all Aislen is capable of now.

Sion felt useless.

Tomas stirred behind him, groaning as he stood and stretched, muttering something about his back and the curse of aging in the mountains. Maera was already up, kneeling by the map again, her expression tight with some unspoken thought that hadn't left her since the dreamwalk.

And Thess... she still wasn't here.

Sion felt that ache every time he turned, every time he half-expected her voice at his shoulder with a sarcastic quip or a comment meant only for his ears.

He missed her laugh. Missed calling her "Trouble" just to hear her groan.

Damn it, please let her be alright.

He cleared his throat and moved back toward the others, kneeling to pack up what remained of their supplies. "We should head out soon," he said. "The trail's going to get harder the longer we wait."

Kael looked up from where he was crouching near his bedroll. "And what exactly are we looking for?"

Aislen rubbed her eyes, sleep still clinging to her like mist. "The place where the wind stills. Where shadows listen."

"Right," Sion muttered. "Because that makes sense. He couldn't have been less cryptic?"

"It's the best lead we've got," Tomas offered, tone more optimistic than convincing.

Sion gave a humorless chuckle. "So we're walking toward what? A void? A magical silence? A haunted ravine, waiting to see if we taste better when afraid?"

"That's enough," Kael snapped.

But Aislen touched Sion's arm gently. "He's scared. We all are."

Sion's throat tightened. He nodded, jaw clenched. "Yeah. I am, she's one of my best friends. One of our best friends."

No shame in that.

Just Thess's face, burned into his mind, wild and furious as she was dragged away by something they hadn't even seen. That's what haunted him, the not knowing. Not seeing. Not stopping it.

He blinked, forced the image away, and stood straighter. "If we're being hunted, we need to act like it. We take the high ground where we can. Stay in each other's sight. No wandering off. No splitting up. I mean it."

"Agreed," Tomas said, shouldering his pack.

Maera finally stood, folding the map with care. "Then we head east. The ridgeline should start within the next three miles. If the Queen's creature is laying bait... that's where we'll start to feel it."

Kael frowned. "That was... almost poetic."

Maera didn't smile. "It wasn't meant to be."

Sion looked at each of them in turn. Kael with his protectiveness on a knife's edge, Maera still haunted by her dream, Tomas trying to keep everyone stitched together, and Aislen... gods, Aislen looked like she was carrying the weight of the realm on her shoulders.

But still, she stood.

Still, she pressed forward.

He felt something stir in his chest. It was not hope exactly, but something like it. A spark of belief that maybe, just maybe, if they held together long enough, they could outrun the trap tightening around them.

Sion reached down, picked up his blade, and slid it into the loop at his hip. "Let's move."

The forest waited.

And so did the creature in the dark.

* * *

~ Aislen ~

They were on their way.

The trees thinned slowly, like they were being peeled away by invisible hands. The shadows stretched farther apart, branches growing sparse until there was nothing left to block the light. Ahead, the forest gave way to an open field. It was vast, wild, and blanketed in tall grass that swayed like a sea of golden-green silk under the rising sun.

Aislen stepped into the clearing first, the grass brushing her hips, then her waist. It tickled her skin and clung to her cloak, whispering against her as if trying to tell her something only her magic could hear.

The others followed behind, blades half-drawn and eyes scanning the horizon, but it wasn't the threat of ambush that made Aislen's pulse quicken.

It was the pull.

That familiar hum beneath her ribs. It was the faint, invisible thread that had been quietly tugging at her since she woke.

It was stronger now.

Subtle, but steady. Like the earth itself was trying to speak.

"Thess would hate this," Tomas muttered behind her, swatting at a stalk of grass that had slapped his cheek.

Kael gave a faint snort. "She'd be grumbling about how the universe is trying to kill her with pollen and hidden ankle traps."

Sion chuckled under his breath. "She'd call it 'nature's ambush' and insist she was too pretty to get eaten by grass."

Aislen smiled faintly, but it faded too quickly.

Because Thess wasn't here to complain. Her voice wasn't filling the air with sarcastic color. And now this field, this bright, open expanse, felt more like a wound than a reprieve.

She paused, turning slowly in place as her fingertips brushed against the stalks. The tug on her magic deepened, no longer a whisper but a quiet pressure behind her ribs, like something calling her name without sound.

It wasn't painful. Just... insistent.

They were walking east, toward the ridgeline her mom remembered. But something in her gut told her this wasn't the right direction.

Not anymore.

She hesitated, letting the others pass her, their shapes parting the grass like ghosts as they trudged forward. Kael caught her eye briefly, frowning, but she shook her head and looked away before he could ask.

What are you trying to show me? she thought, reaching inward.

The bond with the earth beneath her feet pulsed faintly. It was alive, aware, almost... hopeful.

This wasn't fear guiding her. Not this time.

It was instinct.

She turned her head slightly, glancing to the left where the grass seemed to ripple differently. Not in the wind's direction, but against it. A quiet current moving opposite the natural flow, like a hidden tide just under the surface.

Her breath hitched. *It's there.*

Aislen stopped walking.

And suddenly, the silence around her felt sharper.

The others hadn't noticed yet. Not Kael, who was already several steps ahead, eyes narrowed at the distant edge of the field. Not Maera, deep in quiet thought. Not Sion, who still wore the tension of the morning in his shoulders.

She didn't know how she knew, but she was certain.

Whatever came next... started in that direction.

Not the one drawn on a map.

Not the one built on memory.

288

But this one, one whispered by her magic. It pulled at her. It told her she was going the wrong way.

She inhaled through her nose, grounding herself. Her heart thudded once, hard.

She didn't want to pull them off track. She didn't want to make the wrong choice.

But she also didn't want to ignore the call she knew she was born to follow.

She lingered where the grass thickened, letting the others pass her one by one like leaves drifting downstream. No one noticed at first, Tomas caught up to Maera murmuring something low. Kael was looking down at the map, distracted. Thank the gods, if he would have seen her lagging behind, he never would have let her go. Not alone.

Sion was next, eyes flicking sideways as if he felt something too, but he was too caught in his own storm to read hers.

And then... Fenric.

The last.

His sharp eyes met hers for half a second, unreadable beneath his furrowed brow. He slowed just enough that she thought he might say something, but instead, he just gave a curt nod and moved on, disappearing into the field with the others, grass swallowing his boots in waves.

She stood very still as the distance stretched between them, letting the quiet settle back around her like a shroud.

Her heart was pounding now, not from fear, but from that strange, rising certainty in her blood. The pull on her magic had grown bolder, humming through her like a plucked string, and now that she wasn't fighting it, it was impossible to ignore.

A current, just beneath her skin. Ancient. Familiar.

I shouldn't do this.

She swallowed hard and looked over her shoulder once more, watching the heads of her companions vanish into the sea of gold. Kael would be furious if he found her missing. Sion would panic. Her mom... Aislen didn't want to think about that look of worry that would fill Maera's face.

Not again.

But if I call them now, I'll lead them away from the path. And if I say nothing, I might lose the one chance I have to understand what this is.

Her fingertips brushed the stalks of grass as she turned slightly, adjusting her weight toward the pull. It came from the left, just past where the light shifted. It was barely perceptible, like the world had been bent ever so slightly in that direction.

Something in her blood thrummed in response.

Not danger.

Not safety, either.

Just... truth.

A thread in the tapestry, beckoning her hand to weave.

She took a breath and let it out slowly. "Alright," she whispered. "Just for a moment."

And then she stepped off the path.

The moment her foot left the flattened trail the others had carved, the world changed. The air grew still, dense somehow, like it held its breath with her. The grass rose higher here, brushing her collarbone, and shadows lingered beneath it, though the sun hung high overhead. She pushed through carefully, feeling her magic grow more alive with every step, not wild, but *aware*. Watching. Guiding.

It wasn't leading her blindly.

It was *escorting* her. Inviting her.

The thought made her chest tighten with a strange mix of awe and dread.

I should turn back.

But she didn't.

She couldn't.

Because whatever lay ahead, whatever secret hummed in the quiet rhythm of her earthsong, it had been calling for her since before she even knew who she was.

The pull didn't fade. If anything, it grew stronger with each careful step she took.

She'd been walking for... gods, maybe thirty minutes now, pushing through knee-high grass and uneven terrain, her senses sharpened to every shift in the air. At first, the tug on her magic had been like a whisper. Like a soft invitation. Now, it thrummed like a heartbeat in her bones. Louder. More urgent.

Aislen slowed, her hand outstretched as if she could touch it, trace it, grasp whatever invisible tether was winding itself around her soul.

Her breath hitched. "I'm here," she murmured aloud, the sound swallowed by the silence around her. "But where is... here?"

She turned in a slow circle, searching the stretch of field that had narrowed into a shallow dip between rising rock outcroppings. The wind had stilled completely, and the grass stood too still. Unnaturally still. The birds had gone silent again. The only sound was her own uneven breathing and the soft shuffle of her boots in the dirt.

What am I supposed to be seeing?

Her magic pulsed harder. She knelt, brushing aside blades of gold-threaded grass, running her fingers across the dry soil. Nothing. She stood and scanned the rise of a stone nearby. It was moss-covered and worn by time. She moved closer.

And then... something flickered.

Not in the light.

In her *magic*.

Her head snapped toward the largest boulder in the cluster. It loomed at the edge of a ridge, its base half-buried in tall grass and shadow. Aislen frowned and stepped toward it, brushing her hand along its cool surface.

There, just beneath a ledge of jutting stone it was a small, jagged opening. It was almost invisible unless you were looking right at it.

No wider than her shoulders. Low to the ground. Easily missed.

Easily hidden.

Her stomach dropped.

She crouched, sweeping grass aside. Dirt and roots had gathered around it over time, disguising the hole as little more than erosion. But now, with her magic pulsing hard and hot in her veins, she saw it for what it was:

An entrance.

A path.

A secret someone didn't want found.

She leaned forward, peering into the dark. The scent that drifted up was cold and damp, earthy but tinged with something else, something stale and metallic.

Her throat tightened.

Is she in there?

She couldn't know. Not for sure. But her magic was practically *buzzing*, the air around her thick with some ancient energy that tugged at the wild, primal corners of her power. It was telling her—no, *begging* her—to pay attention.

This meant something.

She didn't know what waited in that hole. But she knew one thing for certain: going in alone would be yet another foolish mistake she's made.

And she's had enough of those.

She stood quickly, heart hammering, and reached into her satchel for a ribbon of blue thread from her mother's cloak and tied it to the nearest tree limb. Then another, and another, like breadcrumbs for anyone who might come looking.

Then she took off running.

The path she'd made wasn't much of a trail, but she retraced it as best she could, dodging tufts of thick grass and the occasional thorny snag. The wind had picked up again, tugging at her cloak, biting at her face like it, too, was scolding her for her recklessness.

Please don't be too far. Please still be close enough.

She didn't know what she'd found, but she knew it was important.

* * *

~ **Kael** ~

It started as a whisper in his chest.

A subtle shift. Barely there.

But Kael felt it.

The bond.

Faint and silken, usually humming like a second heartbeat beneath his own was suddenly stretched thin. Like a thread pulled taut.

Too taut.

He froze mid-step.

Aislen wasn't near him anymore.

His head snapped to the side, scanning the ridge behind them. Nothing but golden grass and the flutter of cloaks as the others trudged forward, unaware of what was happening.

Kael's heart slammed against his ribs.

Aislen.

The bond strained again.

No panic. No pain. But it was pulling away... *she* was pulling away.

His stomach turned to ice.

He spun, scanning the line they'd crossed, eyes narrowed.

"Aislen's not here," he barked. "She's gone, I feel her moving away from us."

Sion turned, startled. "She was just behind me—"

"She's not." His voice dropped, low and sharp.

The wind shifted. So did the tension.

Maera froze mid-step. Tomas immediately turned back, eyes raking the horizon.

But it was Fenric who spoke, calm as ever.

"She veered off not too long ago," he said. "Back near the boulder line. Looked like she was following something."

The world tilted.

Kael slowly turned to face his father.

"You *saw* her walk away?" he asked, voice razor-thin.

"I assumed she sensed something. It didn't feel like an emergency—"

He didn't finish.

Kael launched forward, grabbing him by the front of his cloak and slamming him into the trunk of the nearest tree with a sound like thunder cracking through bark. The branches above shook.

"What the *fuck* do you mean," Kael growled, his voice trembling with rage, "you *saw her* leave—*and did nothing?*"

Fenric's expression barely shifted. "She's not helpless."

Kael's arm pressed harder. "I don't care. She's my *mate*. And I deserve to fucking know when she leaves this group. We. Do. Not. Separate."

The words tore from his throat before he could stop them. Raw. Wild. Terrified.

He'd been keeping it in for so long.

But not now.

"She is my mate, and you let her disappear alone into godsdamned *enemy territory?!*"

Fenric's hands stayed open at his sides. "She wasn't dragged off. She walked. Confident. She wasn't in danger."

"You think *I* care how confident she looked?" Kael's grip shook. "She shouldn't have gone alone. Not now. Not after what we saw. Not with that thing still out there!"

"Let him go, this isn't helping us" Tomas warned, stepping forward.

Kael didn't.

His pulse was roaring in his ears. The bond was still there, but distant. A thread pulled too thin.

What if it snaps? What if she's already—

No.

No.

He forced himself to let go, shoving Fenric back with one last hard glare. His father stumbled but stayed silent, brushing off his cloak like it hadn't just been stained with betrayal.

Kael stepped back, chest heaving. He closed his eyes.

Find her. Find her. FIND HER.

He reached inward, deep into that place where her magic curled around his. The bond pulsed again. It was faint, but clear. He could feel her heartbeat. The shape of her magic. That quiet tether that said *I'm here. I'm trying.*

Kael's breath caught.

She wasn't panicked. Not yet. But she was too far.

Too far from him.

And he was done waiting.

"She's northeast," he said suddenly, already turning toward the thick grasses they'd crossed earlier. "I can feel her."

"Wait," Maera called. "Don't go alone!"

"I won't be *alone*," Kael snapped. "I'll be where *she* is."

And then he ran.

Faster than fear. Faster than thought.

He let the bond guide him, burning through the landscape like a storm in motion. Every thump of his boots against the earth was a prayer. Every heartbeat was a promise.

I'm coming, Aislen.

You are mine.

And nothing takes you from me.

* * *

~ Aislen ~

The tall grass parted around her legs as she ran, breath shallow in her chest, arms pumping to keep her momentum. The path looked familiar now and she knew she was close. The others couldn't have gone far.

She hoped.

Her heart pounded louder than her footfalls.

Please still be close. Please.

She crested a small rise in the earth just as the wind shifted, fast and sudden, brushing her cheeks like a warning.

And then—

"*Aislen!*"

She didn't have time to react.

A blur of movement came crashing through the field, and before she could make sense of it, Kael was there, arms locking around her so tightly it knocked the air from her lungs. Her feet left the ground for a moment as he buried his face against her neck, trembling with something wild and unspoken.

"Kael—what—what's wrong?" she gasped, clutching his tunic. "I was just—"

He pulled back just enough to look at her, his eyes ablaze with anger, yes, but mostly fear.

Real, bone-deep *fear*. She could sense it coming off of his body in waves.

"*What's wrong?*" he echoed, voice sharp and ragged. "What do you mean, *what's wrong?* I thought I *lost* you!"

Her lips parted in confusion, but he didn't let her speak.

"You can't just disappear like that, Aislen. Gods—" He raked a hand through his hair, stepping back just to pace, then storming forward again. "You *can't* just vanish. You didn't tell anyone, you didn't leave a sign, you didn't... hells, I *felt* you getting further away, and it was like—like—"

He broke off, his chest heaving.

"I don't care if you leave everyone else behind," he said, quieter now, but no less intense. "But don't you ever leave *me* behind. Never again."

The last words cracked at the edges. Vulnerable. Raw.

"I can't lose you."

Aislen stood frozen, breath caught somewhere between her lungs and her throat. He looked like he'd been shattered and barely stitched back together. Like he'd crossed fire and storm just to reach her.

And she hadn't even realized.

She stepped forward and placed her hands on either side of his face, forcing him to look at her.

"I didn't mean to scare you," she whispered. "I thought... I thought if I could just follow the magic, I'd find something useful without dragging everyone into another dead end."

Kael's eyes closed, lashes trembling. He leaned into her touch like it was the only thing anchoring him to the ground.

"*You* are useful," he murmured. "You're everything. But you're not allowed to go missing. Not like that. Not from *me.*"

She swallowed hard, heart aching with guilt and something else. Something she didn't know how to name. The bond between them pulsed again, not just magical, but human. Hurting. Real.

"I found something," she said quietly. "I didn't go far, I swear. I just... I couldn't ignore the pull. And it led me to a tunnel. It was hidden, only someone searching would've seen it."

Kael opened his eyes again. "A tunnel?"

She nodded. "I marked the spot. I didn't go in. I was coming back to get everyone—*to get you.*"

That softened him.

Still fierce, but not breaking anymore.

He nodded slowly, jaw working like he wanted to say more but didn't have the words. Instead, he pulled her against his chest once more, pressing a kiss to the top of her head.

"I thought I'd have to tear the world apart to find you," he whispered.

Aislen closed her eyes and held on tighter.

"I'm right here."

Aislen pushed up on her toes and grabbed his face. She saw the terror etched into his eyes, and she knew she never wanted him to feel that way again.

She pulled his face down to hers and kissed him slowly.

Their lips came apart, but their foreheads stayed together.

"I love you Kael, with every fiber of my being. But please, I really need your help. We need everyone, now."

Kael searched her face before nodding. He took her hand and pulled her towards the others.

They moved quickly.

Kael didn't let go of her hand the entire way back, his grip firm like he needed the contact to believe she was still beside him. She didn't mind. Her nerves hadn't stopped buzzing since she first felt the tug of her magic, and now, with the path ahead even darker than before, she needed the grounding too.

The others were on high alert, watching for their return, as they made it back.

Maera stood first, her eyes narrowing sharply. "Aislen?"

"I'm okay," Aislen said, breathless as they reached the clearing. "I found something."

Kael added before anyone else could panic, "She followed the pull of her magic. It led to something hidden, something we would've missed if we stayed on the trail."

Maera's expression shifted from fear to wary interest. "What kind of something?"

"A tunnel," Aislen replied. "Cut into the side of a boulder. Low to the ground. I almost missed it myself."

"You really went alone?" Tomas asked, his voice a mix of relief and frustration.

"I came back," she said. "I didn't go inside. But... I marked the way."

Sion had already slung his pack over his shoulder. "Then what are we waiting for?"

They followed her back through the tall grass and winding trail she'd taken earlier, with Kael beside her, Maera and Tomas close behind. Fenric said nothing, though Aislen felt his eyes on her more than once.

When they reached the clearing where the stone jutted from the earth like a buried relic, they slowed.

"There," Aislen said, pointing toward the base of the boulder. "Just under that edge. See it?"

They all stepped closer.

The tunnel wasn't much. It was just a jagged opening carved by time and maybe something else. Moss grew in clumps around the entrance, and the earth itself seemed to hum faintly with magic, so faint that only those attuned to it would notice.

"This place is old," Maera murmured, kneeling to brush aside some leaves. "Very old."

"And very well hidden," Tomas added. "No wonder no one found it before."

Kael crouched beside it, staring into the shadowy hole. "It could lead anywhere."

"Or nowhere," Fenric muttered from behind them. "Could be a death trap. Who even says this is where we're supposed to be?"

The others had taken to ignoring Fenric ever since he let Aislen go off alone.

Sion stepped forward and raised his palm. A soft white glow sparked to life, a flickering orb of light dancing between his fingers. He held it toward the opening, trying to cast it deep inside.

The light drifted in, illuminating jagged roots, dust, and stone. But after a few feet, the glow was swallowed whole by the dark.

Sion frowned. "It's too deep. Too old. My light barely scratches it."

A chill crawled up Aislen's spine. She didn't know what lay ahead, but her magic had led her here for a reason. She could *feel* it, the same way she had in the Veiled Vanor. Like something was waiting. Watching.

Kael stood slowly. "We'll have to go in."

"One at a time," Tomas said grimly. "No way we'll all fit shoulder to shoulder. Not in something that narrow."

"Then we choose an order," Maera said. "And we stay close. If anything moves, we signal back."

Fenric crossed his arms. " If we can even make it back. What's wrong with you people? We don't even know if she's in there."

"Stop. We don't have a choice," Aislen said softly. "But I *know* this is the right place. Are you all with me or not? I can do this alone if I need to, but I want you all with me. I needed you all with me."

Sion looked back at her, his voice steady. "Then we trust you."

She blinked at him, surprised. But then he gave her a small, firm nod, *Thess* still echoed behind his eyes.

"Let's get ready," Kael said. "Whatever's waiting… we face it together."

And one by one, they prepared to step into the dark.

Thirty-Five

"The Betrayer"

~ Tomas ~

The mouth of the tunnel yawned before them like a secret the earth had been trying to forget.

Tomas stood at its edge, wind biting at his coat, the chill settling deeper than just his skin. It wasn't the cold that made him shiver. It was what waited beyond that jagged dark, the not knowing. The silence. The weight of everything they still didn't understand pressing in from all sides.

Aislen had found it. Of course she had.

Of all the people in this realm, of all the paths fate could twist and tangle, it was her. His little girl with soil-stained fingers and stubborn eyes who unearthed what even magic tried to bury. And now she wanted to walk into it.

No. Not wanted.

Needed.

He could see it in the way her jaw was set, in the way her shoulders squared even when her hands trembled. She was afraid. But she would still go.

Because that's who she was.

He swallowed hard, the motion thick with emotion. Gods, she wasn't even supposed to be here. She was supposed to be hidden from the Courts for her protection. And now here she stood, a beacon of power and light, on the edge of something ancient and terrible, and Tomas couldn't do a damned thing to stop it.

But he could go first.

He shifted his stance, took one slow breath, and said, "I'll lead."

They all turned to look at him.

Aislen blinked. "Dad—"

"I'm not asking," he interrupted gently. "You can follow. Kael can protect. Sion can light the way. But I'll go first."

He didn't have powers. Not like the others. No illusions. No starlight. No ancient bloodline humming in his bones. What he had was grit. Loyalty. And love so deep it terrified him.

He'd carried her in his arms as a baby through snowstorms and across flooded valleys. He'd stood between her and misunderstood villagers who muttered about the color in her eyes. He'd kissed bruised knees, soothed fevered skin, told her stories to help her sleep when even Maera couldn't calm her tears.

He was her father in every way that mattered.

And if something waited in that dark to take her, it would have to go through him first.

"You sure?" Sion asked, voice low.

Tomas nodded. "Not even a little. But I'm still doing it."

Aislen stepped forward and touched his arm. "You don't have to prove anything. You've already done everything for me."

"I know," he said softly. "But this... this is one more thing I can do. Let me do it."

He saw her hesitate, and then she nodded, once. Trusting him. Always trusting him.

That alone made his spine straighten, even as the dread clawed higher in his throat.

Behind him, Sion rolled his shoulders and muttered something to his light, coaxing it into a pale, steady glow. "I'm second. You'll need to see, and I'll need to be close enough if something happens."

"Third," Aislen said.

"Fourth," Kael added, never taking his eyes off her.

Maera merely stepped forward and said, "I'm not staying behind."

That left Fenric.

The male had been quiet since the tunnel was found, brooding near the edge of the field like a hawk that didn't quite trust the sky. Now he moved toward them with measured steps.

"You all go," Fenric said, arms crossed. "I'll stay behind. Watch the entrance. Make sure nothing follows you in."

No one argued.

But just as Kael moved to follow the others, Fenric put a hand on his shoulder.

"You don't have to go," he said quietly. "You can stay here. You don't have to follow her into this."

Kael froze.

Then turned slowly, fire sparking in his eyes. "I go where Aislen goes."

Fenric studied him for a long, unreadable moment. Then, he gave the strangest, softest smile Tomas had ever seen on the man's face.

"I knew you would say that," Fenric murmured. "But I was really hoping I was wrong. I love you, son."

Kael blinked. "What?"

But Fenric only stepped back, nodded once, and said nothing more.

Tomas overheard it all, but knew it wasn't his place to respond. Something was going on with Fenric, he wasn't the same male he had known over all of these years. They were friends, not the best of friends but they were cordial. They had a drink from time to time, but that was it. Even then, he knew something wasn't right. Something in Fenric had always felt like a blade with no sheath.

He faced forward again, toward the hole in the earth that seemed to breathe shadow.

One step. Then another.

Tomas ducked low, his boots crunching over dried roots and grit as the light from Sion's magic flickered at his back. He put his feet in first, and then his legs. He slowly inched his body in until he felt his feet touch something solid.

He let go and let the rest of his body drop through the hole. The air shifted the moment he passed the threshold, cool and still, thick like forgotten breath. Each inch forward felt like a thread pulling tighter.

But he didn't stop.

He had a daughter to protect.

* * *

~ Aislen ~

The moment they all slid their way inside the tunnel, the world changed.

The air grew dense, thick with old magic and damp stone. Each breath tasted of dust and time, as if the earth itself had been sealed shut for centuries. The narrow corridor was barely wide enough for them to walk single file, and even then, they moved with shoulders tucked and heads slightly bowed.

Sion's light hovered between his fingers, casting just enough glow to see the packed dirt under their feet and the jagged curves of rock overhead. Shadows crept like fingers along the walls, refusing to scatter even in the light.

Aislen's pulse quickened, thudding loud in her ears. The only thing telling her she was right was the steady pull of her magic guiding her forward.

They were in the belly of something ancient.

No one spoke. The silence was too sharp, like even a whisper might wake something best left sleeping. Her footsteps felt too loud, her breath too fast. She kept close to Sion's back, one hand brushing the damp wall for balance, the other curled tightly around the leather strap of her satchel.

Kael was right behind her. She could feel him. His presence was steady and tense, like a coiled storm waiting to break. Her mom followed him, and behind them... nothing but darkness.

Except for the unease clinging to the back of her neck.

They'd only gone a few paces when a noise echoed from the entrance. They could hear heavy footsteps, then a muffled voice calling out from behind.

"Wait—do you hear that?" Sion whispered, lifting his light higher.

Aislen turned, heart lurching.

"Father?" Kael's voice cut through the quiet. "What is it?"

Then came the voice, clearer this time. It was sharp and unapologetic as it echoed through the tunnel like a dagger flung into their backs.

"I'm sorry it's come to this," Fenric called. "But thank you... for the map. It will help me finish this journey."

A beat of silence.

And then a deafening rumble.

The earth trembled. Dust rained from the ceiling. Aislen stumbled back as the sound of grinding stone and splintering roots filled the space. The ground beneath them shuddered violently.

"Back! Move back!" Tomas shouted, shielding her with his arm.

But it was too late.

The entrance behind them collapsed with a final, bone-jarring roar, sealing them inside in a storm of falling rock and debris. The tunnel darkened. Sion's light sputtered, then flared brighter as they all backed into each other.

Silence returned, but this time, it was suffocating.

No exit.

No retreat.

Aislen's lungs constricted. The dust burned her throat as she coughed, heart slamming wildly in her chest.

He... he left us.

Kael was already moving forward, pounding a fist against the fallen stone wall. "FATHER!" he roared. "You bastard—what the hell did you do?!"

Aislen stared at the wall of debris where the entrance had once been. Her mind raced, disbelieving.

He took the map. He *planned* this.

The betrayal sank like ice into her blood.

Her mother swore softly behind her, voice shaking with fury. Tomas looked like he wanted to throw something, but his shoulders slumped with the weight of something deeper. Disbelief. Grief.

"He waited until we were inside," Maera muttered. "He knew we'd follow her magic. He knew we'd trust it."

Aislen's throat closed. "He used me."

"No," Kael said, stepping back from the rubble, breath ragged. "He *used* all of us."

Sion's light flickered again. "What now?" he asked hoarsely.

Aislen forced herself to breathe. To steady the trembling in her fingers. They had no choice now.

Forward was the only direction left.

She lifted her chin, eyes burning as she stared down the tunnel cloaked in shadow. "We keep going," she said, voice firm. "We don't stop. We find whatever's waiting for us in the dark, and hope it leads us to Thess."

Kael moved behind, his hand brushing hers. "And when we get out—"

"—we find him," she finished. "And we make him answer for this."

The tunnel stretched ahead, cold and silent.

But Aislen's heart burned now. With anger. With betrayal. If one of them got hurt, she would get her vengeance on the one responsible.

Trying to calm her breaths, she looked forward into the darkness.

The tunnel seemed to breathe around them.

That was the only way Aislen could describe it. It was as if the stone and soil themselves exhaled every time they stepped forward, whispering secrets through the cracks.

It wasn't just claustrophobic.

It was *watchful.*

Every few steps, the walls shifted ever so slightly in color. There were patches of damp moss, veins of silvery quartz pulsing faintly with what could only be old magic. Sion's light bobbed ahead like a fragile flame in a sea of ink. The deeper they went, the less the world felt like their own.

Kael was so close behind her, she could hear the grind of his boots on stone, feel the tension radiating from him like heat.

She didn't speak.

Couldn't.

If she opened her mouth, she wasn't sure what would come out. Rage maybe? Grief? Panic?

They had trusted Fenric. Kael had trusted him. That was his father, and yet he still was betrayed by him. He waited until the perfect moment to turn that trust into a cage.

The worst part?

He hadn't even sounded cruel. Just... resigned. As if betrayal was a thing he regretted, but still chose anyway.

Thank you for the map.

Those words clawed at her skull.

Ahead of her, her dad moved carefully but steadily, his shoulders squared despite the dim light, despite the tremble she could see in the clench of his fists. He'd gone first because of her. Because he loved her.

And now they were all trapped.

Because of *her.*

Her magic had pulled them here. Her trust had led them to Fenric. Her instincts... gods, were they even right anymore?

She reached out, brushing her fingers along the rough wall beside her. It was slick in places, warm in others, as if parts of the tunnel had a heartbeat all their own.

"I don't like this," her mom whispered behind them.

Kael grunted softly. "Understatement of the year."

"We keep moving," Tomas said over his shoulder. "Stay alert. No gaps."

They pressed on. Every step forward felt heavier.

The air grew colder. Wetter.

The light didn't reach far, and the shadows twisted unnaturally at the edges of Sion's spell, like something *moved* just beyond its reach. Aislen tried not to look too long at the shapes dancing in the corners of her vision.

She was almost certain they were just illusion made of stone and tricklight, but something about them felt *intentional*.

The tunnel didn't curve naturally. It *guided*. From the looks of it, it was created by someone a long time ago. Maybe centuries.

It felt like a maze. Sometimes they were guided forward, while other times they were met with a dead end with no choice but to turn.

"Do you feel that?" Kael asked quietly.

Aislen nodded before she even realized she was responding. "It's like the air around us is watching."

His hand brushed hers. She took it.

They moved deeper.

No one spoke for several minutes. The only sounds were their breathing and the muffled rhythm of boots on damp stone. Aislen felt like her heart was too loud. Like the shadows were listening to it.

And then the tunnel shifted again.

The walls opened wider, just enough for them to walk two across now, but the darkness thickened. The light seemed to bend strangely in this space, casting long shapes that didn't match their bodies.

Tomas halted suddenly.

Sion almost ran into him.

"Wait," he whispered.

They froze.

Ahead of them, the tunnel widened again into a small chamber, just barely visible in the glow of Sion's light.

Something glittered along the walls. Not moss. Not stone.

Markings.

Runes.

Aislen's breath caught.

"They're old," Maera said, stepping forward to touch one. "Older than anything I've seen since I left the Celestara Court."

Aislen stepped forward, eyes wide. "They look... familiar."

The symbols pulsed faintly under her hand, like they *recognized* her.

"Because they're tied to your bloodline," Maera murmured. "These were crafted with faelight. And if they're active..." Her voice trailed off.

"It means someone's still using them," Kael finished.

Aislen turned slowly, scanning the chamber. The walls formed a nearly perfect circle, and at the center, the floor was slightly sunken. It looked almost like a forgotten altar, or a gathering space. The air here was colder. Sharper.

It smelled like metal and ash.

"Something happened here," Sion said, frowning. "Recently."

Aislen's skin prickled. Her magic stirred restlessly beneath her ribs.

"This is only the beginning," she whispered.

The tunnel beyond the chamber yawned open. It was black as ink and utterly silent. A gust of wind blew through it, cold and unnatural.

Tomas turned, his jaw set. "We rest here. Just for a few minutes. Everyone drink something. Eat if you can."

Kael didn't let go of her hand.

Aislen stared down the new stretch of tunnel, heart pounding.

They were in the dark now, truly in it.

And whatever lay ahead wasn't just old, it was powerful.

It was waiting for them.

She could feel their eyes.

* * *

~ Thess ~

Darkness wasn't the absence of light.

It had a *weight*.

Thess had never understood that until now.

She couldn't move. Couldn't see. Couldn't even tell if her eyes were open or closed. The black around her was thick and *alive*, pressing in against her skin like it was trying to remember what she felt like.

How long had she been here?

Her hands were numb. Her lips cracked. But her mind... her mind still burned.

They took her.

She remembered that part.

The pull. The scream. The hands, no, not hands... *claws? Shadows?* Something cold that gripped her ankle and dragged her through the fog.

But nothing had touched her since.

Not physically.

Not yet.

Something whispered sometimes. Not in words. In memories that weren't hers. In colors she'd never seen. It scraped at the inside of her skull like claws on wet stone.

She wasn't alone.

Not truly.

Whatever *it* was, it was waiting.

Studying her.

She didn't scream anymore.

She couldn't tell if her throat was too raw or if she'd stopped trying. What was the point? No sound traveled in this place. The air swallowed it whole. The silence was a predator.

Still... she clung to one thing.

His voice.

"Trouble."

The way Sion said it, like it meant *more.* Like she was *more* than whatever darkness wanted to make her.

She held onto it like a thread between her fingers.

If she moved wrong, it might snap.

But she wasn't broken yet.

Not completely.

Not yet.

Thirty-Six

"Lured"

~ Aislen ~

The deeper they went, the more the tunnel changed.

It wasn't just the temperature, though the air grew colder with each step. It was so cold her breath began to fog. It wasn't just the walls, which shifted from packed earth to smooth stone veined with silver and gold that shimmered under Sion's soft, hovering light.

It was the feeling.

Something ancient coiled in these depths, her magic just couldn't tell what it was.

They hadn't spoken much since finding the rune-marked chamber. Each of them had pulled tighter into themselves, silence becoming a kind of armor. Even Kael, who usually stayed within arm's reach, gave her a little more space. It was as if he sensed the weight she carried and knew it couldn't be lifted. Not yet.

Aislen's fingers brushed the wall, rough and warm in some places, icy and smooth in others. It felt like the tunnel had a pulse, one that beat slower than any living thing.

She paused when her foot caught on something. Looking down, she expected stone. Instead...

"Wait." She crouched, brushing aside a film of dust.

There, just beneath a cluster of moss, was fabric.

Threadbare. Torn. A strip of something dark blue, stained and frayed.

Kael was at her side in an instant. "What is it?"

She held it up, hand trembling. "This... this looks like the sash Thess always wore on her pack. The one with the little crescent stitching."

He leaned in, eyes narrowing. "It is."

Sion, hearing the exchange, stepped forward and sent a brighter flare of light down the tunnel. The glow stretched into the dark, illuminating bits of scuff marks in the stone. A few strands of hair, lighter than Aislen's and nearly golden were snagged in a crack.

He immediately grabbed Thess's pack from his own back, searching for the sash.

"It's gone," he said. "Do you think she tore it off when she was taken? To try and lead us in her direction?"

"Maybe... All we know for sure is she was here," Aislen whispered. Her voice broke. "She's close." She could feel it with every fiber of her being.

A soft echo carried back to them. A sound like laughter, warped and stretched too thin.

It wasn't real. It couldn't be. But Kael stepped in front of her anyway, shielding her with his body as his shadows rippled at his shoulders, ready to strike.

Maera murmured something under her breath, most likely another prayer, and Tomas raised his staff with a hand that shook just slightly.

Only Aislen noticed.

She frowned, stepping closer to him. "Dad... are you okay?"

"I'm fine," he said quickly. Too quickly. He avoided her eyes. "Just tired." He tried to smile. But it didn't reach his eyes.

He'd gone first this whole time. Kept pace with us the entire time, even when some of our fae feet move quicker than his. She could tell he was determined to prove something. And yet he was still trying to act like he was fine.

Guilt twisted through her. She reached out, squeezing his hand. "Let me take the front for a bit."

"No," Tomas said gently. "I said I'd protect you. I meant it." Tomas met her eyes and all she could see was exhaustion.

Kael turned slightly at the words but didn't interrupt. There was an understanding there between them, something older than titles or magic. The love a dad has for his daughter was different than the love between two mates. She wondered if her birth father ever loved her the way her dad did.

Aislen said nothing more, but she didn't let go of his hand.

They walked like that for another hour. Maybe more. Time felt strange down here, like the tunnel warped it alongside everything else.

The tunnel forked twice, forcing them to backtrack and choose new paths. The walls began to narrow again, the ceiling dripping with condensation that echoed like falling needles in the quiet.

Then, they found a mirror.

It was set into the wall like it had been swallowed by stone. Cracked and fogged, it shimmered faintly when they passed. Not silver-backed, but starlight-backed.

Who would have put a mirror like that under ground? It was almost... elegant. Very out of place in the shadows.

Aislen stopped. Her breath caught.

In the glass, her reflection blinked, but not in time with her own.

It smiled faintly, like it knew something she didn't. Like it wasn't afraid of the dark ahead. Her reflection put her finger up to her lips as if she had a secret, one she was not ready to share.

Kael's hand found her arm. "Don't look at it too long."

Sion stepped up beside them. "That's veilglass. Dream-mirrors. They reflect... not what you are, but what you desire."

She turned away, heart pounding as she wondered what else it could show her.

"Did Thess come this way?" Maera asked, scanning the edges.

"There," Kael pointed at some scratches along the wall. They looked fresh, like someone had scraped metal across the stone. "She must've passed through here. But she was fighting."

More fabric. More strands. The air smelled suddenly of ash and lavender. Thess.

Aislen closed her eyes and let her magic flow through her. She was trying to sense Thess, or something that could lead them to her.

"She's closer," Aislen whispered again. "I can feel her presence."

Her magic pulsed faintly beneath her skin, not guiding anymore, but sensing. Thess's pain. Her fear.

But underneath it, something darker stirred. Something ancient.

They were walking straight toward it. They knew it would be a trap, but knowing something is ahead waiting for them made the hairs on the back of her neck stand up.

And still, Tomas didn't say a word about the sweat now slicking his brow, or the way he winced when he moved too quickly.

But Kael noticed too.

As they paused at a small ledge to drink, Kael pulled Aislen aside and said, voice low, "Watch him. Something's not right."

Aislen's stomach sank. She looked toward her dad, who had taken a seat against the wall, eyes closed for a moment too long.

She nodded. "I will."

They pressed on.

The tunnel darkened further, and in the distance, a faint light flickered. Not their own. Not magic.

Something ahead. Someone waiting.

Thess?

Or maybe whatever had taken her.

All they knew was that there was a trap awaiting them.

* * *

~ **Maera** ~

313

The others were gathered near the tunnel's curve, half-hunched against the cold, while Sion's flickering light orbited slowly overhead like a tired star.

But Maera's eyes weren't on the walls.

They were on Tomas.

He sat against the stone, a little apart from the others. Not far, but just enough. His shoulders sagged, one hand resting on his knee, the other curled around his side like he was trying to quiet something that ached beneath his ribs.

No one else seemed to notice.

But she did.

She always had.

Maera crossed the narrow space slowly, crouching beside him without a word. The shadows clung to the edges of his face, highlighting the lines she hadn't let herself trace in years. He looked tired, deeper than bone-tired. If that was even possible. Like something had been drained from him, and he was only now realizing how much he had left to lose.

She didn't say anything right away. Just pulled a waterskin from her belt and held it out to him.

He didn't take it.

"Tomas," she said softly. "Don't make me force it into your hands."

His lips quirked, barely. "You never had trouble doing that before."

She didn't smile. "Don't change the subject."

"I'm not." His voice was quiet. "I'm just… tired."

"Exhausted or hurting?"

His gaze flicked to hers. That answerless look a male gave when they were too proud to admit they needed help and too in love to lie.

Maera exhaled and sat beside him, careful not to crowd his space. The ground was cold, but it didn't matter. "Drink," she said again, pressing the waterskin into his hand.

He accepted it this time. Took a slow sip, then let it rest in his lap.

She studied him in the quiet, her sharp eyes catching every little detail. She noticed the tremble in his fingers, the way his left foot hadn't stopped tapping against the ground, the pale sweat clinging to his neck.

"You've been pushing too hard," she murmured.

He didn't argue. That alone terrified her more than if he had.

"I need to keep going," he said finally. "She needs me."

"She needs all of us," Maera replied. "But not at the cost of you breaking apart. You've already given everything for her. Let us carry the rest for a while."

Tomas glanced toward the others. Aislen had curled beside Kael, their heads bent close as they spoke quietly. Sion sat cross-legged, reinforcing the enchantment on his light, while his magic danced faintly across his knuckles.

And there, etched in Tomas's face, was the ache of every father who knew his time in that child's life was changing. Diminishing.

"She's not my little girl anymore," he said after a long moment. "I see it every day... In her magic, her voice. In the way she stands up to danger like she's known it all her life."

Maera's voice was barely more than a breath. "She learned that from you."

He looked at her then. Not the passing glances they'd shared over the years. Not the familiar silence of two people who'd weathered too many storms together. He looked at her like he used to, like he wanted to remember everything.

"I'm not ready to let go of her," he admitted, hoarse.

"You don't have to," she said gently. "You just have to let her stand beside you. That's all she's ever wanted."

Tomas nodded, slow and silent.

She placed a hand on his arm, felt the tremor beneath his sleeve. His pulse thudded, strong, but strained.

They sat like that for a while, wrapped in dim light and the ghosts of a life they had almost shared.

When the others finally gathered to regroup, Kael glanced over and asked, "We good to keep moving?"

Maera looked to Tomas.

He straightened, forced a deep breath, and stood without complaint. "Yeah," he said. "Just needed a minute."

But she saw it.

The slight hesitation. The grit in his voice. The pain he wasn't willing to admit to.

Maera rose beside him, brushing dust from her cloak. Her heart ached in ways she couldn't explain. Something in the air felt thinner now, more fragile.

And as they began to walk again, deeper into the dark, toward whatever waited at the end of this twisted tunnel, Maera silently, desperately hoped...

That one minute would be enough.

Thirty-Seven

"Sacrifice"

~ **Tomas** ~

The tunnel was too quiet.

Not the kind of quiet that came from peace, but the kind that followed something terrible. The kind that made your skin itch, like you were walking into the aftermath of a scream.

Tomas moved forward anyway.

He kept his hand on the damp wall, using it for balance more than direction, the uneven stone grounding him with every step. Each breath he drew felt heavier than the last. He didn't know if it was the stale air down here, or if something deeper had started to fray inside him.

His legs were tired. His shoulders ached. But none of it compared to the hollow weight in his chest. It was the feeling that something was coming, something evil.

He looked up ahead, to where Aislen walked with Kael and Sion close on her heels. She kept her chin high, like she always did when she was scared. Gods, she had no idea how strong she was.

It had been hours since they'd entered the tunnels. Time didn't move right in here, it didn't feel right either. There was no sun, no sky, just one foot after another in this endless, watching dark. And though he said

317

nothing, Tomas felt it. It felt like the stone was testing them. Studying them.

Testing *him*.

His heartbeat skipped when he stumbled, just slightly, and caught himself against the wall.

Maera was beside him in an instant. "Tomas?"

"I'm fine," he said, too quickly.

"You're not." She didn't accuse, she never did. Just quietly offered the truth.

He gave her a weak smile. "Just tired. Long walk for an old man."

She narrowed her eyes. "Don't you dare."

He blinked at her, feigning innocence.

"Dare what?"

"Try to laugh it off. You've carried half of us through this journey more times than I can count." And then quieter, "you're exhausted. I just want to help."

He reached over, brushing a bit of dust from her cheek. "I'd carry you still, if you asked."

Her face softened, and she took his hand in both of hers. "Sit. Drink something."

He didn't argue this time. He sat against the wall, letting the cool stone steady his breath. Maera passed him a flask of water, and he drank slowly. The silence around them was still too loud. His ears strained for something, *anything*, that would break it.

That's when he heard it.

A sound. A whisper of something *different*. Not stone shifting. Not wind moaning. Something human.

"Wait," Aislen called from ahead. "I hear something."

Everyone froze.

Tomas stood, heart leaping to attention.

Then a groan. A soft, raw sound of pain. Barely there, but real. Familiar.

Sion darted forward, light glowing brighter in his palm. It illuminated the walls ahead. There were markings etched deep into the stone, and a small recess, almost hidden, behind a jagged bend. A door. It blended so well with the rock that only someone looking for it would find it.

Kael pressed his hand to it, and it *gave.* It held a slow, grinding sound as its ancient hinges creaked open.

The air changed instantly.

Colder. Damper. But also, the most alive it had been within these tunnels.

Inside, on the floor of a narrow room, curled in a heap of torn fabric and dried blood, was a body.

"Thess!" Aislen cried, rushing past the others.

Sion was right behind her, Kael too, and Tomas followed, heart slamming as they reached her side.

She was barely conscious. Skin pale, lips cracked, eyes fluttering.

"Gods," Aislen whispered, falling to her knees beside her. "Thess, can you hear me? Please—please wake up."

Sion knelt too, gently lifting Thess's head and cradling it against his chest. His illusion light hovered above them, casting a pale gold over her face.

"Water," Kael barked. "Give her water."

Maera passed him the waterskin. Aislen tilted it gently against Thess's lips, whispering her name over and over. Sion brushed matted hair from her face, his jaw clenched tight, like he was trying not to fall apart.

"Come on, Trouble," he said softly. "Don't let this place win."

At first, she didn't move. And then, *then,* a small sound escaped her throat. A cough. A breath. A faint groan.

Her fingers twitched against Aislen's sleeve.

"Thess," Aislen gasped. "You're okay. You're safe now."

Thess's eyes fluttered open. Dazed. Distant. Her mouth opened, the movement dry and slow. The words came out like a sigh.

"She... she's coming back..."

Everyone leaned in.

"Who?" Aislen asked, barely breathing. "Thess, who is coming back?"

A new voice cut through the air.

"That would be me."

Tomas turned.

And there, at the mouth of the chamber, wrapped in golden light that turned the very shadows to ash, stood the Sun Queen.

Virel was here.

* * *

~ Aislen ~

"That would be me."

The words sliced through the chamber like sunlight through silk, both soft and searing.

Aislen's breath caught in her throat as she turned toward the voice.

There, standing just beyond the threshold of the hidden door, was the most horribly radiant creature she had ever seen.

The Sun Queen.

Tall. Regal. Dressed in molten gold that clung to her frame like liquid light. Her hair was sunlight braided with flame, her eyes a burnished bronze that seemed to glow with their own fury. She looked nothing like what Aislen expected. Like she could have been different in another life. But here she was, locked in on some evilness she couldn't let go of.

There was no madness in her gaze. Only a terrible stillness. It reminded her of a blade being held just before the strike. That made her even more dangerous. Madness could be unpredictable. But this... this was something colder. Calculated.

"Thess..." Kael growled, stepping protectively in front of her. "Aislen, stay behind me."

But Aislen couldn't move. Her heart pounded like thunder. Her magic surged under her skin, of both fear and fury igniting every buried thread of it.

The Sun Queen stepped into the chamber, unhurried. Unbothered. "I must admit, you made it further than I expected."

"Why?" Aislen choked out, stepping forward before Kael could stop her.

"Why take her? What do you want from us?"

The Queen's gaze flicked to her mom before it settled on her, and for the first time, Aislen felt it, the enormity of her power. Not the gentle hum of earthsong or the wild dance of starlight. No. This was the kind of power that scorched the bones of the world and smiled as it watched them turn to ash.

"You," the Sun Queen said. "You are what I want. The heir with starlight in her blood. The star-forged flame. Your blood sings louder than any song I've ever heard. Did you think the realm would let something like you walk free?"

"I'm not yours," Aislen spat.

The Queen tilted her head. "No. You're his."

Her voice curled like smoke, low and bitter.

"You bear his light in your blood," she continued, taking a slow step forward, her eyes narrowing. "His magic. His legacy. Even your defiance is his. Do you know what it cost the rest of us, when he chose your mother over duty? Over his Court?"

Aislen's breath caught.

The Sun Queen's lip curled, her fury barely contained. "He was meant to bind our Courts under one. To stand beside me and burn the rot from this realm. But he disappeared, I didn't give him a choice. And now, I see it all again. His stubborn hope, his impossible dreams—all of it reflected in your face."

She lifted her hand.

"I should've scorched you from the moment you were born."

Something sharp flickered in her tone. Contempt wrapped in something far older. Older than Velastra. Older than any of them.

And then, without warning, the light came.

A blast of sunfire erupted.

Straight for Aislen.

She barely had time to raise her hands. Her magic surged, but it was too slow, too shocked. She closed her eyes bracing herself for the burn, for the pain.

321

…but it never came.

Aislen opened her eyes only to see her dad.

He threw himself in front of her with a roar that shattered the air.

The sunfire struck him in the chest with a sound like a thunderclap. The light consumed him in a golden flare that burned so bright Aislen had to shut her eyes.

And then nothing but silence.

"Aislen," he gasped, voice raw. "Are you okay?"

He was on his knees.

Smoke rose from his body. His tunic was scorched, his chest seared through with light. He turned to her slowly, his face twisted in pain, blood already blooming under his ribs.

And he smiled.

A weak, broken, father's smile.

"I told you I'd go first."

"No," she whispered, stumbling toward him. "No—no no no—Dad—*Dad*—"

She dropped to her knees beside him as Kael lunged forward, shielding them both with his body, his own power flaring to life in a glow of silver-blue. Sion pushed Thess back against the wall, his face a mask of panic and rage.

Maera screamed.

But Aislen couldn't hear any of it.

All she saw was him.

Tomas.

The man who raised her. Who taught her to plant seeds and told her stories about stars that could sing. The man who taught her how to be brave even when she was afraid.

Her dad.

His hand found hers. His fingers trembled.

"You're okay," he murmured again. "You're okay."

"Why would you do that?" she sobbed, clutching him. "Why—why would you—?"

"Because you're mine," he said. "You've always been mine to protect."

Her tears fell hot onto his cheeks.

He reached up, brushing one away with a shaking hand.

"I love you, Aislen. My daughter."

And then his hand fell.

His eyes didn't close, but the light in them did.

She screamed.

A raw, broken sound that filled the chamber and made the stones tremble. Her magic surged, wild and uncontrollable. The ground cracked beneath her, vines bursting through stone, reaching for anything, *everything*.

Kael pulled her back just as another blast from the Queen flew past them, barely missing where Tomas had fallen.

He held Aislen to his chest, shielding her with his entire body as she collapsed into him, sobbing into his shoulder. Her magic tangled with his, violent and chaotic.

"We have to move," Maera said, voice steel over grief. "Now."

The Queen stood, gathering more sunfire.

But something had changed.

Aislen wasn't running.

She was burning.

And something inside her had just broken wide open.

The Sun Queen's gaze faltered, only for a moment, before she smirked. "You should've learned to shield him," she sneered. "You could've been stronger like your—"

A low, resonant sound filled the tunnel.

Not a sob.

Not a scream.

A hum.

The *magic* in Aislen's blood awakened like a sleeping giant. It was called forth by fury, grief, and something deeper. Something ancient.

Light burst from her skin, *not gold*, not moonlit silver, but a fierce, iridescent *white-blue*, tinged with violet at the edges. Starlight surged through her veins like liquid fire, and something else moved with it.

The *earth* shivered beneath her feet.

The tunnel itself reacted. The stone was groaning, the air vibrating with barely-contained force. Runes on the walls flared to life, echoing the wild, unstable rhythm of her heart.

The Sun Queen's smirk faltered.

"You shouldn't be able to do that. How can you do that?" she breathed.

Aislen didn't answer. Her body moved before thought could catch it.

She *blinked*, not with her eyes, but with her whole being. She disappeared from where she stood and reappeared behind the Queen in a burst of shadows. A movement that wasn't walking. It was Kael's, somehow she must've been able to conjure up his magic through their bond.

That was something she would have to consider later when their lives were not at risk.

The Queen barely had time to turn before Aislen's hand, glowing with blinding force, slammed into her back and sent her sprawling forward.

Magic exploded from Aislen like a solar flare. It was burning bright, but cold. It was the *truth* of stars, not the warmth of them. Not sun. Not light. Something older.

The Sun Queen screamed.

Not from pain alone, but from *shock*.

"You shouldn't have come for me," Aislen whispered, voice shaking with raw power. "You should've stayed in the sky where our shadows couldn't find you."

With a flick of her wrist, a wave of starlight laced with crystalline tendrils of earthsong struck the Queen square in the chest. It was not fire, but pure, cracking light that tore at illusions and armor alike.

The Queen staggered.

Her golden crown flickered.

Her form dimmed.

Then, pure panic.

She turned, trying to raise her hand again, but Aislen was already gone, blinking across the space with that strange, ethereal movement again. The magic *tracked* her, surged from the very stone, wrapping around her like the forest had once done in the Vanor.

"You don't belong here," Aislen said. *"Not anymore."*

The Queen's eyes went wide, and for the first time, afraid.

Then, she vanished.

Not in a blaze of fire. Not in triumph.

But like a shadow in reverse, it was burned away by something stronger.

The tunnel fell silent once more.

Aislen collapsed to her knees beside her father, chest heaving, light flickering across her skin like dying stars.

It was over. For now.

But something in her had *changed* forever.

And the realm would feel it.

* * *

~ **Maera** ~

She didn't hear the end of the battle.

Didn't see the Virel vanish.

Because the moment Tomas hit the ground, the world narrowed to the sight of his body, her husband, her anchor, lying motionless in the dirt.

Maera dropped beside him with a cry that didn't sound like her own.

"No—no, no, no—Tomas—"

She pressed her hands to his chest, to his face, to the place the blast had torn through flesh and bone. "Please. Please come back. Breathe, just breathe, just—*gods,* don't do this—"

There was no breath.

No light in his eyes.

Only the smell of scorched leather and smoke and the faint copper tang of blood that shouldn't have been there. Not on him. Not *him.*

Her sobs wracked her body as she bent over him, cradling his head in her lap, running her fingers over his soot-streaked face like touch alone could undo death.

"You weren't supposed to die," she whispered, voice shattering. "You were supposed to walk her down the aisle. You were supposed to plant seeds with her in the spring, tease our future grandchildren, and grow old with me by the river."

She couldn't breathe.

There wasn't enough air in the tunnel. Not enough room for this pain.

And beside her, silent, was Aislen.

Maera turned, hands still shaking, her heart split in two. She saw her daughter sitting in the dust, only inches away, her knees pulled up, her arms loosely wrapped around them. Her eyes were wide and blank. Empty. Fixed on nothing. Not even tears.

Just… stillness.

Like her soul had left with him.

"Aislen," Maera whispered, crawling over, reaching for her. "Sweetheart, look at me. Please."

But Aislen didn't blink. Didn't move. Her hair was wild, her skin still faintly glowing from the magic that had burst from her like a dying star. Her hands… her hands were covered in blood.

Tomas's blood.

Maera's own hands trembled as she cupped Aislen's cheeks, leaning close. "It wasn't your fault. Do you hear me? It wasn't you. He chose to save you because he *loved* you."

Still, no reaction.

Maera swallowed a sob, pressing her forehead to her daughter's. "I need you to come back to me, baby. Please. Don't go where I can't reach you."

Her tears fell freely now. They fell into Aislen's hair, onto Tomas's chest.

Around them, the others stood in stunned silence.

Kael hovered close, his hands clenching and unclenching at his sides, aching to reach for Aislen but not sure if she'd even feel it. Sion had turned away, eyes squeezed shut, mouth moving silently in what might've been a prayer or a curse. Thess, half-conscious, wept quietly against the wall, murmuring something over and over that no one could hear.

And Tomas...

He looked peaceful.

As if he'd already forgiven them all.

As if his final act of love had been the one thing he'd never regret.

Maera bent over him again, brushing her lips to his brow.

"I'll carry her the rest of the way," she whispered. "I'll get her there. I'll protect her now. But I don't know how to do this without you."

A sob wrenched through her chest.

The tunnels, thick with silence, seemed to echo her grief back at her.

But Aislen didn't flinch.

Didn't move.

And Maera, heart breaking anew, held them both.

She heard voices. They were muffled and distant, like they came from underwater.

Sion murmuring something about Thess. Mentioning how weak she was, how they couldn't push forward. Kael pacing. Aislen still silent, unmoving. Someone, maybe Sion, saying they had no choice but to stop. That they couldn't carry both Tomas and Thess.

Maera didn't respond.

She couldn't.

The idea of leaving him, *leaving* him, was unthinkable. Not after everything. Not when his blood was still warm on her palms. Not when his last breath had been spent saving *their* daughter.

Her chest ached like something had cracked inside her and was still breaking, over and over.

Not now. Not like this.

He was supposed to grow old beside her. His body wasn't supposed to lie cold in the dirt of some cursed tunnel, beneath old runes and ancient stone. He should be home. With his boots by the door and his laugh echoing through the kitchen.

And now...

Now he would be a ghost in her bones.

A presence she would carry in silence.

"Maera."

The voice barely reached her. She blinked slowly, realizing someone had knelt beside her.

Kael.

His hand hovered above her shoulder but didn't touch her.

"Thess can't walk on her own," he said gently. "We can't carry them both… and Aislen—" He glanced toward her daughter, voice faltering. "She hasn't said a word."

Maera turned, and her eyes found Aislen again.

She still hadn't moved.

Still sat with her knees drawn in, her face pale and blank, her eyes unfocused. The blood on her fingers had dried. Her mouth was parted slightly, as if she'd been about to speak and forgot how.

She was stuck somewhere Maera couldn't reach, not yet.

And Maera didn't know how to bring her back.

"I'm sorry," Kael said softly. "But we need to stop here. Just for tonight."

Maera looked back down at Tomas.

"I can't leave him."

Kael's throat worked as he swallowed. "Then we won't."

That simple.

Like he knew if he tried to argue, she'd snap.

Like he'd already decided: no matter how dark the path ahead, they would not force her to move on. Not from this.

A slow breath rattled out of her lungs.

Sion was already helping Thess to lie down near the far wall, bundling a cloak beneath her head and murmuring reassurances too soft to hear. His magic glowed faintly between his fingers, casting a flickering light that didn't quite chase away the shadows. He used his healing powers to make her more comfortable.

If only he could've gotten to Tomas in time…

Kael moved back to Aislen, crouching beside her.

She didn't blink.

Didn't breathe deeply.

Didn't seem to register his presence at all.

Maera knew that look.

Shock.

It wasn't just grief. It was the soul's defense against unbearable pain.

She wanted to reach for her daughter, to wrap her in her arms and promise she'd fix everything.

But she couldn't.

Because right now, all she had to give was a broken heart and shaking hands.

So she stayed beside Tomas. Ran her fingers through his hair one more time. Pressed her cheek to his shoulder.

"I'm not ready to let you go," she whispered, her voice cracking.

No one asked her to.

And that, somehow, made her cry all over again.

Thirty-Eight

"What Remains"

~⟨∘⟩~

~ **Aislen** ~

Her mom's fingers had stilled.

At some point in the night, the soft, rhythmic strokes through Aislen's hair had grown slower… and then stopped altogether, her mom drifting into sleep with her hand still curled gently near Aislen's temple.

Aislen didn't move.

She hadn't moved in hours.

Her head lay in her mom's lap, her limbs curled inward, her eyes half-lidded and unfocused, staring at nothing.

She couldn't see him from this angle, and for that, she was grateful. There was a blanket, or Kael's cloak maybe, draped over his body now. He must've done it quietly. Gently. When she wasn't paying attention.

Everything was blurred around the edges.

Sounds dulled. Faces vague. Time… unmeasurable.

The rock beneath her was cold, but she didn't feel it. The ache in her muscles didn't matter. Her throat was raw from screaming, though she wasn't sure when the screaming had stopped. Maybe when her voice gave out. Maybe when her soul did.

Her dad was dead.

330

She hadn't said it out loud. She couldn't.

Because once she said it out loud, it would be true.

And if it was true, then the world had officially fallen apart.

So she stayed silent.

Because silence, at least, was soft.

Silence didn't cut like knives the way words did. It didn't echo like Kael's voice had when he tried to speak to her. Three times. Maybe four. She didn't remember what he said. Only that it sounded like something fragile breaking against the floor.

She hadn't answered.

Not because she didn't want to.

But because she couldn't.

The moment she did, if she turned to actually look at him, or reach for him, or whispered *he's gone,* she'd fall apart all over again.

There was no doubt, no question about it.

And she wasn't sure she'd know how to put herself back together after that.

So she stayed curled up on her side, chest aching, throat dry, heart silent.

The mate bond hummed faintly beneath her skin, a tether pulling gently toward Kael, warm and constant, like a heartbeat in the distance.

She ignored it.

Not out of anger.

But because even the idea of comfort felt dangerous. If she let herself fall into Kael's arms right now, she wouldn't stop crying. She might never stop. She might scream and burn the entire tunnel to ash with the rage coiled deep in her chest.

And she was too tired for fire.

She didn't want to feel.

She just wanted *him.* Her dad.

She wanted him to run his hand over her hair and tell her she was strong. To tease her about her messy braid. To wrap her in one of his worn old cloaks and say she'd always be his girl.

But he was gone.

331

And no amount of magic or fury or starlight in her veins could change that.

Her breath hitched, but she didn't cry.

Not yet.

She could hear the others a few paces away. Sion's quiet voice. Thess's weak reply. Kael's footsteps. They were back and forth, again and again, like he didn't know what to do with his hands. Maera, even in sleep, made soft sounds, the kind you make when you're dreaming of someone you've lost.

Aislen felt like a statue carved from ice, waiting to crack.

She wanted to move. To speak. To reach for Kael.

But the grief had hollowed her out.

She was just an echo now.

And for the moment… maybe that was all she could be.

* * *

She wasn't sure how long she lay there.

Time folded in on itself, looping like threads caught on a spindle. But at some point, soft as a breeze in spring, she felt movement near her. Not loud. Not demanding. Just… *there*.

A shadow shifted at the edge of her vision. A hesitant breath. Then a whisper of cloth dragging across stone.

It wasn't her mom who moved this time.

It was Thess.

Aislen blinked. Once. Twice. Her body refused to react, but her heart stuttered at the sight of her.

Thess looked like a ghost. She was thin, pale, eyes hollow from too much time in the dark. Her skin looked papery in the flickering light, and she smelled faintly of ash and dried blood.

She leaned heavily on the wall as she moved, one slow step at a time, trembling with the effort. Her legs barely carried her. Her lip was split, her cheeks sunken, and her hands shook as she reached forward.

She shouldn't have been walking.

She should've been resting.

But she came anyway.

For *her*.

Aislen's throat tightened, the first crack splintering her wall of numbness. And then, finally, after all the stillness, she looked up.

Right at Thess.

Her voice came out broken, thin as thread. "Thess…"

It was just a whisper. But it was enough.

Thess knelt beside her with all the grace of a collapsing wave and wrapped her arms around her without a word. The hug wasn't strong, but it didn't need to be. It *was* strength. The kind that only best friends carried between them like sacred fire. The kind that said *I'm here*, even when the world was falling apart.

Aislen buried her face in Thess's shoulder, her hands gripping the worn fabric of her shirt. She let out a shaky breath that sounded more like a sob, and Thess just held her tighter.

"I am so sorry," Aislen whispered, voice shaking. "We tried finding you sooner—" Thess shushed her as she wrapped her in her arms.

Thess didn't answer with words. She didn't need to.

They just held each other and cried.

No theatrics. No speeches.

Just grief.

Grief for her dad. For Thess's pain. For everything they'd lost along the way.

They cried until their tears ran dry. Until the only thing left was the space between heartbeats and the quiet reminder that they were still here.

Alive.

Broken, maybe.

But *here*.

A shadow passed over them again.

This time, Kael didn't speak. He knelt beside them, gentle hands easing Aislen out of Thess's arms. She didn't resist. She let herself be lifted, arms curling around his neck like instinct, her body too heavy with sorrow to carry on her own.

Kael cradled her like she was something sacred.

He carried her away from the others. They went down the tunnel a little farther, where the flickering light barely touched the wall and shadows stretched wide. It was quiet there. Cold. But they needed the space.

She needed him. More than she could say.

He stopped near a smooth outcropping of stone and sank down slowly, back against the wall, Aislen still in his arms.

He didn't speak at first.

Didn't ask anything of her.

He just held her, one arm wrapped around her shoulders, the other tucked under her legs. Her cheek rested over his heart.

And it was enough.

The beat of it was steady and grounding. It matched her own like a balm.

His presence was the only thing that didn't hurt.

She didn't move.

Didn't speak.

Didn't even blink.

Kael's arms didn't waver once as he cradled her. His heartbeat thudded steadily beneath her ear, and for a while, that was the only sound.

Then he spoke.

Softly. Carefully. Like if he wasn't gentle enough, the words might splinter her.

"I was seven," he said quietly, brushing his thumb across her arm, "when I broke my arm falling out of that sycamore behind your garden. You remember that one?"

His voice carried a smile, but there was sorrow tangled inside it.

"You were six. You marched right up to the house, banged on your dad's door, and dragged him outside like it was *his* fault I was an idiot."

She didn't react, but his hold around her tightened just a little.

"Tomas didn't panic. He didn't yell. He just looked at my arm, nodded, and said, 'Guess it's time to teach you how to wrap a splint.'" Kael huffed a soft, brittle laugh. "I cried. You didn't. You held my other hand and told me I was brave… even though you were the one being strong."

He paused, his voice dropping lower.

"He didn't treat me like some fae warrior's son. Or like a problem. He just… saw me. Like I was one of his own."

Kael leaned his head back against the stone and let the silence stretch a little before speaking again.

"He's the one who taught me how to build a fire from damp wood. How to make tea that doesn't taste like bark. How to tell if someone was lying by the twitch in their eye. He told me once that the best males aren't the loudest. They're the ones who stay when things get hard."

Another pause.

"He always stayed."

The lump in Aislen's throat ached so much it felt like she might never swallow again. Her eyes burned. Her chest cracked beneath the weight of Kael's voice.

"He made the hardest things seem simple. He was a good man, and I know he was proud of you," Kael whispered, brushing a strand of hair from her face. "He never said it like your mom did. He was never loud or dramatic, but he looked at you like the stars bowed to you. Like you were his whole world."

She trembled.

Kael didn't push her to speak.

He just kept talking. Kept *remembering*. Because it was the only way he knew how to keep her with him when she was drifting so far away.

"I don't know what comes next," he murmured. "But I know this, you don't have to carry all of it alone. You don't have to be strong for us right now. Just breathe, Aislen. Just stay here with me."

Still, she didn't answer.

But slowly… carefully… she shifted the tiniest bit closer.

And that was enough for now.

Her eyes finally closed as she drifted off to sleep for the first time that night.

* * *

The tunnel vanished.

She wasn't awake.

Not fully.

But she wasn't exactly dreaming, either.

The world around her shimmered with the softness of starlight, a sky painted with violet clouds and galaxies that pulsed like slow heartbeats. She stood in a field of long grass, the wind quiet, the horizon hazy.

It should've felt peaceful.

But it didn't.

Not with the grief tightening like a noose around her throat. Not with the weight in her chest that had no name because *loss* wasn't big enough for it.

She turned, ready to run—

And froze.

There, standing just a few paces away, was a male cloaked in silver and midnight blue. His silver streaked blonde hair shimmered faintly with stars, his eyes an impossible pale violet that mirrored her own.

Her father.

Aislen shook her head with disgust, the only father she truly had was dead.

"Aislen," he said softly.

Her breath caught.

His expression flickered. It turned hopeful yet uncertain. "I've been trying to reach you again. The Veil is thinner when you sleep. I felt your magic pulse… like a beacon."

But she didn't step toward him.

She stepped back.

"You don't get to be here," she whispered, voice tight. "Not *now*."

He blinked. "Aislen—what's wrong?"

"You don't get to show up now," she choked. "Not after everything. Not after—after *he* died."

Confusion knit his brow. "Who—?"

"My dad," she hissed. "The man who raised me. The one who loved me *before* you even remembered I existed."

His face shifted into shock. Grief hadn't reached him yet, but she watched it start to bloom, slow and sickening.

"I—I didn't know," he said quietly.

"No, of course you didn't," she snapped. "Because you weren't there. You're *never* there. You appear in dreams, in riddles. You send me cryptic warnings, but where *were* you when I needed you?"

The air around her pulsed, her starlight magic rippling outward like cracks through the dream.

"You could've helped him. You could've stopped her."

His shoulders fell. "The Sun Queen?"

"Yes," Aislen said, shaking with rage. "She was going to kill me. He—he jumped in front of her magic. And now he's *gone*. Because I wasn't strong enough. Because I didn't see it coming. And you—you just waited."

Alarion stood frozen in the misty dreamscape, agony beginning to settle behind his eyes. "I never wanted this," he said. "I've been searching for you since the moment Maera left. But I could only search so far... you know I am confined to my Court."

"Well, surprise," she spat bitterly. "I'm here. And now everything is broken."

"Aislen, I didn't know. I knew there was something coming, I tried to warn you. But I didn't know what it was," He sighed. "Tomas was a good man, and I am proud of the person you have become because of him. I will never stop being grateful for him being there when I wasn't."

"Don't say his name," she said, voice cracking.

Silence settled between them, sharp and cold.

"I'm sorry," he said finally, barely above a whisper. "If I could trade places with him, I would. If I could bring him back to you…"

Tears welled in her eyes. She didn't want to hear it. Didn't want apologies. She wanted *Tomas*. She wanted her dad. Her real dad, be damned where her blood came from, she knew who she belonged to.

But she looked at Alarion, this stranger with her eyes, and saw something else, too.

He *meant* it.

Even if it didn't fix anything.

Even if it never would.

"You don't get to be my father just because we share blood," she whispered. "He already was."

"I know," Alarion said, his voice like breaking light. "But if you'll let me… I'd still like to be *something* to you."

She didn't answer.

The dream began to fade, slipping away like fog in sunlight.

And before the stars blinked out above them, she said the only thing she could:

"I don't forgive you."

"I don't expect you to," he said gently. "We'll talk more soon, daughter."

And then he was gone.

Thirty-Nine

"Still Here"

~ Kael ~

They moved in silence.

The kind that pressed in closet and was thick and suffocating. It clung to their skin and filled the space between every footfall. Not even Thess spoke, and she was never quiet for long. Ever since they found her, her voice was still. Quiet. Her sharp, sarcastic, always-alive buoyant voice was gone. He never thought they would miss her sarcasm as much as they do right now.

She hadn't yet talked to them about what she went through, if she ever would.

She leaned heavily against Aislen as they walked, one arm wrapped tight around her shoulders. Her other hand trembled slightly, fingers curling every so often like she was trying to ground herself. As if she was still reaching for a wall in the dark. Her skin was pale, her steps uneven. But she was alive.

Kael had seen her dead in his mind a dozen times over these past days. This… this was a mercy.

But it didn't feel like a victory.

Not with the weight of Tomas's body hanging between him and Sion.

Every step was an effort, not because of the weight itself, but because of what it meant. Kael's shoulder ached, his arm burned from the strain, but he didn't complain. He would carry Tomas to the ends of the realm if he had to. If it gave Aislen even a shred of peace.

They hadn't spoken much since the battle. Aislen's voice hadn't returned after whispering to Thess. But her hand had found his in the dark again. That was enough for now.

He glanced toward her as they walked. Her face was almost as pale as Thess's. Her lips were pressed into a thin line, eyes distant. She was holding herself together, barely. But he knew the cost.

Sion hadn't spoken either. His jaw was clenched, shoulders rigid, light magic still humming softly around his fingers. He was more than ready, he was protective. He hadn't let it go dim once since they found Thess.

They walked like that for what felt like hours. Just the steady rhythm of boots on stone, breath and grief moving beside them.

Eventually, the air shifted.

The tunnel widened again, the stone giving way to earth. A faint glow filtered in from ahead. It was distant, but it looked natural. Not starlight, not magic.

Daylight.

Kael's heart gave a painful lurch as they reached a wall of thick, curling vines. They covered the end of the tunnel completely, obscuring what lay beyond, but he could see the shimmer of water reflected in the light that crept through.

Sion slowed first. "We're here, we're out. Thank the gods."

Kael let out a slow breath and glanced toward Aislen. She didn't speak, but nodded once, helping Thess to sit against the wall as gently as she could.

Kael and Sion knelt with care, laying Tomas's body down beside them. He was still wrapped in the cloak that Kael had placed over him.

They paused there.

No one said anything. No one moved for a moment.

It was Aislen who stood first, moving toward the wall of vines. She touched one gently, as if afraid it would vanish at her hand. And then, she pulled it back.

Light spilled in. It was soft and golden as it filtered through mist and trees. The tunnel had opened up at the edge of a hidden pond, the water glittering like glass under the overcast sky. It was quiet here. Still. Untouched.

Kael's chest ached.

It felt sacred. Like the land itself had kept this place hidden for a reason.

The others followed slowly. One by one, they stepped out into the open, blinking against the light, the shock of fresh air filling their lungs.

Kael walked to Aislen's side, brushing her hand with his fingers before crouching near the water's edge. He filled a flask and brought it back to Thess first, kneeling beside her. "Drink slow."

She nodded, voice hoarse. "Tastes like freedom."

He gave her a small smile. It didn't reach his eyes.

Aislen stayed by the vines, silent. Staring at the trees. Her hand touched her chest, right over her heart, right over where her mate bond pulsed between them. Kael could feel her grief like it was stitched into his own skin.

They didn't speak.

Not because there wasn't anything to say, but because there was too much.

Sion sat cross-legged near the water, head bowed, arms resting on his knees. The strain of carrying Tomas for so long had settled into his muscles, his shoulders sagging now that the weight was off his back. The light he'd held flickered gently at his fingertips, dimmer than before, like it too was tired.

Kael lowered himself beside the trunk of a twisted tree that curled over the pond's edge, letting his head fall back against the bark. Every bone in his body ached. His legs, his back, his heart. All of it was exhausted.

Across from him, Thess sat with her arms wrapped around her knees, tucked into herself. Aislen had draped a spare cloak over her, and she leaned slightly to one side, too weak to sit upright for long. Her eyes were half-lidded, but she stayed awake, lips parted like she was still trying to take in this moment. To believe it was real. That she was safe.

She glanced at Kael once, just once, and he nodded. It was enough.

Aislen remained by the water's edge. She hadn't moved since they arrived, crouched beside the pond like it held answers she couldn't quite reach. Her reflection shimmered in the surface. It was soft, flickering, blurred, but still as devastatingly beautiful as he always saw her. Her eyes were open, but distant.

He could feel her through the bond. Tired. Fractured. But still there.

Kael let out a breath through his nose and closed his eyes. Just for a moment.

She wasn't speaking yet. But he would wait. He would carry her through this, too, if that's what it took.

The sun was hidden behind thick clouds. The water barely moved. The trees around them whispered softly, branches swaying in the wind. But none of them spoke.

They just sat.

Together.

Silent.

Breathing.

Surviving.

* * *

~ Sion ~

The pond shimmered with a dull stillness, the surface broken only by the occasional ripple of wind or the distant plop of a falling leaf. It should have felt like relief, like sanctuary. But the weight in Sion's chest didn't ease.

He sat a little ways back from the others, just far enough to watch them all. His legs were stretched out, boots caked in mud, muscles throbbing from hours of carrying Tomas. The ache should've been unbearable. Instead, it grounded him.

His gaze never left Thess.

She sat close to Aislen, wrapped in that cloak like it was armor. She was smaller than he remembered, like her time in the tunnel had hollowed her out. Her hair was a tangled mess, her cheeks sallow, lips dry. She hadn't spoken since they'd arrived. Not really. A few words here and there. But mostly... she just stared into the distance. As if it the daylight might vanish. As if *she* might vanish.

Sion rubbed the heel of his palm against his chest. That terrible pressure still lingered, like fear had wedged itself between his ribs and refused to let go. He kept watching her, like she might shatter if he blinked. Like if he looked away for too long, she'd slip right through his fingers again.

He wanted to go to her. To pull her into his arms and tell her she was safe. That he was here. That she never had to be alone in the dark again.

But something in him held back.

She wasn't ready.

And gods, neither was he.

The air shifted beside him. Heavy footsteps.

Kael dropped down onto the mossy patch beside him, breathing hard. They didn't speak at first. Just sat shoulder to shoulder in silence.

It was the kind of quiet only grief could shape, fragile and sharp-edged.

Sion finally broke it. "You holding up?"

Kael exhaled through his nose. "Define holding up."

Sion nodded. "Fair."

They sat for another beat.

"She looks like hell," Kael murmured, nodding toward Thess. "But she's alive."

Sion's throat tightened. "Barely."

Kael glanced sideways at him. "You okay?"

"No," Sion said honestly. "But I will be."

Kael grunted. "Yeah. Me too."

The silence returned, thicker this time.

Sion picked up a stone and turned it over in his palm, studying the rough edges. "I thought she was gone."

"I know."

"I *felt* it, Kael. When she disappeared… it was like the ground disappeared too. Like someone took out my spine and left me standing anyway."

Kael didn't reply.

Sion tossed the stone into the pond. The splash was small, but the ripples spread wide. "She won't talk to me. Not really."

"She will," Kael said after a long pause. "When she's ready."

"I don't know how to help her."

"You're helping her just by being here."

Sion huffed. "Feels like not enough."

Kael gave a tired, crooked smile. "It never does."

They fell quiet again.

After a while, Kael leaned back against the tree and closed his eyes. "We keep going tomorrow."

Sion nodded. "Yeah."

"I was thinking… I wish Tavien would have come with us. Or even Lira. I wish we would have had time to ask one of them. We could have used the extra warrior backup… maybe if we had it…" Kael didn't finish his thought out loud.

Thankfully, Sion knew what he meant. What he wouldn't dare say.

He looked over at Thess again. She had leaned into Aislen's side now, eyes barely open. But they were focused. Blinking. Present. And that was something.

He would wait.

As long as it took.

He'd stay right here watching her, steady and silent, until she was strong enough to look at him again.

Until she was ready to let him hold the pieces.

* * *

~ **Aislen** ~

344

Thess had finally fallen asleep beside her, curled in tightly like she was trying to fold herself into a place the dark couldn't touch. Aislen stayed still for a long while, just watching the rise and fall of her friend's chest, listening to the faint whistle of her breathing. Each inhale, each exhale, felt like a promise: *You made it. You're still here.*

But eventually, the ache in her legs and the weight in her chest forced her to move.

Gently, she eased her arm out from under Thess's shoulders, careful not to wake her. Thess stirred once but didn't wake, only sighing and nuzzling deeper into the cloak. Aislen rose slowly, brushing her palms over the back of her dress as she stood.

Their sad excuse of a camp was quiet, worn, and beyond broken. Everyone was resting in whatever silence they could carve out.

Her gaze found her mom sitting under a tree not far from the water's edge. Her mom's hands were folded in her lap, her eyes distant and red-rimmed. She didn't cry now—she looked like she'd run out of tears.

Aislen's feet moved before her thoughts could catch up. She had been to the water's edge so many times now, her feet moved on their own accord.

She crossed the short distance and sank down beside her mom, arms wrapping tight around her. Maera startled for only a moment, then melted into the embrace with a soft sound that wasn't quite a sob.

"I love you," Aislen whispered into her shoulder. The words felt too small, but they were all she had.

Maera kissed her temple, then pulled back just enough to cup her face between her hands. "I love you more than you will ever know."

Aislen nodded, blinking back the heat behind her eyes. "I'm sorry. About dad."

Maera's breath hitched, but she shook her head. "Don't you dare apologize. He wouldn't want that. He did what he always said he would do, he protected us." Her thumb swept gently beneath Aislen's eye. "And he would want you to keep going."

They sat like that for a few breaths more, tangled in quiet, until Maera tilted Aislen's chin gently toward her.

"Go to him."

Aislen blinked. "Who?"

"Kael," Maera said softly. "He's been waiting for you. He doesn't know how to reach you right now. And it's killing him."

Aislen looked away, throat tightening.

"I know you're hurting," her mom continued, voice a whisper now. "I know you feel like if you let go of the pain, you're letting go of your dad. But that isn't true. He's with you, always. And Kael... he needs you. Just as much as you need him."

The words sank into her bones like sunlight in winter. Slow and warm and almost painful.

Aislen swallowed, wiping her sleeve across her cheeks. "Okay."

Maera gave her a soft smile and pressed another kiss to her forehead. "Go."

So she did.

She turned toward the edge of the camp where Kael now sat alone near the trees, hunched forward, hands resting loosely over his knees, gaze fixed on the pond. As if he could will himself into stillness. Into strength.

But she saw the cracks beneath it.

And for the first time in what felt like days, Aislen let herself want something. Not for herself, but for comfort, for warmth, for *him*.

One foot after another, she crossed the space between them.

Toward healing.

Toward love.

Toward *home*.

Once she reached him, she collapsed into his arms.

Kael caught her without hesitation, his arms locking around her like the answer to a question neither of them could ask.

Her mom was right, they needed each other.

Forty

"Release"

～～～⚬♡⚬～～～

~ Aislen ~

They moved on.

They had been walking all day before the trees began to thin.

At first, it was just a small break in the canopy, the soft golden haze of late afternoon bleeding through the tangled branches. But then the ground evened out, the underbrush grew sparse, and the wind shifted, carrying the scent of something different. The scent of smoke, bread, and daily life.

Aislen stumbled to a halt, blinking against the sudden light.

There, just beyond the ridge, a village unfurled like a forgotten prayer answered.

Her breath caught in her throat, and for a heartbeat, she couldn't move. After everything they went through with the tunnel, the loss, the aching crawl through darkness, they had finally found light. More than just daylight, but hope.

It wasn't grand, just a scattering of weathered rooftops and curling chimney smoke nestled in a shallow valley. But to her, them, it was a miracle. The warm flicker of lanterns hung from crooked posts. Wooden carts creaked along a narrow dirt path. She could hear the distant bark of a dog. A child's laugh. The clang of metal on metal as a blacksmith worked somewhere unseen.

Thess stepped up beside her, her chest rising and falling heavily. Her hand found hers without a word. They both needed the comfort in that moment.

Behind them, the group came to a slow, stunned stop.

Sion and Kael still carried Tomas between them, his body still wrapped in a thick cloak from the tunnel. The outline of him was unmistakable, and yet, somehow, it didn't seem real. As if any moment he'd groan and shift and complain about how cold it was.

But he wouldn't.

And that truth pressed in like a second skin.

Thess leaned against Aislen's side, her steps steadier than the day before, but her strength still fading fast. Her cheeks were hollow, her lips cracked, but her eyes... gods, her eyes were wide and stunned, locked on the sight of the village with a desperate kind of awe. Like she wasn't sure if it was real.

Neither was Aislen.

"We made it," she whispered. The words didn't sound like hers. They were shaky. Small.

No one answered.

Because no one wanted to break the moment.

Even Maera slowed beside her, letting out a quiet breath that shuddered in her chest. Her eyes glistened in the sunlight. "It's closer than I remembered," she murmured. "We're almost there."

Aislen's legs trembled beneath her. Her boots were caked in mud, the leather cracked from days of wear. Her clothes hung loose, heavy with dust and dried sweat. But none of it mattered now.

They were safe.

Or close enough to believe it for a while.

The walk down into the village was quiet.

Not somber exactly, just... still. Reverent, in a way.

No one rushed.

No one spoke.

They passed worn wooden signs and stone fence posts crumbled with age. The village looked like it had stood for centuries without ever growing. A patch of farmland flanked the south side, golden with late-season wheat. Chickens scratched near the road, unconcerned with the strangers who limped past.

A few villagers glanced up as they entered. Some of them pausing mid-task, eyes narrowing in confusion. Others froze entirely when they caught sight of the body between Kael and Sion, or the frail human girl being half-carried.

But no one screamed. No one turned them away.

And that alone almost brought Aislen to her knees.

They made their way to the center of the village, where a crooked little inn stood beneath a sagging wooden sign carved with the shape of a bear and crescent moon. Smoke poured from its chimney. Light spilled through the windows. It smelled like stew and bread and warmth.

A man stepped out from the front door, drying his hands on a faded apron. His hair was gray at the temples, eyes sharp but not unkind.

He took one look at them, at their torn clothes and blood-streaked arms, at the death and the silence and the weight of it all, and said, "You'll need a room."

Kael's voice cracked when he spoke. "Two. Please."

The innkeeper didn't ask questions. He stepped aside and waved them in.

The moment Aislen crossed the threshold, warmth wrapped around her like a promise. The fire was low but steady in the hearth. Wooden beams arched overhead. A few villagers sat at tables with steaming bowls in front of them, but they all fell silent as the group entered.

It didn't matter.

Aislen's legs gave out.

Kael had just sat Tomas's body down when he caught her before she hit the ground, scooping her into his arms as if it was nothing. She didn't protest. She couldn't. Her head fell against his shoulder, and for the first time in days, she let herself exhale.

They were safe.

They had made it.

* * *

The room was small, but it didn't matter.

There was a bed. A real bed. A basin in the corner. A copper tub half-filled with water Kael had already asked to be brought up and now worked quietly to warm with his magic. Small flickers of moonlight danced along the surface, chasing away the chill.

Aislen stood near the door, arms wrapped around herself. She hadn't said much since they arrived. She couldn't. Not with the weight of everything still pressing on her chest.

Kael turned toward her slowly, gently. "Come here."

Her feet moved before her brain caught up.

He reached for her cloak first, tugging it loose with careful fingers. Then her tunic, her boots, her dirt-streaked trousers. He undressed her like he was afraid she might break, though she already had. Her body felt like paper, like smoke. Fragile and ash-soft.

He didn't say a word as he helped her step into the tub, one hand steadying her as the warm water rose to her knees. It wasn't deep, but it was enough. She sank down slowly, water lapping at her shoulders, heat curling around her aching limbs like a balm.

Kael knelt behind her.

"I can do it," she whispered, reaching for the washcloth.

But he didn't let her.

"I know you can," he said softly. "But let me."

His voice cracked at the end.

She didn't fight him.

Kael dipped the cloth, wrung it out, and ran it gently down her back. Over the curve of her shoulder. Down her arms. Every pass was deliberate, slow. His fingers trailed behind the cloth, grounding her. Her hair was matted and tangled with dirt and blood, and still he threaded his fingers through it like it was made of silk.

"Do you remember," he murmured, "when we used to sneak to the river in spring? You hated the cold, but you always went in first."

She closed her eyes. "You always pretended it was freezing when you followed me."

"It was freezing," he said with a quiet laugh. "But you were there."

Silence settled between them again. It was soft, not heavy this time.

Kael leaned forward, pressing his forehead to the back of her neck, his breath warm on her skin. "I keep thinking if I'd done something different… if I'd reached him faster…"

"You didn't do anything wrong," she whispered.

"Neither did you."

Her eyes burned.

She turned her face, and his was already there. Waiting.

The kiss wasn't rushed. It wasn't fierce or desperate. It was reverent. A shared ache, a silent promise. His lips tasted of salt and moonlight. She reached for him, cupping his cheek with her damp fingers.

"I need you," she whispered, her voice trembling. "I don't want to think. I just… I need to feel something that isn't pain."

He didn't hesitate.

Kael stood slowly, lifted her from the bath with arms steady and strong, water streaming down her body. He held her close to his chest, as his hands gripped firmly onto her bottom.

His hands there jolted something else awake in her. Instead of her chest aching, she began to ache somewhere else.

Kael didn't speak as he carried her towards the bed, water streaming down her bare skin like liquid moonlight. His arms were steady, strong, but the way he held her felt almost fragile. As if she were something sacred. Something breakable.

She didn't feel sacred.

She felt cracked and raw, splintered in ways she didn't have words for. The grief sat heavy in her chest like wet stone, but wrapped around it, pressing through it, was *him*. The bond. The heat. The *ache* to be closer, to be anywhere but alone inside her skin.

Kael crossed the room slowly and laid her down on the bed like a prayer. Her heart beat unevenly, a stuttered rhythm that felt too loud in the silence.

He didn't say anything at first.

He just looked at her.

Looked like he couldn't believe she was still here.

His fingertips ghosted down her arm, raising goosebumps in their wake. Then over the arch of her hip, along the slope of her ribs. Reverent. Worshipful.

"Aislen," he breathed.

She could feel how much he wanted her through the bulge in his pants.

He was holding back for her, but she wanted him to let loose. She needed him to.

She reached up and slid her hands beneath his shirt, pushing the fabric up his chest until he pulled it over his head. Her hands found his skin again, and with it, the grounding hum of his heartbeat. Steady. Fierce.

"I need you," she whispered, her throat tight. "Please."

"You have me," he said, his voice breaking. "You've always had me."

He bent to kiss her. It was soft at first, like a question waiting to be answered. She answered it with a kiss of her own, deeper, hungrier, all trembling breath and parted lips. The bond throbbed between them, a warm pull behind her ribs that pulsed in time with his touch.

Kael's mouth trailed down her throat, over her collarbone. His hands followed, learning her curves like a map he already knew but wanted to memorize again. His tongue swirled over one nipple, his hand cupping the other breast, and she gasped, her back arching off the bed.

Heat coiled low in her stomach.

He moved lower, kissing a line down her stomach, slow and aching and deliberate. When he reached her thighs, he paused as his eyes flickered up to meet hers.

The desire in his eyes unmistakable.

"Tell me what you need."

"You," she said again. "All of you."

He groaned like it hurt to hold back, and then he dipped between her legs.

His mouth was fire.

Soft lips and skilled tongue moving with devastating precision. Her body jolted at the first stroke, and then melted as he found a rhythm that unraveled her from the inside out. Her fingers fisted the sheets, her cries breaking loose with every pass of his tongue, every flick and suck that left her trembling.

She came with a gasp that was sharp and raw. It had stars bursting behind her eyelids.

But Kael didn't stop.

He kissed her inner thigh and made his way back up, pressing kisses to her hips, her ribs, the valley between her breasts. When he hovered over her again, their eyes locked.

"I love you," he said. "So much it terrifies me."

Aislen reached up and cupped his cheek. "Then show me."

He hesitated for a single breath, his thumb brushing the curve of her jaw. "I will."

He positioned himself at her entrance, breath trembling, the bond sparking like starlight between their skin. Slowly, he slid into her, inch by inch. He was stretching her, filling her, until she thought she might shatter from how perfect it felt.

They both moaned. Hers was ragged and full of need, but *his*, gods, his was guttural.

The sound alone made her melt.

He stilled when he was fully inside her, forehead pressed to hers, chest heaving. "Is this okay? If I am hurting you, I can stop…"

She wrapped her arms around his neck. "Move, Kael. Please."

He did.

Slowly at first, drawing out the slide, making her feel every inch of him. Her legs wrapped around his waist, and they found a rhythm that was equal parts reverent and unrelenting. With each thrust, their bond pulsed brighter. Magic flared in her veins, her body glowing faintly with starlight where he touched her.

The moment shifted, tipping from sacred to full of pure need.

Kael surged deeper, faster, the sound of their bodies meeting lost beneath gasps and moans and whispered names. His lips found hers again, swallowing every cry she gave, every breathless plea.

She clung to him like he was the only real thing left in a world that had broken her.

And maybe he was.

"I've got you," he rasped, lips brushing her ear. "I'm right here."

She felt the bond *snap* open.

Not break, but bloom.

Magic exploded inside her, a pulse of light and power that arced through her spine and flared across her skin in waves of heat. Kael cried out, his body shuddering as he came undone inside her, their bond surging with the force of it.

They rode it out together. Breathless, burning, *bound*.

And when the tremors faded, when their bodies stilled and all that was left was the sound of their hearts beating in sync, Kael collapsed gently against her, still buried deep.

She held him there.

Held him like a lifeline.

For the first time since the darkness, she felt *real*. Felt like herself. Not whole, not healed, but *here*.

And that was enough.

* * *

Kael lay beside her, one arm tucked beneath her neck, the other resting lightly across her stomach as if afraid she might drift away if he let go. Their legs were tangled beneath the blanket, skin pressed to skin, and for the first time in what felt like forever... she felt safe.

Not untouched by pain.

Not healed.

But wrapped in something stronger than either... *love.*

His thumb traced slow, idle circles across her ribs, and she closed her eyes, letting the rhythm of his heartbeat lull her into a soft haze. They hadn't spoken since the bond had burst open between them, wrapping their magic and emotions in a silken, unbreakable thread.

It was there before, strong. From the mating ritual.

But they never got the chance to consummate it up until now. She didn't realize how much of a difference to their bond it would make. The strength between the bond they shared almost doubled. Even now, it pulsed between them. Pushing them together.

Leaving her wanting more.

She turned her head slightly, cheek brushing his chest. "I didn't know it could be like that."

Kael's breath caught, and he tipped his chin to look at her. "Like what?"

She tilted her face toward him, eyes still glassy from everything they'd been through. "So... soul-shattering. So intense." Her voice dropped to a whisper. "It felt like something inside me exploded. Like I was seeing stars with my *whole body.*"

He gave a quiet laugh and pressed a kiss to her temple. "You *were.*"

She smiled, cheeks flushing. "Is that what it always feels like with mates?"

"I mean, I've never had one before," he said, his voice low and rough. "But if that's what it's supposed to be, then... *gods,* I'm glad it's you."

Silence settled for a beat, warm and slow.

Then Aislen turned toward him, mischief glinting faintly behind the tenderness in her eyes. "Do you think..." She leaned in closer, brushing her nose against his. "We can do that again?"

Kael's answering grin was slow and wicked.

"You don't even have to ask."

He rolled on top of her in one fluid motion, kissing her deeply as her laughter was swallowed into his mouth. His hands slid down her sides, anchoring her beneath him, and her breath hitched when he pressed his hips to hers again.

Heat bloomed between them, slower this time, but no less consuming.

He kissed her like he was already addicted.

And just before the fire flared again, before her thoughts scattered into starlight, she felt him whisper it against her lips:

"I love you."

She whispered it back.

Then there was no sound at all but the hush of breath and the whisper of magic wrapping around them once more.

Forty-One

"Always"

~ **Maera** ~

The scent of fresh bread nearly broke her.

It shouldn't have. It was just a smell. A smell of yeast and warmth, tinged with herbs and smoke. But after days of blood and rot and dust, after dragging her husband's body through the dark with her daughter barely breathing beside her, the smell of something so *normal* felt like a knife.

Maera stood in the doorway of the tavern, hand clenched white around the strap of her satchel. Aislen was beside her, Kael just behind, his palm steady on her lower back. She didn't know how long they'd been standing there, staring into the dining room where a fire crackled low and chairs scraped across wooden floors.

Thess was curled in a bench seat beside Sion, her small frame tucked in close. She looked better. Not good. But better. Her cheeks had lost the gray pallor. She was sipping broth, slow and deliberate, and though her eyes flicked toward every movement like a rabbit ready to run, there was something solid in her now. Something rooted.

Maera's gaze swept past her and landed on the chair beside Sion.

It was empty.

Tomas would have made a joke.

He would've limped to the table with some crude comment about how they needed a real cook and not just charred rations and root water. He would have squeezed her hand under the table. He would've stolen Aislen's bread, just to hear her protest.

But his chair was empty.

And that truth lived in her chest like a knife turned sideways.

Aislen moved first. Quiet. Almost like she was floating. She slid onto the bench beside Thess and murmured a soft hello. Maera followed, slower, and sat stiffly, as if the weight of everything might crush her if she let herself settle too far into comfort.

The food came quickly. They received generous bowls of stew, buttered bread, roasted squash, and even some honeyed tea. The kindness of strangers who didn't ask questions. Who didn't recognize who they were. Who didn't know the Celestara Court was just beyond the tree line, shrouded in glamour so fierce it had erased an entire kingdom from memory.

Maera barely touched her food. Her fingers curled around her mug, the ceramic warm but not comforting.

After making sure no one was in earshot, she needed to talk to the others. It was eating at her.

"I made a plan," she said after a long silence, her voice as dry as the bread she hadn't eaten. "Once we reach the Celestara Court... we bury him."

Kael glanced up. His face was still bruised, his eyes sun-shadowed and quiet. "The king might not allow—"

"He will." Maera's voice cracked like stone. "And if he doesn't, then he can be damned. Tomas gave everything. *Everything.* For our daughter to be where she is today. He owes us. His body will rest beneath the stars, where his daughter walks and where his love still lives. Tomas will not be left forgotten in the shadows."

Nobody argued.

Not this time. They did'nt have it in them.

Kael nodded once. Sion bowed his head. Even Aislen's eyes shimmered as she turned her face toward the hearth. The silence wasn't heavy with discomfort anymore, it was reverence. It was grief.

She felt the pulse of it in her bones.

Later, Kael suggested they rest until sundown and travel beneath the cloak of night. Fewer eyes. Less risk. A plan she agreed with, if only because it gave her one more day to keep her husband close.

They wouldn't leave him behind.

They *couldn't*.

When the meal ended, Aislen wandered toward the window, watching the children laugh in the dusty street, the vendors calling out about root vegetables and thread spools and goat cheese. It was life. Ordinary. Unscarred. Untouched by Courts and prophecies and death.

And in that moment, Maera hated it.

Then she loved it.

Because her daughter deserved this too. Someday.

She rose slowly, knees aching, and crossed to stand beside Aislen. Her daughter didn't speak. Just leaned into her side, and Maera looped an arm around her shoulders.

They didn't say goodbye to Tomas when they left him upstairs for supper. They couldn't.

But when they reached the Celestara Court... they would.

No matter what the king said.

* * *

She lay in bed long after the others had made their way back for the next meal, the afternoon light now softened through the curtains, casting pale shadows against the wooden floor. Her eyes were closed, but sleep didn't come.

Instead, she reached for memory, groping blindly for something familiar to hold onto.

What did he smell like?

She thought of the earth after rain. Of smoke curling from the hearth. Of pine needles and old parchment and something warmer beneath it all—safety.

She swallowed hard and pressed her face deeper into the pillow.

What did his voice sound like again?

She reached back. Not for the end, but the beginning.

The first time she ever heard it.

And then it came. It was not the laughter in the garden, nor the comfort in the dark. But *him.*

She closed her eyes and remembered it all.

It had been almost twenty years ago.

Maera was running, stumbling through a forest soaked with fog and moonlight. Her cloak torn, boots caked with mud, and blood. Gods, so much blood, trailing down her body. Not her own. Not entirely.

She was barely two months pregnant.

The night she fled the Celestara Court, everything changed. Who she would've been was gone. Her future gone. Everything she had planned for... worked for. Just gone.

All but one.

She had crossed the ridge back into the mortal realm, into the hills near the border village of Valebrook. She hadn't made it far before her knees gave out. Going through that glamour alone had been hard on her body.

She collapsed near the edge of a stone wall, breath ragged, clutching her belly.

She remembered thinking, *Let it end here. Let the cold take me.*

But then there was a voice.

Rough. Gentle. Alarmed.

"Hey—hey! Are you hurt?"

She'd blinked up through strands of hair, barely able to see him. A tall man, broad-shouldered, with dark eyes that didn't narrow in suspicion but widened in concern.

"I... I can't..." she whispered.

He didn't ask her name. Didn't question her torn dress or the dirt on her face. He didn't even flinch when he saw her ears.

He just knelt beside her.

"Come on," he said, sliding his arms under her like she weighed nothing. "I've got you. You're safe now."

He brought her into his home. It was just a small cottage then, barely more than two rooms, and a fireplace that smoked if the wind turned wrong. He laid her on the bed and fetched water, bandages, and broth she could hardly stomach.

When she woke again, her wrist wrapped, her brow cool, he was sitting at the edge of the room carving a piece of wood. Whittling helped him think, he told her later.

That first night, she gave him a false name.

The second, she didn't speak at all.

By the third, she told him nearly everything.

She expected him to turn her out. To call for the guards. To fear her.

But instead, Tomas had only nodded, leaned forward, and said, "You don't have to run anymore."

He'd loved her before her name was Maera. Before she was a mother. Before she knew how to be any of it.

He fell in love with her when she was nothing but fragments and fear.

And slowly, he helped her become whole again.

She didn't want to, but Maera opened her eyes.

The pain wouldn't go away.

The ache in her chest swelled until it pressed into her ribs. But for a moment, she welcomed it.

That was where they began.

Not in some perfect kiss or warm summer night, but in blood, fear, and the quiet kindness of a man who saw her and didn't run.

She turned onto her side, curling into the pillow that still smelled faintly of pine and soap.

"I should've thanked you more," she whispered. "I should've told you every day."

But maybe he knew.
Maybe he always had.
She hoped.

Forty-Two

"Threshold"

~⚬⚬⚬⚬~

~ **Maera** ~

Night cloaked the village in stillness, the stars scattered above like old memories, both familiar and far away. Maera stood at the edge of the tavern's small courtyard, cloak drawn tightly around her shoulders as the others prepared behind her. The pack on her back felt lighter than it should have, even with all they carried. Maybe it was because the real weight wasn't in what they held. It was in what they had lost.

Tomas.

The name ached just to think, sharper now in silence.

She didn't turn as footsteps approached, she didn't need to. She could hear the soft drag of Thess's steps, the steady thump of Kael's boots beside Sion's. They had taken up the burden again without complaint, Tomas's wrapped body cradled between them. Kael hadn't spoken much to anyone aside from Aislen since they left the tunnels, his jaw set, his shoulders locked. Sion, too, wore his grief quietly. Only his eyes betraying the cost.

Maera swallowed down the burn in her throat.

"It's time," she said softly. "Follow me."

No one questioned her.

They passed through the village like ghosts, slipping between alleys and around sleeping homes. The small lamps that lit doorways flickered dimly in their wake, as though the very air recognized what passed through it.

As they reached the outskirts, the road began to narrow into a footpath. Trees leaned in close, their branches whispering secrets to the dark. Maera led them through thickets and past old farmland long gone to seed, the scent of night soil and wet leaves clinging to the air.

And then... she saw it.

The path curved, just slightly, and there, half-covered by wild ivy and memory, stood a cottage.

Her steps faltered.

Her heart seized.

It hadn't changed. Not really. The roof sagged now, the stone walls moss-covered and cracked, but the bones of it were still his, still theirs. She could almost see herself in the doorway, a hand on her swollen belly, Tomas laughing as he patched the chimney with far too much mortar. He'd made a mess of it. But gods, he'd been trying.

Maera closed her eyes.

She hadn't been looking for a male that day. She hadn't even been looking for help. Just a place to disappear. And yet, he let her in. He let her into his heart, and his home. No questions. No judgment. Just eyes full of quiet strength and hands that knew how to hold things gently.

And somehow... that had been enough.

"Aislen," he'd said when she finally let him touch her belly. "That's her name. I don't know why... but I know it's hers."

She'd cried then.

She nearly cried now.

But the wind stirred and the moment passed, slipping from her like mist.

Kael stepped closer, eyes watching her cautiously, protectively.

Maera turned away from the past and kept walking.

"This way," she said, voice stronger than she felt.

The land shifted as they neared the edge of the forest. A faint mist crept up from the ground, unnatural and clinging to their boots like cold fingers. Just ahead, a small rise in the earth curved sharply upward. It looked like jagged stones breaking free from the roots like half-buried bones. At its base was the structure.

To the untrained eye, it was nothing.

A ruin. A pile of old stone and tangled vines, partially sunken and wholly forgotten.

But Maera knew better.

The glamour was thick here, woven into the air itself. It shimmered faintly if one looked from the right angle. Like heat waves. Like deception.

Thess slowed, clinging to Aislen. "What is that?"

"A lie," Maera said. "One that's lasted long enough."

She paused, staring at the structure, the veil between them and what they'd come so far for.

Behind them was death. Loss. The path that had carved each of them down to their rawest selves.

Ahead... was truth.

And whatever came next.

"Rest," she said. "We'll need what is left of our strength to pass through. This glamour is strong. It is going to try and keep you from going through it. Your mind will be redirected to a task you long forgot about, but it's a lie. Ignore what your mind says is true and keep going."

They all shared a look as they sat down to take their final rest.

"Well, can't go back now." Thess said. "Anything beats that damn tunnel."

They all sighed collectively in agreement as they made what was hopefully their final campfire.

* * *

~ Kael ~

The fire crackled low, sending flickers of amber light dancing across tired faces. The warmth should have been comforting, but it felt too small, too fragile, against the weight of everything pressing down on them.

365

They sat in silence, gathered loosely around the flames as if the closeness might hold them together. Thess leaned against Aislen's side once more, as she finally fell asleep again. Maera hadn't spoken since they stopped, eyes fixed on the wrapped form laid gently near the tree line. Tomas's body was still. Sacred.

Sion stared into the fire like he was trying to read the future in its embers. Each glance towards Thess didn't go unnoticed. Kael could feel it too, the strange tension in the air. It wasn't just grief. It was something else.

He was tired. Not the kind of tired that could be solved with sleep. It sat in his bones, heavy and splintered. He hadn't let go of his blade all day, and even now, his fingers twitched against the hilt.

They were almost there. Just one more stretch.

The night had gone quiet, almost too quiet. Even the insects had hushed. The fire cracked, brittle and loud in the stillness. Kael shifted his gaze toward the trees, heart pounding for a reason he couldn't name.

But Kael couldn't shake it. The feeling.

Like maybe they weren't alone.

He stiffened, his eyes narrowing into the trees beyond the firelight.

There.

A shift. A flicker of movement too fluid to be wind.

Kael surged to his feet, blade drawn before anyone else even registered his motion. He took three long strides forward, nostrils flaring. His shadows curled around his shoulders like they sensed the threat too.

Then he saw him.

The male who was no longer his father.

Fenric.

Standing just beyond the edge of the firelight.

Watching.

Kael didn't think. He launched forward, knocking over a log, shadows slamming outward with a soundless force. The older male barely had time to react before Kael's blade was at his throat and he was slammed against a tree.

Thess flinched, half-rising to her feet before Aislen gently caught her wrist.

Sion stood too, muscles taut, eyes never leaving Kael. He said nothing, but his own shadows flared just once, ready if needed.

"You should be dead," Kael snarled, his voice low and shaking. "You should be in the dirt with the rest of the traitors."

"Kael—" Fenric rasped, but Kael shoved harder, the blade nicking skin.

"You left us. You *used* us. You locked us in and *walked away.*" His voice cracked. "And because of you, Tomas is dead."

That name landed like a blow.

Fenric flinched.

He didn't speak right away. His mouth opened, closed. His eyes, gods, his *eyes,* finally shifted to the body near the fire. Wrapped. Still.

Kael didn't miss it, the guilt that flickered there. The sharp breath. The slackening of his shoulders as if he'd been punched.

"That wasn't..." Fenric swallowed. "That wasn't part of the plan."

Kael's grip tightened. "What plan?" he spat. "What twisted game was worth *his* life?"

"I just wanted to find the Court," Fenric said hoarsely. "The real one. I thought the map would show me. I thought if I got there first, maybe I could—"

"You could *what?*" Kael shouted. "Claim it? Own it? Sell it to the highest bidder?"

Fenric shook his head. "No. Not like that. I just... I didn't want you to follow me. I thought you'd find another way out."

"You left us in a fucking *maze,*" Kael hissed. "You knew how dangerous it was. You *knew.* And still you walked away."

He almost did it. He almost let the blade press deeper.

But then he heard Aislen's voice behind him, quiet and shaking.

"Kael..."

He didn't look at her. Couldn't. His hand trembled with rage, but slowly, very slowly, he stepped back. The blade hovered one last heartbeat at his father's throat before Kael yanked it away. And then he felt the gentle touch of his mates hand on his shoulder. His breathing calmed, if only a fraction.

"Leave," he growled. "Before I forget why I didn't end this here."

Fenric took a shaky breath, rubbing at his neck. "I didn't want this. Not... *this*." His eyes flicked once more to Tomas's shrouded form. "I swear, son."

"Don't call me that," Kael said coldly. "You don't get to call me son anymore. You are no longer my father, Fenric." Kael spit on the ground, as if his fathers name was a foul taste in his mouth.

"When mother finds out what you did. When she knows you left your child and everyone else to die, you will be alone. Just like you deserve." And with that, Kael pushed his dad away from him even further.

Silence stretched between them.

Then Fenric stepped back into the shadows.

Kael didn't watch him go.

He just stood there, breathing hard, blade still in his grip, as the others slowly came to their feet behind him. The air was thick with judgment. With grief. With too many words unsaid.

Maera didn't speak.

Aislen didn't move.

And Kael? He just stared at the place where his father had vanished and felt... nothing.

Nothing but the fire in his chest and the memory of the male who had taken his place as a father years ago, and who now would never speak again.

He stood there long after Fenric had disappeared into the trees, the night air cold against the sweat on his skin. His hands were still clenched around the hilt of his blade, knuckles white, chest heaving like he'd just finished a fight he hadn't truly won.

He should have killed him.

He *wanted* to kill him.

But then she said his name.

She gave him just the briefest of touch, and all the anger started to melt away.

And now...

Now his body was trembling, not with rage, but with the ache of all that had been lost. Of everything his father had stolen.

Then, ever so softly, arms wrapped around him from behind. The touch was warm and certain.

Aislen.

Her cheek pressed gently to his back, her fingers splaying across his ribs like she was trying to hold him together.

He exhaled slowly, lowering the blade inch by inch until it rested against his thigh. His head dropped forward, the weight of it all crashing into him at once.

She didn't say anything.

She didn't have to.

He turned, slowly and carefully, and pulled her into his chest. Wrapped his arms tight around her, one hand cradling the back of her head, the other splayed across her lower back.

He buried his face in her hair and *breathed*.

Violets.

Summer rain on warm forest soil.

The scent of her wrapped around him like a balm, grounding him in something real, something still his. Something *good*.

He inhaled again, slower this time, letting her soothe the burning in his chest, the roar in his ears. Her scent settled the storm inside him, chasing away the bitter sting of betrayal and grief until all that was left was her.

She was silent still, her face tucked beneath his chin, fingers fisted gently in the fabric of his tunic.

And gods... he didn't realize how badly he needed this.

How badly he needed *her*.

"I'm sorry," he whispered into her hair. "I'm sorry you had to see that."

Aislen pulled back just enough to look at him, her eyes shining in the firelight, soft but steady.

"He deserved it," she said quietly. "Every word."

Kael swallowed hard and nodded. "I just... I couldn't let him walk in here like he hadn't torn everything apart."

"You didn't," she murmured, reaching up to touch his jaw. "You said your peace. That's what matters."

He leaned into her touch, closing his eyes for a long breath. Her fingers were cold but gentle, tracing along the edge of his face like she was memorizing him in this moment.

"I'm right here," she whispered. "And we're almost there."

Kael opened his eyes and stared at her. In front of him was this stubborn, strong, heartbroken girl who somehow still glowed in the dark.

"Stay close tonight," he said softly.

"Always."

He kissed her, slow and steady, just a press of lips that spoke every word he didn't know how to say. Her arms tightened around him, and for a heartbeat, everything else faded.

Not gone.

Not forgotten.

But quieter.

And in the silence between them, Kael finally let go of the last of the rage.

Because she was here.

And that meant he could keep going.

Forty-Three

"Home"

⚜

~ Aislen ~

They were already a short distance from the entrance.

Their camp had been close, intentionally so. But not too close. No one dared test the reach of ancient glamours until they had no other choice.

From a distance, it didn't look like much. Not after the Hollow Mountains, not after the tunnels. Not after the blood, the silence, the grief. Just another half-forgotten ruin cloaked in vines and dust and stories left untold.

But as Aislen stood at the edge of the clearing, staring toward the shimmer cloaking the ruins, seventy-five feet felt like the longest distance she'd ever have to cross.

The shimmer rippled faintly in the air, like heat over stone. Light that wasn't quite visible, but not quite invisible either. It pulsed with something old. Something living. She could feel it pressing against her magic, stirring deep inside her as though it remembered her even when she did not remember it.

Kael stood at her side, his hand brushing hers, his body rigid with readiness. Sion shifted Tomas's weight beside him, his face drawn with quiet strain. Thess leaned against Maera for support, each breath a silent fight. The five of them—six, if you counted the man they carried—stood still, suspended on the edge of something vast.

No one spoke.

Because none of them wanted to admit what they already knew.

It was working.

The glamour.

Aislen could feel it creeping along the edges of her thoughts. A whisper in the back of her mind urging her to turn around. That she'd forgotten something urgent. That she didn't belong here. That she was trespassing in something sacred.

She swallowed hard and stepped closer to her mom.

Maera stood at the head of the group, calm and rooted. But there was tension in her shoulders, in the way her fingers hovered just beneath her cloak. She reached inside and pulled free a silver amulet. It was simple, elegant, shaped like a crescent moon. Embedded in its center was a shard of starlight.

Aislen felt her magic react before her mind caught up.

She recognized the amulet, but from where?

It hummed in the air, soft and unmistakable.

Her mother noticed the flicker of confusion in Aislen's eyes. Her voice was quiet as she said, "Your father gave this to me the night I left the Celestara Court. In case I ever wanted to return... it would let me back through. Even after all of these years, his magic lives in it still. If we remain physically connected, it should shield you too." Maera looked up at the others around them, "All of you."

Aislen's breath caught.

"Does it help with just the wards, or the glamour too?" Aislen questioned.

"It should help you all with both, but I only need it to bypass the wards to enter. The glamour keeping it hidden does not affect me like it does the others." Her mom hesitated, as if she was scared to say too much.

"I don't understand, why aren't you affected by it?" she asked.

Maera met her gaze, violet eyes dimmed but unwavering. "Because I belong to this place. This Court. I never stopped."

Her voice trembled only slightly.

Aislen didn't press. Not even as she saw the sadness creep into her mom's eyes.

Maera cleared her throat as she shifted the conversation, "Okay, everyone let's link up."

They followed her words without question, without doubt. Maera reached for Aislen's hand. Kael stepped in behind her, one arm wrapped tightly around her waist, his other hand helping hold up the body positioned between him and Sion. Behind Sion, offering the little strength she had regained, was Thess. They all formed a chain, and together, they stepped forward.

The moment Maera's foot crossed the threshold, the glamour reacted.

Not with a blast.

But with a wave.

Aislen's breath left her lungs as something unseen swept over them. Not pain, but doubt. Not pressure, only forgetting. Her limbs felt heavy. Her thoughts scattered like windblown ash.

She forgot why they were walking.

Forgot where they were going.

Forgot the grief coiled like a knife in her chest.

Kael's hold tightened around her waist. She leaned into it, anchored by the weight of his love, his bond, the steady rhythm of his breath against her spine.

Sion swore behind them. Thess whimpered.

The glamour pulled harder.

Fingers of magic slid through their minds, unweaving memory, loosening threads of purpose and will. Guilt rose. Then fear. Then the soft ache of something she didn't want to name.

But still, they walked.

Step by step through a fog thick with forgotten stories and the weight of ancestral silence. Her magic screamed against it. Not in fear, but in recognition.

Starlight.

This place bled starlight.

And her bones remembered.

She didn't know how long they walked. It could have been seconds, minutes, or even centuries. But at last, the pressure ebbed. The wave broke. The glamour fell away like a second skin.

And they stepped into silence.

The shimmer behind them vanished.

And the ruins?

They weren't ruins at all.

Where crumbled stone had once stood, silver arches rose. Where vines had once choked windows, flowering blossoms bloomed beneath moonless starlight. The towers stood tall, whole, dusted in silver-blue. A soft light, not from the sun or even the moon, lit everything.

Alive.

Waiting.

Sleeping as they waited for not only her, but the return of her mom.

Aislen didn't realize she'd dropped Kael's hand until he reached back for her again.

And that was when the shimmer behind them rippled once more.

A crack of pressure broke the stillness.

A figure stumbled through.

Aislen spun. Kael's growl was low and guttural as he pushed her behind him.

Fenric.

Bloodied. Panting. But unfortunately, alive.

He was still chasing them.

Still haunting them.

Kael surged forward, fury in his step, but Maera beat him to it.

She strode forward, chin high, voice low and lethal as she slapped him across the face. "I trusted you. TOMAS trusted you. We were friends, Fenric."

Fenric's sneer twisted his mouth as his hand rubbed the blooming red mark on his cheek, "I have no friends. Friendship only weakens you."

"No. I don't believe that. You sat by my Tomas side by side sharing food, drinks, and laughter," she said. "And now he's dead, my love is dead and IT'S YOUR FAULT," she shouted. "I don't understand. What happened to you, Fenric? When did you become so—so wretched?"

Fenric spat at the ground. "He was always a liability, just as you are. None of you could see the truth. Not even my own son," Fenric glanced at his son as he said, "And he deserves everything coming his way."

A blade glinted in his hand.

He stepped toward Maera, as he drew it in her direction.

And then—

"*Stop.*"

The word itself wasn't shouted, but the way it was spoken, it shook the stars.

The very air cracked under the weight of it.

A figure stepped forward from the silver archways, robes dark as midnight threaded with the pulse of constellations. His face was still young due to his fae heritage, but his hair was both silver and blonde.

His eyes on the other hand, his eyes were violet. Just like hers.

He radiated command. Power. History.

Despite only seeing him in the dreamworld, she knew who he was the instant she heard his voice.

Her father.

Alarion, the Starlight King of the Celestara Court.

Everything froze.

"How dare you step foot in my home. In my Court." Alarion growled, "And then have the utter audacity to threaten my family." His eyes never leaving the coward in their presence.

Fenric bowed under his gaze.

"We all heard the whispers, but we didn't believe them to be true. You—you're really still here. Wait until everyone kn—" He didn't get his final word out as Alarion drew his own blade. A large sword the color of night.

His voice was lethally quiet as he whispered, "No one will know. Traitors to my Court, to my family, have no say here. Especially the ones who threaten what I love. *Who* I love."

"She's going to doom us all," Fenric whispered.

Before he had the chance to utter another word, the Starlight King plunged his sword through Fenric's throat.

* * *

~ Alarion ~

The traitor had dared raise a blade.

In *his* Court. To *his* queen.

He knew she was no longer his, but seeing her now, it was much harder to grasp. She was just as beautiful as the day she left.

Alarion didn't shout. He didn't scream.

He simply walked.

And the earth obeyed him.

He hadn't expected to spill blood today. Not now, not in front of them.

When the air calmed, Alarion turned.

He saw the grief on their faces.

Maera. His beautiful Maera.

She looked broken.

And Aislen... Aislen looked more ragged and exhausted than she had when he visited her dreams last. When her grief shook him through the dream itself.

And he stopped breathing.

There were no crowns. No armies. No power that could shield a male from the ruin and pain carved into their faces.

He took a step.

Then another.

He reached the fae who held Tomas's body on his own. As gently as he could, he took him from his arms. He felt so light in his arms, as if the days since his death stole not only his soul, but everything else that made him a person. His laughter. His voice. The weight of his presence that made him

376

real.

Alarion knew there was a lot he couldn't make up for, but he had to try. And he was going to try with this.

He began walking slowly away as he held the man that cared for his family when he couldn't.

He couldn't bring him back, but he could give him the final resting place he deserved.

Forty-Four

Epilogue

⌇⌇⌇

~ Aislen ~

Dawn came quietly to the Celestara Court.

The strange, silver starlight that had filled the sky since their arrival began to pale, touched now by the first blush of sunrise. It was the first time Aislen had seen true sunlight here. It was soft and gold, filtering through the high canopy above the courtyard, gilding the leaves and casting long shadows across the stone.

The garden was still, too silent for birdsong. No wind stirred the ivy climbing up the ancient walls. Even the fountains seemed to hush themselves, as if the entire Court held its breath.

Aislen stood at the edge of the grass, her bare feet pressed into damp earth, the hem of her dress whispering against her ankles.

Before her, a grave had been prepared.

Simple. Circular. Ringed in stones etched with glowing runes she didn't know how to read, even though her magic did. They hummed softly beneath her skin as she stepped closer, reverent and alive.

Tomas's body lay within, wrapped in a pale cloak woven from moon-thread and starlight, the same one he had used to cover her shoulders on cold mornings as a child. Someone, her mom most likely, had placed a single blue flower over his heart before he was enclosed forever. She shivered slightly, though there was no wind.

Aislen couldn't cry anymore. She had done that already, in Kael's arms, in silence, in sleep. But the ache had changed. It had settled deeper now, into the marrow of her bones, quiet and constant.

"He would have liked it here," Thess said beside her, her voice hoarse from sleep and grief.

Sion stood just behind her, his hand resting on her back. He hadn't said much, not since they'd arrived. Not since Tomas's name had been carved into stone.

Maera knelt beside the grave, her hand pressed gently to the edge. Her eyes were red, but her spine was straight.

"I promised him peace," she whispered. "I will keep that promise."

Kael stepped forward with a torch, his face unreadable, though his jaw was tight with held emotion.

Alarion stood to the side, silent, regal. Respectful.

This wasn't his ceremony to lead. This was theirs.

And when Maera nodded, Kael stepped forward and lowered the torch.

Flames sparked gently across the circle. The runes ignited blue, then silver, then white. The entire ring glowed, and slowly, the ground began to shift, the stone beneath Tomas's coffin descending as if guided by the Court itself. The earth moved to cradle him, vines curling like fingers around the shroud, wildflowers blooming in his wake.

Aislen knelt, pressing her hand to the soil as it settled.

"Thank you," she whispered. "For being my dad when I needed one. For being brave. For loving us all."

And when she stood, her knees trembling, Kael caught her, arms wrapping tightly around her waist.

They didn't speak.

There were no right words.

Only love. Only memory.

Only silence.

Ever so slowly, the others drifted back toward the heart of the Court, footsteps hushed, giving space where it was needed most. Aislen didn't move.

Not until Kael's hand slid gently down her back, anchoring her to the moment.

"You okay?" he asked softly, his voice low enough that the wind nearly swallowed it whole.

She turned to him, her heart still clenched tight in her chest. "No," she admitted. "But I'm standing."

"That's enough for now," he said, brushing a lock of hair from her cheek.

The courtyard around them was quiet again, save for the faint crackle of the still-burning runes and the whisper of vines settling into the soil. Tomas's grave had already begun to bloom with tiny pale flowers budding where his name was carved in stone.

They stood in silence until Aislen reached for his hand and gave a gentle tug.

"Come with me," she murmured.

He didn't ask where.

He just followed.

She led him through one of the side arches, down a narrow corridor half reclaimed by nature. Moss grew between the marble cracks, and distant starlight spilled down from broken ceilings above. She stopped when they reached a small room tucked just beyond a set of carved doors. It had once been a garden atrium, but it was now open to the sky, overgrown with climbing roses and veined with silver roots glowing faintly beneath the stone.

It felt safe here. Still.

She sat on a stone bench beneath the arch of flowering branches and pulled him down beside her.

Kael didn't speak, but his thumb traced soft circles over the back of her hand, grounding her.

"He's really gone," she whispered after a long moment. "I knew it before. I felt it. But seeing him… seeing him vanish into the earth, into this place, made it real in a way I wasn't ready for."

Kael nodded. "I know."

Her throat tightened. "He loved me like I was his own. He never once made me feel like I didn't belong. Not even after he knew."

"He was your dad," Kael said, voice fierce in its quiet. "No bloodline changes that."

She leaned into him, her head resting against his shoulder.

"I feel like I'm made of fragments," she said. "Pulled between who I was and who I'm supposed to be. Between the human life I thought I had and the magic I am growing into. Between grief and... this." She gestured around her.

Kael turned and pressed his lips to her forehead. "You don't have to choose. You get to be both. All of it."

She exhaled a shuddering breath. "I'm so afraid I'll break."

"You won't," he said, cupping her face. "Because I'll hold the pieces if you do."

Aislen's eyes shimmered, but no tears fell.

Instead, she kissed him. It was slow and searching, a kiss that asked for nothing but comfort and gave everything in return.

When they pulled apart, she pressed her forehead to his. "Thank you," she whispered.

"For what?" he breathed.

"For being here. For seeing me. For not leaving."

"I'll never leave," he promised. "Not even if the whole world burns."

He picked her up and carried her back to their room.

Their room was beautiful, something from a dream. It was tucked away in one of the upper towers of the Court. It was private, quiet, and overlooking the gardens that bloomed only under starlight.

The walls of the room were veined with silver and quartz, pulsing faintly with ambient starlight magic. No torches or candles. There was just a soft, natural glow that shifts with the night sky, ebbing and flowing like breathing. Some walls were arched with high, open windows. No glass in the windows, just delicate, warded glamour that lets in the breeze but keeps the cold out.

Her favorite part was the small reading nook built into the curved wall, with shelves of ancient tomes and one of her bookmarks tucked between pages.

But their bed, their bed was a close second… It was a grand, carved canopy bed made of pale moonwood entwined with starlight vines. Draped with translucent fabrics that shimmer faintly when touched. The mattress is impossibly soft, layered with furs and silks in deep indigo, silver-gray, and muted violet. Kael always slept on the side nearest the door, out of instinct.

An instinct he wouldn't lose any time soon.

It was all perfect.

Once she was finally nestled in between their blankets, with Kael's warmth by her side, Aislen closed her eyes and let herself believe him.

Finally let herself rest.

But when sleep finally came…

It did not come gently.

* * *

The sheets were warm from Kael's skin, the soft rise and fall of his chest steady against her back. His arm curled protectively around her waist, fingers tangled in the hem of her nightdress. Her head rested beneath his chin. The moonwood bed creaked softly as he shifted in his sleep, breath slow, deep.

Aislen didn't remember falling asleep.

But the moment she did, the world changed.

She was no longer wrapped in warmth and heartbeat and quiet.

She was standing barefoot in a scorched field beneath a sunless sky.

The stars had fled. The trees were blackened husks. The earth cracked beneath her feet like it had been weeping for centuries.

A sickly golden light began to drip from the horizon, bleeding into the sky like ink spilled into water.

She turned—

And there she was.

The Sun Queen. Virel.

Tall and terrible, with hair like wildfire and a crown of burning thorns. Her golden robes whipped around her like flame licking through a dry forest. Her skin shimmered with power... too bright, too unnatural. Her eyes glowed molten, and when she smiled, the world flinched.

Aislen tried to speak, but no sound came.

The Sun Queen's voice cracked through the silence like a blade against bone.

"I offered you mercy..."

"But instead, you spat in my hand."

Aislen backed away. Her feet sank into ash. Her magic stilled inside her, like it was caged.

The Sun Queen stepped closer. The sky warped behind her.

"You wear your father's blood like a crown. Do you think it will save you?"

"Do you think *he* will?"

She lifted one finger and the image behind her rippled.

Aislen saw Kael, on his knees, bleeding.

"No," she whispered.

Thess, sobbing in a crumbling garden.

Sion, screaming into a storm, reaching for someone who wasn't there.

Her mom, standing on the balcony of the Court, surrounded by fire.

"Come to me alone," the Sun Queen whispered, voice low and deadly sweet. "Come to me and pay the price."

She smiled. It was somehow both horrible and soft.

"Or I will tear every Court apart. I will burn the Lunaris Court to dust. Drown the Thalor Court. I will find and shatter the Celestara Court and salt the ruins so your ancestors scream in their graves."

The wind rose like a howl.

"You have three moons."

"Then I start with your mate."

And Aislen screamed.

But the world cracked—

And she woke.

Her breath tore from her lungs as she shot upright in the bed.

Kael jolted awake, grabbing her shoulders. "Aislen? *Aislen*—"

She was shaking. Her hands clutched the sheets like they could anchor her to reality. Her skin was clammy, and her chest wouldn't stop rising and falling like she was still tumbling through the dream.

She didn't speak at first.

She couldn't.

Her breath was still lodged in that burning dream.

Kael's arms wrapped around her again, pulling her tightly to his chest. "It's okay," he whispered, again and again. "You're safe. I've got you."

But even as she melted into him, her nails still trembled against his chest.

Because she knew something the others didn't.

The war wasn't over.

It hadn't even begun.

About the Author

Sierra McCallister is a wife, a mother to five wild and wonderful boys, and an early childhood educator with a heart for stories that linger. When she's not teaching or writing, you can find her on the sidelines cheering at her children's sports games, or curled up with a book in one hand and coffee in the other.

She writes in the quiet, in-between moments—often late at night—spinning tales filled with slow-burn romance, emotional depth, and magic that feels like memory.

Beneath the Bond is her debut novel and the first in a sweeping romantic fantasy series. Sierra writes to explore the ache of longing, the fire of love, and the power of found family in worlds where even the stars have secrets.